The Secret of the Scrolls

by

James Best

For my children, who represent my life and inspiration.

To the prolific writer, J.H.Brennan, without whose critique, in the period 1999-2001, Gareth Emery, the lawyer, would never have been transformed into James Best, the writer, and this book would never have been published. www.jamesbest.co.uk

British Library Cataloguing in Publication Data.
A CIP Catalogue record for this book is available from the British Library.

ISBN 0-9550203-0-1

Printed in Great Britain by Cox & Wyman Ltd.

Published in Great Britain in 2005 by Emery Publishing Limited,
"The Gables", The Paddocks, Groesfaen,
Mid Glam. CF72 8LE.
www.thesecretofthesrolls.com

PREFACE.

This book was first written and re-written many times between 1999 and 2003, whilst still carrying out substantial legal work to pay the bills. In an early (obviously inadequate form), it was submitted to various publishers and rejected in this period. Even my original title was used by another popular writer, so has been changed.

It attracted attention from the Submissions Editor of a large London Publishing Company who wrote indicating it was very enjoyable and readable and a cut above what she normally received. Nevertheless, she could not convince a Senior Editor to publish it. A Literary Agent took the time to see me and offer advice. The Editor of a BBC Radio Wales programme liked the novel sufficiently to be invited onto the programme and a Senior Editor at another large publishing company spoke highly of an earlier draft on the same programme, indicating "I think he has it in him to be a writer". David St John Thomas, then Editor of Writers News, encouraged me after reading an early draft. All have motivated me to overcome the obstacles placed in my path.

There have been many scholarly, academic and theological writers who have stirred my imagination and created the inspiration, which has resulted in 'The Secret of the Scrolls'. I pay homage and acknowledge all of them, for they are too many to mention.

The Gnostic Gospels found at Nag Hammadi had a resonance of truth. Of course, since I first began submitting this book to various publishers, (including Bantam, New York, in December 2001), the Da Vinci Code has been published. Hopefully, this only emphasizes the fact this book is ripe for the time. I, too, have used the thriller genre, but in a different style, written on two levels. I hope it appeals and provokes as much. Embrace the path to 'Sophia'.

I pay tribute also to another teacher and writer of the mysteries, Dolores Ashcroft-Nowicki, who helped me on my first faltering steps on the mystical path.

INTRODUCTION.

Esoteric knowledge and Initiate wisdom have traditionally been hidden from the masses. Even today, when more 'forbidden' material than ever before pours from the world's printing presses, the central secrets remain – buried beneath the sheer weight of words that wrap around presentation of seductive nonsense.

How refreshing in such circumstances to see the old truths re-emerge, communicated clearly and succinctly in a highly palatable form.

Fiction has a long and honourable history as a teaching vehicle. And it is a vehicle James Best drives here with considerable panache and skill. *The Secret of the Scrolls* is disguised as a thriller, carrying its readers from the darkness of the great Knights Templar persecutions to the implications of their demise in the present day. But in reading it for pleasure important spiritual lessons are absorbed.

The process begins on the very first page where we are told of those who 'live in a destructive cycle of repeating patterns of behaviour until they awake from their hypnotic dream to realize it is only fear that separates them from the truth'.

And we are also presented with the kernel of the book itself: it is Love that is the key.

James Best is a vivid writer and his work will transport you to distant realms of place and mind. When you emerge, your soul will be the better for the trip.

Enjoy.

Herbie Brennan.
County Carlow.
Ireland.   2004.

Extract from first scroll: "...Within the peace and silence of my being, inner-plane teachers guide me, as I write. Free will is granted to humanity, but only those who have access and knowledge of the consciousness of the soul exercise it. For them, there is no separateness from the spirit and they understand why the outer world always reflects the inner one. They know if they want to get what they want, they must first be the person they ought to be. When we transform our nature first, we transform our world afterwards, as our instincts change and the allure of superficial pleasures of the moment wane. It is love, infinite and universal, rather than personal, which is the key, as it is the only truth. Everything else is illusion. All others live in an unconscious and blind, destructive cycle of repeating patterns of behaviour, until one day they, too, will awake from the gloom of their hypnotic dream and realise it is only fear, which separates them from the truth. At that moment, we shall discover the unity of life and touch the truth with a timeless ecstasy and joyous inspiration and pay homage to the knowledge which sets us free. It is this understanding and essence of the real, rather than the illusion, which is the power and impetus of the spiritual quest. It lifts us above the rage and daily degradation to a vision of what the splendour of life can be. When the inner transformation is complete, there is an awesome understanding of our true being. Only then will we understand that we are not our experiences and so are not bound by memories from the past. This will establish a harmony and balance within our world and we will remember who and what we really are. Until then, karmic ties will bind us to the physical and the material and disguise the real nature of the spiritual reservoir, in which we live and breathe and have our being."

PROLOGUE

More than six years had elapsed since his crucifixion, but the wounds still wept and ached. Dislocated shoulders permanently disfigured his shape, despite crude attempts to push them back to their original position. The three days lying in a shroud, hovering between life and death, were a blur, though the horror and agony preceding it was the stuff of nightmares.

Human frailty meant even the knowledge of the righteous path he trod, and his likely martyrdom, could do little to comfort him as deep archetypal fears stirred. He needed a purity of spirit and clarity of intellect to defend his principles and beliefs.

Death was the price demanded. He knew nothing could prevent his inevitable fate, though acceptance of it remained difficult, as his mind spiralled within a tangled web of memories, emotions and thoughts.

***

Gulls strutted and screeched, then flew above them, drifting in the breeze beneath a chill March sky. Occasionally, one darted down to feast on the remnants of a hawker's stall, at the side of the street, where a labyrinth of hovels lined the route. The pungent smell of fish wafted into the nostrils, mingling with the stench of an overburdened sewerage system. The familiar sound of prisoners, grimy and unwashed in their prison rags, being carted unceremoniously to their public trial generated raucous interest. Banter and laughter filled the air. People of both sexes young and old alike, spilled out of ale-houses and alleyways, trailing the forlorn figures on their final journey to a destiny they had not anticipated, in their imperious years of influence and power.

He grimaced, as the cart taking them along its cobbled-street route hit another pothole, jolting his ravaged body. In the distance, he could see the square at Notre Dame, with its scarlet awnings, faded with the sun, jousting boxes and benches of Inquisitional figures set up as a court to administer the King's will. He sat imperious and arrogant with his retinue of robed figures around him to do his bidding. A line of gendarmes protected the King. Ministers, courtesans and general lackeys dressed up in their silk finery and chains of office allowed baser instincts to bay for bread, wallowing in the misfortune of souls more evolved than theirs. Peasants, merchants and persons of lesser nobility created a humm of noise around the square. It swept over him like a torrent, in his attempts to create an objective detachment from the event.

One day, he mused, the world would acknowledge the mockery and injustice of this Court. Beyond the square, the intimidating sight of a stake and pyre reminded everyone of the price for defiance. His heart sank and with it dignity, but pride remained, though all traces of vanity had long disappeared.

In the square, fellow Templars huddled and kneeled, chains cruelly cutting into their wrists and ankles, shackling them to each other in one withering undignified mass. Such a motley remnant of a unique, once-formidable Order made it impossible to realise their legacy, though a political arm, which had initially inspired their spiritual quest would still remain. Hopeless glances exchanged, as they were taunted with their confessions of heresy, the ugly scars of their harrowing persecution and scourging, a testimony for all to witness. Some lay prostrate on the floor, terrified and openly penitent in the abyss where fear had led them, others prayed or wept, creating a cruel spectacle, manipulated by the Chief Inquisitor for the benefit of the King.

How could he forget the appearance of the dreaded "Holy" Inquisition with the Chief Inquisitor in his red silk, trimmed with white ermine at the neck, cuffs and hem. His arrogant colleagues, in their dour black robes and white-lined hoods, anonymously protected the ugliness and savagery of their torture? How could such cruelty be perpetuated in the name of religion? To be hauled onto the Temple door and crucified was inhuman. In the torment, as they opened and shut the door, he would have confessed to anything. He grew faint at the mere memory of it.

"For posterity, I want to make this my proudest moment, but if only I could wish time away. I become sick at the prospect of the ordeal I must endure," he said, grimly.

His great friend Geoffrey de Charney lay slumped alongside him in the cart. He looked up at Jacques, his eyes locking with his. "I want to recant my confession, but courage may desert me." He spoke in muffled tones, never imagining the charismatic Grand Master of the Knights Templar, Jacques de Molay, so gaunt and dishevelled and only a shadow of the great man he once knew. His full beard remained, but it had turned white, as had his hair. His sunken eyes squinted out of dark sockets and tears trickled down his grime-stained face, as he struggled to cope with direct sunlight again. The stench of prison showed scant regard for his position and still oozed out of his pores.

This was supposed to be the final humiliation of a great and innovative Order, sworn to uphold truth, whatever the sacrifice. Unfortunately, the

Catholic Church could never acknowledge a truth about Christ, which would destroy its fundamental belief structures and its power. Instead, he hoped an underground movement, perhaps spawned by the Priory de Sion, could sustain the integrity of a spiritual way of life, more important than any religion. The reputation of the Order had been built on the bravery of the Knights Templar, in fighting against superior odds, but only a bedraggled few remained after three thousand had been arrested, tortured and imprisoned in France. The others had fled the country in haste, as suspicions of the French King's purge grew.

"I must retract my confession too. It's my responsibility as the leader and Grand Master." His voice cracked, as he looked towards Geoffrey.

"I'll do the same, but do you know the consequences?" Geoffrey asked.

"They'll burn us and King Philip will do it slowly, with oil on our feet and private parts first. I've seen his handiwork before."

Geoffrey groaned and heaved vomit over the edge of the cart. His body and feet already bore witness to the terror of his suffering on the notorious iron bed, with his feet and legs, in particular, roasted over an open fire. "So much for the name of Philip le Bel. It will be synonymous with treachery for centuries."

Jacques leaned towards him, placing an arm around his friend. He loved him, as a brother, and didn't want him to suffer. " He'll rot in hell, but if you ratify your confession, then you'll simply be imprisoned. It is enough that I take the martyr's course."

Geoffrey shook his head. "I don't want to live in this disabled body, incarcerated and unable to walk again. It's not life they offer me." He lifted his cloak and showed Jacques a small bloodstained cloth bag. A distinct odour of old dried blood permeated the bag and small bones protruded from it."

Jacques recoiled. "What's that?"

"These were the bones they took from my feet. I intend to throw them on the ground, so the people of France will know the evil their King perpetrates, in their name." He dropped his head.

Jacques nodded. "If the worst has happened, the scrolls and our Journal will already be in the Vatican vaults in Avignon."

"Jacques, Jacques," a familiar voice shouted from some distance behind the cart.

He turned his head and noticed the scarred face and long dark hair of an old friend, Jean Claude, a troubadour, who had journeyed with him throughout Europe. He acknowledged him.

"Jacques, these are dark times for our countrymen." He lumbered forward, his giant frame devouring the distance to the cart in no time. Flushing with the effort and placing his arm over the side of the cart, he squeezed Jacques' arm with obvious affection. "Where are the scrolls recovered from beneath Soloman's Temple in Jerusalem? And the Journal, are they safe?" He asked.

"I don't know," Jacques replied sadly. "Copies have been made and despatched, with some of our treasure, and the holy relic, in nine ships, which sailed from La Rochelle, in anticipation of this purge."

"Where did the ships sail to?"

"To the Isle of May, in Scotland, where they'll be safe. Other ships sailed south to Portugal and across the great sea to the New World. The maps and charts, discovered with the scrolls, show them the way. Perhaps there, a better way of life can be created based on religious tolerance, liberty and freedom from persecution."

For a moment, he allowed himself to escape in daydream, until stark reality dragged him back. He turned to Jean Claude again. "The rest of our wealth is with the Pope's nephew, our commander in the Languedoc, so it should be safe. For political reasons, His Holiness the Pope may have conspired with the King, but he'll protect his own blood."

Geoffrey shook his head. "It doesn't augur well."

Jean Claude nodded, as he struggled to keep apace with the cart. "Perhaps the original scrolls and Journal should have gone to Scotland too."

Jacques lifted his head. "But if our fears had been ill-founded, there'd have been an outcry." He hoped history would judge him favourably. "The King resented our rejection of his application to join the Order. With hindsight, it may have been a mistake, but we couldn't have allowed him to know the truth behind our discoveries. If the knowledge we've protected had reached the King, it would either have destroyed the Papacy or our Order. We were still not strong enough. How could we have taken the risk?"

"Friday the 13th October 1307 is a date which history will remember with sadness," Jean-Claude said, as he ran alongside the cart and recalled the day of their arrest and torture.

"You must protect the secrets of our Order," an urgency reflecting in the tone of Jacques's voice. "Liaise with Sion, but be wary and help our colleagues overseas set up a new network. Let each group give the gravest of oaths never to divulge the hidden truths, for which we've been the guardians these last three centuries. We must become an occult order, with a verbal tradition, which can pass from the initiated down to the apprentice. This must never happen again. We can remain a Society of Secrets. You must tell them that this is my wish."

Jean Claude's grip slipped away from the cart and he stumbled to the ground with a thud. "We'll not allow the truth to be buried, I promise." He shouted, as the cart drove away from his prostrate figure. He said something else, but the words drifted away in the breeze.

As his destiny loomed nearer, he searched within himself for a well of courage. The terror he felt, overwhelmed him, and strangely expanded beyond himself to another place. He trusted nobody could smell the fear, which must have seeped into every drop of perspiration. He took another deep breath in hopeless surrender and held his head high.

He turned to Geoffrey again. "They made me confess to worshipping a demon called Baphomet." Even in this adversity, he smiled. "They didn't recover the simple Atbash code, so they had no comprehension it could be reduced from the Hebrew to the Greek word Sofia or Father of wisdom. If only the people could understand the truth and abandon anything which attempts to institutionalise spirituality. We can prove the Church's persistence in preaching Christ's bodily assumption to Heaven is a lie, but it's not enough to say they're wrong. In their bigoted and arrogant eyes we'd still be heretics."

"I know, it doesn't help," Geoffrey moaned.

"Nothing does," Jacques looked down, all hope sapping from his ageing body.

"I confessed to much worse than worshipping a demon," Geoffrey confided, "but though they may destroy my body, they'll never take my spirit."

Jacques winced and sighed at the prospect of the ordeal ahead of him. He had far too often witnessed the pathetic, writhing spectacle of a burning and its charred victims to believe there was any glory in it. He trembled. "It hurts me when a French Pope presides over this perversion. If they burn me, as they will, I'll curse him, the King and the Chief Inquisitor in the flames and they'll all meet me before a higher Court, before the year is out." He knew there could be no turning back and a whole gamut of human emotions washed over him, as he recalled his life's work. He had prepared himself for this moment, since his torture and incarceration more than five years previous.

"I suspected the invitation to Paris, for the wedding of the King's sister, was simply a ploy," Geoffrey said. "He's always sought to plunder our wealth, to bolster his flagging finances, ever since he sought refuge in our Temple."

"But I couldn't refuse," Jacques replied, philosophically, lifting his head again. "The name of the Knights Templar had to remain unblemished. Others will take up the mantle of our virtuous cause. Our Journal and the scrolls cannot be suppressed forever, but I hope centuries don't pass before the glorious truth is revealed. I fear the blood of true Christian martyrs will flow, until the scrolls heal all sectarian wounds, as has been prophesied."

The allegations against the Knights Templar echoed, eerily and unreal, across the square, choking in the cold morning air amongst the buzz of a thousand voices. "Do you confess and acknowledge your guilt?" The Chief Inquisitor, a fat and squalid little man, pompously demanded an answer.

Jacques stood, lifting himself to his full height and the throng hushed for a moment. He tried, vainly, to project his spirit to the blessed release, which he knew lay beyond this nightmare. The choice may have been an ignominious one, between an agonising death and imprisonment for his lifetime, but honour had to prevail, whilst the whiff of courage lay within reach. He cherished the Templars' heritage and believed in his teachings and spirituality, which was higher and more pervasive than any religion. The ultimate sacrifice had to be made. Anything else would be a betrayal of his beliefs. Inevitably, he had to publicly declare the integrity of his Order, as he had carefully rehearsed during his years of captivity. It had to be done with dignity. In a way, which would not make him sound like a deranged peasant.

"I confess I am guilty of the greatest infamy, but the infamy is that I have lied in admitting the disgusting charges against my Order. I declare, and I must declare, the Order is innocent. Its purity and saintliness have never been defiled. In truth, I have testified otherwise, but I did so from fear of horrible tortures."

* *

Further extract from the First Scroll: "....I declare the wisdom teaching in this treatise is the remnant of an oral tradition taught to me in the Mystery Schools of Egypt, where the learning of the ancient mystery religions were closely-guarded secrets. In truth, the secrets guard themselves, for those who are not ready will not understand or accept them. Do not waste time in theological debates with those who are not ready. It is pointless. My origins and family are of Royal blood. My mother is of Pharoic descent. I have been commissioned by the Essenes at Qumran, who have allowed me access to their teaching methods and knowledge, to reveal the secrets of our graded learning systems and to make a written diary of these spiritual truths, as a chronicle of my ministry. Future generations must venerate and hold these truths, navigating a path away from contaminated ideology, which would take the world into a dark age of ignorance, where propaganda would be passed off as history. I offer truth and not rhetoric and shall not be tempted by external power, which always risks degenerating into authoritarian institutions and dogma. The body is in the Cosmos, yet the Cosmos (as consciousness) is in us and when the mystical reunion of the male and female awakens the final mystery, then you will enter the Kingdom. No one has yet reached the finality of what truth is, neither I, nor any other spirit, which has manifested in this world. Similarly, language is finite and rhetoric cannot accurately express the infinite, so do not be bound by too literal an interpretation of my words. Literalists would create a dogmatic religion based on history and not the mystery. If any religion encourages or condones a breach of the commandments, then that religion is already corrupted and leads man away from the path of true spirituality. Gnosis, through Love, is the key. I seek no personal adoration or following. My reward shall be the knowledge that I follow a path, first recorded by Soloman, which takes me towards a more beautiful place, a dimension where there are many mansions. The mystically enlightened soul moves towards the Light, where there are no limitations. It recognises its essential nature as god-like and Gnostic initiation awakens in us a lifetime of recognition of our shared divine essence. On death it communes with and has become a God."

CHAPTER 1

"Just imagine the scene, John," the Cardinal said, after relating this story with an anguish, which mimicked the suffering. "Such wretched cruelty. This frail old man, a great man, being dragged in chains to an agonising and ignominious death, as a pariah, rather than betray a truth, which would have been regarded as blasphemy. This same liberating truth must now set people free." He stooped, round-shouldered, lethargically pacing his high-ceilinged study, sadness anchoring his body and restricting movement. Though he was a man with such gentleness of disposition, the burden of the world weighed so obviously and heavily on his ageing frame.

For a moment, he stopped pacing and lifted his head, looking towards his nephew through weary, hooded eyes, which silently appealed for help.

"I had to end the bigotry and hypocrisy within the Church, so I've taken them," he said, vaguely, but intensely. " I've taken them," he repeated as if I hadn't heard him.

His opportunity to reveal the documents and scrolls, in his possession, had passed. The failure haunted him. It was time for someone with more energy and freedom to take up his cause. His nephew, a defrocked priest, had developed a significant reputation as an investigative journalist. It would work in his favour, but they were credentials, which would still be challenged and the abandonment of vows would not help his cause. In the past, he may have relied on dark good looks and charisma to open doors, but this time he would need all his instincts and intellect to succeed. He knew the Vatican had a Department Head devoted to suppressing unpalatable truths and the new Pope had an intransigent attitude on doctrinal matters.

Vatican institutions had been infiltrated by an intelligence elite, which wielded power greater than that of governments. The ailing and late Pope John Paul II may have wanted to keep a hold on these influences and had taken a hard line, but the strength or will to fight this battle diminished with his illness and was bound to persist long after his death. It had been the reason for this strange conundrum in that the he hated authoritarianism, yet he himself crushed all dissent and became so authoritarian himself.

The Cardinal knew now why it had been necessary, but the floodgates would soon open with his departure. He also knew his nephew had a determination, bordering on stubbornness, but this was a quality of character he could lean on, if he would accept the burden of responsibility he was about to thrust on him.

I had received an urgent summons to his London residence, an imposing, but antiquated, three-storey Victorian building, badly in need of decoration and refurbishment. I fidgeted uncomfortably in an elegant Edwardian chair, within a study dominated by shelves full of books and articles and a large, cluttered, mahogany desk

3

with carved legs, baroque style, which took a quarter of the room. I puzzled, with some concern, at what could be so important as to require my immediate attention. My uncle was not accustomed to making cursory demands of me, at a time when it was difficult to make holes in twelve-hour working days. I sat next to a white marble coffee table with venetian finish, arcing away at the sides. The study had fading lemon walls with white borders, which only served to emphasize the lack of cleaning. A mirror on one wall had an opulent gold-leaf frame, adding a little depth to the room. The chairs were mainly Edwardian with maroon fabric and brocade edgings.

"Jacques de Molay must be avenged! It was the cry from the banks of the River Seine that fateful day, again at the time of the French Revolution, when the curse on the Royal House ended with the death of the last Bourbon King at the same location. It's as true today." His hands moved rapidly, almost eloquently, in animated fashion, developing a mind of their own.

"This all sounds too mysterious?" I said, sceptical.

"John, I fear for my life and I need your help. It happened then and it may happen now."

"I don't understand," I clutched at a handkerchief as a sneeze, triggered by the dust, took me by surprise.

I loved my uncle and enjoyed our discussions on esoteric subjects, but I had never seen him agitated. I liked his disciplined passion and integrity, always stemming from a deeper aura of tranquillity. He had been my inspiration to enter the priesthood, but as I had been determined to study and contemplate the mystical texts of all the great religions, he had rightly questioned my motives. I found limitations in my life to be vexatious to the spirit and ignored the luxury of compromise. It had been one of the causes of serious differences of opinion with the Church Establishment and, subsequently, in my marriage. My disillusionment with the Church, though, could be attributed to many factors, not the least of which being deep-seated personality flaws, which made me totally unsuited to a life of the cloth.

My uncle walked around his desk and sat down heavily on an old and worn leather chair in the corner by the French windows. I had to turn to face him. "I've witnessed immense secrets. They're contained in sacred scrolls and a Journal, which have been locked deep within the vaults of the Vatican for centuries. This is the reason I explained their origins." He stared, starkly, his mouth opening and closing again, but he said nothing.

"Surely, many others would have seen them too. Why would this place your life in danger?" I asked, puzzled.

"Because I've taken the scrolls. This is the problem." He raised his voice, but spoke in a matter of fact way, belying the gravity.

"Oh my God." My jaw dropped. "Are you going to return them?"

He hesitated. "The world must know I've been a party to their delusions for too long. If something happens to me, you'll know it's not an accident."

"Why would something happen to you?" I asked, surprised at his paranoia.

For a moment, he placed his head in his hands, before standing and pacing the floor restlessly again, then looking out of the French windows towards his garden. He kept his back to me as he spoke. "Those with vested interests have already begun their work."

"Begun what?" I asked.

He turned around to face me. "After a meeting between a Cardinal and someone well-connected in Sicily, one of only two men, in whom I'd confided, has been found dead in Italy, crucified to a tree in his garden. The symbolism was clear enough. The second person died of a heart attack, even though he was only in his late thirties. These intelligence organisations can introduce a chemical agent into food or drink, which can create an embolism, and for all intents and purposes it would appear as if he had a heart attack."

"You're serious?" I asked.

"Of course I am. Do you doubt me?"

"No, but perhaps it's just coincidence. These type of things happen all the time down there, it seems." I said, if only to alleviate the paranoia.

He shook his head, his craggy face revealed his submission to the unmerciful ravages of age. "The man who had been crucified had a SAS-trained bodyguard who disappeared and, despite an emergency call to the Police, they took two hours to arrive at the scene, by which time it was too late for rescue. I'm sure they know I have the scrolls. I've even been ordered to return to Rome, but I refused. I may have little time."

I shook my head. "How did you manage to take these documents?" As a former priest, I knew the extent of the security there.

He smiled. "Before I became a Cardinal, I worked in the Vatican for ten years, I never told you or your father about my precise position there, but, due to my linguistic skills, I was assigned to the secret archives."

"I didn't know."

"By this time, you had your own problems, having left the priesthood, leaving a trail of emotional debris in your wake. My situation was never discussed.

Furrows in my forehead tightened. "I don't understand. You can't just walk out of the Vatican, with such important artefacts."

He nodded, a crooked smile appearing, then disappearing almost as quickly. "You'd think so."

"How can I help?"

He looked around furtively. "I have a meeting shortly and I don't want to discuss matters in the house. Can you come back tomorrow? We'll walk in the park or perhaps go out into the garden. There are things I must tell you."

I nodded. "Not a problem."

I stood up and we walked towards the door. My uncle turned towards me. "You know, even under torture De Molay never revealed the nature of the Wisdom Tradition at the heart of the inner circle of the Knights Templar. There were always two streams of history."

*　　　*　　　*　　　*

It had been a hot day by March standards, but shadows now lengthened in the small village, just fifty miles south of Rome. Away from the main drag, the older men of the village sat lazily around tables, in the square, discussing women, wine and sport, though not necessarily in that order. The weathered church, perched precariously on the hill above them, had always been there, though its crumbling structure may have seen better days. This familiarity meant no attention was paid to its visitors, though David felt out of place and sticky in designer suit and shirt, recently purchased from the expensive Via Condotti in Rome. He hadn't come prepared for this sort of heat in March. His shoes, with a metal plate on the back of the heel to limit wear, clicked machine-like at every step he made.

Yet, even as he passed middle age, he could not compromise the upright walk. It reflected the confidence of his character and he willingly portrayed it to the world. It was the confidence of an expert in diplomacy and surveillance, someone who was respected by his peers and his superiors.

As with so many Italian churches, it imposed its authority on the inhabitants, almost subconsciously, from indoctrination as children. Inside, years of incense use and ritual gave it a smell and feel of such a distinct nature that nothing could compare. The energy empowered its adherents because they believed in its authority and potency. It had been a living witness to the events within it and perhaps even those attempting anonymity outside its dignified walls.

The echo of whispering voices at the far end of the church, offering prayer, and heavy footsteps on the aisles gave it an eerie atmosphere of ghostly proportions. In the dusk, and with candlelight to illuminate the path, David was led to a small room at the back, where an Italian Cardinal waited in the shadows. The room was bare and stone-floored, though three chairs and a desk had been placed on the one side. A small window in frosted glass at the far end shed only the faintest of light from the increasing darkness. Once the door had been shut behind him and they were alone, the Cardinal spoke, nervously at first.

"I've been waiting patiently," he whispered.

" I came as soon as I received the message Cardinal R……"

The Cardinal placed a finger to his mouth. "Sssh. Don't mention my name. Even here, we must keep our voices down and be on our guard."

"If you say so," David replied with the disdain of someone who had worked in the shadowy intelligence community all his life.

8

"These are dangerous times and the intelligence organisations keep files on everybody, including me. There are sophisticated transmitters everywhere and this room has not been swept."

"I understand." David patronised him, though he felt like saying 'so what'. "How can I be of assistance this time?"

The Cardinal turned away, coughing into his hand, a hand wrinkled and sun-damaged from years of abuse by the climate. "There's been a breach. A breach of such magnitude that I need you to devote your entire staff to ensuring there's a satisfactory conclusion." An intensity of feeling reflected in the weight of his words.

David thought the Cardinal looked smaller, wearing only dark trousers and jacket, rather than robes of office, though his ring gave away his status. The dark clothes complemented his silver hair and leathered complexion. Brown marks, almost like large freckles stained his face. He could have passed for a Chief Executive of a multi-national conglomerate or even a lawyer, but then he remembered, his initial training had, in fact, been as a lawyer. He smiled to himself.

"What's happened?" He asked, looking down on the Cardinal.

"Certain documents belonging to the Church have been removed from the secret archives within the Vatican vaults. Such is the information within these documents that cataclysmic damage to the Church will be the consequence of their disclosure, if they surface."

"Will they surface?"

"You must prevent it happening, at whatever cost."

"At whatever cost?" David sought clarification.

9

"Yes. Do you understand what I'm saying?"

David nodded. He should have retired by now and really didn't want to dirty his hands with this unsavoury work anymore. He shifted and repositioned his black-rimmed spectacles. "I think you've made it abundantly clear, but there've been breaches in the past. Can't you manage the situation the same way you've managed it in the past. Discredit and misinform."

"It's more complicated than that."

David shrugged. "You've the links with the media at the highest levels to restrict damage?"

He shook his head. "The documents must never surface. It must not be a question of just restricting damage."

"This is more serious than I had imagined." David said.

"It's of a greater magnitude than anything you have ever done before and, unfortunately, we're living in an era where it's not so easy to discredit through the media."

David nodded. "These documents must be dynamite."

The Cardinal took a deep breath. "I must emphasize we simply cannot risk these materials being made public under any circumstances, even if there is collateral damage in the process."

"I think I understand," David said, dutifully.

"Such is the importance of their suppression, contractors from other agencies have already been used, but I have asked that they suspend their activities. They have one further task involving the Cardinal in London. If they have to be pulled back in at some stage in the future, I'll ensure they liaise and work with you."

"I don't understand why do you need my help? What is it you think I can do, which they can't?" David asked, still reluctant to take on the responsibility and believing he should be allowed to pasture.

"You're one of us, they're not. Besides, they may have contacts with the Police in England, but not to the extent of our network and you've the personal connections with British Intelligence."

David grimaced. "I understand, but I get nervous when other agencies are involved. I never know if I'm their next target, after the contract is complete. They like to cover their tracks."

"You've nothing to fear. I'll control them," the Cardinal said. He picked up a file from his desk and handed it over to David.

"If only the public understood the extent of influence your people have in the corridors of power," David spoke scornfully, before opening the file quickly, with a resignation to the task he was duty bound to perform. He scanned the first page and appreciated immediately the significance of the material. He lifted his eyebrows spontaneously and turned to face the Cardinal.

"Now you understand why this must be done?" The Cardinal said quietly.

David nodded.

"As soon as you're outside, you must memorize and destroy this file. The address at the bottom of the first page was handed to me only this morning from one of our contacts in London. Once there has been a resolution with the person in possession of the material, which will take a couple of weeks, the contractors will withdraw. The nephew is a greater concern. He's unpredictable and has some contacts. We can't take any chances"

11

"What do you know about him?" David asked.

"If you read on, you'll find everything you need in the file. Just make sure the situation is contained. There can be no mistakes. The Church faces the greatest risks since its early history and we're relying on you to protect us. It's what you've been paid to do for all these years."

"I'll do the job, but if there are difficulties do you want me to liaise with you?" David asked.

"You've everything you need. Don't have difficulties and don't contact me. I must deny ever meeting with you tonight. The only way you must contact me is in the gravest of emergencies."

"Any special code?" David asked, matter of fact.

"Do it the usual way, but use the expression red code. You've done it before, so you know the procedures."

"It may not be that simple."

"It has to be that simple and it has to be done. Will the girl do what you ask?"

David sighed. "She'll do what I ask her to do."

"Good," the Cardinal said, turning and opening the door. He marched briskly down the aisle and out of the Church and into a car waiting for him. David followed, his heart heavy with the usual task of mopping up other people's dirty work. He had been disillusioned with his work for some time and determined he would not destroy the file. He already knew too much and had seen too much. This would be his insurance. He wanted to enjoy his retirement and had, for some time, been secreting documents, which would guarantee his place in the sun. His sleep had become fitful and his conscience troubled him. He reasoned that he deserved better recompense for the nightmares, which accompanied the territory, and he knew how to demand it with one final big payday.

13

Further extract from the First Scroll:-"….There is a time in the scheme of things when the fruit has ripened and is ready for harvest. At that time, there will be a quickening of knowledge, of life, and in the rush, which follows, all things will be possible. I fear that time is not nigh. The natural laws of attraction embrace everything, but there is often too much ignorance and arrogance in this world of illusion for these laws to work their magic. I am consoled by the knowledge that nothing real can be threatened and nothing unreal exists. It is for this reason, I bear witness to the great wisdom within the work of the Mystery Schools, which have synthesized all the ancient wisdoms of the East and the West. There will be a time, I am sure, when there will be an opportunity for unity in this world, for the spirit always unites, even when the darkness within man divides and instils fear. Until that moment, false teachings and sterile dogma will be imprinted in the subconscious of our children, which will prevent the assimilation of truth. Evil will masquerade as righteousness, ironically in the name of God, and "martyrs" will murder for the inflation of ego, as if one religion is better than another. Repetition of truth does not diminish it, but repetition of dogma hardens hearts. Instead of love and tolerance, selfishness and hypocrisy will allow conflict to arise in its place. The light of the spirit cannot be expressed from whited sepulchres. These churches contain a dead faith and are at best a debating chamber for flawed theological doctrines. This will be a serious obstacle to bringing unity and peace to our world, for they will be incapable of holding ideas. Instead, ideas, in the form of dogma, will hold them. Dogma demands you accept it without reason. Your intelligence will tell you this cannot be. You will recognise truth when the harvest is ready, but it is offered on one basis, that you may, in accordance with free will, either accept it or reject it. If you are spiritually ready, something deep within you will intuitively recognize and resonate truth. No one may compel you to accept their truth on any other basis. Theology and dogma comes from the mind of human beings, whereas revelation comes from God. Which does your intelligence inform you should be followed?

CHAPTER 2

My uncle pointed to the garden, opening and ushering me through the French windows and onto a patio area, with a rockery beyond it. He picked up a spray gun he used for protecting his roses from greenfly. In the distance somewhere, I could hear the muted sound of dogs barking, but for London this remained a peaceful oasis away from the frenetic city pace, from which I had scurried some thirty minutes before. As I stepped onto the patio, I inhaled the different fragrances from flowers and a garden nurtured with love over many years. Negative energy dissipated magically and I could be at peace with myself again. The earth and the cycles of nature always had the same effect on me. It was real in an unreal world, but I shied away from its influence, burying myself instead in the unconscious demands of everyday living.

I leaned towards my uncle intimately. "Since our meeting yesterday, I've been thinking about what you've done. You must have been mad…"

He smiled again, "You're right. It's a sensitive post and, as you know, one in which you give an undertaking of utmost secrecy, as only the highest echelons had knowledge of some of the documents in the vaults. Even the Vatican's scholars are not allowed to see whole texts, but are given perhaps every third or fourth page."

"I'd heard as much," I replied. His sprawling garden, already awash with daffodils in this first weekend of spring, gave my uncle such pleasure. The air chilled the bone and I shivered, but not from the temperature. Rather some cold fingers of fear had reached its tentacles out to touch my soul. I recovered quickly, remaining close, as his voice drifted away in the breeze. We passed a silver birch tree to the side of the path. Though it remained half-naked, its delicate new leaves almost glittered in the sunlight.

"You'll be aware, there are Cardinals with greater influence and knowledge of these things, than the Pope."

"Yes, I understand. He concentrates mainly on the spiritual task of tending to his flock and leading the Church. The late Pope, despite his failing health, had fought significant battles with his advisors. He even acted against the wishes of many Cardinals in meeting with the leaders of other faiths and religions."

He nodded. "Yet he could not bridge the gap between the faiths, as he had publicly set out to do, and he was the one of the greatest of Popes. What hope is there for his successor."

"There may never be such a strong moral voice in the world again and with the dwindling number of priests and falling congregations, where does the Church go from here?" I shook my head.

"This has led me to take the course of action I must now take. The new Pope has to match his predecessor, but how can he walk with the same humility and courage. His predecessor made public admissions seeking forgiveness for the sins of the Catholic Church and referred to the Church's hostility to other religions and the divisions within the Christian Church, apologising for the Inquisition, the Crusades and significantly to women."

"I was impressed, but, as always, it's only now, with hindsight, we appreciate him," I said, reverently.

"There was humanity and fallibility too. He preached unity, but he sparked such division."

I thought for a moment. "But they now call him the Pilgrim Pope because he held the Church together and expanded it to distant lands."

He sighed. "Did I tell you, I've had these scrolls for some time. I always wondered whether my possession of these scrolls, their reference to the source and unity of all religion and the importance of the feminine, may have influenced some of the decisions." He said softly, furtively looking around, as he spoke. "You know I'm surprised it has taken them so long to do anything about it. Perhaps they were waiting for the demise of the old Pope before reverting to the old ways."

I found myself unwittingly copying the gesture and looking around, with paranoid eyes. "I don't believe they're ready to open up their archives yet."

He stopped momentarily, almost absent-mindedly, looking back at the house, before walking away from the patio. "There's still much work to do," he said, dryly.

I stayed happily by his shoulder. "Uncle, I understand all of these things, but are you overreacting?"

He glared sternly, through haunted eyes. "You must believe me. I'm not overreacting." His voice, though firm, remained calm. He had a square face and could look angry some of the time, if he chose. "The Papal Institute for Christian Archaeology and the Vatican's new guardian and prefect of doctrinal orthodoxy will hold on to the old traditions. In fact, they will now have more freedom than they have had for some time."

I smiled. "But we have a new regime in place and anything could happen."

He chuckled, stress lines disappearing for a moment. "All we need is for the next Pope to give himself the name of Peter and Malachy's prophecy regarding the end of the Catholic Church, may be nearer than we think."

I sighed. "It's sad how the world suffers. The fanatics and terrorists destroy human life, gloating as they do, even trying to justify their evil and misguided actions in the name of religion. The wounds they create will cause greater divisions, when healing is required. I had such high expectations twenty years ago," I said, looking down.

He nodded. "The darker the hour, the more light we must shed. When each of us is at peace with the person we see in the mirror, then peace between nations is bound to be a consequence. As we change our perception, so we shall change our experience and reality."

I looked up at my uncle with respect. "I suppose so."

"It was the late Pope John Paul II who pressurised one of his Cardinals into the publication of the apocalyptic third secret of Fatima, in its original Portuguese text," he smiled. "Of course, that Cardinal is the old enforcer, Cardinal Ratzinger, and we now know him as Pope Benedict XVI."

I laughed. "He had his name sorted within thirty minutes of being elected by the Conclave and a long speech in Latin followed."

My uncle bent over slowly, grimacing at full stretch, as he pulled up a stray weed, which had lazily encroached onto his territory. "He is an intelligent man, with powerful influence and a hard-liner. If you under estimate him, it will be at your peril."

I raised my head, turning towards him. "I have no dealings with the Vatican anymore, so it is of no consequence to me."

"But things will change," he said calmly, with no change of tone. He looked straight ahead, failing to make eye contact.

"What do you mean?" I asked, placing my hand on his arm, so he was forced to look at me.

"In time, in time," he pointed down the garden again and I released my hand.

For some moments, neither of us spoke. I wanted to change the subject, being uneasy at the direction our conversation had taken. "Why didn't you attend the funeral of the late Pope or the Conclave?"

He shrugged and his voice cracked. "I told them ill-health prevented me from travelling and offered my apologies," he hesitated and cleared his throat. "But I have lost friends over it."

I placed my arm around his shoulder. "You have served the Church well for many years, so don't reproach yourself."

"But I do, I really do."

I gave my uncle a squeeze of affection and reverted to our earlier conversation. "What's your view of the third secret of Fatima? It's the forty pages of explanation and interpretation, with which I take issue. The vision can just as easily represent the collapse of orthodox Christianity. Even the image of an angel, with a flaming sword in his left hand, may well reflect the threat of judgment looming over the Papacy, rather than the world."

19

"It's possible the death of the Pontiff, which was seen in the vision, may be symbolic of the death of his Church." He shook his head. "Who knows, but I would still prefer divine revelation to man-made theology."

"The one thing we both know is that without truth, the Antichrist will flourish in the vacuum." I said, pausing for a moment to reflect on the consequences of giving up the cloth.

"Even though it's an illusion, it can be a powerful one, which may hold sway in this world for what may seem an eternity."

I walked slowly alongside my uncle and mentor, as I had done so many times before. He had always epitomised the essence of responsibility and self-discipline. I still found difficulty in imagining him breaking any rules, unless for reasons of strict conscience. I was the rebel in the family, who always broke the rules, including my vow of celibacy. Absolution, after the confessional, was supposed to relieve me of the sin and the guilt, but I battled with the principle of instant absolution. It was no discouragement to sin, if you knew you could be absolved of the burden afterwards. Perversely, I shouldered my guilt manfully, both in respect of the failure of my vows, as a priest, and with regard to my private life subsequently. Occasionally, I tried to project the guilt to someone else, but more often than not it followed my every footprint, like uninvited guests at a party creating a nuisance.

"When did you take the scrolls?" I asked.

"I copied the Journal over a long period, then took one small scroll at a time, until I had twenty-four. I could never manage to hide the Journal, it was too large, but I've copies of their entries. The announcement of my elevation as a Cardinal meant

I had little time. In the few months before I returned to England, I began secreting the scrolls. I thought I'd managed to avoid detection, but it's obvious, I failed."

He paused, shaking his head persistently. "I tried in vain to reconcile my position. I thought of going to the Pope himself, but he's guided on all edicts of consequence. Anyway, he couldn't condone what I'd done. He's a mere figurehead, in the line of Popes from Peter."

"At least, we're led to believe the Papacy started with Peter" I said. "Though doesn't the Church's own Apostolic constitutions suggest the first Bishop of Rome was Britain's Prince Linus?"

"You're right. He was appointed by St. Paul in AD 58, even if his name only appears second in the list, publicly exhibited, in the museum at St. Peter's Basilica in Rome." His eyes looked down. A sadness lingered there and drained life away from his body

"Pope John Paul II had been a good man, though conservative, but his health deteriorated with the struggle"

"It's self-evident to everyone." I said.

"The scrolls will undermine the religion I served all my life, but it'll prove the lie behind orthodox Christianity and shed light on its pagan origins. Without these documents, I knew I'd be ridiculed as a heretic. As it is, I can't publish them now. I've delayed too long."

"Surely, your reputation will prevent them calling you a heretic and you haven't left the Church?" I asked, even though I suspected the answer.

A faint smile deepened creases around his mouth. "The cardinals at Anagni in the thirteenth century defined heresy, as each man choosing for himself the teaching he thinks best."

He looked up, as the noise of an aeroplane in the distance reminded us of the house's proximity to one of the flight paths to Heathrow. He took a deep breath. I found myself synchronising and imitating him. The aroma of mint swept across from the bottom of his garden. Its sweetness saturated senses, already heightened by these revelations.

"John, you know perfectly well, heresy is to diverge from Holy Scripture, as interpreted by the popes, hierarchy and 'divines' on Earth." He drifted away, distracted by his garden, pulling out weeds and tending his rose bushes, spraying them carefully with the spray-gun he had picked up from the patio, before returning and carrying on where he had left off. "They're deemed to be inspired by the Holy Spirit. So you can be a heretic, even if you've not left the Church."

"Yes, but what's the message in the scrolls?" I asked.

"Ironically, it's identical to orthodoxy in one respect. The promise, after the death of the corrupted body and the resurrection of the uncorrupted soul, of an afterlife in the next world."

I shook my head. "It was once heresy not to believe the Earth was flat. Like so many false truths, which are supposed to be at the base of Christianity, it's ludicrous," I said, tetchily. I had entered the priesthood with such faith, but soon became disenchanted and corrupted by the bureaucracy, which took the Church away from the people, for whom we were meant to serve. Consequently, I remained highly sensitive to the injustices created by the hierarchy within the Church. In truth, I knew I had also been corrupted by the immense power of sexuality. When you take something away, you miss it more.

He placed his arm around my shoulder and pulled me closer. "In their eyes, I'm a heretic. Look at what happened to such an eminent theological scholar as John Allegro, when he tried to expose the cover-up over the Dead Sea Scrolls. They denigrated him and treated him like a leper."

"You're right", I said. "I sometimes wonder whether anyone can succeed against the Church, with its power and infiltration within governments and the media."

"Research one of his published letters in 1959. He wrote of being convinced, if anything affected the Roman Catholic dogma, the world would never see those scrolls and Father De Vaux, who headed the mainly Catholic team, would send the lot to the Vatican, to be hidden or destroyed."

"Presumably the same principle can apply to any of their secret archive material?"

"Precisely." He looked around again, but other than the trickle of a brook at the bottom of the garden and birds rustling gently in the trees, I heard no sound. "There's much truth in Allegro's statement. He knew there was a conspiracy to delay and spread misinformation about the scrolls, but he didn't know the whole truth."

I regarded my uncle as one of the sanest, most stable of men. He was an example of a man capable of goodness, compassion and true spirituality.

"I've known a bureaucratic tendency to cover up mistakes, but few examples of genuine conspiracy," I endeavoured to reassure him.

"I've seen it at first hand," he replied.

I shook my head. "Why are you telling me this? What can I do?" I had many questions.

"In time, the truth within these scrolls will emerge. It must or it will hasten the hold of the

Anti-Christ in these apocalyptic times. I believe the last of the Four Horsemen of the Apocalypse may already have been released on an unsuspecting world."

"What a frightening prospect". I said sadly, reflecting on my own weaknesses. "I sometimes fear, by walking away from the Church, I've abrogated my responsibility in this battle."

"Well, the answer is simple, isn't it?" He said.

"What do you mean?" I asked.

"Welcome back to the fight. It can be fought both inside and outside the structure of the Church. This is the reason the new century has to be a global one, in more ways than one. It must apply to religion too. Why is it so difficult to overcome politics and understand the unity of all things, that we're all global brothers and sisters. It's a fundamental duty to ensure one religion does not fight another. I think it was Gandi who said that in Heaven there is no religion."

"I agree wholeheartedly, but…"

"There are no buts".

I persisted. "But these are chronically unstable times and surely one man cannot make a difference?"

"What if everyone took the same attitude and, anyway, you don't believe that."

"Perhaps not." I could never win an argument with my uncle. He knew me too well.

"It would be a dereliction of the truth of all spirituality, which pervades all religious people if we don't stand up and be counted," he said.

"The world survives all of its perversions," I said, taking in a deep breath.

He tilted his head one way and then the other. "Some years ago, I was part of a forum, when some liberal young lady suggested no right-minded person could be a Catholic, when they had sided with destructive right-wingers, such as Franco, Salazar, Hitler and Mussolini. I found it difficult to answer, other than to revert to core beliefs. " He hesitated. "She was right."

"But you stayed within the Church. I couldn't, though I still believe it's the spiritual reality, which underpins the world of the senses and surprisingly, I remain emphatically in awe of Catholic ritual. Yet violence is constantly perpetuated in the name of religion."

"All human beings are imperfect, whether they are inside or outside the Church. All of us can become the gullible prey of evil. We all search for meaning and purpose and often find it in a cause, even if that cause is fatally flawed."

I remained in awe of his integrity and idealism, particularly as mine had been so easily corrupted and abandoned, in the heat of temptation. I had lost respect for myself and sought to hide from the pain, by rooting an existence away from spiritual matters. He had a resilience, which I could only envy.

"The problem is, uncle, you have one passage from the Koran, which states there is more truth in one sword than ten thousand words and its true symbolism of action, rather than words, is lost and misconstrued as justification for violence. Though many extracts emphasize a non-violent creed, where human life is sacred, people with limited intellect clamber over the one line they remember. Whether through personal injustice or inadequacy, they then build a destructive life on this false foundation, a life which inevitably crumbles into the dust in tatters, causing a further cycle of pain and havoc, in its wake".

He nodded and took hold of my arm. "I knew I could reach you."

"You always could," I replied, taking his arm and pulling him close. "Though I still find it difficult to believe what you've done," I added.

"I thought my position gave me immunity, whilst I struggled with my conscience. The scrolls were rarely checked and there are so many documents in the vaults, but I've been naïve. You must help me."

I shook my head again. "You're a cardinal. They're not going to ex-communicate you. It would create a scandal and draw attention to the documents. I understand, more than most, the deficiencies of the Church, but there must be a limit to what they would do."

"They've sinister connections who'll do their dirty work. I'm sure they've no intention of ex-communicating me, but I'm being followed. They've installed their staff within my household. I've no choice."

"What do you mean?" I asked.

"One man systematically checks all my paperwork. He even cross-examines my assistant Rachel and there are constant quarrels. She deserves better. I hope she earns it."

I recalled meeting Rachel on four or five occasions. She was an elegant girl, stunningly attractive in that classical pretty way of simple lines. Her perfectly proportioned body triggered my imagination. If I analysed her carefully, I would have noticed an imperfect elfin-type face, which in the excitement of lustful thoughts, could assume almost supernatural beauty. In fact, she was the sort of woman every man wanted to know better. She had a distracting habit, though, of avoiding eye contact, yet with such gentle velvet eyes, I could forgive her. Nevertheless, it puzzled me. I suspected she had a hidden side.

I had become distrustful of pretty girls. They had caused me too much pain, but my inability to resist their attraction made me feel inadequate. It was my problem, but I always feared they had they would scuttle off, like spoilt children, to the next man in the queue at the slightest ill wind. I should have treated certain emotional experiences in my life as an opportunity for healing and growth, but I had too many imperfections and resented their control of a relationship. I needed a woman in my life, someone who would take time for some intellectual self-analysis, but I had rarely been afforded such luxury. I had come to believe women were a different species, with different needs, which I could never understand. Perhaps the Venus/Mars analogy was accurate enough, but part of the problem, I realised, related to my choices to court overtly sexually-active, frivolous women. I loved courtesans, but they rarely developed into loyal consorts. Consequently, the destructive patterns of behaviour repeated themselves, with pain for everyone concerned. My little drama and pretence involved refuge in bachelor status, with no commitment to frighten me. By generalising, I could find escape and bury my pain. A similar insane drama had driven me into the arms of the Church, though ignominiously leaving it, to pursue marriage, had proved an equal disaster. At least, two delightful daughters gave me a legacy from the debacle of another failure. They gave me love, inspiration and no little pride, all of which had given me the will to persevere in my career, even if I treated it as another hiding place. The escape route lay in burying myself in work.

"John, I need you to do me two favours," he said. Furrows in his face tightened with a stubborn intensity, as he assessed my reaction.

Concentration jolted back. I nodded instinctively, a strange act for a journalist, but respect outweighed natural instincts.

"Let's go to the gazebo, at the bottom of the garden. It's one of the few places I feel safe from prying eyes and listening devices."

"Are you sure you're not being paranoid?" I asked quietly.

He laughed. "Is that what you think?"

"Well, you must have been on the brink of madness to take the scrolls," I smiled.

"Perhaps" He still held my arm tightly, tugging me gently in the direction of the bottom of the garden. He then took his hand from my arm and placed it on the small of my back, pointing with his free hand away from the patio. I indulged him and we walked slowly down a crooked path, which straggled slightly downhill towards the gazebo. The branches of some shrubs, badly in need of pruning, overlapped the path and brushed against us as we walked. At one point, I almost slipped as leather-soled shoes caught damp foliage stuck to the path.

"I 'm about to change your life forever," my uncle whispered, as we arrived at the gazebo.

Extract from the second scroll:- "The gates of Paradise will be re-opened in the New Age for those with faith. Take pride in the knowledge that humility will open them and ancient soul memories will be recalled. At that time, the Darkness, which relies on fear and the veil of ignorance for its power, can be banished for those with courage to follow the mystical path. The courage will arise from love, for it is only the lack of love, which is a sin. Fear, hatred, resentment and revenge are all cancers of the soul, which will result in cancers of the body. Perhaps in some future time, but sadly not in this, people will accept their birthright and move into the Light. From that moment, we shall realize we are all one consciousness with the privilege of experiencing itself subjectively. Be vigilant and do not fear the battle, but embrace it with joy, for victory is assured with faith, courage and the knowledge that the dark is but an illusion and there is the treasure of a harmony to be mined. Take heart in the knowledge that you cannot be defeated and that in time all can escape the prison of the senses, for many illusions are created for the imprisoned consciousness. The warriors of the New Age will find the peace that passeth all understanding, but only after they have stood alone and have been tested. We must renounce the lesser for the greater, for there are no limitations. Others will meekly accept mediocrity, believing they are taking the easier and more comfortable choice, but in the sacred places within their heart and within their soul, a dark hole will appear. At a deeper level, they will be aware they have lacked the courage to face their destiny. They will know that something will always be missing from their life, though they may bury and turn away from all such instincts, which speak to them of a spiritual connection. In fact, they may fiercely deny

*it, but the more energetically they argue, the more
you can be certain they fear the truth, for the
Darkness and the ego will fight for its survival.
Eventually, Light must be drawn to these dark,
empty places, if the demons of the Darkness are not
to hold sway within their souls. They can exist only
if you believe they can. In this sense, true reality is
a polarity between light and darkness, as it is
perfect harmony, where every part is an expression
of one indivisible whole. Simplify the way you
contact God and believe everything is possible. You
are deserving of everything and must dare to dream.
Do not inflict suffering on yourself and take solace
in the knowledge that you are worthy. You are,
indeed, a ship built for heavy seas."*

CHAPTER 3

David struggled up the final narrow iron steps to the
rooftop garden of his Hotel, the Pace Helvetia, in the
centre of Rome. His knees creaked with the onset of
arthritis and breathlessness revealed the price he
paid for a decadent lifestyle. Too many lunches at La
Rampa or at the piazza Campo di Fiori. Long
dinners at Trastavery and too much alcohol did not
help, he thought. He slung his designer blazer over
his right shoulder and hung onto it with his right
hand. Under his other arm he carried a plastic folder
tied with red tape. The exertion caused perspiration
to drip unpleasantly from the hairline at the nape of
his neck and under his arms, but he knew etiquette
would be no problem this morning.

It may have been a strange venue for a
meeting of such import, but he loved the views from
the top of the Hotel. He could look across at the
wedding-cake architecture of the Victor Emmanuel
building immediately in front of him and to the

Forum and the Coliseum to his left. If he looked right from the Piazza Venetia, he could see the awesome structures of the Vatican and St Peters Basilica in the distance, even more stunning when illuminated at night. Unlike some cities, everything of significance in Rome was within walking distance. The touristy and incongruously located Fontana de Trevi was five minutes walk away from the Hotel and the Piazza Novona, a mere ten minutes walk.

The sun was already pleasantly high in the sky as he listened to the heavy and familiar footsteps of one of his soldiers of Christ. For one of their better customers, the concierge had promised privacy. A cloth table and two chairs had been carefully arranged, with coffee, biscuits and a carafe of water set out neatly. He greeted the man with an embrace, as a father would greet his child, before matters of business and strategy took precedence.

His soldier was a man of few words and little intellect, yet great persuasion. "What's gone wrong?" He asked, declining the chair and leaning across the balustrade and taking in the view. David stood alongside him, amused at a young girl sunbathing in a bikini on one of the nearby rooftops. The noise of the bustling city could be heard only as a low hum in the distance and hardly intruded.

"There's a greater urgency for the recovery of the documents and their suppression. There must be no publication of their contents." David replied.

"I understand. Is there a problem?" The soldier walked to the table and poured a glass of water, almost demolishing it in one go.

"I have instructions to resolve the issue quickly, one way or the other, though we're not to get involved with the Cardinal at this stage."

"Why? Is anyone else involved?" The soldier asked.

31

"I've been told that another agency has been engaged." David sat down on the chair at the table with a sigh. "This is not a normal person of little significance, but a Cardinal for God's sake."

"If there are other agencies, it could get messy and they'll get in the way."

"Precisely, but I'm not surprised, this is arguably the biggest threat to the Catholic Church in the modern era and they were never going to take any chances."

"I've been ready to move since you first told me you'd infiltrated people onto his staff to monitor the situation, but I thought this was a softly, softly approach."

"It was supposed to be, but contractors from the other Agency have already been used in Sicily and they want them involved with the Cardinal. I am told they will then step down, when we take over."

"I've heard that before," the soldier turned and stretched, like some feline creature waking up to the challenge life would bring.

David shrugged. "I'm not happy about it either, but some things are out of my hands. I've had enough. I'm too old for the front line."

"Is this going to be your last job?"

"I hope so." David took some of the water and sipped it quietly, looking out over the eternal City. "I'm tired and I deserve a simple retirement, for all the dirty work I've done for them over the years."

"Are there any other complications?" The soldier asked calmly, as if matter of course.

"There's one." David handed him the plastic folder he had been carrying. "His name is John O'Rourke, he's the Cardinal's nephew. A former priest, but he's now an investigative journalist, with a reputation for taking on dangerous assignments. He has some influence within the media and he may become a nuisance, so he's not to be underestimated. Read it."

The soldier took the file and began to read, before looking up. "How much independence do I have on this?"

"I don't want you to do anything without my approval on this one. His photograph is there and all the other information you're likely to need. There are voice-activated transmitters in his car and at his house. I can give you access to relevant tapes, as and when the need arises. I may even have to stay with you on this one, which is not ideal from my point of view. Too many risks, but I can't make any mistakes this time."

"Fair enough. Are we to meet in London?"

"The usual place, the day after tomorrow. I have a meeting in the Vatican this afternoon. I'll be flying back in the morning." David stood up with a groan and, after a handshake, moved towards the stairs.

**

"Not for ourselves, Lord, not for ourselves, but for the glory of your name," the Cardinal spoke quietly, as if in trance.

I looked strangely towards my uncle, as we continued walking to the gazebo at the bottom of his garden. "Sorry," I said almost apologetically, as if I had not heard what he had said.

He looked back at me and smiled. "It was the motto of the Knights Templar. They knew they had to be of service and be soldiers of the Lord. This is why you're here."

"I don't understand," I replied meekly.

"You will," he said and paused. "How's your wife?" He asked, suddenly changing the subject.

I drew back. "Uncle, Katie is my ex-wife, not my wife. You see, I even believe in divorce now."

"And your two beautiful girls? I don't see them as often as I used to."

"Neither do I, but they're all fine. The girls seem well-balanced and cope better with the break-up than I do."

"You should spend more time with them." He gently reprimanded.

"It's not easy, when you don't live with them, and have a career to follow."

"Take time from work."

"If I don't work, I can't support two homes, so I'd be criticised again. It's a no-win situation."

"For your sake, forgive Katie. It's necessary for healing. An inability to forgive and guilt are two of the major causes of illness and misery. Christ preached about sins being forgiven, because he saw health in terms of inner wholeness."

"I don't have any guilt," I lied impulsively, feeling my face redden and pulse increase. I hated lectures, even from my uncle. "She's the one who betrayed me. I was always loyal to her. I felt as if my heart had been torn out, when she admitted having a series of affairs. They're such dishonourable transactions between selfish people. Yet she intrudes into my dreams uninvited, even now, and it still gnaws away at jangled nerve ends. It makes you feel emotionally retarded. I have little respite from it and dare not make myself that vulnerable again."

"But you must, you know you must," he replied, emphatically.

"If I said I forgive her, my feelings would betray the truth. It's not how I feel."

He looked disdainful, whilst I feigned indifference. "You're tied to her. You trained as a priest and you know better. The wounds will bond you, until you forgive. I'm sure she didn't intend to betray you."

"Some things were wilful and I can never trust her again. Love is easy and lingers. It's not a love, which stood the test as the great attracting force of the Universe."

"Then it's over and forgive her," he replied, as if it was a simple matter.

"Forgiveness is possible with time, but respect and trust are damaged beyond repair."

He shook his head again. "Like so many people, she allowed life to control her and followed instincts. Some people, and you're a prime example, have to learn from events, rather than any intuitive teaching."

"That's unfair. Where's your compassion?"

" If you feel unjustly treated, you're being ego-driven and are losing sight of the only source of true reality and authentic power." He spoke calmly and with a conviction, which was unnervingly and annoyingly compelling.

"Perhaps so. I understand we must always revert to the unity of all things, whether physical and spiritual, science and religion, men and women, but when trust is broken, it's impossible to repair."

"That's a different matter, but I believe everything is possible," he replied. "Many women crave for the love and affection they had from their fathers, even if circumstances of everyday living don't allow such constancy. When they feel they've not had it, they look elsewhere, but confuse sex and love in their search for wholeness."

"I understand that, I've been there and worn the t-shirt."

"Then you know it's an ego-based, conditioned reflex. It becomes their nature. They've lost sight of their spiritual home. That's all it was."

"But Katie had me. Why would she seek love elsewhere?"

"Have you asked her?" He stared unblinking.

"It's not that simple. You've never had to suffer betrayal."

"In truth, it is that simple. There may be betrayal, but afterwards there has to be forgiveness."

I shook my head. "Maybe in time."

"John, I'm not judging you. People in pain want relief, not moral reflection."

I nodded. "I always preached how the root of every argument in a relationship is the belief that the other party doesn't love them enough. Unfortunately, though I could often help others, I didn't have the strength to overcome the negativity, which swamped our marriage, and help myself."

"Is it too late?" he asked.

"It's hardly any consolation for me, but it's taken away all hope for change," I shrugged and looked away momentarily, uncomfortable with the expression of deeper feelings. "I've created the perfect woman in my mind, but, of course, I understand it's unreasonable and unattainable."

"Then compromise. Life is full of them. It's an imperfect world."

"But I still strive for this perfection, as if it's a need of my soul?" I rubbed my hand on his arm and smiled. "I knew, as a dancer, Katie had a chequered past, but it was the past and I didn't care. This is different. I love long-legged girls and I didn't mind her kicking her legs higher than anyone else, as long as it wasn't wider too."

"That's not funny."

"If I don't laugh, I'll cry." There was little relief for me in humour, when emotions remained raw. "She had two children to think about. Like

36

everyone else, I didn't want the original good-time girl, had by all." I said, more seriously.

"John, patronise me. If you react strongly and emotionally to things I suggest, then it's probably true. If you can reasonably and quietly consider what I say and dismiss it, then it probably isn't true and I'm wrong"

I looked back at sad, weary eyes, which made me feel uneasy. "I'm not ready to move forward yet, I still need to grieve. When children are involved, you can't just walk away and I resent the fact I no longer share their lives."

"I can see that."

"I want to make a greater contribution and have been deprived of the opportunity."

"You're right, of course, but a soul is often drawn to another for their healing potential."

"I understand, but it's not that simple," I repeated, impatiently.

"Well, if things have run their course, you should be glad, not sad."

"I want to believe something wonderful is about to take its place, but it's difficult.

My uncle tended another rosebush, turning his back on me, but carried on talking. "Trust in God. If you hang on to the negative emotions the experience has created, it will immobilise you. You'll attract the same energies in your life. It would be foolish. I keep reminding you, we are the consequences of our thoughts."

"Uncle, I don't want to fall out with you, but I don't have time for this. I must work this out my way and in my time. Please respect my wishes." I said, obviously not ready to face painful analysis. I carried on walking towards the gazebo, leaving my uncle behind.

37

He finished the pruning of his roses and began walking quickly, catching me as I neared the gazebo. "You're sounding more and more like a victim. If you're not careful, you'll be one."

I turned back to face him. "I really don't need this," I said.

"Very well, but I need your help and I want you strong. You'll need courage in the face of the challenge. You're no good to me, if you're emotionally disabled in this way."

"You're going around in circles."

He shivered and began rubbing his hands together. "Remember, the emotions are a portal of great energy between the physical and spiritual dimensions, so you must remain in control of them."

"I understand that," I said, screwing my eyes painfully. "But what challenge do you mean?"

For a few moments, he didn't speak, but gathered thoughts. It gave me time to take in my surroundings. I inhaled deeply, pulling in the energy of Nature all around. It always invigorated me, such simple pleasure and available to anyone. There was a time I could live every day with joy, but life had taken its toll. I looked beyond the brook, which trickled timelessly at the bottom of the garden; it backed onto another large garden, where buds had already begun to sprout. The emerging foliage had always symbolised new life for me. I liked spring, with its regeneration and promise of warmer days and balmy nights, but it had been a long time since I had communed with mother earth or attempted to synchronize my life with the cycles of the seasons.

I turned to my uncle. His face revealed the ravages of age; worry lines betraying a heavy burden. We sat down in the gazebo, which nestled magically and peacefully beneath a canopy of trees, beginning to leaf again. The seats were cold and hard, like my mood. I loved my uncle, as he had been more of a father figure to me, than my own. I couldn't imagine danger lurking in this innocuous environment. I looked down at mud-splattered black shoes. A dark blue suit, with red tie on a white shirt may have been ideal for the image of dynamism for the City, but appeared incongruous and inappropriate here.

"Your late father and I followed different paths." His eyes were noticeably haunted by anxiety and the creases in his forehead were deeper than I remembered. "I criticised his lifestyle, but he was a gentle man who couldn't cope with the exasperation and hopelessness of personal circumstances, especially after your mother's death."

"I understand all that."

"You're a stronger individual and have the spiritual understanding to find meaning and harmony in your life."

"I'm not convinced about that at the moment. In my darker moments, I feel as if I may have inherited more of my father's genes."

"The more evolved you are, the more you're tested, but you must eliminate fear from your life. It gives potency to evil and you're still afraid."

"It's not that I'm afraid, I just don't want to be tested. Don't I have free will in this," I raised the pitch of my voice and sighed, sitting back and waiting for the next question.

"Do you know how to exercise it? Leaving the Church was never going to prevent your struggle. You've gone too far down the path to stop now." He smiled weakly.

"But I don't want the struggle," I said defiantly.

He ignored the response, but his eyes caught mine. "I couldn't have wished for a better son, even if you'd been my own. I always felt you became a priest for the wrong reasons."

"Then why didn't you say something?"

"I did try to dissuade you on one occasion, but, as ever, you were headstrong and determined, with too many preconceptions of the nature of your ministry."

I resisted the censure. "Possibly, but I had to find out for myself."

"I understand. Your achievements and success in your new career have given me much satisfaction, even if sometimes I worried because you were like a car with no brakes."

"Not really. It's been work for which I've had a passion, that's all."

"For a young man, only forty years of age, to have won so many prestigious journalistic awards does you credit, but a greater destiny may now await you."

I touched his arm. "And I respect and love you, as if you were my father. You know I run my life barely adequately, so I'm certainly not ready for any other commitment and, with the greatest of respect, would like to choose my own destiny."

He placed his arms around me and squeezed. "I'd like you to take Rachel as your assistant. You've met her and I think you like her. She's safer with you and deserves protection."

"Why does she need protection?" I asked, curious.

He cleared his throat. "I'm not sure. I'd initially been puzzled by her decision to work for me. It didn't make sense."

"In what way?"

"It was as if she was running away from something, or acting against her will, but I didn't pry. She's passed on certain information to me and it's time for her to leave."

"You make her sound mysterious, but I don't really need an assistant."

"If it's the money, I'll continue to pay her salary, as if she still worked for me."

"No, you know better than that, it's not the money, that's of little consequence. It's just that…."

"I've disclosed more to her, than has been prudent and it may place her in jeopardy. I've entrusted a document to her possession. If she stays, I fear for her safety. I can only turn to my favourite nephew."

"Uncle, I'm not only your favourite nephew, but your only nephew."

"I'd forgotten," he smiled gently, as if he already knew the answer.

"I can never refuse you."

I liked Rachel. She must have been thirty-five years of age, but looked younger and so feminine, in that fragile, vulnerable way, which ensnares the unattached. Her large saucer-shaped eyes hid deeper emotions, as if she struggled with the harsher realities of life. I sensed it, but the magnetism remained obvious. I remembered watching her willowy and well-proportioned figure and dark bobbed hair swing, as she walked and felt an instant attraction. She could tell I had been looking; all women had the same sixth sense, when a man was on the prowl, but this was something more. She had the ability to break a man's heart.

A nagging sensation hit me in the centre of the forehead. An intangible feeling she would play some part in my life. A rational part of me promptly rejected it. Either she feared me or perhaps feared men generally, but she had shown little interest in me during the twelve months she had worked for my uncle. I had always been aware it was the woman who picked the man, not the other way around, so logically I thought there could be no risk of emotional involvement.

"What about Rachel? Does she want to work for me? I don't think I made a good impression on her and you don't get second chances to make a first impression."

"I'll speak to her, but I needed your consent first. Don't be deceived, there are depths to her, though she struggles with her sexuality. Something you know all about. It's a battle she can't win, if she works for me."

"She sounds dangerous."

"Perhaps, but being cloistered here is causing some type of problem and solves nothing. I've been selfish, but I feel you've something in common."

"I like her, but you make her sound like a nun."

He laughed, a deep-throated infectious laugh. "Most people are insecure and are running away from something."

"I'm not sure I agree, but I think I'll keep on running."

"It's true. We must increase our capacity to embrace pain, but few do."

"I'd rather not. I've had enough to last a lifetime."

He stiffened, an expression of reprimand on his face. "It's part of a learning process, which has many intricate facets." He paused momentarily. "If she'll agree, I'll ask her to start tomorrow, there's no time to waste. I can be very persuasive." He chuckled again. "By the way, she certainly could never make a nun."

"I'm pleased to hear it, life would be too boring. Now, what about the second favour?" I asked, suspiciously.

His face soured quickly. "This is more difficult and you'll think I'm paranoid. Dark forces must be overcome. You must take the scrolls and my file, before it's too late. It will include a copy of the Journal and a number of other items, which I've copied. They must be brought to the public's attention and I want you to publish them."

I was momentarily lost for words.

"Will you do it?" He pressed me.

"Why now and why me?" I asked, in deliberate firm tones.

"You've the integrity to write the truth, whatever the cost. You'll make a decision from a spiritual perspective."

"Is there something you're not telling me?"

"There will be significant risks and I don't want you to underestimate them."

"But this is really a bad time for me, right now."

"There'll never be a good time. John, you're my closest friend and kin and a journalist I admire." He spoke quietly and slowly, in contrast. "You're a strong man physically, but more important, you've a strength of character, which has helped you overcome significant obstacles."

"Uncle, please stop the bullshit."

"I mean it. The moral dilemmas and obstacles you've faced would have broken most men. You'll need all of these qualities of character. If the information is to be published, someone who commands public respect must write it. Every experience and all the knowledge you've accumulated in your life, makes you perfect for this task. I've confidence in you, but it will need courage."

"What if I said no?"

"Whom else would I turn to?"

"There has to be someone better motivated."
"There isn't."

"I don't like the sound of this," I frowned. "I have enough problems."

"Everybody does. It's the human condition."

He shrugged. "You must promise me you'll do all in your power to publish this material. If you need assistance from theological scholars, be careful with your choices, as I've made mistakes and I'll have to pay the price."

His love for me blinded him to my weaknesses. I may have been intrinsically loyal and strong in adversarial situations, but I had a sensitivity and tenderness, which made me vulnerable to pain. It brought on feelings of anger, resentment and frustration when people were insensitive to my needs or lacked love. There lay my humanity. It had been a problem in my marriage. I recognised it. Yet I felt huge reluctance to disappoint my uncle, though instinct warned me of dangers.

I sneezed as the aroma of wild herbs attacked the nostrils. I had become more used to exhaust fumes in the City, than the living natural world. I realised, in that moment, how far I had deviated from the spiritual connection with the earth, which constantly expressed its universal image of creativity and wholeness, mainly with people ignorant of it. I was no different.

"Now, tell me how would you propose to publish the material?" He asked, bringing me back to a different reality. His tone assumed my consent.

"I don't know about this."

"You'll overcome your doubts, but I need your expert opinion."

"What's wrong with the Internet?" I replied, failing to resist the assumption, my wandering mind returning to focus. "Anyone can do that for you."

He shook his head. "There's so much deception and scams on the Internet, it'll easily be dismissed. Laymen of high-enough standing can successfully publish the material, but if they're not experts, it increases the risk of the work carrying no weight."

"I'm still not convinced about this," I said, realising how easily I was being sucked in.

He placed his hand on my arm and looked into my eyes. "Please do it for me, my conscience troubles me. The Church and the Establishment are one and they will do all they can to keep this out of the public domain. I know it's not an easy task."

"Which is why it's inconvenient at the moment," my tone still reflected reluctance.

He sighed heavily, his head dropping. "The scrolls will reveal the common roots behind Judaism, all Christianity and Islam. It will show their origins in Sumeria, immediately after the Flood, then Mesopatamia and Egypt. If you succeed, perhaps it'll prevent the prejudices behind many of these fundamentalist groups and fanatics, which plague the planet. Your path will be fraught with danger, but isn't it a prize worth fighting for? It'll reveal we're all brothers and sisters, with the same spiritual origins."

"I don't doubt you, but I'm not sure I'm your man."

"I'm sure," he replied emphatically.

"You know I've no truck with the evil and destruction these fundamentalists perpetuate, whatever the legitimate grievances, but look at it from my point of view. As a priest, I failed to convince even Catholics about God."

"That isn't the reason your ministry failed and you know it."

"But I've tried to leave religion behind. Most of the bigots are beyond redemption or, at least, beyond reason. Trying to suggest to them that all paths to God are equally valid seems a waste of time and energy."

"John, even the Koran suggests Mohammed was a reincarnation of another spiritual master, Jesus Christ, so it doesn't necessarily involve such a quantum leap of faith."

"I don't believe I can do what you ask and I don't want another failure."

He shook his head again. "Failure is only another experience on the path to success. I want you to try." I had forgotten how persistent my uncle could be.

I took a deep breath and grunted. "Very well, I promise." The words slipped out of my mouth inevitably, before I had time to consider the consequences. As a matter of integrity, I would never willingly break a promise. Unfortunately, my uncle knew it too.

He struggled to stifle obvious pleasure. "I knew you'd do it," he said.

"You're the only person on this Earth who could have persuaded me to do this, but I need to know more, if I'm to get involved."

"I understand. You've read the Gnostic writings, but what do you know about the cult of the Black Virgin and its connection with Mary Magdalene and the Knights Templar?"

The implications and commitment this promise involved impacted slowly and I stared blankly ahead, eventually recovering my voice. "I've read the popular books and I'm aware of some of the theories, but not of any substance behind them."

He leaned towards me, his hands animated, with words tumbling out of his mouth in a hurry. "There's an ancient tradition of wisdom, which will lead to a new bond between man, woman and the earth. It has links to dark secrets from the past.

Christ transmitted his secret doctrine through Mary Magdalene."

"Isn't that to do with the worship of the Goddess?"

"It's much more than a continuation of the pagan goddess worship, its symbolism derives from the ancient Egyptians, where it was the female, significantly, who always carried the royal bloodline, contrary to popular belief."

"Didn't you tell me before, the cult of the Black Virgin was associated with esoteric wisdom and schools of initiation?"

His eyes sparkled. "It'll take us back to the instinct of love and we'll understand, more clearly, the whole purpose and meaning of life."

I picked up his enthusiasm. "You also told me Bernard de Clairvaux, the Cistercian, who wrote the rules and constitution for the Knights Templar at the beginning of the twelfth century, is thought to have either perpetuated the cult, or inherited it, in some way."

"There was also a strong Arab influence in their philosophy."

I strained my memory of old theological studies. "In some way, the Priory de Notre Dame de Sion was politically involved with the Knights Templar and with the cult." I hesitated for a moment. "Though isn't there some evidence of a manipulation of the facts."

"He nodded. "Scholars have refuted some of their assertions, as far as I can recall, but seek out material, which will link it. I never found the opportunity."

"Will you help?"

"If I can, but I've told you, it'll be difficult and my time may be limited. You must do more

research yourself, so you can show their origins."
His eyes shone, but still masked anxiety.

"How will it be difficult? I can always see
you for advice."

"I may not always be around. The moment
they can locate the scrolls, I'll have no future. I'm
certain of this."

I grimaced. "Now you're frightening me."

"I don't mean to, but there are certain
realities you must face. You know I do not fear
death, it is only a walk within our mind.
Consciousness cannot die or cease to exist, so why
should I fear it?"

"Where are the documents?" I asked,
resigned to my obligations.

"They're secure. I'll have to bide my time
before recovering them, but I'll try to have them
here by the end of the month. I dare not keep them
in the house for more than twenty-four hours. Please
come here immediately I contact you."

His words were hardly comforting, but as
with all secrets, I craved for their knowledge, once
my appetite had been whetted. My course was now
irrevocably set.

"What happened to King Philip le Bel?" I
asked, reverting to the historical origins of the
scrolls.

"The Pope, Clement V, died within weeks of
bowel cancer and King Philip IV fell off his horse
and died seven months later. Even his Chief
Inquisitor was dead before the year was out. Just as
De Molay prophesied."

My face contorted. "It adds to the legend?"

"I mentioned to you yesterday that
throughout time, there has always been two streams
of history, the outward one visible for all to see and
the underground and esoteric one, which was known

only to Initiates. As with all esoteric hierarchy, only those initiated at the highest levels knew the whole truth."

"How did De Molay manage to protect the information?"

"Through this system of Initiation and by using a code."

"But he must have confessed to everything under torture," I suggested.

He shook his head. "He never revealed what they'd discovered about Christ, from the scrolls recovered during the excavations at the Temple in Jerusalem."

"Are there copies of the scrolls?" I asked.

He hesitated for a moment. "I've copied the scrolls carefully, so as not to damage them, and I'll supply copies of the interpretations. If you need further copies then copy the copies, not the originals. You must take great care of the originals and keep them in the silk, which protects them. Temperature control is essential to prevent damage from humidity.

"I understand."

My uncle took two folded sheets of paper from his inside pocket and unfolded them. "These are photocopies of the first two pages of the Journal, written by Hugues de Payen in the year 1100."

"They're in French," I said.

"What did you expect? It's about time your expensive Cambridge education came in useful."

"Shall I read them now?"

He gestured with quick movements of his hand, pointing to them. "You can read them later. I must believe there's a pattern of events, which will eventually bring a unity of purpose between all religions, rather than one faction constantly battling with another, all in the name of spirituality. It's brainless." He said, his passion for truth as unflinching as ever.

"Uncle, the problem is the minute you bring in religion, there are rules and boxes, which attract all the human flaws, whereas spirituality bypasses religion."

"I forget who once said if God existed and cared about us, he would never have given us religion."

"You're right, of course," I agreed.

He tilted his head towards me. "As you'll see from the scrolls, the essence of the true teaching of Christ is that you don't need an intermediary between the individual and God."

I smiled. "You can imagine the Church's view on that."

"But evil in all its aspects must be exposed for the impostor it is."

The smile subsided. "Unfortunately, I suspect there may be some dark times ahead before that happens."

His expression monitored the more serious side of his nature and his eyes looked down. "Perhaps eventually spirituality will shine through."

"I've never heard you be negative before, Uncle."

"You're right. I must be getting old."

"Not you. You'll never get old." I smiled again.

He reciprocated, looking up again, taking a deep breath. "The Knights Templar were wary of the Roman Church and so must you. They did the Church's bidding when necessary, such as the conceding of the Kingdoms of England and Ireland to the Catholic Church in King John's Charter of May 1213, two years before Magna Carta."

I lifted my eyebrows. " I do not recall that part of my history lessons."

"Everyone remembers Magna Carta for the rights it bestowed, but forget that the King had already conceded these kingdoms to Pope Innocent III and the holy Roman Church some two years before for himself and all his successors and heirs forever and as an acknowledgment of it, even agreed to pay one thousand pounds a year."

I shook my head. "Surely, this is not taken as binding in this modern era?" I asked, scornfully.

He stiffened, wagging his finger and I listened silently, as he raised his voice. "Don't underestimate their power and influence or all will be lost. They're not just a religious organisation. There are sinister aspects to their connections."

"There you go, frightening me again."

"John, when have you ever known fear? It's alien to your nature."

I turned towards him. "Believe me, I've had my moments."

"You must remember what happened to the Order of the Solar Temple. They were close to a wisdom path, but were infiltrated and their work undermined, as a consequence. This is what they do."

"You mean corrupting the truths and publishing misinformation?"

"Worse. Sixty nine of their members have subsequently been killed, many were known to have been murdered, yet despite an investigation by the French Police, ongoing since 1994, there have been no prosecutions."

"I'm sorry." I said, recoiling. "What about the Knights Templar, what else can you tell me about them?"

"Do your research and we'll talk again." He replied.

"You've told me they had secret contacts with the mystical sects of the Jews and the Arabs." I coaxed a response.

His reaction delayed a second or two. "They refused to take part in the Albigensian Crusade against the Cathars in the south of France, as their beliefs were similar, though they were far more secretive about them."

"Didn't some of the Cathars become Templars?" I asked again, recalling past reading.

"Yes, even the Tarot can be traced back to these times. It had certain symbolism, used by both the Templars and the Cathars in their quest for archetypal energy. Its twenty-two trump cards corresponded to the twenty-two letters of the Hebrew alphabet and cabbalistic Judaism."

"Is this why the Church continues to undermine it?" I asked.

"Jung understood it's true archetypal significance, as a form of psychological transformation."

"Where do I start my research?" I asked. "The British Museum and the Natural History Museum in London or do I go to Paris and the Musee Du Louvre and the Bibliotheque Nationale? I also need to know about this relic?" I could never ask one question, when three needed answering.

He pondered, before replying. "You'll probably have to do research at all of these places, but read the documents I'll give you first. It's critical you understand there are still significant tracts of scriptural and cultural documents, which were not included in the Bible."

I nodded. "I understand that more than most, uncle. They were omitted for various reasons of vested interest. Through the centuries, the academic establishments strategically ignored them and fiercely persecuted anyone who may have openly canvassed the heresy."

"As long as there were people of courage like De Molay, they could never destroy the truth," he said.

"As you know, it's a cabbalistic principle that what is concealed is always more powerful than what is manifest," I reminded him.

He looked up, as a shirt-sleeved member of his staff walked across the patio and down the path, stopping some fifteen feet away.

"You've business to attend to," he said coldly, no respect or humility in the address." He turned and walked back up the path.

"These are the problems I'm facing here," he whispered, pointing towards the house. He stood up slowly, groaning with the effort. "We can discuss these things in more detail when I see you next. In the meantime, you'll do well to remember the same vested interests will conspire against you, even if their methods are more subtle than the Inquisition."

"You're still trying to frighten me, aren't you?" I narrowed my eyes.

He shook his head. "Not at all, but you must exercise discipline and it's critical you don't underestimate the power of these vested interests."

"I hear what you say," I said too dismissively, "but you make it sound as if we're back in the Dark Ages, with persecution for anyone canvassing heresy. "

"John, you said that as if you don't believe me, but you must. There are still bigots and they still have far-reaching power."

"Very well," I replied, lifting my right hand, as an acknowledgment.

"Good. When you do your research on the relic, bear in mind its existence is rumour and unproven, but you must follow the scholarly path others have trod and study the Journal."

"It's what I do best," I replied.

He nodded and spoke in deliberate, monotonous tones. "If you refer to the scriptures, you'll understand the challenge we all have to confront. 'The two Beasts appear at the threshold, where the ways of men cease and the ways of God begin.' "

"I never quite understood what that meant." I confessed.

He smiled for a moment. "We have free will and man has the choice between a change in spiritual attitudes or the destruction of the Planet. Which choice will we make?" He paused for a second or two, looking at me quizzically, before reciting another biblical prophecy. "The Fourth Horseman of the Apocalypse, the Pale Rider, has already been unleashed. His name is Death and perversely it waits for no-one."

***

It must have been three weeks later, when Rachel came into my office, stern-faced. "Ronan, one of the Cardinal's staff, has just telephoned."

I stopped what I was doing and turned to face her. "What did he say?"

She hesitated. "Your uncle is gravely ill. He asked if you'd go to him at once. There's apparently no time for delay."

Further extract from the second scroll. "… I, Jesus, of the Nazarene sect, attest for all to witness. I am a mortal man. Only human beings can contemplate and in reflection come to know God, though I recognize that to use the word God immediately limits God. The purpose of human life is to rise above our human nature and awaken to our divine nature. We do this by learning to give and share, in a way that is against our instinct, and is, in fact, uncomfortable. No rules, regulations, politics or manner of worship are necessary to touch this all-consuming, awesome bliss, this stillness of the One. When we realise God is everywhere and in everything, then we can become one with him and it is through the heart that we connect with this Oneness and develop conviction. This is the potential for our spiritual journey and the potential to transform our world. To know God, we must become like God. Those who choose the path of the Mysteries are always tested, for only the best will do for Initiates of the mystical way. Evil and Darkness are the negative thrust-block for this testing. Overcoming it, is part of the test for the transformation of the individual spirit. The transformation of each such spirit takes us one step further towards the transformation of the world. The Pharisees may, for political reasons, wish to conspire with the Sanhedrin and see me portrayed as a God, for this will enable them to attack my teachings as blasphemous, but they are hypocrites who seek recognition for earthly motives. As with all institutionalised religion, which seeks control over the people, they become lethal and arrogant and blight true spiritual knowledge. I fear many want me to pronounce myself as the long-awaited Messiah or even to create another myth of a resurrected God. I write so all will understand, I am not Osiris or Dionysus reincarnate. My message of rebirth is the knowledge of our immortality. There is a myth, which explains the descent of the soul into the physical body and the return along the spiritual path back to God, but it is a mere allegory. It is this alone, which guides us to the redemption of the soul. The soul may appear to be incarcerated within the body, but to escape our suffering we must be reborn in spirit. The mission I have undertaken is only to teach the way of Light and the integration of the Personality, away from the clutches of the Darkness. I acknowledge a risk, as with all who have tried to create a universal spiritual brotherhood uniting all spiritual traditions as one, that I will also be put to death for reasons of dogma. I must accept my destiny, though human frailty may test my resolve."

CHAPTER 4

Rachel and I shuffled quietly into the darkened bedroom, but the ambience of death seeped in before us. It mingled with the faint smell of unwashed linen and disinfectant, which permeated the room, closing in around me, clinging to my skin and to the particles of air in my breath. My uncle still lived, but barely. A Doctor propped him up on pillows in a large bed and acknowledged us in hushed tones.

"A Priest has administered the last rites," he said, quietly.

"Is there any chance he'll survive?" I asked, equally softly.

He shook his head. "He'll not last the night," he whispered, as he left. "It's a miracle he's lasted until now. I'm not sure, but I think it's the presence of a toxin, probably ricin," he added.

"Can you make a report to the appropriate authorities?" I asked.

He nodded, before closing the door behind him.

I knew many would mourn his passing, but none more than me. It saddened me to listen to his laboured breathing. Despite being a regular visitor, I had never seen inside his bedroom. A fading claret bedspread sprawled haphazardly across his bed. Even the lined claret curtains had seen better days. The furniture was mainly mahogany, with strong corners, except for an oak cupboard, alongside the bed. On top of it, a brass-stemmed table lamp, with a black shade, perched precariously. Three lights clustered at the centre of the high, ornate ceiling. A statuesque figure on the other side of the bed carried a hooded lamp-shade, creating eerie shadows across the pillows, with its harsh light, deepening the creases of pain on my uncle's face. The claret and cream wallpaper had obviously been expensive, in its day. A combination of prints and old framed-photographs had been fixed, almost in mathematical sequence, on the wall opposite the window, above the old bureau. I noticed photographs of my father and two of me amongst the collection.

I pulled up an old upright chair, with rope edgings, and sat down beside the bed. It was uncomfortable and creaked in complaint. I gently placed my hand in his. "I'm here, as I promised."

A faint smile lit his face and I squeezed his hand.

He looked across towards Rachel. "My dear," he said, softly. "How is John treating you?"

She appeared uneasy, carrying her head low. Her eyes looked down. A dark pinstriped jacket and skirt gave her an attractive executive image. Her blouse buttoned high at the neck, but the skirt had a vent revealing a glimpse of slender legs, which always tantalized me. "Like a gentleman, sir." She looked up at me, then my uncle.

I didn't want to be a perfect gentleman. "She's the consummate professional and I already depend on her." I said.

He looked towards me. "John, you know my concerns. Protect her, at all costs."

"I'm able to look after myself," she interrupted immediately. Her face flushed. She had a steely presence when she needed it. "Would you prefer me to wait outside? You'll have things to talk about."

My uncle turned his head back to her. "You make a good couple."

She blushed faintly, but said nothing.

He pointed towards a chair. "Rachel, sit down, where I can see you."

I detected reluctance, but she sat silently.

He looked at me with a wide-eyed scrutiny. "John, I've got the file with the scrolls and a copy of the Journal. I collected them yesterday."

He coughed weakly and wheezed, until all life drained from his face. I cringed, brushing away a tear. "Perhaps you should rest."

"No, no, I must tell you, even if it takes the last breath in my body. I'm not afraid to die. It's a mere transition. You know that." He pointed to a cupboard at the side of the bed and struggled to remove a key from a chain around his neck. His trembling hand stretched out to me, before I could assist. "In the cupboard, by the side of the bed, is a locked green metal box. Use this key to open it."

"They'll never allow me to take that box from the house." I said.

"Ye of little faith," he scoffed.

"Then tell me how I'll do it," I replied.

58

"I've told one of my staff you'll take this box with you. If you've any problems, Ronan will help you. He's the only one I trust. He succumbed to pressure once, but it'll not happen again."

I indulged him, for what I knew would be the last time. I found the metal box, scratched and dented. I moved it to the floor at my side and opened it. Inside I counted twenty-four large, musty envelopes, which had been sealed in the old-fashioned way with sealing wax. A larger bundle of papers, contained within a file, had been placed underneath the envelopes. The file had been bound and tied with purple ribbon.

"Place the contents of the box by my side," he said.

I nodded and emptied the contents onto the bed.

He tried and failed to lift himself up, so this time I helped him. Damp blood on his pyjamas smeared against my hand and I took out a handkerchief to clean it.

He pointed to a number of sealed envelopes. "Those twenty four sealed envelopes must be taken to a vault or some other place for safe-keeping," he said, unaware I had been distracted by matters of hygiene.

"I will," I said, folding the handkerchief. "No problem."

"You must use the utmost secrecy, as these will reveal the truth, which must be published. Without them, you'll be savaged and I'll be ridiculed as a senile, disloyal old man."

"I understand."

He nodded. " Inside the envelopes the ancient brown leather scrolls are wrapped in silk to avoid deterioration, so take great care with temperature and humidity."

I nodded.

He pointed to a separate bundle. "Those are the interpretations."

"And the file?" I pointed to a red file.

"In a moment..." He stopped, as black blood, mixed with bile, trickled from the corner of his mouth. His left eye twitched. I noticed a damp flannel at his bedside and mopped it from his chin.

"When did you begin to feel unwell?" I asked, my voice cracking.

"Yesterday, soon after returning with the box. It's no coincidence."

"Perhaps someone has tampered with your food or drinks."

"I suspect I've been poisoned. They're obviously not natural symptoms and nothing other than a fast-acting toxin could make me so gravely ill, so quickly." He grimaced. "They may not trace it, but I've asked the Doctor to do his separate toxicology tests. He may even call in the scientists at Porton Down."

"What can I do?" I asked, helpless and desolate.

Rachel's face drained of all colour and her eyes dampened. "This is awful," she whispered.

My uncle looked at her quizzically. "Don't grieve for me, my life is unimportant."

"But it is," she insisted.

"I never did believe this insignificant physical body was anything other than a temporary structure for the spirit. It was never my understanding of the Christian teaching. As Origen once said, Christ crucified is teaching for babes."

Rachel turned away, unable to look.

He glanced towards her and back to me. "You must think this is the paranoid rambling of an old man, but it isn't. John, I trust only one man, other than you."

60

"Who is the other man?" I felt compelled to ask.

"He's from the old country. The others are Establishment men, who'll do the bidding of the Vatican."

"You make them sound formidable."

"You mustn't underestimate the extent of the influence of the Vatican. It has become a right-wing organisation, which will cling to power."

"I always felt the Vatican was becoming sterile and cold, but always benign," I suggested.

He shook his head. "Anything, but benign."

"Surely, they wouldn't stoop to such depths?" Rachel turned back, finding her voice again.

"My dear, the Doctor can find no natural cause for my symptoms, but he knows my rapid deterioration precludes any hospital scans."

"I'd be surprised if it was anything deliberate," she said.

"Don't be. It's too late for me and there are more important considerations, than my death."

I squeezed his hand. "If you were to die I could arrange an autopsy, if you wish?" I hesitated at my indelicacy.

"If you do, they may try to cover it up and you may be forced to hand over the scrolls and the documents." He struggled with ragged breathing, talking in staccato tones, his voice rising at times of anguish. "You must keep a low profile. Trust the Doctor to implement the necessary procedures. You may not even be able to use your home, until the scrolls are published."

"This seems all cloak and dagger to me." I said.

"You'll find out soon enough."

"You paint a damning and frightening picture." I said.

61

He nodded. "First, open the red file. I must explain them."

I untied the purple ribbon, which had been bound many times over with a number of knots. Inside the file was a substantial bundle of papers, all containing what I recognised as my uncle's handwriting. It looked as if this bundle had taken years to write. Some documents had already begun to fade and many different coloured inks had obviously been used during the painstaking exercise.

My uncle slowed in his speech. "It was only in the last five years of working as an archivist did I discover these scrolls and the Journal. I haven't had the courage to divulge their contents to anyone, other than one member of my staff, but I must soon face my conscience, free from the shackles of this worn-out body. Perhaps there'll be peace of mind, if I pass this responsibility to you. It's my only salvation." His voice began to break and he gestured towards some water.

"Thanks a bundle." I took a glass from the bedside and lifted it to his lips, so he could sip it. A flicker of a smile etched on his face, before a wheeze prematurely stopped it in its tracks. A burbling cough took all his energy and I waited patiently for him to recover.

"You may come to curse your visit tonight and your friendship with this old man," he spluttered. "Your life may now be in constant danger. Don't underestimate the risks, you'll need...." He gasped, pain creasing his face into something ghoulish, which I hardly recognized.

I took the damp flannel from the top of the bedside cabinet again, folded it over and mopped a cold brow, beaded with perspiration. He took a deeper breath and spoke again, weakly. "These scrolls and the Journal originally came from the Hall of the Popes in Avignon."

"Presumably, they were taken there in the 14th century, during the purge of the Knights Templar in France."

He hesitated and groaned. As he bent forward, I instinctively held my hand out and placed his head back on the pillow. "Do you have to tell me these things, you should rest."

"You don't understand their importance," he said. His eyes opened wide, almost catching fire. I melted back into my chair, chastened.

"It was to the credit of De Molay that in public he recanted the confession, as being obtained under torture." He gritted his teeth.

"Were the Knights Templar heretics?" I asked.

"Depends on your point of view," he whispered. "The scrolls pre-date anything in the Bible and were authentic enough. They stemmed from the cabbala and the Egyptian mystery schools."

"I thought the cabbala was an esoteric or mystical aspect of Judaism?" Rachel asked, her face looked puzzled, but she was obviously listening attentively.

I nodded and smiled, appreciative of the fact she was surprisingly well-informed.

"Tell her, John," my uncle said.

I turned towards her. "It considerably pre-dates Judaism, which suggests the source of all religion is the same. Over time, separate schisms have caused divisions within the religion."

"In the same way that there are cultural demarcation lines between peoples?" She said.

"Similar," I smiled again.

"Man-made creeds have been preferred to divine inspiration," my uncle intervened.

"Diversity should never have meant alienation, with all the injustices it creates," I raised my voice.

"Simple human flaws," he dismissed the comment.

"Why was the Church afraid of the Templars?" I asked, shifting uncomfortably in my chair.

"Part of the reason is they perpetuated a direct route to the Kingdom," he replied.

"Back to the same problem for the Church. They were not needed as an intermediary."

"Precisely," he concurred. "The power of the priests would have been diluted."

"It's why the Nag Hammadi scrolls are not recognised by the Vatican."

"The Gospel of Thomas within those scrolls suggests that the Kingdom of God was within you and all around you."

"But the other reason they feared the Templars?"

He doubled up in pain, grimacing and taking in sharp breaths. "There's a mystery, in which time itself is transformed into space."

"I don't understand."

"You will in due course. De Molay knew the Knights Templar weren't heretics because he'd read the scrolls and the Journal of his Grandmaster predecessors. He knew the scrolls were authentic, though some may have originated from a time long before Christ, the majority were written by Christ and his Nazarenes. They stem from the cabbala, which, as you know, forms the basis of the true western mystical tradition and pre-date anything written in the New Testament, mere sanitized and political versions of the Gospels."

It was six o'clock in the evening and a shaft of light from a sunny spring day squeezed, almost reluctantly, between partially drawn curtains, draping one part of the bed from the window, some five yards away and creating a splash of colour in the room. He must have known he wouldn't see the light of the sunrise again. Death seemed so final, even if my training had supposed to teach me otherwise.

"What scrolls is he talking about?" Rachel whispered, in the lull in conversation.

I looked at her. "They're the scrolls discovered by Hugues de Payen beneath the Temple in Jerusalem, at the end of the First Crusade in 1100. He had located the secret passages, which took them many metres deep beneath the Temple."

"I still don't understand."

"Significantly, he went on to become the first Grand Master of the Knights Templar. History suggests they were formed in 1118, but it's more likely they were formed seven years earlier in 1111. Their clandestine work started from the discovery and their deception was essential for self-preservation."

She nodded and I turned back to my uncle, pain constantly reflected in his face. "Can I get you anything?" I asked.

"Another six months," he wheezed, in a futile attempt at laughter, but recovered his composure quickly. "The hand-written file is a copy of a narrative, the original of which remains deep in the vaults of the Vatican. I was unable to remove it because of its size. So over the years, I copied it laboriously in my own hand-writing and took the copies out with me, page by page." His legs thrashed out, as the suffering increased. "Doesn't remove sound much better then steal?" He looked at me quizzically.

"What's contained in the Journal altogether?" I asked, bright-eyed and attentive. "I still have the copy of the first two pages."

He sighed and groaned again, louder than before. "The rest is various accounts written by the Knights Templar Grand Masters, between 1100 and 1307, and other parts written by Bernard of Clairvaux, obviously intended to record the accurate history of the Knights Templar, their beliefs, rules and exploits."

I opened the file, but skipped the first two pages and began to peruse random parts, listening to my uncle at the same time. "Interesting."

"You'll see their purpose wasn't to protect pilgrims on the road to the Holy Land, as stated in their constitution. This may have sounded grand, but impractical, even absurd as…Oh No, No!" A pained expression crossed his face, as the agony of death drew closer.

"What does he mean, impractical?" Rachel leant over.

I placed my index finger to my lips, before replying. "As there were so few of them it was hardly plausible. In fact, it was quite absurd. There were only nine of them at the start, with others joining later to make up the mystical thirteen they wanted."

My uncle joined the discussions again. "They intended to denounce the Catholic Church's interpretations of the Virgin Birth and the Resurrection."

I aided him in the explanation. "Just as the Nazarene Church of Jesus had done, centuries before. They believed his religion was to be found in his teachings, rather then his veneration, as a figurehead or as the Son of God."

I turned to my uncle. "But what's in the twenty four scrolls themselves. Have you interpreted them all?" I asked.

The creases of pain in my uncle's face eased for a moment. "Yes, I have, but a little patience, my boy." A gurgling in his throat intensified and his voice scratched out an explanation. "The Knights Templar had to protect a verbal heritage or be destroyed as heretics. They knew the Jewish Cabbalists had protected their mystical heritage by word of mouth using the Tree of Life as a meditation glyph and a memory system in the process."

A series of short staccato breaths interrupted his explanation and an attempt to clear the gurgling in his throat, by coughing, failed. Nevertheless, he persisted, words almost strangling in his throat. "The Templars used a code similar to that contained within the Dead Sea Scrolls, even though they weren't discovered until hundreds of years later. It's where the mystical saying that there is nothing hidden which cannot be seen, originally derives." A belch prevented further speech and more blood seeped from his mouth.

I handed the flannel to him. I could never hide my feelings and shook my head, involuntarily. A clock chimed eerily in the hall outside his bedroom, as if counting down the time to his demise. Though somewhat muted, I could hear the sound of much activity downstairs, with internal doors banging shut, whilst cupboard drawers opened and closed and occasionally raised voices exchanged views heatedly.

"Interesting isn't it?" He found his voice again, apparently oblivious to any noise outside his bedroom. "You may be sceptical, but read the interpretations and consider the evidence. There's no leap of faith. The Templars protected their special knowledge with symbolism and a complex system of secret cells, each with its own oath of secrecy, within separate degrees of initiation."

"Is this how the modern-day Masons began?" I asked.

"The Masons have lost their heritage, but any serious investigation of their history will take you back to the Knights Templar. You just have to look at the original Scottish Rite, but I don't have the time to talk about...Aah." He gasped, as words seeking expression withered in muted expulsion.

"I'm sorry," I said, bowing my head. "Do you want us to leave now?"

"No, no. I must go on. They tried to destroy the Knights Templar and their records. They wanted them tainted as heretics." He paused for breath, grimacing as the talking aggravated his condition.

"I don't like to see you suffering," I said. "Is this necessary?"

"Yes, it is," he replied, his voice steadying again. "There are things I must say. I used scholars in different Universities to assist me with the English interpretations, including here in England and the Ecole Bibliotheque. By giving each the odd random page in isolation, just as the Vatican do, I thought I'd be protecting their source. Obviously, I was wrong."

"Didn't they ask about the origin of the documents?" I asked.

"I wish they had, but I made a mistake using the Israeli-funded research facilities at their archaeological museum and the Hebrew University in Jerusalem, for part of the Hebrew translation."

"Too close to Mossad," I suggested.

"With hindsight, it's easy to say."

"I agree. The Israeli government will not take on the Vatican, they need foreign support, particularly America." His whole body heaved, as he moved his head violently from side to side, before regaining his composure. "I assumed, as a Cardinal, they simply accepted this was an isolated document in the possession of the Vatican. With the history of bloodshed and deception involving the Dead Sea scrolls and other important artefacts, I should have known better. Only the Nag Hammadi scrolls stand up to scrutiny."

"They would have known that the Congregation for the Causes of the Saints would never have released such a document outside the Vatican," I said.

"It's easy to see it now." He pointed to the scrolls. "They'll provide an impetus towards truth. The Nag Hammadi parchments have already aroused interest in the Gnostic teachings. These will corroborate their accuracy."

"But what is the origin of this special knowledge and these scrolls?" Rachel asked.

"They were passed down from the original Jerusalem Church." He wheezed heavily. "From Christ and Mary, the Apostle of the Apostles, not from Paul's corrupted and distorted version of Christianity or Peter, who had no authority at all. He hated women and tried to exterminate the Church of Mary, but only succeeded in driving it underground."

"I understand," she replied, settling back into her chair again.

He nodded. "Even Paul said, in the Epistle to Timothy, that a Bishop should be married and have children and would be better qualified to take care of the Church."

He hesitated, catching his breath.

I squeezed his arm. "It's my understanding of the mystery teachings that it was Mary who was the Archetype of Wisdom, who linked Heaven and Earth as the great mediator," I said, pausing and releasing his arm, as his breathing stabilized again. "This is the energy behind the general background of Catholic mystical thought and not Mary, mother of God." I suggested.

"I'm not sure I understand," Rachel said, a puzzled expression on her face. "Is this the Goddess principle?"

"In a way, yes. The Knights Templar, the Cathars and the Celtic and Grail legends kept the feminine alive," he said, wheezing between the sentences. "But in symbolic form, for reasons of self-preservation."

"Why don't more people understand this?" I asked.

"The Inquisition left deep scars," he replied. "But formal religion, which gives subservience to doctrine has no value."

"Then what is the connection with the Crusades and the cult of the Black Virgin?" I asked.

"She was the original black Isis, but too quickly, too much," he still struggled for every breath. "You must read it, all of it, no more questions please. If I'm not allowed to talk, there may not be enough time." He hesitated, lifting a trembling hand and pointing. "Some water please."

"Forgive me," I said giving him more water and more time. "You know impatience is a flaw in my character." I bit my lip.

A flicker of acknowledgment showed in his eyes. "Too many Christians think more of temporary position and favour, than truth. I should have spoken out sooner." He sighed, but energy flowed from somewhere and he laboured on. "Jesus was a Nazarene who wanted to overthrow the Roman occupation of Judea. When his brother, James the Just, became the head of the sect, Paul and Peter resented his influence and that of Jesus's wife, so plotted against them."

Rachel repeated "Jesus's wife?"

I had read much heretical material speculating on Christ's marriage to Mary Magdalene, and was not surprised at my uncle's conversion, for it was not even controversial anymore. Most historical theologians accepted it was most likely and the evidence is overwhelming. The Priests had always known, but from the fourth century had more or less been given freedom to preach whatever they wished.

"Yes, Jesus's wife." My uncle placed emphasis. "Why are you so shocked, my dear?" he asked, his voice breaking up. "This has been common knowledge within the Church, especially since the Dead Sea Scrolls and Nag Hammadi scrolls were discovered. Jewish Rabbi were mainly married men. Even if he came from Egypt, Jesus is called 'Rabboni' by many of his followers and by Mary Magdalene in the New Testament. She had to flee Palestine after Paul, the 'spouter of lies', had killed Christ's brother, James. It was Mary who generated the legends of the Holy Grail. It was the reason the Arthurian tradition was condemned by the Bishops and why the writings of Merlin were formally blacklisted at the Council of Trento. It wasn't the Holy Grail itself, which was significant, but what was contained within it. Your research, if it's thorough, will discover a connection between the Holy Grail and the Black Madonna's. Remember black is associated with wisdom."

"Is this the reason for the Black Madonna's?" I asked.

"Par of the reason, but you may discover the reference to Magdala of Ethiopia and remember both Jesus and John the Baptist lived in Egypt for many years, though modern scholars try to link it with the town of Magadan on the shores of Galilee."

"This is something of which I am unfamiliar," Rachel whispered, "and I'm lost with all this talk of Nazarines and a Christian ideology I can hardly recognize."

There was no immediate response from my uncle, so I turned towards Rachel and interceded. "The Nazarenes wanted to overthrow the Roman occupation of Judea. This is all factual history. It was Jesus's brother, James the Just, who became the head of the sect."

"Why aren't we taught this?" She asked.

"Because the Church would lose all its power."

"Perhaps that Peter and Paul resented James's influence with his brother and his brother's wife. If the Church is based on Peter, where does that leave the Church?"

"You're painting a picture, which I don't recognize."

"You don't have to, but remember that Paul and Peter plotted against Mary and wrote her out of history and tried to pass misinformation to discredit her. Even the Catholic Church, when they gave Mary sainthood in the sixties, admitted that Mary Magdalene's standard image as a reformed prostitute is not supported by the text of the Bible. They separated Luke's sinful Mary of Bethany from Mary Magdalene."

"Nothing changes with misinformation," she replied.

"The Eastern Orthodox Church has always treated Mary Magdalene and Mary of Bethany as separate characters," I said.

There was silence and Rachel looked towards me. "Perhaps the word prostitute may have been used in the sense of the temple prostitute or whore, who were used by men to experience ecstatic, divine, mystical or religious revelation."

"Possibly", I said. "This may have been what Carl Jung or Joseph Campbell would have seen as universal archetypes and myths of sacred unity between male and female."

For a moment, my uncle's eyes closed completely and I feared the worst. There were some shorter shallower breaths and a spluttering in his throat, as he gasped for breath. A harsh vibration in the body signalled the death rattle beginning, but a feeble cough suggested life still endured. I willed the spirit to remain in its disintegrating body long enough to pass on its knowledge.

He groaned and his eyes opened. "There's a reason you could never reconcile yourself to the vow of celibacy."

I turned back to my uncle. "And what was that?" I asked.

"At a deep level, you still felt separate from God," he murmured. Every sentence took huge effort and his chest heaved again.

"This is Gnostic stuff again."

He gently nodded. The precepts of ecclesiastical discipline were drawn up to suppress the marital status of Jesus. It's why the Catholic Church instituted a rule of celibacy for its priests and why, centuries later, it became law, so feel no guilt, John."

"So celibacy is only a recent concept?" I asked, feeling some genuine consolation with the knowledge.

"Mm," he replied.

"Interesting."

He pointed to the sealed envelopes. "In there, you'll find the evidence of the highest sacrament and the 'secret of secrets' of the Templars. When you read the details, you may understand your problems from a different perspective."

"Is this why the Catholic Church refers to the Gnostic texts as the work of the Devil and sought to denigrate them, as they did with Mary Magdalene and the sacred feminine?"

He groaned again. "The spiritual state is androgynous, this is the urge for unity. The perfect union between the sexes is a spiritual urge. The Templars had a deeply sacrosanct ritual, which brought together the union of the two halves of the human spirit. It posed a serious threat to the Church."

"The Gnostic Gospel of Philip deals with the theme of androgyny," I recalled.

He hesitated, taking in another deep painful breath. "The Church had to destroy these teachings, if they wanted to retain their status."

He raised his shaking hand from the bed and gripped my arm. "This sacrament will be misunderstood and corrupted by many. It may leave you vulnerable to criticism, but if there's a groundswell of opinion, backed up by evidence, it could flood the Vatican. They'd never recover, but even some of the Gnostic teachings have their flaws. It's an imperfect world."

"Perhaps we can force open the doors of ignorance." I said.

"Truth always has a price to pay," Rachel interrupted firmly.

"But is John prepared to pay it?" My uncle asked her.

"If there were less religions, there would be more spirituality." Rachel said, a sincerity reflecting in her tone and in the serious expression on her face.

"Different religions are all flawed by human hand, but essentially they're only different ways to access spirituality," my uncle replied. "It's critical you remember the common source behind all the major religions. It is childish to pretend that some of the pagan and eastern ideas that filtered their way into Eastern Mediterranean thought do not have value or validity."

"And history teaches us that the spiritual truths perpetuated by the founders of all the great religions are often buried by those who claim to be followers," I said.

The sound of the chiming clock in the hall callously kept counting down the minutes of my uncle's life, as it ebbed away, and there was so little time.

"What will people do when they realise they don't need the Church?" I asked, rhetorically.

"People are already discovering the answer. You can always try to justify a lie, but something spiritual must replace it or there could be dangers in the vacuum," he strained for breath. "This is exactly the argument the Church uses to underpin their deceit."

I placed the file down on the bed. "Is this the reason you cultivated my interest in the Cabbala and the heresy of the Gnostic teachings, after I left the Church?"

He smiled weakly. "I knew you'd be interested and I was right." An attempt at laughter failed. Instead pain crossed his face like the crack of a whip, his head jolting up from the pillow for a second. I empathised, but looked away. I caught Rachel's eyes, still damp with tears. Underneath the hard exterior was a sensitive girl finding it difficult to come to terms with a good man's suffering.

I looked back at my uncle. "What can I expect to happen?"

"You're a theological scholar and a tenacious reporter, but you can expect the relinquishing of vows to be used in propaganda against you. These people control the media at the highest levels. All of your qualities of character and reputation will be essential if you're to succeed. I hope you're not easily intimidated, because I'm depending on you. Search out the Order of the True Rose-Croix in France. You may need..." He stopped abruptly, coughing up blood, which dribbled down his chin.

"But what can they do?" I asked.

"More than you think. Even the crime syndicates have infiltrated the banks and the Vatican Institutions."

"I've done articles on the crime syndicates, so I've a starting point."

"I remember them, but this will be different," he replied.

"Are you saying that there are malevolent forces at work within the Vatican hierarchy?" Rachel asked, firmly.

"There are sinister powers at work within the Vatican, which few people understand. They may be in a minority, but their influence is malignant," he replied.

I cleaned his chin and left the flannel on his bed within easy reach. "I understand, I'll do all in my power to do as you ask."

"Good, I've so little time. It takes a great act of will to fight the urge to drift away."

"Then go with it," I said.

"There is much to tell you, but I've seen the brightest light imaginable and instinct pushes you towards it. In the midst of darkness, the soul essence does lift up into glorious light. Where music plays, joy can be felt."

His eyes lit up for a moment, as if some faint glimpse of bliss dissolved all the pain or became part of it in a way that is essential to our being. "Nature's places of beauty raise the soul away from the suffering of a physical existence, etched in misery," he said.

I leaned forward. "What can you tell me that isn't in these documents?"

"You must research yourself, but the documents will show you the path. Do not be distracted by ..." I squeezed his hand again, as his voice tapered off.

"What can I do?" I asked, inadequacy echoing in the tone.

"Do you want us to leave?" Rachel asked again, anxiety furrowed into her face.

His eyes opened wider again. "No, you must stay whilst there's still breath in my body. I know my time is close."

"I'll stay to the end, if you wish," I said.

He nodded. "Human beings are unique in their awareness of death and it's this awareness, which always motivated me towards transformation. I've nothing to fear from it."

For a moment, silence crowded the room, before he grasped some energy again. "It's only recently that the Vatican has found the courage to make a formal declaration exonerating subsequent generations of Jews from responsibility for the murder of Christ."

"I never knew," Rachel said.

I looked at her, then at my uncle. "They'll deny this material, as they've done throughout the centuries, but they're already releasing some documents relating to the Inquisition. Perhaps we can give them a gentle push, but it may be the beginning of the end."

He nodded, then pointed to the file. "You'll find a copy of Joseph Boullan's Cahier Rose with these papers."

"Couldn't I just apply to the Vatican for a copy," I asked, aware they reputedly had the original.

"Don't be naïve. If you did, it would be refused, but it's not as shocking as they'd have you believe."

"But wasn't he ostracised by the Rosicrucians?" I asked, scouring old memory banks.

"They didn't condemn him for what the document contained, but rather for the act of making it public."

I nodded. "Didn't you tell me previously, he corrupted the rites?"

"The man had no self-discipline." He grimaced and gritted his teeth.

I felt hopelessly ineffective at reducing his pain. "What do you mean?"

"He fell into the trap that so many of us do. The problem is that real sharing, which involves giving not getting or taking, goes against the reflexive urges of our human nature. We have to look at everything from a spiritual perspective and that's not easy."

"The lens of ego distorts the truth," I said.

"That's right. Now. I must go on, before it's too late," he said.

I sat back in the chair and listened.

"The true Christian teachings will take you back to the pagan principles of ancient Egypt. You'll soon appreciate the significance of Mary Magdalene and John the Baptist." He paused, each pause lasting longer, but his eyes remained focused on me. "Look for the contradictions and the omissions in the approved versions of the Gospels. Many important writings were not selected for New Testament inclusion for a reason. Look also at some of the Gnostic texts, including the ones found at Nag Hammadi. At least, scholars were unafraid to publish them."

"If you mean the Gospels of Mary, Philip and Christ's brother Judas Thomas, I've read them." I said.

"They are part." Pain distorted his face.

I placed my free hand on the crown of his head to give him energy. I visualised a gold and white light and mediated its power in a healing ritual I had learnt in my time in South America. Where organic change had taken place, I had discovered that it seldom worked for me, but perhaps the problem was my faith, not the ritual. "If you need to let go, then do it, nothing is worth the pain," I said.

"Oh, but it is." he replied, immediately, in short breaths. "I must have peace of mind before I meet my maker. Being a coward in life doesn't stop me having courage in the face of death."

I waited patiently, but with an inevitability, which the shadow of death casts.

"Much was saved when the great Library at Alexandria was destroyed and burnt. The unique City blended many traditions. Some documents remain in the Vatican vaults. The evidence is there and must be made public, even the Great Work of the alchemists."

"The troubadours, who accompanied the Templars, concentrated on poems and songs of erotic mysticism and the feminine principle. Is this significant?" I asked, when a lapse in dialogue allowed interruption.

He nodded. "Look for the cross-fertilisation between the mystery schools of Islam and Christianity.

79

You must...." There was another pause, as he conjured the effort to speak. "If only people appreciated the pagan symbolism in the Gothic Cathedrals." He smiled feebly and his eyes lit up for a moment. "The Catholic Church won't be forgiven for its hypocrisy and the sham of its faith. It's in its death-throes."

Rachel shook her head. "Do you really think he can do anything in the scheme of things?" She asked rudely. "You're asking him to take great risks."

I looked sternly at her. "Rachel," I said firmly. "It's my decision, not yours. Why are you afraid? Do you know something I don't?"

She quickly dropped her head, silent again.

He smiled weakly. "Great couple," he whispered.

"I'm sorry," I apologized for her.

"Rachel," he took another intake of breath. "He's the only person I know who could make a difference, but you're right, of course. I'm looking for peace of mind to know I've done something, even if it's at the end."

"In what way can he make a difference?" She said, her face reddening again. "It's not fair."

He looked at Rachel, compassion showing in his face. "He'll understand, with his scholarship and his training, the significance of some of the scrolls." He said, calmly, but with conviction. "I can think of no one better to undertake this task, it's his destiny." He turned to me and I felt the weight of his will on my shoulders. He heaved two heavy breaths. "Patronize me and give me your vow on this."

"Uncle, I'm not into vows anymore, but I promise I'll do my best to publish the material."

He nodded, but all colour drained from his face.

"Shall I call for assistance? I asked, numbed into helplessness.

"No, not now. Remember Christ was an occultist in the true meaning of the word, in the sense his teachings were "secret". He was an Initiate of the Egyptian mysteries and eventually had to play the part of the archetypal resurrected God, because that was his destiny." His voice dropped almost to a murmur. "You must research the cult of Isis, which will explain so much. It's already in the public domain. The Church may condemn so-called occult practice, yet two astrological horoscopes have been found amongst the Dead Sea Scrolls. They would be wiser to acknowledge the truth."

I sat back, releasing my hand. "People will not believe it. They'll accuse me of blasphemy. There must be the clearest of evidence."

I looked at him starkly, but the pain took his breath away. Rachel stood up and squeezed onto the chair with me. It creaked again, barely coping with the weight. I placed my hand on her thigh, offering a subdued smiled. I looked back at my uncle, as he struggled for every breath. "At least heresy is no longer a crime against the state."

He nodded. "There are repositories of esoteric knowledge, in places other than the Vatican vaults," he mumbled. "You may be tempted to abandon this task, as you'll be tested as never before to take the line of least resistance, but it's critical you publish this material. Persevere, for my sake." He pointed to the scrolls. "You've all the evidence to support you. Once published, there'll be a momentum towards truth. Ronan can authenticate…." He stopped again for breath.

Rachel placed her hand on my uncle's forearm. "If it's his wish, I'll help him to do it," she said.

"Wasn't the Buddha searching for truth when he found spirituality?" I asked.

"Hmm," he squeezed a flicker of a smile. "You're definitely the man for the task." A lone tear trickled slowly down his cheek and anxiety, perhaps for me, lurked somewhere behind haunted, narrowing eyes. "The Vatican moves so slowly."

"You're a good man," I said, lovingly and with respect. "They're deceiving themselves if they believe the impetus can be resisted."

"I recognise I didn't have the courage in my life to do what I'm asking you to do," he whispered, eyes widening again. "People in authority will tell you quite openly the Vatican will prevent the publication of these documents, but you must defy them." He raised his voice, but the effort etched pain on his face and he doubled over, coughing blood onto the duvet.

"I think I have enough," I said, hoping he would relax and preserve what little strength was left.

He shook his head. "We must return to the path of the Mysteries and the religion of love, not strict obedience. You'll have to be so careful."

I moved my head closer to hear him. "The Church will lose all its power, if the truth about Christ is known," I said.

"It's not an excuse," he said, quietly again, his face a pale and gaunt yellow. "Because you cannot excuse the terror and brutality they've used. I feel sadness for my part in the perversion. It grieves me, now I'm about to appear at the ultimate altar of truth."

"I still find this all difficult to believe," Rachel said, quietly.

"You don't have to, but check the facts. Even in the second century, Bishop Clement of Alexandria removed a section of the original Gospel of Mark suggesting that not all true things are to be said to all men."

"How little times change," my uncle said.

"What did he remove?" She asked.

"The reference to Jesus and Mary Magdalene being married," I replied.

He shook his head. "I'm so ashamed at the part I've played. I knew the truth and did nothing."

"Don't blame yourself. You're doing more today than any of your predecessors have ever done," I reassured him.

"It isn't surprising the established catholic religion is in decline," Rachel said.

His eyes half-closed, but he whispered a reply. "It's critical the vacuum isn't filled with a greater perversion of the truth. There'll literally be Hell on Earth, if it is."

"There's so much I didn't understand," she said, with genuine sincerity echoed in the tone.

His eyes flickered shut and then half-open again. "John, I'm making a judgment of your character and, in this final act, I hope to atone in some part for my own..."

I couldn't watch his agony. "Please rest now," I pleaded. "I've all I need and I promise this material will be published. I'll not allow anything to stand in my way."

"Our cultural heritage must return to conscious awareness," he turned to me again. "Soon I'll discover the source of all harmony." His face lit up for a moment and the distortions in his face subsided. "There'll be less pain, if I know I've done something to move the world towards true spirituality, even if it's away from recognised religion. Search for allies, you'll need them. Remember, I love you very much." He stopped sharply and there was no intake of breath. The words "forgive me, forgive me" left his lips in one last sigh, then a whimper and a shuddering, before all life expired.

I whispered my reply into the ether; "I forgive you." I released my grip and shouted for assistance, knowing none could be given. I quickly gathered all the documents together in the green metal box and grasped it tightly.

Rachel took my free hand nervously and we moved towards the door, passing the large clock in the hall, strangely silent now. She pointed to the box. "How are you going to take that with you?"

"Easily," I replied.

"Why don't you leave it here and collect it later."

I stared coldly at her. "No-one will take it from me," I said, sternly. "We must leave quickly, before anyone can question us about these things."

Help arrived from a bespectacled, middle-aged Irish Priest with thick white hair and bushy black eyebrows. "My name is Ronan. I've worked with the Cardinal for ten years. I intend to seek sanctuary in St. John's seminary, near Guildford. I hope you've no need to contact me again."

"Why will you be seeking sanctuary?" I asked, puzzled he should tell me where he was going, if he did not expect to see my again.

"The Cardinal confided in me and I know your purpose, though I'll deny it. I'll honour promises I made to your uncle, but I can do no more at the moment. You must go immediately or you may encounter some difficulties." He led us out of the hall, allowing me to retain the documents in my custody.

One person placed his hand out as we reached the front door. "Can I have a word with you?" He spoke firmly, with no compassion for the moment.

"Not now." Ronan replied, before I could respond. He placed his hand between us. "Perhaps, this is a time for grief, for all of us?" Whilst they glared at each other, my path cleared. I left urgently, almost rudely, furtively looking around and over my shoulder, as we walked away, still clutching the metal box tightly under my arm.

Extract from the third scroll. "... If, as part of my teaching mission, I can point the way for the salvation of the personality, then I shall have succeeded. Let it be known that only by creation, through the consciousness of the soul, can a world evolve of any value, free of illusion. It is this unfolding of consciousness, which is the mystery. The personality and the soul must be consciously merged and unified as one. It is necessary for the personality to awake to the potential of the soul. This is the need of the soul for healing and this, and the path towards the Light, is my true mission. It can only be achieved through the one energy, which derives its source from the soul and therefore is indestructible. The energy is love. It is felt as pure ecstasy and is life itself. Unconscious evolution, with no knowledge of our sacred essence, will create a destructive and material world, full of destructive and superficial people, who react by instinct, not choice. It is a world where holy conflict and Jihad will be manipulated by forces of evil to galvanize support for religion, to the detriment of the spirit. It is my destiny to bring the worlds of the personality and the soul together in harmony. Its absence is the dour perpetuation of the myth of the Fall. If fear taints love, then evil is the inevitable consequence, though logically and paradoxically evil is a creation of God, for it enables us to choose and move away from our instincts. Nevertheless, it is an illusion. This is what makes us a special seed and differentiates us from the animal. The Physical world must again be touched by the knowledge and light of the soul. It will soon resonate beyond its mere potential, but this resonance is the stillness within your heart. This pilgrimage to the spiritual realm, the Kingdom, is a difficult path and is not to be undertaken lightly. Those who take this path will

*find, as with all ancient wisdom, it is the true
sustenance for life and the institutionalised aspect,
the Church, its mere imperfect shell. Seek out
knowledge. Purify your heart through wisdom and
in the abundance of your intellectual potential,
investigate the mystery of existence, for when the
heart has conviction, the head can manifest at will.
It is this investigation, which can awaken cosmic
spirituality and keep it alive."*

CHAPTER 5

I had driven back to the centre of London by instinct
and the light in my third floor office shone starkly,
like a beacon in the night sky. It made me feel
vulnerable. I copied only the interpretations of the
scrolls, as instructed, but the telephone rang
insistently. I left the documents by the photocopier,
so Rachel could finish the copying, and answered it,
but no one spoke. A chill ran up my spine and I
knew I had little time. I replaced the receiver.

"Who was that?" Rachel asked, pausing
from the routine work for a moment. There was
something strange in her eyes, which I could not
fathom. It wasn't fear, but rather some barrier,
preventing anyone from clambering inside her head.

"Probably a wrong number." I lied.

My voice lacked conviction and I wandered
around the office, vacant eyes revealing the clue that
my mind hovered elsewhere. A cloud of self-doubt
clung heavily, paralysing my thoughts. Fear
intruded, and the isolation creeping alongside it,
confusing the senses. The remnants of some
primitive, mystical instinct hinted at lingering
dangers unforeseen. The dynamism and focus, such
a feature of my career, now scattered haphazardly in
different directions.

Twenty minutes or so must have elapsed, without a word spoken. Rachel appeared as deep in thought.

I garnered what energy I could and wound myself up for action. I begged a favour of my lawyer Julian, a good friend, and within an hour the original documents and a letter were in his custody, with instructions to keep them locked and secure in a temperature-controlled environment. He would open them only in the event of my death. His unflappable and reliable nature bred confidence. I handed him letters for the Police and the Coroner. I hoped the letters, written as the next of kin, would cause an autopsy to confirm or deny my suspicions. I referred them to my uncle's Doctor, in the belief he would support me.

The photocopies had been slipped into a plastic folder and placed underneath a loose carpet in the wardrobe in my bedroom. I needed a safe place, whilst I considered my position and it was as good as any. This had to be a huge story, yet any elation had been tempered by grief for my closest adult relative and friend. Nevertheless, time was of the essence and I could not afford indulgence. I hid my concerns from Rachel and knew it would be wiser if she distanced herself.

I drove away from Julian's office, still trance-like, relieved the scrolls would be safe. The windscreen-wipers swished heavy rain back and for across the windscreen. Their sound and motion enhancing the hypnotic effect on a psyche so uncertain of its direction. I turned to Rachel. The jewellery she wore was understated and simple, an expensive gold watch with an Italian black leather strap and pearl-studded earrings. She sat elegantly in the front passenger seat, but her eyes looked down, haunted by some deeper anxiety. I touched her arm, but she pulled away sharply, almost instinctively.

"I'm sorry," I said.

"No, it's my fault. It's been a long time since a man touched me. I'm not used to it." Here eyes refused to hold mine.

"I understand," I said, sympathetically.

" Perhaps we can take one step at a time, together," she said, as if she meant it.

I nodded. "At some time, I must go to the Bibliotheque Nationale in Paris. Perhaps now is the time to start my research," I suggested, taking in a deep breath.

She folded her arms and smiled weakly.

I leaned forward in my seat. "I don't want you to take any chances. Perhaps it would be wiser if you remained here or took a holiday," I said.

Her eyes opened wide and her nostrils flared. "Do you really think I'm prepared to let you go alone?"

"But I'm thinking of your safety."

"I'm safer with you and I haven't been to Paris for a couple of years. I get withdrawal symptoms."

"It's not going to be a holiday," I reminded her.

"You don't understand, I can't stay here," she insisted, her face muscles contorting. Her tone had finality, but she had to know the risks.

I looked at her earnestly. "I don't want you to get hurt. I couldn't live with that on my conscience. This is no ordinary research project. There'll be dangers, some I suspect we can't even contemplate yet."

"I know. I'm not a fool," she replied, tension echoing in her voice. "But believe me, I can't stay at home." Her arms and ankles remained tightly crossed.

"Then give it more thought," I said.

"I have. I'm a big girl now, and would worry more, if you weren't there, by my side."

"You must understand the risks."

Her voice changed to a more gentle tone. "I care about you and I want you to keep your promise to the Cardinal, but I don't want you to be hurt either. It's possible I can prevent it."

"How can you do that?" I asked.

She hesitated. "Who knows, but if I'm around, there would be two of us to deal with, instead of one. It's bound to help."

I reached over with my left hand and squeezed her arm. I needed to plan the mundane things. This time she acknowledged me, with a flicker of a smile, a faint one, but it was a start.

"Why is this happening to me?" She sighed, almost to herself.

"There's no such thing as coincidence. Life has a pattern to it and we eventually discover our destiny." I said.

She nodded, but said nothing.

"If we're leaving, let's pack quickly, collect our passports and the photocopies at my house, it's nearer than yours. We can drive straight there. It'll be safer if we leave the country immediately."

I needed time and space to read the photocopy documents and the interpretations of the scrolls. Those documents in Latin and French I could understand, but ancient Hebrew scrolls would have been impossible. A terrible price had been paid for an interpretation, but I needed to authenticate them, pending publication.

"If my uncle found scholars in ancient Hebrew to decipher random pages of these old manuscripts, then he must have been determined to publish them," I said.

90

She pondered, for a moment. "I remember him asking me to contact a foreign university and a museum to seek help, on the basis of some research being undertaken, but I didn't pay any particular attention to it at the time."

"It would help if you could remember which one."

She tilted her head. "I think it was in Jerusalem, but my file will be at your uncle's residence."

"That's going to make it difficult," I replied.

"You don't think I should go back there?" She asked.

"Definitely not. Just try and remember which institution, it could be helpful, but let's do Paris first. If we're careful, we can return next week to investigate unresolved matters."

She made eye contact and I held it, the tension creating furrows in her forehead. The thought of a trip to Paris with Rachel stirred emotions, if I could only trust them. Like most men, I tended to think with my loins and not my head. It worried me, knowing I could not trust my judgment.

"OK, sounds good to me," she turned to me and smiled.

"Is there anyone you must contact, before we leave?" I asked.

She took a deep breath, running delicate fingers through her hair, before it fell obediently back into place. For a moment, sadness stained her face. "I must tell my father I'll be out of the country on business and I need to go to the hole in the wall, for cash."

"How long will it take you to pack?" I asked.

"Not long. I always have a suitcase half-packed for the times I went out of the country with your uncle, but I need an excuse to buy things in Paris."

"Good." I hated routine and, as a freelance, mainly avoided it. "I'll speak to my ex-wife. I want the two girls to know why I'll not be visiting for a while."

"Can you trust her?"

"I suppose so and I've no idea how long we'll be away. I've spare cash to hand. Beyond that I'll use my credit cards. If I need larger sums of cash, I can ring my bank. They'll transfer it quickly."

Rachel looked ashen and distant. "How long do you intend to be away?"

I shrugged. "I really don't know."

"If I'm likely to be away for more than a week, I'd want my father to know "

I smiled. "Not a problem, but I can't be sure how long. The mobile phone will be with us, so we can communicate with him, if it's more than a few days. If I take the laptop, we can be in touch on e-mail, wherever we are."

"I worry about my father. He still thinks he's a young man and lives life in the fast lane."

"Why don't you ring him now?"

She hesitated for a moment. "O.K. We can make the calls on the move," she said, taking the phone. "I'll catch him on his mobile, as he won't be in his office."

Her conversation appeared slanted, one-sided, and lacking in emotion, but I paid little attention. Some ten minutes later, as we neared my home, I noticed a large black Mercedes parked outside. It had tinted windows. I didn't want to take chances, so I turned the car around. It would follow or else I had become utterly paranoid.

I pointed to the car and one of the windows pulled down four or five inches. A face, almost discarnate, pressed vaguely against the window, like the caricature of a puppet in a show. "I'm going to drive away to be safe. It's probably coincidence." I spoke calmly, even if my stomach churned. The face followed the movement of my car as I quietly accelerated.

"I thought there's no such thing as coincidence", she replied. I looked at her, quizzically. I hated women with a healthy memory.

Within what must have been no more than three or four minutes, the Mercedes had overtaken me, cutting across and forcing me into the kerb. The power of the action sprayed such an amount of rainwater over the windscreen that the wipers were unable to cope. All I saw was a blur of movement, as I braked heavily to a standstill. Before I could remonstrate with the driver, two large men, dressed in sober business suits, had emerged from the rear of the car and dragged me out of mine. A third man jumped into the front of my car and took hold of Rachel.

"She's just a friend, don't touch her," I demanded, forlornly struggling.

"This is not the time to tell us what to do, sir," the older man said.

Fear enveloped me, from my head to the pit of my stomach, even my legs buckled beneath me, as I realised their purpose. I willed my body to resist and blood surged to my face. I felt the veins in my temple throbbing wildly, but I could appeal to no one and taut muscles had nowhere to run. I needed to think, but I felt out of control and physically overwhelmed. Though adrenaline pumped into my body, a numbness soaked the senses, devouring any remnants of courage.

I memorised the number plate, as they searched my car systematically. These were professionals. I may have been out of my depth, but as long as the documents were safe, they needed me. The thought was comforting.

One of the men appeared about ten years older than the other, of particularly large build, with longish straggling dark brown hair, greasy and in need of washing. He had a craggy face, which looked as if life had been a struggle for him. He had a scar about three centimetres long across the bridge of his nose. A confident and arrogant manner suggested he usually had his way. He spoke, quietly at first, whilst his companion began frisking me aggressively.

"We work for Special Branch and I've reason to believe you may have documents in your possession of a sensitive nature. They've been stolen and must be returned. Come with me." He grabbed me tightly by the upper arm and forcefully took me to the black Mercedes, swaggering as he walked, before dumping me unceremoniously onto the back seat. One man sat either side of me.

I felt helpless and weak, but a semblance of courage welled up as I recalled my uncle's faith in me. "Can I see your warrant card please?" I asked, coughing to disguise the cracking voice.

The man with the scar and the craggy face looked as if he wanted to place his hands around my throat. The driver in the front didn't turn around or say anything, but they looked towards the mirror constantly, as if needing his authority. This man would have been in his early sixties. He wore tinted spectacles, which masked narrow-set eyes and his skin, though dark, was sun-damaged. He was certainly not a driver by occupation; neither did he work for Special Branch. He removed the spectacles for a moment and I caught his eyes in the mirror. They remained fixed and unmoving, revealing what I thought must have been a stubbornness in his nature.

The one with the craggy face continued to do the talking, but this time louder. "I'm sure you want to co-operate. I can take you straight to headquarters under arrest and detain you for at least twenty-four hours. All we need to do is tell the custody sergeant we're making further enquiries and won't be ready for interview, until they're complete."

"That's nonsense," I said. "You'll have to tell him on suspicion of what charge and I have some influence myself."

"The charge would be theft, of course. We can even search your house with our powers under the Police and Criminal Evidence Act. This allows us to use force to gain entry, in circumstances where a suspect has been arrested."

"I've not stolen anything."

"Well, is this what you want?" He leant across and ran his fingers under the lapel of my jacket.

"There's no need for that," I insisted.

"Now, we're asking you nicely for your assistance." He smiled, exposing yellow stained teeth, decaying at their roots. "Do I assume you'll cooperate?"

"I've done nothing wrong." I said, firmly.

"Look here," he said, impatiently at first, then more calmly, "The owners of these documents have reassured us there'll be no prosecution, provided you co-operate and return them, intact, together with any photocopies. They may want a promise of non-disclosure, but with common sense, this can be resolved amicably."

"I need to know what documents you're talking about?

"You know perfectly well. Don't treat me like a fool. There'll be a D Notice preventing publication, so why don't you be sensible?"

My head ached. "I want to speak to a lawyer for advice. If you let me do this, I'll come back to you, by midday tomorrow." I said, with sudden inspiration and waited.

"You must be reasonable, you don't really want us to arrest and lock up the young lady too, do you?" He repeated an obviously rehearsed line.

"I want to be reasonable." I said.

The third man leaned forward, towards the driver and a whispered exchange took place, before the driver spoke for the first time. "Who's your lawyer?" His accent seemed cosmopolitan and difficult to place, but the voice had authority. The reply suggested they didn't know. I felt reassured.

"I don't know. I'd have to ask a friend to recommend one." I straightened my tie and sat up in the seat, gaining confidence.

The man with the craggy face looked at his colleague, then at me. He spoke slowly and firmly. "If we agree, you must understand we'll keep you under surveillance. If we find you've acted in bad faith, you'll regret it. That's a promise."

I felt relief, almost surprise that they would agree. "I understand. Tell me what documents you want and where I should meet you?"

"Tell him Marco." The driver said to the man with the craggy face.

"The documents were in the possession of the late Cardinal O'Rourke, but they didn't belong to him, as I'm sure you know," Marco said, sternly. "Now do you understand?"

"I think so," I replied.

"Good," he said, firmly and with a tone of exasperation. Patience was obviously not one of his better qualities.

"There are legal questions involved and I'll take advice. You must appreciate it's necessary, as his next of kin, to go through all of his effects first. I don't know the extent of them, at the moment." I trawled for any ideas, which flitted into my head.

"This is not a time for excuses or explanations."

"Where do you want me to meet you and who should I ask for?" I asked.

"We're undercover police officers." Marco replied. "That's all you need to know, at present. We'll meet you at your home at noon, promptly please."

"I may be a little delayed. You'll have to show some forbearance."

"You'll be given no further extensions of time. Don't try to communicate with anyone, other than your lawyer, or we'll not wait until tomorrow. We'll follow you home, to ensure you arrive safely."

"But I must take the young girl home afterwards." I pointed to the car. "You're spoiling my social life."

"I want to spoil your social life. Why don't you leave the girl alone?" Marco responded, strangely.

"What's it got to do with you."? I said, belligerently.

I felt a blow to the ribs and bent forward in pain.

"Marco, No." The driver shouted, too late.

I searched for breath and instinctively rubbed my sore ribs.

"We'll follow her home afterwards too," Marco said loudly.

He ushered me out of the vehicle more gently, though I still crouched from the blow to my ribs. As I left the car I looked towards the driver. "Can I have your name?"

It brought a smile, as he turned to face me. A Windsor knot in his silk tie and what looked like a Valentino shirt suggested this man had more sophisticated tastes than Marco. "Certainly, my name is David, it's all you need to know for now, but the name will be of no use to you. If you make any enquiries of Special Branch, they'll not tell you anything, but we'll know. I'll take it as an act of bad faith on your part. Do you understand?"

I nodded.

Back in my own car Rachel was white, unable to even look at me.

"Did he hurt you?" I asked, leaning across and hugging her. She still trembled from the ordeal.

"Not now." She pushed me back, in a gesture of rejection, her eyes darting nervously towards the other vehicle. She noticed my surprise. "I'm sorry, I shouldn't have done that. He just took hold of my arm and was rude that's all, I'm a little upset."

"I understand," I said, sympathetically. "If something is guaranteed to make me stubborn and bloody-minded, it's bullies. I've not bowed to violence before and I'm not starting now." I felt my face flush. "Let's go back to my place first."

Driving off, I looked in the mirror. The Mercedes followed. I had time to think, but not much, and I had no idea what I could do.

In these situations, as in all investigative journalism, I knew from experience the critical step was the first one. By gathering facts, one step at a time, the fog dispersed and the clarity eventually allowed reasoned judgments to be made.

Rachel reached across, touching my arm. "I'm fine now. The last thing I want to do is reject you and I don't want to be on my own."

"In any other circumstances, I'd think you were making a pass at me," I teased, reassured by the more friendly response.

"Well, if I did, you wouldn't recognise it," she replied. A glint appeared in her eyes again.

"Now that's funny." I said.

"Well, they say retaining your sense of humour keeps you sane in adversity." She smiled, at last, and winked at me.

"Careful," I said, in my most boyish tone. "Don't lead me on, if you don't mean it. I get excited too quickly."

"No, I won't," she replied, looking ahead straight-faced again.

"We're almost home. Take the mobile phone and cable from the glove compartment and hide it in your bag." I said.

"But we'll be travelling in your car, so what's the point?" she asked, furrows highlighting in her forehead.

"No. They'll be able to trace my car far too easily. Anyway, how would we evade them, they'll be waiting for us the moment we get in the car. We must leave on foot, take a taxi to your house and drive your car or we'll hire a car with cash. I can sort out the paperwork later."

As I arrived home, I parked the car in a visible position on the drive, rather than garage it. Mature trees surrounded the house, like sentinels, embracing it, giving the house a secure feel, though on this occasion, perhaps not secure enough. Its Tudor design made it appear older than its age. When I walked through the double doors at the front, the hall expansively led to an open dark-stained hardwood staircase, with a gallery at the top. Off the hall, to the left, was my study and library; to the right my lounge, dining room and kitchen. Everything had a familiarity, which normally felt reassuringly safe. The pastel colours of the interior walls contributed to the softness, essential for its purpose, as a retreat and escape from the rigours of everyday life, though telephones littered the house, as testimony to its demands. Even the freestanding, grandfather clock in the hall somehow rendered stability to the place. Untidy, it may have been, but only in a haggard way, which reflected the personality of the owner. It was a bachelor's house.

I ducked my head instinctively beneath the chandeliers in the hall and began looking for signs of forced entry, but none were apparent. I placed my index finger to my lips, until I felt secure. Rachel nodded in acknowledgment. I quickly checked to ensure the photocopy documents remained safe in their hiding place. They appeared untouched.

"Come in here." I took Rachel's hand, pulling her towards the main bathroom at the top of the stairs. She resisted nervously, but I encouraged her. I turned on the taps in the bath and the washbasin. "If they've bugged the place, they'll not hear anything now."

She began giggling uncontrollably. It was the first time I could remember her laughing spontaneously.

"What's the matter?" I asked, eyes narrowing. "You're demented."

She composed herself. "When you took my hand, I thought you were being amorous." Her voice tapered off, as she sank to the floor, giggling again. Her infectious laughter triggered a similar response in me, as I sat down beside her.

"If the place is bugged and they're listening to this, they'll be wondering what the hell is happening,"

I said, snuggling closer, enjoying the excuse for intimacy. As time passed, I found myself becoming less hesitant and uncomfortable in her presence. She smelt divine. I placed my face against hers and deliberately inhaled deeply through the nostrils to make my feelings, if not my intentions, clear.

"There are stranger noises than laughter." Her eyebrows rose.

"Are you flirting with me?" I asked.

"I wouldn't dare," she replied.

"Perhaps tonight is a night for serious thought," I said, still tempted by the thought of a sexual encounter, but trying to be sensible, whilst my discipline lasted. "After all, I'm looking for Mrs. Right, not Mrs. Right now."

"Passion-killer." She leant over, kissing my cheek.

"Well, I'm not convinced I want to make love to you with someone listening to every word and every groan." I said, feeling the need to explain my reluctance to take advantage of the opportunity.

"Oh, I don't know," she teased.

I smiled. "You're doing wonders for the fragile condition of my ego." My hand strayed onto her thigh with a familiarity of instinct and from that moment any control over my actions dissolved. She realised and immediately gripped my hand, shaking her head firmly.

"No, no, I don't think so." She sat on the edge of the bath, placing my straying hand back into my lap.

"Spoilsport," I said robustly, making no attempt to disguise my disappointment at that moment.

"Be serious, now is not the time."

"Perhaps you're right, I said, in a tone lacking any conviction.

She changed the subject quickly. "I was curious at what you and your uncle found so amusing about the pagan symbolism on the Gothic Cathedrals. What did he mean?"

I sat alongside her, placed my arm around her shoulder. "Well, the shape and layers of the entrance arch of these Cathedrals were intended to represent the vulva and in many instances you'll find a small circular window or ornate engraving just above it, representing the clitoris. Strangely, an organ whose only function is pleasure."

She laughed openly again. It brought a smile to my face.

"You're winding me up," she said. "In a Cathedral?"

"No, I'm perfectly serious. Bearing in mind the Catholic Church's view on sex, it's a strange paradox, because sex is anathema to them."

"It's bizarre," she agreed.

I laughed. "I don't think I should mention the pagan origins of the cock on the church steeples or else you really would believe I'm telling fairy stories."

"Seriously, I'm interested in how you broke your vow of celibacy?" She asked, cleverly sliding an intimate and provocative question in, almost surreptitiously.

"Just like a woman," I scoffed, shaking my head. "There's nothing to tell. I was feeling lonely and isolated, in a strange country and somehow far from God. I was weak and a beautiful woman consoled me in my loneliness."

"That doesn't sound too bad to me," she replied.

"No, I suppose not, but she did console me rather frequently, which made it worse." I caught her eyes with mine and smiled.

"Just like a man," she smiled back, resting her head on my chest.

"Sometimes I wish I could return to South America, where the natives live a simple life. Sex is no big deal to them. If they like you, they have no guilt about sexual matters."

"Perhaps you should," she said.

"But it would just be an escape and life has obligations. Remember, I have children. I want to be around as they grow and I want to contribute to their lives. I'll never go back."

I felt protective towards Rachel. Other feelings stirred too, but this was definitely not the time. I stood to move away. "Come on girl, let's organise ourselves. I'd like to linger, but we must leave quickly."

"I suppose so," she said, taking a deep breath and standing, all assertiveness and ego evaporated. "I'm unsure if I can manage this situation." She began shaking, revealing a vulnerable side to her I had not appreciated. "I was never the adventurous type." She looked at me with doleful eyes. "I didn't mind being your personal assistant, doing your typing and research, even your shopping, but I'm afraid I may get in the way. I've a bad feeling about this."

I moved close. She clutched my arm and rested her head, this time against my shoulder. "I want you to honour your promise to your uncle, but I can't stop shaking and I'm really worried."

"I'll look after you, if you're sure about me, but I think you should stay, unless you're absolutely certain." I hesitated, gently pulling her chin up. "But I can't leave you in my house on your own, so help me get out of this place."

She took a deep breath. "Yes, you're right, but I want to be with you. Don't leave me behind."

She still hung on to my arm, preventing me from moving away.

" I promise, I'll not leave you behind," I gave her a gentle squeeze, encouraging her to leave the bathroom.

"Do you know why I've had no boyfriends in the last two years?" She asked, as she walked with me into the living room.

"You've probably been too busy, " I said, flippantly.

She pushed me away. "I was being serious. I was in a relationship with an older, violent man for a number of years and had no confidence to break away from it." She waited for a response, but none came. "It had given me a modicum of security and like many women, I wanted the impetus of something better to come along first. I feared for the future otherwise."

"I understand," I said, sympathetically. "Though you don't need the prop of another relationship. Why women have to wait for another man first puzzles me. This always causes more pain with the breach of trust, which is difficult for men, but I'm not the one to preach to you. I have my own flaws."

She nodded, but insisted on opening her heart. "Well, he forced me to have an abortion, when I became pregnant. I desperately wanted the child. I've been racked with guilt and never allowed myself to become involved with anyone since."

"Why are you telling me now?" I asked. "I don't do the confessional anymore."

She followed me around, as I closed down appliances and central heating systems. "Because I've been afraid to live life and I want you to know the truth from the start. I've been a coward, unable to embrace the pain in my life and I've forgotten how to trust. These habits aren't easily shed, but I'm determined not to be a burden to you." The shaking subsided, but transmuted to a gentle sob. When I placed my arms around her and held her close, she cried openly, like a fragile bird, hesitant to leave a cage, which had been its prison.

I felt her sadness, but took a deep breath and kissed her cheek. "I promise you'll be fine." I offered my little finger and hooked it around hers, as a token of the promise. "I'll never let anything bad happen to you." I enjoyed her warmth, indulging the embrace. When she regained her composure, she dried her eyes with a tissue, checking in a mirror to ensure no mascara had run, with the tears, to stain such a pretty face.

"I want to go to Paris with you. I know I can help you, but how are we going to escape from here?" She slung the strap of her bag over her shoulder.

"I'll leave some music on low on a timer and turn on one of the table-lamps. I know how to get into my neighbours' garden, then away at the side of his property, without being seen," I replied, confidently.

"We can't just walk quietly out," she said. "How do we get to my house? There are bound to be people at the back of your house."

"Trust me." I smiled.

"I've heard that before," she said, cynically.

"Part of my neighbour's house will be out of sight from the rear. I'll ring Tom's Taxis. He's a friend. Perhaps we'd better use the call box; it's only half a mile away. We may also have to take extra care at your house."

"You're being very optimistic," she said, in downbeat tone.

I shrugged. "There are bound to be risks. If you feel safer at home, it isn't a problem. I've told you."

"OK, point taken," she said, more firmly. "I'm going with you."

I nodded. "I'll just collect the laptop and case. I can place the copy documents there. I'll throw some things in my holdall. What I don't have I'll buy," I said. A few minutes later, I opened the patio doors at the rear intending to make our escape, but noticed a torch flashing in the bushes at the bottom of the garden. I immediately pushed Rachel back inside and slammed the doors.

"Well, we can't go out that way," I said.

"But there's no other way." Her voice rose and creases stretched across her forehead.

"There's a side entrance, but I don't know how to get there without being seen." I walked to the kitchen. "I know." I said with sudden inspiration. "I'll place some rubbish in the bin and if I move it to the right it'll obscure our exit." I spoke with confidence; on the basis it is the first step to assuming it. I took a plastic bag of rubbish and went through the kitchen door, before placing it in the large green rubbish bin. I then moved the bin, so it obstructed much of the pathway. I returned to the kitchen and signalled Rachel to extinguish the main lights, taking her hand and easing her out through the side entrance.

"Ouch!" She shrieked in the darkness, her hand slipping away from mine.

I saw a shadowy figure grab her. I immediately dropped the holdall, thrusting a punch in its direction. It landed with a thud, which hurt my hand and must have hurt my victim more. He sank to his knees.

"Come on." I shouted to Rachel, grabbing her hand again.

"I can't," she cried. "Help me!"

He hadn't completely released his grip on Rachel, although this time he had grasped her leg. A surge of adrenaline coursed through my body in a rush of feeling. I summoned all my energy and stamped on his leg, somewhere around the ankle. I heard a crack. This time he squealed in pain and slumped to the floor completely, releasing his hold immediately. I picked up the holdall with one hand and pulled her with the other. We both ran through my neighbour's garden and away, leaving our anonymous assailant groaning in our wake. I looked back, but no-one pursued us.

Rachel sobbed again. "Did you see that? He grabbed me, not you. He wanted me." She took a breath. "I don't understand."

"You were probably nearer," I lied again. "Anyway, I bet he's regretted it now. Let's hurry."

From research I had undertaken for articles written about the international organized crime syndicates, I knew about the existence of a powerful intelligence elite, extending their sinister influence beyond governments. The clandestine, intelligence services had mutated from less sophisticated origins, by alliances with underworld structures, bonded for profit. They had ceased to be accountable to the Executive, from the moment they had set up private security corporations, with the backing of large banking institutions in certain countries. Access to satellite and surveillance facilities gave them a power they were reluctant to relinquish. They could fund drugs, extortion, smuggling, political assassinations and terrorism, create wars for the arms industry and supply the illegal weaponry, which went hand in hand with it. As with all intelligence services, this private third force had more subtle ways to blackmail, even influencing world economic conditions. Its control of the media gave it the power to discredit and assassinate presidents or prime ministers, so what chance did I have? I knew they had links all the way to the Vatican. Yet some vanity within me, made me believe I could take them on with immunity. I had to be a fool. They had their dirty money laundered through concessions with the banks, casinos and ownership of racetracks and other gambling institutions, which fronted their evil empire. If the Vatican used this kind of power, my chances of publishing the scrolls were minimal.

Nevertheless, in our innocence, we scuttled and stumbled along the road, propelled by a mixture of excitement and fear, which drove us forward, but which would also stalk every footstep. Perhaps the prospect of intimacy added to the unusual concoction. Even taking Rachel's car had been easy. In my mind, I felt it was too easy, but by morning we were through the Tunnel and in Paris.

Extract from a later scroll. " *...My brother James fears Paul, as he continues to collaborate and conspire with the Romans. He is a stooge, who has been educated by the Pharisees. He may understand many spiritual truths, but he seeks personal and external power, rather than authentic spiritual empowerment. There is no limit to his ambition. Ironically, he may want me as a figurehead for his 'new religion', but he would have me gloriously crucified, if it helped him to create the myth of the resurrected God. I am determined to avoid this fate. He would have to destroy James too, for he is the true leader of our Nazarene sect. Once Paul travels west to Rome, he could create a momentum, which would be difficult to control. His philosophy is flawed and I must endeavour to persuade him of his error. If not, he must be stopped, before it is too late and he corrupts the true path of the Mysteries, which is inward, not outward. If he is not careful, he will create an institutionalised religion, where everything, which people hate in another culture or in another's tradition, becomes a projection of what they hate in themselves. Spirituality should not be a test of where you are born or what is your culture, but what is truth. The way to redemption is not the acquisition of power for its own sake, but rather by knowledge and service. All true spirituality has common roots and is radical, but it can never be violent. This leads to err. In turn, error leads to a misunderstanding of our spiritual traditions. Evil and darkness is bound to follow, as light follows darkness, but in the physical world, it may only be the knowledge of it, which leads us back to the Light, a Light more glorious for its absence. In the spirit, there are always paradoxes and knowledge of them is the only insight. So all is one and one is part of All, just as* *everything that is above or within is also reflective of everything which is below or without. It is only by descending into the darkness below, can we rise up into the glorious light above and dissolve into a mystical communion with the Spirit, which is and always has been."*

CHAPTER 6

The haunting sound of La Vie En Rose, being played on a shiny piano accordion at a pavement café on the Left Bank, evoked everything familiar about Paris. A resurrected Edith Piaf could have been serenading me. It still brought tears to my eyes. I loved the flavour of the City, even the smell of the Gitanes cigarettes and strong coffee, which wafted across most street corners in this part of the city, reflected its soul. The unforgiving smell of garlic from the bistros, and from the breath and pores of the inhabitants, all added to its character, perversely. The waiter arrived with a belated breakfast and I quickly brushed away the tears, which had dampened my eyes. There was much to do.

"What's the matter?" Rachel asked, reaching across to touch and squeeze my arm.

"It's this silly tourist tune. I'm sorry, it's stupid of me."

"No, it shows you have depth. I should know, I've known too many superficial men." She smiled, though not condescendingly.

"I love Paris." I said, admiring the architecture around me, so peculiar to the city. Though the larger tree-lined boulevards had their own character and history, this part of the Left Bank, where the narrow streets straggled haphazardly without any semblance of design, added somehow to its de rigeur. I took a large sip of fresh orange juice. "It's so different from the rest of France."

"Me too, but it's been some time since I enjoyed its hospitality. I always loved the unique ambience and decadence of the place." She said, taking a deep breath and relaxing back into her chair.

I sighed. "We must remember our purpose. I'd like to read the copy of Boullan's Cahier Rose today. I also want to make some inroads into the scrolls." My eyes were heavy and I yawned, as a more urgent need intruded. "First, I need sleep, then I'll plan." Road noise still echoed in my head and I ached for the need to lie down. "I can't stay awake much longer."

"Do you know a quiet hotel, not too central?" She asked.

I thought hard. "There's a hotel the other side of the Eiffel Tower in Rue du General de Larminat. Hotel Ares. It'll be ideal, as its inconspicuous."

"How big is the hotel?" She asked.

"It's small and basic, but very comfortable. The owner and his staff are charming. I had a pleasant time there one year, when I visited Paris to see the Prix De L'Arc De Triomphe at Longchamp. It's one of the top horse races in Europe."

"I should have known it would be horseracing, you Irish are all the same," she laughed.

"Even Catholic priests make the pilgrimages to the Cheltenham National Hunt Festival in March every year, unless they wait for the Longchamp meeting in Paris in October. Is there anything more important?" I asked, seriously and straight-faced.

"Anything you say," she shook her head. "What about this hotel?"

"The important thing is the hotel isn't in a prominent position, so no-one will think of looking for us there."

"Do you believe they'd even know we're in France?" Her voice wavered and she withdrew her hand from my arm.

"It's important we take precautions, that's all," I replied.

"I want the truth," she said, firmly.

I never knew when people really wanted the truth. "Well, the Church is part of the Establishment and there may be organisations which would assist them. There may even be more support in a Catholic country like France, than in the U.K." I said.

Her head dropped. Perhaps she wanted the delusion, after all.

"I'm sorry," I said, inadequately, regretting my candour. "There could be a chance that the Vatican, its bank and institutions had outlived its usefulness to the private corporations. If so, they could benefit from any destabilisation of the established Church. Their research groups and Think Tanks, in various countries in the western world, are able to plan precisely the social trends, from which they could profit, often years in advance." I offered a little hope to combat the doubts, self-evident in her face. "This intelligence elite have funded obscure cult and metaphysical organisations and there were attempts on the life of the late Pope John Paul II."

She lifted her head again. "I really did want the truth, so I know where I stand. Are you still determined to keep the scrolls?" She asked.

My eyes narrowed and I felt my face flush. "I don't believe you're asking me that question, when you know the answer."

She looked away for a moment, before turning back. Some darker side hovered under the surface, but I couldn't grasp it. Her old habit of avoiding eye contact worried me.

"If you're not with me, then you're against me," I said, harshly. For a moment, she did not reply. I banged my fist on the table. The glass and the cup rattled. The coffee spilt. People at adjoining tables looked askance.

"I'm with you." She raised her voice. "I'll help you, you'll see, but

be more laid-back. I've known too many obsessive men who wanted to share their anger with me." She leaned away.

I took a deep breath, ruffled my hair and told myself to relax. "Point taken, but I'm tired and irritable. I must sleep and I need you on my side."

"I understand. Now you'll not have time to go to the Bibliotheque

Nationale today." She changed the subject.

"I'll devote the whole of tomorrow for that." I said, relaxing again.

"What can I do?" She asked.

"Well, there's an occult bookshop near Notre Dame Cathedral. They'll have the addresses of the esoteric organisations we need, including the Order of the True Rose Croix. Can you find a contact name and address? There should be addresses of Masonic Lodges there."

"No problem." She tucked into croissants and strong coffee. "That's the organisation the Cardinal mentioned," she said between mouthfuls. "Would it help, if I do it whilst you're sleeping? At least, I've been able to sleep in the car, when you were driving."

"I sometimes forget how efficient you are." I said, smiling. "But don't give your name or the hotel where we're staying, just in case, and be careful."

"You believe they can trace us, don't you?" Her eyes widened, stern-faced.

"No," I reverted to lying. "But I want to take all precautions. We must approach this, as professionally as anything we've ever done. If you notice anyone following, go into a shop or restaurant with two exits or use the Metro. It's so busy in the daytime you'll have no problem losing them, then return to the hotel."

"How far will these people go?" She asked, wiping her mouth elegantly with her napkin.

"I don't know. What do you think?"

I drank the rest of my orange juice. I recalled my uncle's comment about our lives being in danger, but this was not the time for brutal honesty.

"It's only that I care about you," she said.

"I don't think we'll have a problem, but I'll not take any chances. It's too important," I said.

"Then I'll be cautious," she agreed.

"Let's book into this hotel. There's a taxi over there," I said, pointing to it and leaving twenty-five euros on the table.

"Sure." She ran her fingers through her hair, before offering her hand, spontaneously. I willingly took it.

The taxi drivers in Paris were marginally better than Rome and less animated. At least they understood their vehicle was not a Ferrari, something Italian taxi drivers would never acknowledge and drove as if they could prove it to you.

"I must warn you," I said, during a lull in the journey. "I'm fearful about proper relationships at the moment and vulnerable. When I fall in love I'm blind, yet the women in my life always seemed to have their eyes half-open. It worries me, so please don't hurt me."

"I understand and I'll try not to hurt you," she replied, sympathetically.

"Don't try, just don't do it."

"Point taken." She raised one hand in acknowledgment.

* * *

The old hotel had been built in traditional stone, with the top floor squared off in typically Parisian slate. It sheltered in a nondescript road, with high buildings either side of it. I could not imagine anything more perfect for our purpose. The double doors were open and a porch area allowed guests to escape inclement weather, before entering the main reception area on the left. The interior was just as typically French, even down to the narrow stairs, which twisted around to the first floor. A single lift barely allowed two people and a suitcase to enter, without risking significant intimacy. The hotel room was pleasant, but basic, as I remembered. Soon I succumbed to sleep, leaving my enthusiastic assistant to do the legwork.

It was late afternoon, when I awoke, with no sign of Rachel. I looked at my watch. It was five o'clock. I felt the same unease, which a parent has when their child goes out alone for the first time. At least, I had time to read the copy of the Cahier Rose. It fascinated me and I understood how primeval energies could be tapped and stirred. According to the ritual, the Priestess brought down the spiritual power and I needed one or else frailty would prevail. After a knock on the door, Rachel appeared, cheerful as ever.

"Are you feeling better?" She asked.

"Yes, I am. I needed the sleep."

She handed me a piece of paper. "I found the occult book shop, such a small shop. I was expecting something much bigger. Anyway, the owner was helpful and gave me the contact name and address of the Order of the True Rose Croix."

I read the name. "Jean DeValois de St. Clare."

"Yes, that's it. I also have the addresses of the Masonic Lodges in Paris." She placed a bag on the bed and handed me another list. "There's some water and fresh fruit in the bag. It's all you need, until we find a bistro."

"I'd prefer to go to Le Grand Café in Opera. It's one of my favourite restaurants, the turbot is good and I've never had to wait more than thirty minutes for a table. They'll even give us a free Kir, whilst we're waiting."

"Sounds good to me, when do we leave?" She asked.

"Shall we say an hour? I want to tell you about the Cahier Rose and I know how long women take to get ready."

"Yes, tell me about it. Is it really so shocking?"

"Not at all."

She moved towards the bathroom. "Tell me after I've had my bath." She shut the bathroom door firmly behind her. I heard the lock click.

I consoled myself by relaxing on my bed. Rachel had given me cause for optimism by allowing me to book one room, rather than two, even if she had insisted on twin beds. Within minutes the telephone rang. I jolted myself upright. "I'll get it, it's probably Le Patron." I called out to her, calmly. "I suspect he's finished with my passport. He said it would be ready late afternoon."

"Yes." She muffled.

116

I picked up the phone and spoke in my best French. "Bon Soir."

"I have someone asking for you, monsieur. Shall I put them through?"

Coldness swamped my body and my jaw dropped. "Mais, oui." I replied, hesitatingly. "But are you sure it's for me?"

"Certainly. He asked for Monsieur O'Rourke."

"Merci."

"What's the matter?" Rachel shouted from the bathroom.

"Nothing," I shouted back, placing my hand over the telephone, and then removing it.

"Hello?" I spoke into the telephone. There was no reply. "Hello?" I repeated, but again no response. I replaced the receiver, my mind racing. Rachel, sensing a problem, came out of the bathroom, dripping wet with a towel around her. Anxiety lines showed in her face and those doleful eyes looked pitiful. For a moment, she looked like a little girl.

"It's probably nothing." I said.

"That word 'probably' worries me." She ran to me and began crying. I reacted instinctively, holding her tight, giving her the warmth and security she obviously needed.

"We must be professional and strong. I'll not let anything happen to you." I placed the palm of my hand on her head, until her crying subsided. "Come on, let's go out and eat. There may be many reasons why the telephone rang. Perhaps it's connected to your visit to the occult bookshop and the enquiry about the Order of the True Rose Croix."

"I don't believe that and neither do you. I gave no-one our address." She took a tissue and dried her eyes. "I'll apply some mascara and dress.

117

I suppose they'll not harm us, if all they want is the scrolls and the copy Journal?"

"Yes," I agreed. "If they harm us, they know they'd never recover them."

Rachel moved towards the bathroom, turning around at the door. "Would you be prepared to give them what they want, if our lives were in danger?"

"I don't know." I thought for a moment. "The problem is I couldn't be sure they'd be satisfied with just the documents."

She shrugged and slipped into the bathroom. Within fifteen minutes we were leaving in the car.

It was a typically bustling and moody Paris evening, as we crossed the bridge over the Seine, leaving the Eiffel Tower behind us. Cars jammed most of the roads and hordes of people rushed around, as if their lives depended upon it. I pointed to the Palais de Chaillot opposite. Imposing buildings loomed up, in every direction. "I'll turn right here and we can follow the road alongside the Seine and exit before the notorious Pont D'Alma underpass." Every taxi-driver repeated 'Diana', as they drove through. "If we turn left there, we can travel along Avenue George V, before reaching the Champs D'Elysees." I said. "Tomorrow, I'll go to the new Bibliotheque Nationale in Bercy, in the south-eastern outskirts of the city, first thing. I'll also ring Jean DeValois and ask him if he'll meet me later."

Rachel seemed in melancholy mood. "Just like Diana, I have premonitions, which recur. I'm convinced I'll die young and there'll be violent circumstances surrounding my death. It's why I always avoid conflict if I can."

There was a lingering sadness about Rachel, which permeated the essence of her being, in some strange and intangible way. I had a duty to teach her that fear became a self-fulfilling legacy and attracted the very thing she feared. I leant across and squeezed her arm. "I promise you nothing will happen to you when you are with me, so you had better ensure you stay with me."

"You're right. Look around us," she said, lifting her spirits and gesturing with her arms. "We must forget our problems. This is Paris."

I smiled. "I agree. Did you know that the Thai people have a wonderful custom at one of their full moon festivals on the beaches or on the canals. They light a candle and place it on a boat made of banana skins and flowers and as they let it drift away on the water, they believe their problems float away with it. Sometimes they'll also use candles in small cloth balloons and you'll see the sky littered with these burning candles, like giant fireflies. It's an effective spiritual ritual. We must do something similar, but something that lovers do."

"You're an easy man to love."

"But complex, I assure you." I laughed.

She thought for a moment. "We must light a candle at the Sacre Coeur and make a wish. Imagine all of our problems disappearing. As the candle extinguishes, so will all the obstacles in the path of our being together."

I nodded. "That would be good."

We slowly edged past the opulent Hotel George V on our left and the famous Crazy Horse on the right. It was still light and the sky remained clear. The crisp evening air tasted of Paris. Soon we reached the most celebrated tree-lined boulevard of all, almost unique to the City, as far as the eye could see. The setting sun filtered through the trees, like a cathedral, with shafts of light through stained glass. We circled the Arc de Triomphe and drove back down again, taking the view of the Champs D'

Elysees into the distance. At the top of this unique Parisian boulevard, bars and pavement restaurants, crammed with tourists and the young of France, bulged outwards, almost onto the road in places. Further down the bars disappeared, but crowds still paraded in their finery, as they had done for centuries. Courtship rituals of a different kind took place and lovers held hands, touched and played serious games of l'Amour. Similarly, birds sang and courted in the trees, which bordered this boulevard, finding little respite from the frantic nature of City life. Those whose duty was not to serenade the lovers, who laughed oblivious to them below, would have sought refuge in the more profuse greenery of the nearby Bois de Boulogne.

Rachel looked more relaxed, eyes sparkling, occasionally smiling. Even if you weren't French, the temptation to burst into a rendering of La Marseillaise could be overwhelming, as one recalled the victorious marches of history along this route. At every junction, well-known landmarks thrust out to keep us in awe.

"In the hotel, they told me there's a Brazilian drum-band playing at the Place De Tertre, in Montmartre, and in front of the Sacre Coeur. We can light the candle there and see the drum-band before we eat. It's something to do with their football team being in Paris," I said.

She nodded, more cheerfully, and why not? We were free to enjoy the City made for lovers. I drove through Pigalle, then left up and around to the Sacre Coeur and Montmartre. Long before we reached there, we could hear the samba beat of the drums. We parked the car and followed the beat. Young males and females were inching around from the Place de Tertre to the front of the Sacre Coeur, swaying provocatively in unison, as they played, all displaying an intoxication with their music. It took the breath away, with different drums for different sounds. It was impossible not to sway with the harmony created by the spectacle and the rhythm, though it was impossible to match the natural rhythm of the young Brazilians. Individual drum rolls broke up the continuity. The excitement of the ritual, and the energy generated took me off-guard. A Brazilian cameraman and his associates pushed us to one side and Rachel separated from me, amongst the milling crowd. Within seconds, I could see a familiar face reaching out towards her.

"John, John!" She shouted, an octave higher than usual. "Help me!"

I saw her grabbed from behind. Her scream ripped through the twilight. I charged into the back of the cameraman, with no restraint. He stumbled on the steps of the Sacre Coeur, trying desperately to protect his valuable equipment. The crowd gushed forward in the subsequent mayhem. I jumped over one prone figure towards Marco, his scar and craggy face unmistakable. Rachel leant back and pulled against him. It gave me enough time to reach him and jump on his back. I placed my arm around his neck, with no thought for my safety.

"Leave her alone." I shouted.

I felt my heart pumping, but I had no time for fear, only instinctive action. Unfortunately, Marco appeared more used to this situation. Almost immediately, I flew over the top of his head and onto my back. He landed on top of me, piercing his elbow agonisingly into my solar plexus. I couldn't breathe, but in that moment of release, Rachel ran to a man in a security uniform, pointing to me. He moved towards Marco, who leered and manoeuvred himself, so he faced the both of us, but directed his comments only at me, as I lay writhing on the floor.

"I can pick you off or the girl, anytime I choose," he said venomously. His face twisted with all the ugliness of the egotistical bully he had become. This was now his nature and he didn't have the intellect or the desire to change. He pointed his finger into my face. "My boss wants to see you. He'll call at your hotel at ten o'clock in the morning. This time, do as you're told."

At that moment, the security man arrived with Rachel. He placed his hand onto Marco's wrist, but simultaneously it was twisted, so the security man became the victim. Two straight fingers poked into his throat, beneath the Adam's apple, and he collapsed, like a baby, on the floor.

"Keep the appointment tomorrow. I warn you for the last time." His eyes bulged and hatred coloured his face, but something more. He smiled, obviously enjoying this part of his work, being in his element in conflict situations. He trained for it and people needed him for his expertise. Only in the fulfilment of this need, did he feel wanted. I realised, in that moment, the sadness in the man's life, even if no sympathy would pass from me. I disliked him too intensely for that.

He turned away, walking slowly to a parked car, some forty yards away, where another man held open the rear door. Rachel tended me, as I placed my head between my knees, gradually regaining my breath. Then she turned to assist the security man, still rolling on the ground, coughing and spluttering. She helped him to his feet. "I'm so sorry," she said. Turning back to me, she caressed my head and cried. "I'm afraid," she sobbed. "They always try to snatch me away from you. How can the man be stopped?"

I placed my arms around her, giving her time to compose herself. They either wanted to take her, as some kind of hostage, or she knew something important, but I couldn't tell her. I couldn't think of any other reason, but I hadn't appreciated her vulnerability, being selfishly too concerned about mine. Perhaps my journalistic career had made me too hard-nosed or maybe I still found difficulty in accepting personal responsibility for anyone.

"We're safe tonight. They want to speak to me tomorrow morning and I'll protect you until then." I tried, in vain, to reassure her. "We can still light the candle." I pointed back towards the Place De Tertre. "Afterwards, we can eat at one of the bistro's and still be back in the hotel in an hour or so. We don't have to go to Le Grand Café."

She nodded, wiping the tears away with the back of her hand, before slipping her arm tightly around my waist. Her bobbed hair covered half of her face, as she pressed it against my shoulder. "I could do with something strong to drink, rather than eat," she stuttered. "I'm not sure the lighting of a candle will help, but I'd like to try."

"Then let's do it," I agreed.

Within a couple of hours, we were back in the hotel, having lit our candle and imbibed in a stiff cognac. We bribed the receptionist to give us another room, with a promise to keep it secret from anyone enquiring. We didn't want any more disturbing telephone calls. It may have been only a semblance of security, but I needed to make a token gesture, for Rachel's sake.

"What are you intending to do in the morning?" She asked, throwing her wrap on the bed.

I shook my head. "I may have to give them the copies, but I'll not tell them the location of the originals. In fact, it may be safer if I don't say anything at all, but I'm not running away again." I sat on the bed alongside her.

She placed one hand on my arm. "You must do as you think fit, but remember what happened to your uncle. If you want to honour the promise you made to him, I'll support you one hundred percent." She spoke boldly, but her huddled body language and lowered head exposed the inner anxiety. She needed to be hugged and wanted the comfort of my arms, but each of us had some reluctance. Together in the moment our thoughts coincided.

"I've been celibate for two years," she confided again, but her eyes didn't engage mine. "I suppose it's the reason I took the position with your uncle."

I seized the opportunity. "I'm beginning to fall in love with you," I said, pulling her closer. Even if I found it impossible to believe a woman, with such sexuality and magnetism, could be celibate for such a time, I buried the thought.

"You used to avert your eyes every time you saw me. It puzzled me." I said.

She lifted her head and looked at me. "I'm not averting my eyes now. Perhaps I may have been afraid of my feelings."

"I never avert my eyes. That's the problem. My ex-wife had no objection, in principle, if I looked at the opposite sex, except she became embarrassed if I began to drool and salivate. I think she hugely exaggerated," I said, jokingly. "After all, I was married, not blind."

She laughed. It made me laugh. I couldn't help it. "I think it was Socrates, who first likened the male sex drive to having a sex maniac chained to your back, whose persistence, it was impossible to ignore," I said.

She snuggled closer, nuzzling into my neck. "I suppose I just wanted to avoid men, but it didn't solve the problem did it?" She wanted an answer, but I had a vested interest in the reply.

Extract from one of the scrolls. "... There will always be a quest for the meaning of life and an instinct for truth will drive mankind towards spirituality. The polarity of male and female must be understood in this context, in the sense that it transcends religion and attains knowledge of the spiritual realms. The physical union of a man and a woman, with spiritual awareness and reverence, is a reflection of pure spiritual energy and the highest sacrament. Its harmonisation is a creation of optimum spiritual energy, as it reflects the merging of the Consciousness of the Cosmos with the body in an explosion of feeling. It becomes a sacred unifying partnership in a bond of love. We are then One in God and only God. This process of reproduction is made a holy loving sacrament to acknowledge the marriage of spirit and matter. We must all make our contribution to the building of the Temple and the creation of a dynasty of priest-kings who will perpetuate the appreciation of truth, goodness and beauty. We share in God's creative powers and participate in the work of creation. In this way, we are part of the Vessel, which continues its struggle to resolve its dual nature. If this knowledge is lost, then the striving for it will contaminate marriage and undermine the feminine and the spiritual aspect of marriage will be misunderstood. The place of the Mother, alongside the Father, in a Holy Trinity, with the power of the Son, must be completely understood, in its complementary nature. In the Greek, this female energy or wisdom is known as Sophia. If the significance of this energy is repressed, then the balance and harmony needed for healing is also lost. As Nazarines and Keepers of the Covenant we have a sacred covenant and duty to retain and pass on this knowledge for the benefit of mankind. The

black-robed Nazarine Priestesses must reach out to
the world and pass on their divine wisdom for they
instinctively know All."

CHAPTER 7

Being a gentleman of sorts, I wouldn't make the first
move, but I wanted the emotional connection. Life
had been too cerebral of late. The thought of some
pleasure, amidst the trauma, fulfilled a need. When
she placed her arms around me, I could hardly resist.
I disciplined myself, so she dictated the pace. I had,
admittedly with some difficulty, learnt to say no,
unless the circumstances were right. It may have
been the man, who used the sexual key, but it was
always the woman who chose when to open the
door. I needed the energies to endure beyond the
immediate experience, as I wanted a constant in my
life and sex within a loving relationship had so much
more depth.

She moved to push the two beds together,
then allowed her head to drop onto my shoulder.
The symbolism was enough and I placed my hands
on the body I had longed to touch.

She lifted her head. "I want you," she
whispered.

"And I want you," I stated the obvious.

She began removing my clothes, kissing me
gently, then more passionately. Finally, naked and
fully aroused, I caressed the figure I had previously
only admired.

"Let me look at you," she said, moving
apart, for a moment, and inspecting me.

I blew her a kiss. "You're teasing me." I
said, embarrassed at the close scrutiny. I moved
toward her again and began removing her outer

126

garments, but she pushed me away, removing the remnants of her underwear herself, ever so slowly.

"Pose for me," I suggested, as she triggered sensual fantasies. She smiled and obeyed, flaunting her body, lifting her arms above her head and moving her legs apart. I quickly closed with her, unable to resist a moment longer. I gently touched the hidden places, now exposed, and took pleasure in the passions displayed. The subtle perfume had become familiar and I wanted her body to become equally so.

"I knew there were hidden depths to you, more than met the eye." I said, nuzzling closer. She had a pleasing softness to her skin and I could taste the moisturizing lotion she had used. It made me hunger for closer contact and thirst for penetration.

"You excite me." I said, gruffness from lust in my voice.

"Good," she replied, eyes widening.

"Everything you see with me, you get. The good and the bad," I said, in a brief respite, as we changed position.

"I know," she replied. "I always knew."

"If this is what it's like to make love after abstinence, then it's almost worth the wait," she said, though continued acting in a whore-like fashion, turning me on, which belied the assertion.

Our writhing bodies explored intimacy. There were ecstatic cries as moist mystical places unfolded. Places I had enjoyed only in my imagination. I searched every crevice of her being and the embrace touched my soul. I needed the indulgence of the pleasure I had sorely missed, since the break-up of my marriage. A few sexual liaisons in meaningless relationships had done nothing for me. A deeper love triggered a surge of feeling. I remembered the ritual of the Cahier Rose, when the energy from one chakra projects and passes to the polar and receptive, sacred chakra of the woman, the womb. How the natural striving for unity and harmony, reflected the rhythms of the universe. It copied the forces and essence of the spiritual experience, with its characteristics of timelessness, loss of ego and communion. I cradled her fragile body and determined to hold the energy, for as long as possible. She began to devour me, moving downwards, kissing different parts of my body in the process, until I could take no more. The urges she created had become impossible to control.

"I must have you now," I insisted, unable and unwilling to wait, all patience and discipline dissolved in the urgency.

"You've got me," she replied, kissing me passionately again.

I needed the exchange of feeling, without the requirement for experiment or delay. The rest happened quickly, but it didn't matter, for the groans suggested mutual pleasure. For a time, the inner explosion of peace, the oneness with life's magnetic impulses, washed over all the stresses and, in that moment, nothing else mattered. Passion and the mists of the imagination excluded all outside influences.

I drifted into deep sleep, but awoke early, as if the subconscious knew important decisions had to be made. I found it difficult to disentangle myself from the physical and emotional warmth Rachel offered, but sober considerations intruded on pleasure. When I awoke happy and content in a woman's arms, not desperate to evict her, then she was the sort of woman I always fell in love with.

"Have you had a chance to examine the interpretations of the scrolls yet?" Rachel asked, pulling the duvet across and getting out of bed, giving me a final glimpse of that naked, lithe body, which so enthralled me.

"I've glanced at some of the scrolls." I said, jumping out of bed and stretching, before opening the curtains, looking out over some of the rooftops of Paris. It was another beautiful spring day. The first appears to be a covenant, for initiates of the Nazarene, or Nazarite sect, as they are sometimes called, to become Servants of the Light and to fight against the Angel of Darkness. They appear to have inherited certain mystery teachings from the Benjamites and before that from Egypt. It emphasises the harmony between the individual and all of creation. We really are made in the image and likeness of God. It also seems that Mary Magdalene, the essence of the sacred feminine, was of royal Benjamite blood. As Christ was also of royal Davidite blood, then any offspring of the bloodline of the two royal families would have been an enormous threat to both the Sanhedrin and the Romans.

"It still sounds innocuous to me and I don't understand what the fuss is about." She sighed, shaking her head and moving towards the bathroom, this time leaving the door open. "I must have a bath, but talk to me, whilst the bath is running." I didn't need a second invitation. "You still haven't told me about the Cahier Rose?" She turned on the old-fashioned taps and water began pouring noisily into an old stained bath. Underwear and toiletries cluttered the bathroom, with little room for my things, but I liked it that way.

"It's a magical ritual, a complex, but beautiful ritual, in which the intention of sexual union is a harmonising with all the cosmic energies. You must also understand that the rose was a symbol of the sacred feminine and was secretly symbolic of the grail. It resembled the female vagina, through which all men must enter the world. The ritual involves an immersion in the spiritual reservoir in which we live and breathe and have our being. It brings down enormous sexual, spiritual energy and sends it back to its source, so mirroring the connection we all seek with our creator, the urge to give, as well as to receive. The scrolls confirm that sexual intercourse, as a spiritual ritual in love, is the highest sacrament. It is at the point of climax that our minds become still for a moment and in the void we sense God. The ancients believed that only with this intimate knowledge of the sacred feminine could the man become whole. It is such an anathema to the Catholic Church and is the reason lust was deemed to be a deadly sin, yet it is a bridge between Heaven and Earth, which celebrates an enormous release of creative energy. It is the very substance of the Universe."

"Sounds interesting." She posed provocatively. "Shall we try it?" She asked, her eyes opening wider.

"Bad girl." I shook my head. "Remember, as with all magical work, the intention is paramount and this must be pure. It must be a gift of the energies to God. Anyway, there has to be an altar, with correspondences representing the Light and the Sacred Quarters for all ritual work. It's complex, involving the expression of union of both body and soul. It's the polarity needed for all creation, in its purest form and a way to commune directly with God, so there was no reason for the existence of the Church."

"I think people in this age are already beginning to understand that the Church is irrelevant," she said, sitting on the edge of the bath. "And I don't think the Church can create the same shame or taboo on sexual matters that they have done in the past. The traditional conflicts they created are disappearing."

"I must confess to still having a problem with it," I confided.

"Perhaps I can help, as I'd like our relationship to be special and pure," she said, her face expressionless for a moment. I believed her, but I was a sucker for a smile and a pretty face.

"It can be if you want it to be, but most people can't pay the price." I hesitated, distracted, as she tested the bathwater and turned off the taps. "Marriage is an imperfect institution and is no longer revered or respected as an institution made by God or intended for life."

"But if you find your kindred spirit or twin soul, it can be that way, can't it?" She asked.

"I'd like to believe it. I studied the mystical cabbala and one of the first lessons is the union between male and female, as reflected in the Pillars of Mercy and Severity in the meditation glyph of the Tree of Life. Its study brings a greater understanding of the role of both man and a woman."

She nodded, as if she understood, but turned frivolous again. "Shame about the ritual. I'd like to have experimented." She smiled, before undressing and leaving her clothes in a pile on the bathroom floor, finally removing her knickers and swinging them around her index finger, with a flourish.

"What am I going to do with you?" I asked, without expecting an answer.

"As long as you let me have my bath first, I'll tell you, precisely. She replied, brazenly. In the meantime, tell me more about the Cahier Rose and the scrolls."

"Well, most people have heard of the eastern mystical tradition and the Tantric sexual rites. This is similar. The ritual suggests God, or the Universe if you prefer, has created physical union and decreed that two human beings should become one. In this way, it's perfectly natural to believe a man and woman can reach the divine through this energy. From the scrolls, the Templars inherited the knowledge from the mystery schools, of which Christ was an Initiate. Their 'secret of secrets' involved the spiritual transformation, by sacred sexual rites."

"The Rosicrucians believed in it didn't they?"

"Do you know about the Rosicrucians?" I asked, impressed at the intellect behind the pretty exterior packaging. "You note the reference again to the symbol of the rose."

"My father studied comparative religions and discussed a number of fringe organisations with me." She tilted her head, her face reflecting a serious side to her nature.

"Well, you'll understand how the Church must take the blame for poisoning the sexual life of the West. It demonised sex and the female generally and has suppressed the people by atrocity over the centuries. The Roman Church was founded in Peter's name and, as he was so at odds with Mary Magdalene, they had to exclude some part of the gospels and treat them as heresy. Other religions did the same for different reasons. The knowledge would have taken away the need for the existence of the Church. The truth, in the form of the Gnostic teachings, remained and went underground." I hesitated, inevitably drawn back to a more basic need and smiled at Rachel. "They can no longer foist their distortions on the unsuspecting population."

Intimacy in the bathroom may not have been an appropriate venue for these serious convictions

132

and changed the subject. "What does your father do?"

At first, she didn't answer, but continued bathing, as if oblivious to my presence and to the question. "He's semi-retired now," she eventually replied.

"It's difficult to engage in serious conversation with you, when you've no clothes on and insist on exposing yourself like this," I said, more interested in the hypnotic effect of her bathing, than debate.

"You can leave and talk to me from the bedroom?" She blushed for the first time, though little contrition reflected in her tone.

"No," I replied, immediately, my concentration disintegrating completely. "I'm simply saying it's difficult to be serious."

"That's OK then, let's not be serious." She smiled again. "Be patient, it'll be worth it."

"Tell me about the Rosicrucians," she asked.

I would have preferred to occupy my mind on more frivolous pursuits, but Rachel seemed genuinely interested. "Their name also comes from a rose and a phallic cross, so it's self-evident. The symbolism is the same with the Egyptian Ankh, with its phallus and the loop representing the vagina. It always relates back to the sacred feminine."

"Were the Knights Templar in search of occult knowledge?" She asked, continuing to sway intriguingly between the serious and the frivolous.

"The Templars had occult knowledge within their inner sanctum. There was an exoteric, as well as an esoteric aspect, to their organization. The Order of the True Rose Croix may be part only of the political thread behind the Templars, as is the Priory de Sion. It has been suggested they helped perpetuate the Grail legends and the Great Work of the Alchemists, each to do with sexual rites."

"So how do these rites work?" She asked, seemingly intrigued.

"You should read it yourself. It teaches a union between the body, the intellect and the soul with what, in cabbalistic terms, they call the Active Intelligence. It is what the Knights Templar referred to as Sophia or wisdom, except using the Atbash code word Baphomet, meaning Father of wisdom, which was so widely misunderstood during their persecution and the burning times. Wonderful imagery is used." I stopped and moved across to kiss her, as she lay in the bath. She had become irresistible and I longed for her.

"That's good," she said, lifting the plug. "I'm just finished. You must realize where there's passion, it really doesn't matter if there's a meeting of minds or whether the relationship has potential for intellectual or spiritual growth."

"It matters to me," I replied, firmly. "It's interwoven, whether you believe it or not."

She acted as if starved of love and affection. I was content to wait and enjoy the anticipation, not averse to a little voyeurism, but needing urgently to play a more active role. Rachel's body was magnetic. Her breasts were larger than apparent, fully clothed. Towel in hand, I shook eagerly as she skipped out of the bath. I assisted with drying, as a gentleman would, but it didn't last long, for passion overcomes discipline.

"What do you want out of life?" She asked, frivolity changing to seriousness, as she fixed her eyes on mine. "Are you looking for a new perspective and a new culture?"

"Well, if you mean this precise moment, I'll give you one guess what I want." I said.

"You're incorrigible, but I'm serious," she said.

"Now it's my time to be frivolous. The passion of love may be the energy and flow of life, but most people suppress it, because pain always accompanies it."

She didn't argue, as I wilfully moved closer. She slapped me on the arm and gently pushed away my advances.

"You know exactly what I mean. Are you happy?" She persisted.

"Happier than most and, at this moment, I'm delirious." I laughed loudly and moved towards her again, nibbling her neck.

She pulled away. "Seriously, I understand if you block passion, you also block the flow of life, but it's the gift a woman brings to a man isn't it?"

"You're right, as always. What's it like being right all of the time?"

She recognized it as a rhetorical question, which did not require an answer. A steely glare made me feel uncomfortable.

"Forgive me, that was unfair," I said.

She placed her arms around me, pulling me close, her warm breath on my face triggering energy I had tried to repress. I inhaled deeply of the fragrance of her body, as I moved towards her. I found myself reciprocating every movement she made. My hands searched out for soft warm areas for enjoyment. I had forgotten how joyful it felt to find release in the love of a woman, with no inhibitions.

"I've wanted you from the moment I first met you," she whispered, her hands moving expertly, creating pleasure at every stroke. "It's as if I'd known you before, in some past life and had been searching for you, ever since. Why do you think I've put up with this perfectionist streak in you, these last few weeks?" She smiled.

All these things I wanted to hear. It brought a surge of feeling.

"I want your body now and your love," I demanded. I kissed her softly first, then more firmly. She responded ferociously. My tongue searched for her essence and moved downwards, enjoying the softness of her breasts and firm nipples, on the way to even more exciting pleasures. My fingers inverted her nipples.

"Don't stop." She groaned.

"I won't stop," I replied, when I had a moment to take breath. My tongue moved between her legs. As her vagina dampened, the unity of the moment transcended to a greater need. I led her to the bed and allowed her to crawl all over me. It was her turn to use her mouth and tongue, until I begged for more.

"I must get inside you now, before it's too late."

"Take me now, all of me," she replied, opening her legs. "I'm yours."

I knew I couldn't enjoy orgasm, if she didn't share it. I determined to ensure a final explosion of passion. Even if we could not undertake full ritual, this was still, in its simplest form, the most powerful ritual I knew. How could words describe this awesome, sweet, most all-consuming ecstacy.

"Help me with this," I suggested, allowing her freedom to masturbate. "That really turns me on."

She pursed her lips and blew a kiss in the air to me.

"I hate the fact, man is the weaker sex. It's unfair, a man should be able to make love forever, just like a woman," I said, knowing I could hardly wait.

"I need you to come with me, now," I insisted.

"Yes, I promise. Fuck me harder, faster. Yes, yes." A shuddering of bodies reflected the feelings, then a release.

"Now, I'm in heaven," I said, rolling over onto my back exhausted, with Rachel alongside me, continuing to kiss and touch me, cleaning me with her mouth.

She looked up at me, her eyes portraying genuine feeling. "That was beautiful. I knew it would be," she said, leaning across, kissing me on the cheek and pulling me closer again. "Never let me go."

"Never." I said, in the moment meaning it. "But you don't make love as if you've been out of practice," I teased.

She hesitated, before replying. "With gadgets available, a woman can manage reasonably well and making love is like riding a bicycle, you don't forget." She spoke slowly, looking away, for a moment.

"I worried about you, when you were out yesterday. You were away for so long, I thought you must have been queuing to see the Mona Lisa, for the time it took."

She laughed. "Rodin perhaps, or even the Last Supper, but not the Mona Lisa or even the glass pyramid at the Louvre, La Pyramide. It's awful. I think the architect, Ieoh Ming Pei, has more critics, than supporters, especially here in France."

I nodded. "But many suggest it has an esoteric significance."

"Perhaps that explains it."

"So where did you go, other than the bookshop at Notre Dame?" I persisted.

She paused and kissed my cheek again, touching it afterwards with one hand. I felt patronised, but I didn't know why. "A girl is entitled to look at the designer shops along Avenue Montaigne, provided she doesn't buy anything too expensive."

"But I wanted to share the atmosphere of Paris with you." I said sullenly, intending the tone to reflect disappointment, rather than paranoia.

She smiled. "Let's go for a stroll together this afternoon along the Jardins du Trocadero, unless you want to take me there tonight, after dark."

"Now that sounds like a good idea," I said.

"Good, then let's have some breakfast," she said. "I don't want you to have this meeting on an empty stomach."

"It may give me an appetite of another sort later."

Her eyes sparkled, but she jumped out of bed, searching for clothes again. "Please take these men seriously, for my sake."

"It's not right that women have such energy after making love," I searched for a more comfortable position on the bed. "All I want to do is go back to sleep."

"But we may have a critical situation today and I want you alert and at your best."

She was right.

* * *

At ten o'clock precisely Marco and David appeared in the reception area of the hotel. They both looked carefully at Rachel. She looked down, gripping my arm tightly. I ushered them towards an unoccupied small room, off the reception area.

"Bonjour," the receptionist smiled.

I reciprocated. A white-shirted waiter passed with a tray of coffee cups, having cleared the room. It still retained the smells of coffee, fresh croissants and cigarette smoke, which so epitomized a French breakfast salon. Once inside, I closed the door, immediately feeling claustrophobic. There was another small door to the kitchen and a small window, which accessed the only natural light in the room. Uncomfortable breakfast chairs made the room barely functional.

"The time has come to pass these documents to me. I'll not tolerate further delays. I'm authorised to use whatever means are necessary for their recovery." David said, almost as soon as the door had closed and before anyone could even sit. He may not have had the menace of Marco, but the firmness in his voice and conviction in the delivery, suggested confidence.

I hoped I could appeal to his intellect. Unlike Marco, who was a man of instinct, he appeared to think, before action. My body tensed. "Forget the fact you may have paymasters who pay you well and help your lifestyle. There are more important considerations, such as truth and spirituality. Aren't they important?" I asked.

"Bullshit." Marco interrupted, rudely.

David lifted his arm and Marco stopped immediately. "What makes you think these documents will benefit anyone at all, they may cause more pain. Don't think you've an exclusive right to truth." He stopped for a moment, but his gaze never left mine. "I repeat. I'm instructed to use whatever means or force as is necessary, to recover these documents."

"But, these documents may help destroy the delusions and hypocrisy in the world. It'll give people a greater freedom." I persisted. I judged he was the sort of man who would at least acknowledge wrong.

"The Church provides some stability in the world and leadership, truth won't change that need.

You're a former priest, you must realise it." So they had done their research. It made me feel edgy. David pointed to the chairs in the room and beckoned to sit. We all sat down. The door may have been closed, but reception was a mere loud call away. I felt reasonably safe, as a consequence.

"When authorised education and teaching within society is at odds with the underlying truth, history has shown it leads to a division of interests followed by the disunity, disintegration and death of that order of things." I said.

Marco grunted disapproval, but David retained a studious expression.

"Society must have its goals, not simply the individual," I added.

"Now is not the time and you're not the person. I intend to recover these documents and I've no wish to debate it with you." David replied, sternly.

"If it's not me, it'll be somebody else who discovers the truth. You'll never stop the momentum. Even Catholic psychics like Malachy confirmed there'll be no more than two popes after John Paul II, so you don't even have to believe in Nostrodamus." I shifted in my chair, looking around at Rachel, who was sitting immediately behind me. She looked away.

"You mustn't underestimate the goodness of the Catholic Church," David said. "You must have witnessed it, before you left the Church. It's a power, which touches the lives of humankind for the better, as does its artefacts. You imagine the vacuum created, if the Church disappeared. Who'll fill it?" It sounded reasonable, but I had a different point of view.

"An institutionalised church can hardly urge people beyond the limits of its institutions. Instead, it simply offers a safe haven from life's fears. Fears they've often created themselves. It isn't liberating them. There has to be a new World Order, based on spiritual principles," I recalled some of my uncle's comments. "Perhaps all the religions of the world will unite, for they all contain an element of truth." I added, more out of desperation, than confidence. "Each is a single representation of something belonging to mankind. The only ultimate truth is spirit."

"If you're suggesting it's time to merge the crescent moon of Islam with the sun of Christianity, then you're quite mad." David said, scornfully.

"In the fullness of time, it must happen," I replied. "Even the Vatican admit to the existence of a manuscript, which are the personal teachings of Jesus Christ. It was always acknowledged that most rabbi in those days kept a chronicle of their ministry. Do you know where it is?"

I anticipated a response from David to the provocation. There was an obvious question, but he said nothing.

"You do understand what I have in my possession?" I asked.

"Does it matter?"

"I think it does and the next step is to allow the people to see the content of these chronicles." I paused. "And I have them, written in Jesus' hand."

David didn't blink and nothing registered in the expression on his face, no surprise, just blankness. I realised at that moment he already knew and had always known.

Marco stared continuously at Rachel. I turned around again and she dropped her head. I looked back at David. "We have to follow Jung's path. He showed the link between religion and psychology."

"These arguments achieve nothing. I'm not going to enter into an intellectual debate with someone who couldn't even honour holy vows. You can't take the moral high ground with me," David said, coldly.

"That's hitting below the belt," I complained.

"On the contrary. It's the truth, as you're so fond of saying." His eyes fixed on me, almost staring, as if he knew something about me, which I didn't know.

I held my arms out, palms upward. "You must accept organised religion is in chaos."

"Don't you understand English? I'll say it for the last time. I'm not debating this with you."

"All I'm saying is that the Church must adapt and synthesise into something better, without the dogma and rigidity. The dynamics of life insist on movement and change. Nothing stays the same. If it did, it would stagnate."

"Why are we listening to this crap?" Marco moved his head to face David.

"You're right, Marco," he said, menacingly. "You explain to him that I'm not going to enter into a debate. He doesn't seem to understand me."

Marco stood up, a smile crossing his face for the first time. Before I could object, one hand was firmly around my throat, preventing me from calling for help, the other on my lapel, lifting me out of the chair, so that my legs dangled helplessly. I kicked the chair over, as I struggled for air, spluttering a muted call for help, until he squeezed harder. As I began to lose consciousness, I heard Rachel, somewhere in the void, scream, then David shout something to Marco. The next minute, I had been dumped unceremoniously and painfully onto the floor. I groaned, as the jolt brought life back into my body, rubbing my hip where I landed awkwardly, but thankful I could breathe again. A worried Hotel receptionist opened the door.

David pointed to the chair on its side. "He fell back off the chair, but he's fine now," he said.

"Are you alright?" She asked, concern etched on lines in her face.

I grunted. "I suppose so."

She left the room, shaking her head, closing the door behind her.

"This is your Christian message is it?" I said, sarcastically.

"I've warned you for the last time," David replied, contemptuously. "Don't you understand? You cannot impose change on the Church, when it would not be beneficial for them?"

I sighed. "If the Church would agree, I'd allow them to publish these documents themselves, even as part of an encyclical letter on the subject, from the Pope. They can reform at their own pace. Isn't that reasonable?"

He didn't reply. "Tell them we could work together on such a project and I'd give them my full co-operation," I said.

David shrugged, his eyes opening wider, but said nothing for a few moments. The silence was deafening, with no softening of the expression on his face. "If you give me the scrolls, I'll undertake to use my best endeavours to try and persuade them," he said, eventually.

I shook my head. "No, it's not quite as simple as that." I said. "Don't take me for a fool."

David smiled, condescendingly, shuffling in his chair. "Look, Jung's modern order would do away with all denominations and creeds. The Church will never sign its death warrant. It'll not happen in my lifetime."

"It's already happening, even loyal Catholics

are questioning its right to pronounce absolute truths," I said, more in hope than expectation.

"You're wasting your energy," he said.

"All religions share certain patterns and themes and they all forget their common roots. Isn't it time we stopped Catholics and Protestants, Moslem Islamic fundamentalists, Jews and Hindus all killing each other in the name of their religion?"

"How do you propose to do that?" David asked.

"Perhaps we can remind them that if they had been born in another culture, then their view could be equally fervent for the tradition they now hate. It is only a reflection of their hate within."

"The time is not ripe for change. Believe me," David dismissed the idea without thought."

"But we must rise above religion and conflict, for the sake of our children and our grandchildren."

He looked towards Rachel, catching her eye, but said nothing.

"If there's a chance to resolve this amicably, isn't it worth a try." Rachel leaned forward in her chair, interrupting eloquently. I looked around. David listened, but neither he nor Marco responded. "Surely, it's worthy of consideration." She added.

David turned to Rachel. "My dear, there are vested interests involved here, which you cannot even imagine," he replied, softly, a strange sweetness in the tone.

I turned back to press the argument. "Even the conservative Pope John XXIII tried to bring the Church into the then 20th century by passing power from the elite to the people. He called the first Ecumenical Council to discuss it, for many years. Unfortunately, he died before it could bear fruit, but how many priests resigned or protested as a consequence of its failure. What does that tell you?"

Marco stood up, moving nearer Rachel, before leaning back against the wall. "Not a lot and we're wasting time."

David turned to me. "If it happens, then it must be from within. You'll not be allowed to change it. If I wanted to do as you suggest, I still couldn't do it and frankly you've not persuaded me. Now are you going to return these important artefacts freely or not?" He fidgeted in his seat again.

"What if I decide I don't want to return them, what will you do?" I asked, looking David straight in the eye.

"I'll take other steps for their recovery and I'll not be responsible for the consequences." He spoke firmly, his expression mirroring the serious tone of his voice. "You should believe me."

"Is that another threat?" I asked, without moving my gaze.

"You can take it any way you want, but I've been reasonable and patient with you. I'm duty-bound to recover these documents and will do so." He said, firmly, his eyes fixed and unflinching.

"I intend to do some research at the Bibliotheque Nationale today. I'm prepared to have another meeting with you, but you'll have to show me compelling reasons for handing over these documents." I said, equally firmly.

"John, I don't want you to get into any trouble and wouldn't it be easier for everybody concerned, if we just co-operated?" Rachel said, sharply.

I turned around and glared, feeling my face flush. She had never seen me angry before and she withered.

"You're getting good advice. Why don't you listen to the girl?" Marco said, smiling.

"Are you prepared to meet me tomorrow?" I asked. "I'm not prepared to make any decision today."

David shook his head and sighed. "We've already been through this before and you couldn't be trusted."

"You were pressurising me then and you're doing it now. I don't react well to intimidation."

"Well, at least, you know you can't run from us, so perhaps you'll honour an agreement this time." David stood up

"So you agree?" I asked.

"I'll give you until noon tomorrow, but you'll not have another chance." He replied. "I want to be seen to have exhausted all possibility of a negotiated settlement to this stand-off. What happens after that will not be on my conscience."

Marco took a further step, so his face almost touched mine. "I don't trust you, so be careful you don't play any more games." He said, pointing his finger into my face.

"Grow up," I sneered, courage welling up in the safety of the hotel.

He stood up, taking a step towards me. David stretched his arm out to stop him. "He gets the message, Marco." He turned to me. "We'll meet you here at noon tomorrow, but we'll keep tabs on you. So keep your promise this time." David held out his hand. "Perhaps you now understand the extent of our intelligence. I'd like your word that you'll be here tomorrow?" he asked.

"Yes, I'll meet you here tomorrow, but I'll make no promises beyond that." I turned my back on him, refusing to shake his hand. After they left, I returned to the room with Rachel.

"What was all that about?" I asked, banging the bedroom door behind me.

"Please don't get angry with me. I don't want this aggravation. I want an easy life," she replied, turning her back on me.

"Then don't betray me and don't turn your back on me." I said, plainly. "You were supposed to be supporting me. Anyone who lies about small things or is disloyal in small things, always end up lying and being disloyal on major issues. I know all about betrayal."

She turned around to face me again. "It did you no harm. I couldn't bear the thought of you getting hurt again, so don't lose your temper. I'm under pressure too."

I raised my voice, missing the subtlety. "It's not the point. Would you try to persuade me to hand the scrolls back?"

"No." She glared back. "You're a stubborn man and wouldn't listen to me anyway."

"I find it difficult to believe we made love in this room only a couple of hours ago. It's a question of loyalty. I must be able to trust you, implicitly. If I can't, I'd rather you leave on the next plane."

She blushed, but said nothing. Instead she turned and grabbed her bag, before leaving the room, slamming the door angrily. Old joists and floorboards shook with the force.

For a moment, I remained rooted to the spot, unsure whether to follow or not. I decided to go after her, but at the entrance to the hotel she was already out of sight. I ran into the road and to the junction. In the distance, I could see her, but a familiar car stopped and a rear door opened. She moved into the car without any sign of coercion. It was the car Marco had used near the Sacre Coeur. It drove off and out of sight. A strange uncertainty punctured jangled thoughts and emptiness gnawed away at my stomach. Not for the first time in my life I was alone.

Further extract. "... As a rabbi, it is time for me to marry and I do so willingly to Mariam (Mary Magdalene). She is a Benjamite of Royal Blood and with my Royal Blood of the line of David, this will be a dynastic marriage, which will have to be kept secret from the Romans and the Herodian tetrarchs. I know one soul is drawn to another, only if there is healing potential between them. Any issue we have, may be at risk from those political factions who would oppose the merging of two royal families. The mutual balancing of energy between us, makes me more certain of our union than anything I have ever known. She is the only woman for whom I have truly lusted. The Torah teaches that lusting after someone is already adultery, but there are worse sins than the sins of the flesh. There is so much distortion of the spiritual truth and many may be contaminated by these falsehoods, if they do not understand or search for the resonance of truth. For they try to subjugate women in order to bury the knowledge of the ancient ways. In this respect, marriage is an institution rooted in carnal needs. The ancient pagan rites of sexual marriage, performed in the tradition of the priests and priestesses of Isis enable a man to achieve knowledge of himself and the Gods. Miriam's dark skin and long hair captivates me and I believe she is the most beautiful woman I have ever seen. Of greater importance is her kind heart, her feeling. She is my disciple of all disciples. I crave for a child by her. It will make our union complete. She encapsulates the wisdom that existed in the darkness of Chaos before the Creation. I know I am nothing without her. I continue to be treated with suspicion and hostility by the Sanhedrin. If I publicly reveal their initiations, then the penalty will be death. They will demand it and suggest I have smuggled witchcraft out of Egypt, rather than healing and wisdom. They want to make a prison out of the Torah, instead of a way to God for those who have spiritual wholeness and freedom. The rise of a spiritual religion will always be restricted more by arrogant dogma than science, though the mystical experience is the inner mystery, which science attempts to understand from the outside. This transformation in the mystical experience involves our essential nature being able to give and share and allowing our essence to become one with the Light, for in the ultimate spiritual truth there is only Oneness."

CHAPTER 8

I raced towards the Metro Station, where I knew taxis waited, stumbling across a cobbled side street and hurdling a piece of antique furniture, placed haphazardly outside one shop. I skipped past dining tables outside a bistro, where familiar smells exuded an invitation, which on another day I would have welcomed. A balding waiter, black waistcoat and apron at ankle-length, already balancing a tray full of food and drink precariously above his head, twisted artistically to avoid this whirling dervish, as I passed. A metro rattled and scoured its way across the overhead tracks and screeched to a halt. Breathless and perspiring, I realised the futility of my actions. Marco's car had disappeared and, with it, any realistic possibility of following them. I collapsed, lungs bursting, in a crumpled heap at the side of the pavement, with exhaustion my only companion.

I returned to the hotel, a morass of angry ideas muddling around inside my head, few worthy of consideration and most desperate. For more than two hours, I waited in the bedroom, until I had examined every blemish and blot on the walls. Every landmark, visible from the window, had been implanted into my memory and I knew the interior colour scheme of attic apartments, fifty yards away, imagining them as my little pied-a-terre in the City. I should have attended the Bibliotheque Nationale, but all motivation for research had drained away, in the uncertainty. When the telephone rang, I jumped.

Rachel spoke, as if nothing had happened. "I'm sorry, I shouldn't have walked out on you like that, but you were winding me up, giving me ultimatums. I can't be controlled again." I detected little guilt in her tone.

"Where've you been?" I asked, impatiently.

"I've been to see Jean DeValois for you."

"But you didn't have his address and contact number, you gave it to me." I said, still wallowing in the doubts, which had clawed away at my psyche all morning.

There was a brief pause. "I went back to the shop, near Notre Dame. I had nothing to do and I needed to get away."

"But I saw you getting into Marco's car when you left?" I said, coldly, unable to use any subtlety and hold back the information for a more intelligent enquiry later.

For a moment, her voice froze, but anger seemed to re-ignite it. "Are you going to cross-examine me like this, all the time. Do you want me to come back to the hotel or not? I can explain everything, but if you don't want me to return, I'll go home."

"Your passport is with me and your things, so you can't just go," I said abruptly. "You know I intended to visit the Bibliotheque Nationale today, as part of my research. I have to examine Les Dossiers Secrets, which are catalogued there. It's so important to me and I've been waiting patiently for you to contact me. I can't wait any longer. If you have an explanation, I'll meet you back at the hotel by five o'clock and listen to it."

She had a magnetism, which drew me to her, despite my reservations. I didn't particularly want to face her, until I had certain things straight in my own mind, but I was falling in love with her, warts and all. Whichever course I took, pain would follow. I knew it instinctively and from experience.

"Don't be like that," she said. "I've arranged for Jean DeValois to meet you at the hotel at five o'clock. He's very interested in the scrolls and enthusiastic about the meeting, but I needed to see you first."

"You shouldn't arrange appointments without discussing it with me first. What have you told him?" I asked sullenly.

"I explained that you've documents from your late uncle, a Cardinal, which you wanted to discuss."

I spoke calmly, though distrustful thoughts intruded. "You'll have to entertain him, if I'm late. I'll see you then." I replaced the receiver, without waiting for an acknowledgment. I needed time to think and do my research, so I missed lunch, eating fruit instead.

At the Bibliotheque Nationale's impressive new building, I completed a myriad of bureaucratic forms, before being allowed to do my work. First, I was guided to a section dealing with mystical texts, and another relating to the Knights Templar. I wrote down what I felt might be significant information and examined copies of more well known texts, including Les Dossiers Secrets. I hoped this would give me some clues, which my uncle had failed to do before he died. As I prepared to leave, an official dressed in a sober charcoal suit, sat alongside me. He had with him the various forms I had painstakingly completed. He must have been about sixty years of age with silver hair, clean-shaven and wearing half-moon spectacles.

"Monsieur, I'm the supervisor in charge of this department. It's my duty to record details of all the research carried out here. Can you tell me what you're actually researching?" He spoke in excellent refined English, with only a hint of an accent.

I frowned. "I've completed numerous forms. You know who I am and what I'm doing here. How many other journalists examine the same documents every day. I can see the forms in your hand."

"But I'm simply asking you to provide me with further information. It's my job, you understand?"

"What else do you want to know?" I asked.

"You say you2're a journalist. Are you doing a story for a particular publication, or are you freelancing?"

"I'm freelancing," I replied, cautiously.

"Do you have any new information or any story which we, as a Museum, would be interested in?"

It appeared an innocuous enough question, but I had to suspicious. In all the years I had attended the British Museum, and previously researched here, nobody had previously asked me questions of this sort. It was inconceivable they asked everyone. "No, but I'm looking at different slants on some aspects of history." I looked into his eyes. He would know I had been researching the Knights Templar and the political threads interwoven with them. Their list of Grandmasters had been one of the documents I had perused. There was more to his questions.

"I'm particularly interested in the Knights Templar," I added. I had also looked at historical data relating to the Order of the True Rose Croix, but discretion suggestion it would be wiser to resist emphasis on this aspect of my study.

He smiled, taking a card out of his top pocket and handing it to me. "My name is Dominique Flaviel. I think I can be of assistance to you. Can I suggest you telephone me and arrange a meeting, at a time which is convenient to you?"

I reluctantly took his card, realizing I disliked this man and his need for subterfuge. The address was unfamiliar. As a supervisor, in charge of that department, it seemed rather strange he should have an office located elsewhere.

"You don't actually work here then?" I asked, gruffly.

"I've an office here, but the government provides me with separate offices, which I use when conducting business for the acquisition of new items for the Museum. Do you understand?"

"I think so." I stuttered.

He turned and walked away, as quietly as he had arrived. I had to leave too, mindful of the meeting Rachel had scheduled.

***

As I arrived in the reception of the hotel, Rachel sat, already entertaining a short, slim man with dark hair, beginning to grey. He must have been about fifty-five years of age. He had nothing of distinction about him, dressing casually and smoking a Gitane. The sort of man you would pass in the street and not notice or remember him, if you saw him again.

Rachel immediately stood and gestured to her guest. He held out his hand, as I walked towards him.

"This is Monsieur DeValois. I mentioned him to you this morning."

"Yes, I remember."

I looked directly at him. He presented a pleasant manner and I courteously shook his hand.

"Enchante, monsieur." He smiled.

"Shall we have some privacy," I said, directing him into the conference room alongside reception.

"What's your position with the Order of the True Rose Croix?" I asked, sitting down and gesturing for him to do the same.

"Well, I'm not sure I am able to say, at this point. Although we're not a secret society, we are a society with secrets." He held up the index finger of his right hand and shook it in the air. "First, I'd like to know what I can do for you."

"I know we've never met, but we're in a Catch 22 situation here, because I'm not prepared to talk to someone who refuses to be candid with me." I said sternly, perhaps rudely. My mood still affected by the morning's events and Rachel's presence.

His expression changed dramatically, the smile disappearing. "This charming young lady informed me you wanted my help. I've gone out of my way to meet you. In the circumstances, I need some integrity, respect and a little trust." His hands moved continuously, as he talked, sometimes spiralling above his head and other times almost pointing at me.

I felt guilty and looked away, needing a moment to think. There seemed little point in hiding facts, which he may have been told already. I looked into his eyes and he held my gaze, so I took a chance. "Very well. Before my uncle, Cardinal O'Rourke, died, he suggested I contact your Order. He's left certain documents, including some ancient scrolls, in my safekeeping and I need to authenticate them. I'm undecided, at this moment, as to my course of action."

His manner became friendlier again. "You've been open with me, so I'll do likewise. I'm the Secretary of the Order and I'll help you, if I'm able, although my authority stems from the members of the Order."

"Then you are familiar with the documents?" I asked, bypassing the semantics.

"We've known about their existence and know their origins. Although we thought the Vatican may have destroyed them. Can I suggest you meet me tomorrow morning at nine o'clock, at my office? We'll have more privacy there and I can discuss your position with my colleagues. They'll have to give me authority to divulge information to you." He hesitated, then added. "At least, you can examine our library, and we can get to know each other a little better. We may be able to help each other. Our Order probably has more scholastic manuscripts and records than you'd suspect."

I had to be interested and the meeting gave me time, before my noon deadline. "Good, I'll be there promptly," I promised, standing up and walking towards the door. I gestured to Monsieur DeValois to walk through ahead of me.

I needed the opportunity of a serious discussion with Rachel. If this man was genuine, then she was trying to help, but she had behaved in such a clandestine manner, particularly in entering Marco's limousine, I would be a fool to ignore her actions. The situation had to be resolved quickly.

We returned to the hotel room. She sat on the bed, facing the window. I remained standing. "You can start by telling me why you went in Marco's car, when you left." I said.

She looked towards me, brazenly. "David and Marco were in the car. They said they wanted to help and wouldn't harm me. So I went in the car." She spoke as if it was of no consequence, but I couldn't handle betrayal. It caused me too much pain.

Despite good intentions to maintain a calm facade, they disappeared as quickly as the sun in a Norwegian winter. "Just like that." I shouted.

"Just like that." She mimicked, sarcastically.

I turned away, taking a deep breath and walked away from the bed. I counted to ten, under my breath, but the atmosphere remained taut. We both knew it. There was something being hidden. I could almost touch it and I had developed a nose for deceit.

"I had nothing to lose," she said, after the pause. "You were angry with me and I thought if I obtained information, which could help, you'd be pleased." She rose from the bed and moved behind me, placing her arms around my waist. She drew me closer. I could feel the warmth of her body. I desperately wanted to respond, but too much was at stake and I had to be sure.

I unclasped her hands and turned to face her. "I can't think, when you do that. At this moment, I'm not sure I can trust you."

She reacted angrily, her eyes looking upwards. "That's really wonderful."

I couldn't speak, turning back to the window.

"It's no big deal," she said, burying her head in her hands.

"Then what did they say to you?" I asked, spinning around again.

She sat on the bed and took a deep breath. "They promised no harm would come to us, if we co-operated. They said we couldn't hide and it would be futile to try."

She looked up, her eyes bulging and face white with either fear or anger, but which one I could not fathom. "There's no way would I ever do anything to harm you." She moved off the bed, sighing as she approached me and placed her hands on my arms tenderly. "You do believe me, don't you?" she looked up at me with those big eyes. Experience had taught me to be wary in these circumstances. It was normally a prelude to betrayal, but my heart and instinct always ruled my head.

"So how long were you in their car?" I asked, sternly, unable to forgive or forget.

"No more than five minutes."

"So you've never met them alone before?"

She hesitated, before replying. It didn't breed confidence. "Of course not. Only when I've been with you."

"I want to trust you," I said, though old emotional scar tissue held me back.

"You can trust me," she insisted.

Those eyes, and the closeness, mesmerised me, dispelling all confusion. This time I couldn't resist and collapsed into an embrace, as my heart and body had longed to do, but my mind resisted.

"Do you think I'd have arranged this meeting with DeValois, if I wasn't trying to help?" She whispered the reassurance, before kissing me, as passionately as ever. My head and body remained in conflict, but my body was stronger. When I made love to her, I felt a world in harmony, with all doubts dispelled. Problems dissipated and my anger with it. It was all I craved for, in that moment.

My problems needed sleep, but pleasure became the priority.

***

Morning came quickly, sunshine piercing a gap in the curtains, draping the room in a spectrum of colours. My right hand nestled comfortably across Rachel's body and on her breast, whilst my right leg stradled hers. Pleasant feelings lingered from the warmth and closeness of her naked body, but I resisted the urge for further contact and disentangled my leg from hers. Doubts resurrected in the reality of the day. Something didn't feel right.

I left Rachel in bed asleep and walked down to reception to use a public phone. David could have had a scanner close by, to pick up any mobile telephone conversations. I spoke to the man from the Bibliotheque Nationale, Flaviel. He agreed to join me for the meeting with David and Marco at noon. I gave him enough information about the scrolls, to whet his appetite, but nothing he would not already know. If DeValois also attended, I'd soon discover whose side everyone was taking. I returned to the bedroom and took brief delight in Rachel until it was quickly time for us to go.

***

"I've an appointment with Monsieur DeValois, for nine o'clock." I said to the secretary, in my best French. Rachel agreed to wait outside.

Within a minute, I was sitting in front of a dented and weary-looking desk, facing him. His office had old hardwood cabinets, which stretched wall to wall. His desk, though, was immaculate, with only a diary opened at today's date and a half-open packet of Gitanes to spoil the symmetry.

"You must forgive my journalist's instinct, but I'd appreciate some information about your Order," I said, plainly.,

He leaned forward and shifted noticeably in his chair. His forehead wrinkled. "I have been as candid as I can. I will do my best to help, but there is a limit to what I can divulge. I can tell you we knew your uncle. He contacted us, some time ago."

I raised my eyebrows. It explained his reference to the Order.

"Follow me." He moved out of his chair, indicating towards two large doors, which we passed and through a small vestibule area, before another set of double doors opened.

It revealed a magnificent Hall with black and white marble squares on its floor. Though not a large room, there was an unusual and unique aspect to it. An altar stood at one end, with correspondences upon it for ritual work, including a dagger and a chalice. Various regalia lay on a large table to the side and a substantial book rested on a lectern. He walked towards it, opening the book.

"Look for yourself," he said, gesturing with his right palm over the pages. The ornate book, with gold leaf embroidered upon it, contained various ceremonies and rituals, recorded on a graduated basis.

"It's similar to Masonry rituals in the U.K." I said, on first glance.

"No, these rituals are closer to the original Scottish Rite, which were outlawed in the U.K. They are still used in the highest echelons of the most secret societies, often as part of an initiation and selection process, including Britain." He pointed to another section of the book and an appendix at the back. "Read this carefully."

I read part of a ritual, similar to the Cahier Rose. "This must date from the Knights Templar." I said, more enthusiastically.

He shrugged. "The knowledge went underground after the purge, but it was always there. A couple of centuries elapsed, before it could be openly recorded again."

"All sorts of hidden knowledge is surfacing," I said.

He nodded. "Perhaps there's not the same fear of persecution in these enlightened times, but there are still vested interests, with significant influence and power. Some will undermine the truth with ridicule and lies, some with violence. Do not underestimate those who are fearful of change."

"I'm well aware of the risks. My uncle emphasized them before his death."

He lit a Gitane and inhaled loudly and deeply, holding the breath to allow the drug to have its full impact. " What do you know about the Isis Cult?" He asked.

I pondered for a moment. "The Isis cult was created with the Hermetic Order of the Golden Dawn, involving Mathers, Westcott, Aleister Crowley, W. B. Yeats and others. It was organised around the 1877 manuscript, Isis Unveiled, by Madame Helena Blavatsky, the Russian occultist and founder of the Theosophist movement. She called for the British aristocracy to organise itself into an Isis priesthood."

"This has already happened and an organisation exists, which has links with government and all the way to the Vatican," he said, extinguishing the cigarette, even though it had only been half-smoked.

I've read Blavatsky's work, as I have H. G. Wells', the Open Conspiracy, that of his proteges

Aldous Huxley and his Brave New World and George Orwell's 1984 and Animal Farm. They were all written as organising, mass-appeal, documents on behalf of a one-world order."

"Tres bon," he smiled, walking over to a bench and sitting down. "You appreciate, of course, that Wells, who was the head of foreign intelligence during World War One, called his conspiracy a one-world brain, which would function as a police of the mind."

I nodded. "I understand even Huxley went on to found a nest of Isis cults in California," I said, beginning to wonder if I was developing my uncle's paranoia.

He smiled again. "The original Order of the Knights of St. John of Jerusalem and the Templars maintained direct continuity with the ancient cult of Isis. They nurtured the Wisdom of the East from the Gnostic and Manichean teachings still prevalent in the Eastern Mediterranean at the time. My Order has shown enduring patience, whilst observing these developments. It has the patience to wait until the time is right. I'm not certain this is the moment."

He appeared frank and held my gaze, as he spoke. There appeared no darker side to him, though I still had little confidence in my judgment of character. Nevertheless, much of what he related, rang true. I needed a kindred spirit and warmed to him.

"What about these stories, which question the integrity of your order and its motives?" I tested him one final time.

He laughed, taking no offence. "I told you they've immense power to control the media."

I nodded. "One day, people may understand the extent of their influence over our lives."

He stood wearily, shoulders hunched. "Most people have an instinct about truth, just as they have for the paradoxes of spirituality, except that in their busy lives it is sadly not a priority."

"I gain the impression, though, you feel battles still have to be won." I said, picking up on his tone.

"Certainly. People have free will and choices, even though there are limitations on it, which they don't understand. We must judge the public mood accurately. My Order will always weigh up its options carefully, but it will make political decisions where it deems it expedient. I warn you, they may not coincide with your ambitions or suit your timescale."

"What do you think about the documents in my possession?" I asked, taking a mental note of the caveat and his honesty.

"I only know what you've told me," he replied, walking over and closing the book.

"I promise you, I do have these documents in my possession, including a copy of the Knights Templar Journal and the scrolls found in Jerusalem, at the end of the First Crusade." The book and Jean convinced me to take a chance, even if the Hall could have been a simple Masonic Hall. "Can you help me?" I asked.

He thought for a moment. "We've been waiting for an opportunity to go public, but it would have to be a decision of our highest grade Initiates, within the inner sanctum of our organization. There are political considerations," he said, pacing across the Hall away from me.

" What political considerations," I asked, puzzled.

He turned back to face me. "All organizations have political considerations and we're no different," he said, vaguely.

162

"Then what can you do to help?" I asked again.

He paced towards me, before stopping. "We've a worldwide structure, capable of supporting the publication of the documents and a sister organisation in America. They've a high-ranking member, who is a publisher and distributor of esoteric material. I think he'll help us and I can contact him, if you wish." He shrugged and threw his hands out in true Gallic fashion. "But do not underestimate the powers of the Establishment. They'll undoubtedly try to stop you and prevent publication. We have some clout, but could not fight the Vatican on our own."

"I'm beginning to appreciate the extent of their influence," I said.

"There's always been political propaganda. The Order of the Knights of St. John, were opposed to the Templars humanist approach in the fourteenth century and wanted them annihilated, but first they discredited them."

I nodded. "Possibly they wanted their wealth too."

"For sure. There may be similar organisations reconstituted and ready to oppose you today," he said.

"Do you know of any?" I asked.

"You may be aware that the Red Cross is officially the charitable side of the Order of St. John of Jerusalem, but this is the same Red Cross, whose political function is often cover for intelligence operations. David Bruce, a direct descendant of the Templar King, Robert the Bruce of Scotland, for example, was chief representative of the American Red Cross in Britain in 1940. One year later, he became head of the Office of Strategic Services operation in Europe, the precursor to the CIA."

I shook my head. "I've a meeting at noon today, with two persons who say they're acting as Agents for the Vatican. One is called David. He'll have a man with him called Marco, an unpleasant man with a propensity for violence. Are you prepared to join me?"

"What problems have you encountered?" He asked, tilting his head.

"Nothing of any consequence."

"Where's this meeting?"

"My hotel." I replied. "I've also had contact with someone called Dominique Flaviel, at the Bibliotheque Nationale. He told me he works for the government, but he seems to know more than he should. He's promised to be there too."

He pondered for a moment. "It'll be a little crowded, but I'll come. Do you want me there before noon?" he asked, turning towards his office.

"Yes, just before noon would be good," I agreed, following him back into his office. He stopped at his desk, smiled and offered his hand. "I must ask you this. Do you have any idea of the value of these artefacts?"

"The monetary aspect of it hasn't been a major concern." I replied, honestly. "But I'm aware of the values placed on the Dead Sea Scrolls, so I appreciate their worth could be significant."

"It doesn't tempt you?"

"Not really." I shrugged.

"Good. I'll meet you in the hotel." He sat down at his desk.

I began to walk away, but turned to face DeValois again. "I think you should know I've reason to doubt the girl with me. Her name is Rachel and she worked with my uncle. Strange things have been happening. She had a private meeting with David and Marco in their car and it concerns me. I hope I'm wrong about her."

He shook his head. "Thanks for telling me, but remember she did contact me. Why would she do that, if she were conspiring in some way against you?"

"I don't know," I replied.

He thought for a moment. "On the other hand, I do remember her mentioning the surname of this man Marco. I think she said it was Rosseli. Does she know him?"

Further Extract. "...The Earth, and everything in her, is a thought expressed by the mind of God, and Nature is the chalice for the recovery of the individual human spirit. Herein lies the secret of the Holy Chalice, which must be perpetuated in symbolism, if these teachings are contaminated. We must all work for the thought of the integration of the truth of all religions, as the energy in the experience of God is exactly the same. It is the only true reality, as it never changes, is ageless and eternal. I fear the orthodox authorities, which denigrate the feminine and its principle, will lose their direction, for the closer we move to the Light, then the more we are tested. Spiritual work must be done with a joyful heart and all I see around me, save for Mariam (Mary), is a dour spiritual hierarchy. The ancient Goddess is a symbol of the Divine Wisdom, which merges both masculine and feminine, in complementary fashion. We must fight to preserve the way of the Priestess, before it is too late. Men and woman may be born equal, but it is the woman who is receptive and draws down the power for the man, the Magus. This is the polarity and this is the unity, which must eventually bring all religion together, if there is to be peace on earth. For all positive energy must have at its polar opposite negative energy, which must be controlled for the benefit of harmony of spirit. The feminine must be receptive to man, but not subordinate to him It is only in this way will we be reunited in the One."

CHAPTER 9

Circumstances and events were propelling me faster than I could control, like a giant boulder, rolling down a steep hill. I feared the magic, which time weaves, could once more cast me as a victim in this absurd theatre of illusion, but I determined to resist its spell.

Just before noon, Rachel joined me in the bustling reception area of the hotel. Guests regularly passed, some leaving, others arriving. One person, sitting opposite the reception desk, browsed literature about the Moulin Rouge, another something raunchier. The receptionist busied herself, simultaneously answering the telephone and handing out keys, whilst fending off an impatient German businessman, jostling for immediate attention.

Our own little drama seemed insignificant, almost like a cameo appearance. I had no preconceptions about the meeting, somehow assuming the correct decision would crystallize of its own volition. One way or another, I vowed to control my destiny, rather than be controlled. David stood waiting, hardly an expression visible to betray emotions, but Marco paced around, his body twitching menacingly, like a coiled spring. Rachel lingered behind me, eyes looking down, as if disinterested. Peripheral sounds filtered into consciousness, the noise of traffic, and a horn tooting nearby, penetrated through the front doors and loud, fast-spoken French. The smell of strong coffee and cigarette smoke hovered unpleasantly in the air.

"I've asked two other people to join us, in the hope this matter can be resolved amicably," I said to David, looking around and noticing the other two invited guests had not yet arrived. He wore a red open-necked designer shirt, Armani trousers and brown buckled shoes. Marco wore denim jeans and an old tight-fitting sweater, which allowed his physique to bulge manfully. It fitted his image.

David looked suspiciously at Rachel. "That wasn't the arrangement." He stated the obvious. "Perhaps I should cancel this meeting."

"I have things I want to say," I sighed. "The least you can do is listen to me."

"I'll listen, but on my terms. It'll be on your own and you'll not have to wait long for that meeting."

"Please don't threaten me, they're experts in this field of research and I must make the right decision. They can help explain my position." I said, vainly and unnecessarily attempting to justify my actions. "They already know about the scrolls, so you've nothing to lose," I added.

David turned, scrutinising Rachel's expression, thoughtfully.

"Don't look at me. I knew nothing about this," she said, dismissively.

He turned to Marco and grimaced, shaking his head.

At that moment, Jean DeValois walked into the reception area. I moved towards him, shaking his hand. "I'm pleased you could come," I said. "Let me introduce you to everyone. You know Rachel, of course." I moved back towards the group. "This is David and Marco." I pointed to each, in turn. "I don't know David's surname."

"Because we've not told you," Marco said, firmly. His face twisting into a sneer, as if force of habit.

"You shouldn't wear your heart on your sleeve," I said provocatively, with the confidence of a public place to protect me.

He stepped towards me, until his face almost touched mine. "Don't ever offer me advice again. It may be the last you give." He spoke, starkly, true to his disposition.

"I understand that it's Mr. Rosseli, isn't it?" I asked.

He didn't respond, but glanced towards Rachel. She looked away.

I turned to David. "Is this the true face of the Catholic Church, with its compassion and dedication to service."

"I'm not a priest," he replied.

"There's no need for unpleasantness," DeValois said, using his arms to push Marco away.

"Now's not the time." David pulled Marco back.

Marco pointed his finger at me. "There's going to be a time ...and soon." I shook my head.

Jean lit a cigarette, cupping his hands expertly, as he did so. He inhaled deeply, and blew the smoke upwards in a confident manner.

I walked ahead and the others followed more reluctantly. "Let's go into the conference room. I've agreed with the Hotel, we can use it, without interruption. They'll send my second guest through, when he arrives."

We moved into the small room, adjoining reception, and I closed the door.

"Jean, perhaps you can tell me whether I can rely on promises from the Vatican."

He shrugged. "It depends on what documentation they provide to support it and any pronouncements, which accompany it."

"I also need to understand the importance and significance of the documents, which my late uncle, the Cardinal, bequeathed me." I said.

He nodded. "If they are what you say, it may change the intrinsic nature of Christianity. They would be hugely significant and should not be buried again for centuries. This is the risk, if you rely on the goodwill of the Vatican." He sat back in the chair, taking a deep breath. "There were undoubted cover-ups and delays in the interpretation of the Qumran material, because of its mainly Catholic researchers and its Catholic leader, Father De Vaux."

"I understand all that," I said, shifting impatiently in my chair..

"There is also clear evidence, some of the material was capable of embarrassing the Christian establishment. The Vatican funded some of the acquisition of material and, consequently, held great sway with the research team."

"But would the same thing happen again?" I asked firmly.

"If they controlled the material, it's likely to be repeated." He hesitated, his eyebrows raised. "Even if they promised to publish it in some form, you can guarantee it'll be edited, more probably it'll disappear without trace."

"With respect, you miss the point," David interrupted, forcefully, shaking his head. "They're not his documents, or even Cardinal O'Rourke's documents. They were stolen from the Vatican and we've archive records to prove it. So any arguments about their significance are strictly academic."

"Boss, do I have to listen to this crap?" Marco stood up, obviously struggling to hold back restrained nervous energy.

"Sit down, Marco," David gestured downwards with his hand.

"But didn't the Vatican, in turn, steal them from the Knights Templar, by force?" Jean replied, glaring at David unblinking and raising his voice to a similar pitch.

"Well, John," David turned to me. "It's your decision, not his. You're the one who'll have to pay the price. I certainly didn't come here for a debate." He wagged his finger in my direction. "I hope the original parchments have not deteriorated. At least, in the Vatican vaults, temperature and humidity are controlled. You'll answer to the world otherwise and to me."

"Is that a threat?" I asked, stoically, disguising the fact that my heart thumped wildly.

"In life, there's always a price to pay for your decisions, you must know that," he replied. "Certainly, your uncle did."

"So you accept responsibility for his death?" I glared at David, my face flush with anger. I should have realised the extent to which these documents would become a focus for vested interests, but I had barely enough time to read them, without considering the wider picture.

He shrugged. "Not at all, but these things happen when people fail to obey the rules."

It still mystified me, how quickly these people had located me. Everything so far had followed gut instinct, but I needed to use my head. Choices had to be made. A knock on the door interrupted my thoughts. It was Dominique, offering apologies for his lateness. He looked around the room.

I introduced him to everyone, explaining his approach to me, whilst researching at the Bibliotheque Nationale. "Do you know any of these people?" I asked, studying his reaction, rather than his reply.

He looked at Jean. "I believe I know Monsieur DeValois, that's all."

"We've been discussing the merits and importance of the scrolls and Journal, which I inherited from my uncle, the Cardinal. Do you have any views on them?" I asked, wondering if he knew what documents were in my possession.

"But I don't know what documents you have," he replied, straight-faced.

"Come on, Monsieur Flaviel," I reacted, angrily, shaking my head and raising my voice. "You wouldn't come to a small Hotel in Paris, to meet someone you hardly know, unless you had a good idea what documents I have in my possession. Let's be candid with each other. What's your connection to these people?"

"He's nothing to do with us," David said.

"Nor my Order," Jean concurred.

"But these are the only people who know I have the documents," I said, studying Dominique carefully.

"You must understand, I have access to intelligence sources, which have provide me with certain information," Dominique said, lowering his gaze. "If it's accurate, then you've documents, which were taken by the French Pope from the Knights Templar, in the fourteenth century. Am I right?"

I looked around the room for reaction. The expressions were studious, though no-one showed surprise.

"You're right, Monsieur," I said.

He raised his eyebrows. "I'm employed by the French government to recover any artefacts, which properly belong to them. If they were recovered by a French citizen or were taken in France, this government will do everything, within its power, to recover them." He looked directly at me. "All the power of the state will be used," he added.

"Nonsense." David replied, dismissively. "The original documents may not even be in France."

"How would you know?" I asked, nervously fretting over the comment.

"I'm guessing," he replied. "In any event, they were allegedly recovered in Jerusalem by Agents, acting on behalf of the Vatican. They've been properly recorded and retained by them. I don't intend to enter into silly discussions like this."

"Well, possession is nine-tenths of the law, they say." I said, boldly. "From a legal point of view, I believe the head of the research team on the Qumran project bequeathed his rights to the texts when he died, even if he didn't own them. It went unchallenged, so the precedent has been set. Isn't this the same situation?"

David sat back, his face a mask of fury. "You can't be trusted." He shouted, pointing his finger again. "Quite frankly, I'm not sure why I'm even discussing this with you."

I had determined not to be bullied. "Well, if you're acting on behalf of the Vatican, perhaps it's because they're oblivious to the march of history or will they again suggest propaganda is history."

"We'll recover the documents, one way or the other." Marco interrupted, angrily.

I heard a faint whimper behind me and turned to see Rachel, head down, with tears running down her face. I stretched out my arm, touching her knee. "Don't get upset," I said, softly. "Why don't you return to the room?"

She shook her head.

"You're the one causing all the problems. They can be resolved at a stroke." David said, stridently.

"If you don't agree, we'll have to help you make the right decision." Marco said, smiling.

I turned back to face him. "Now don't start making threats again. All I've done is keep my options open." I said, attempting to diffuse the situation and realizing I still needed information from them. "David, I need to know Rachel's position?" I asked. "It's time for placing all our cards on the table. I saw her getting into your car, yesterday."

I kept the question clear and hoped for an honest answer.

He didn't reply immediately, looking first at Marco. "We knew she worked for the Cardinal. Yesterday, we asked her for help. It's that simple." No body language was evident, but perhaps he was trained in subterfuge.

"How dare you ask him about me, as if I'm just an ornament in the room," she scorned, still tearful. "I've already explained the circumstances in which I talked to them in the car. Are you calling me a liar?" She turned her face away.

I clenched facial muscles and my stomach churned. "I think those circumstances, and the way in which we were traced to this hotel, warranted the question." I said, unable to disguise my lack of diplomacy.

Marco smiled, a lopsided smile, at my embarrassment. "I'm not interested in your petty domestics," he said.

I took a deep breath and turned to Jean. "Would you be in a position to work with the French government and protect us?" I asked.

Before he could answer, Dominique interposed. "I must make it absolutely clear, I can't promise any co-operation with an independent organisation, such as that of Monsieur DeValois."

Jean shook his head. "I'm not surprised."

"This makes it more difficult," I said.

"I've obtained authority from my government to offer you full protection, whilst you're in France, and ten million francs for the documents." Dominique smiled, confidently. "Does that make your decision any easier?"

I thought, for a moment, waiting for a reaction from the others, but none came. All eyes turned to me. Dominique clearly misunderstood my motives. "It's tempting, but there are matters of principle, which are more important than money, including a promise I made to my uncle, to ensure the documents were authenticated and made public. I wouldn't want a cover-up."

David became agitated, his face reddening. "You're a fool. We can offer money too, but the French government cannot protect you all the time." He stood up to leave. "I assume you intend to return to England, at some stage."

"But you cannot promise me publication and I'll settle for nothing less." I insisted, firmly setting out my stall, with no room for equivocation.

"Do you really think you can depend on promises from Governments," he said. "This isn't the end of the matter."

"Are you telling me that the Church is more interested in power and politics than concerning themselves with satisfying spiritual needs? Let me remind you that one of the recent Popes, when he called the second Vatican Council, made it clear it was spiritual service that took precedence."

David smiled, a sarcastic lop-sided smile. "You forget that elements of Vatican hierarchy would have retained their power base. In any event, his successor made reference to the devil having entered the Church, so who do you believe."

"The Church, sadly in many ways, is spiralling towards obscurity, if I may use the expression of Professor Father Martin, when he resigned his position at the Vatican to write."

"I've had enough of this farce. It's time for us to leave them to their fatuous deliberations." David walked towards the door, with Marco faithfully following in his footsteps.

As he walked out of the door, Marco pointed to Rachel and made the image of a gun with his hand, pulling the trigger with his index finger. She paled, looking down again. The door closed firmly behind them.

"Dominique, I feel I can trust Jean. He's shown me historical documents, which tend to suggest his Order could only benefit from the publication of these scrolls. What assurances about disclosure would you give me, bearing in mind you wouldn't co-operate with his Order?"

" I would have to take instructions on these matters," he replied.

"I'd demand publication, as a pre-condition of the acquisition of these documents, wherever they go." I said.

"I could take advice, but I can make no promises, at this time," he said.

He was a cold fish and I found it difficult to assess him. "As you know, I can make more money in the private market, if I wanted to sell the documents, so any possibility of a sale, without conditions, is remote."

"Then I'll take instructions," he said, nodding his head, but giving no clues as to his integrity.

"Where does this leave me?" Jean frowned.

"I can always make it a condition of sale you should have access to the documents. Perhaps you can assist in the publication." I said. "But I've made no final decisions yet. I cannot afford to make a mistake."

"Well, I'd settle for that, but I'm not sure our friend here will agree," he replied.

"Perhaps not." Dominique grimaced.

"Well, we can't take this meeting any further today. Can I propose a meeting tomorrow, at the same time," I suggested.

Jean nodded. "My office would be available for the meeting tomorrow, if you wish?" Jean looked at me, then Dominique, for a reaction.

"Dominique, are you happy for the meeting to take place at the offices of Monsieur DeValois. Do you know where they are?" I asked.

"Yes, I know. It's satisfactory." He hesitated, before offering assistance. "Do you want me to arrange for someone from the Police Nationale to provide security for you until then. If so, I can do it."

"Do you think it's necessary?" I asked.

Rachel stood up. "I've had enough." She walked towards the door, turning momentarily. "I'm going for some fresh air. I'll see you later," she said, before leaving in a huff. This was becoming a habit I did not enjoy.

"I'm sorry," I apologised for her, in her absence and turned to Dominique. "If you think it prudent, I'll take whatever protection you can offer, but I want the man to make himself known to me. I don't want there to be any mistakes," I said.

"Very well, until tomorrow." Dominique shook my hand and departed, leaving the door ajar.

Jean waited for a moment. "You must understand, I don't know this Monsieur Flaviel. He could be anybody," he said, quietly. " He could even be an intelligence officer of the government, especially as he seems to know my organisation."

Are you suggesting he's linked with the others in some way?" I asked.

"I don't know, but you must be careful not to trust him," Jean looked furtively towards the open door.

I nodded, already appreciating the need for prudence. "I'll contact my lawyer in London and ask him if he could be present at this meeting, tomorrow. I'm sure he'll take all necessary steps to protect me." I had intended to contact him anyway, as Rachel knew the original documents had been deposited with him, and it worried me. I felt confused, as if I was walking through a door, before it was open.

"Do you think it strange, a government official offers you money for scrolls, without first asking to see them, or at least, a summary of their contents?" Jean asked, unblinking.

I shook my head. "Perhaps," I replied.

"For my part, if my Order wanted to pay for the scrolls, they'd want to know precisely what they contained and they'd want them authenticated."

"Yes, it's as if he knew already," I agreed.

"How much of the detail have you examined in the scrolls and the Journal?" He asked.

I anticipated the question from somebody. "I've been wading through my uncle's interpretations. I can provide you with a summary of the various scrolls and their contents, provided you can assist me with the publication. At first, I thought they were innocuous, but I can assure you they're hugely significant."

"Then I'll see you tomorrow." He said, taking a packet of Gitane out of his pocket and lighting the cigarette, as he walked through the door, ahead of me.

He turned around before walking away. "One more thing. If the intelligence agencies are involved, don't connect to the Internet. If you do, they'll be able to download everything on your hard disk." He wagged his finger, knowingly.

***

"I've wanted you inside me for ages." Rachel placed her hands inside his shirt, pulling the shirt out of his trousers, then undoing his belt and unzipping his fly. Her hands were gentle and movements fluid.

"I must have you now," she insisted, kissing his chest, his stomach and then his erect penis, devouring the tip in the process. She looked up at his taut, strained facial expression. She knew she couldn't be innocent of the effect her body had on him, or the fact she indulged his fantasies.

"Have you missed me?" She asked, even though his body already offered a wilful answer. She unleashed passions, which made him tremble.

"If that man has laid a finger on you, I'll kill him." Marco pushed her onto the bed. He needed to control her; it was a flaw in his personality, which was beyond redemption. "You were placed with the Cardinal for a reason. You've not been doing the job you're being paid for." He reminded her of business before pleasure.

"I didn't want the position, in the first place. I only did it because you asked me," she said, sitting upright in the bed. "You wouldn't have known we were in Paris, if I hadn't telephoned you." It may have been a mistake to talk back to Marco, but she couldn't help herself. "Ow!" She shrieked, turning instinctively away from him, as he slapped her across the face.

"What was that for?" She asked, angrily.

"You haven't answered me yet," he said. "Has he touched you?" His face reddened, stained teeth clenching in his anger and jealousy.

"No, he hasn't touched me," she lied. "I told him I hadn't had sex for two years, after having an abortion, so he's left me alone."

He relaxed, laughing loudly. "The man is a fool," he said.

Rachel knew otherwise, but survival insisted she play his game for now.

"But it still doesn't explain why you haven't been doing your job." He pulled his trousers off completely and pushed her flat on the bed again.

"I think he suspects I'm working for you. He doesn't trust me, so he doesn't tell me everything," she said, plausibly. It had become easier to lie with practice, but Marco was not a complete fool, even if he was a bully.

"I need you. Don't ever betray me," he said, with a trace of humanity in his tone.

In a sober state, she found his behaviour undesirable. He wanted sex, but she did not. He obviously thought it would sedate the pain, but it didn't and couldn't. She puzzled over this vulnerable side to him, but still wondered how she could have fallen in love with him, in the first place. At the start, he had appeared so much like her father. His evil deeds may not have made him an evil man, but any empathy, which may once have existed, had turned to revulsion. She still could not understand how he remained so ignorant of this resonance, when it vibrated so loudly from her soul. Perhaps he did feel it, but chose to ignore it. It had been impossible to sustain love in the face of his indifference. Once he may have known his choices were wrong, but he still exercised the freedom of his will to make them. Eventually, his humanity disintegrated into evil, consumed by it, becoming soulless. It had happened gradually, almost insipidly, but its impact hit her suddenly. She may have been confused before, but not now. The worst thing was his refusal to acknowledge his imperfections. She realised, for the first time, he was afraid of his conscience. This fear terrified him and so he, in turn, inflicted terror. She reasoned his lust for power had passed any hope for salvation, by being subordinate neither to any spiritual power, nor to anything higher than itself.

"Now lie back and open your legs, I'm going to give you the ride of your life." He boasted, but she knew better. He first straddled her, pulling off her skirt and knickers, and then forcing her legs further apart as he moved down and rammed his penis inside her, with no foreplay and no sensitivity. He roughly manhandled her breasts, pulling her blouse apart and her bra up. He sucked her nipples in the way he knew would give her pleasure and make her beg for more. Then he used his thumb and index finger on her nipples. She groaned in pleasure and he smiled. This gave him his power over her and he thrust his penis harder inside her. Little did he know the confidence in his lovemaking ability had been so utterly misplaced.

"Do you like it?" He asked, despite only being able to tolerate a dishonest answer.

"Yes Marco, I love you," she replied, more out of habit than spontaneity, but the words were hollow. She had endured sex many times without love and a hot bath afterwards always sedated the emptiness.

He turned her around. He knew she loved a rear entrance and her deep sighs reinforced his belief, but she felt dirty.

"I want you to have two orgasms. Do you understand?" He demanded an answer.

"Yes. Yes." She responded, faking the first one, with groans that would have matched Meg Ryan's fake orgasm in 'When Harry meets Sally'. Her head dropped, hopeless and dead. Sex had originally given her the escape from her humdrum and mediocre existence, but now the price she had to pay was unbearable. It hadn't always been this way. He had shown kindness, even if it had been measured doses, but subtly his control dramas took over. He tried to transform her into an obedient extension of himself. It had begun to kill her spirit and if she allowed it to continue, she could no longer

181

call herself a victim. She had freedom of will, too, and could change the choices and the patterns of behaviour, which created the situation.

Soon the ordeal was over and she felt degraded, as she lay there, entwined in Marco's sweating body. There may have been superficial pleasure, but she knew she had to extricate herself. She had entered into the relationship, as with other men, for all the wrong reasons. It was a destructive pattern of behaviour, which she seemed always to repeat. She had to use her intellect to break the pattern. Her growing feelings for John had already led her to defy Marco. She had not told him where the original scrolls and Journal were located, and actively contacted the Order of the True Rose Croix, to assist John. If Marco found out he could do serious harm and take pleasure in it. If he knew she had made love to John, he would certainly carry out his threat to kill him, but she was used to lying about sexual matters. She regarded it as part of a woman's armoury, but for the first time in her life she wanted to be honest with John.

She wondered if he could take the truth or whether it was too brutal. She agonised as to what she could do. A part of her loved and wanted to help John, but she feared another part was irredeemable. She knew she didn't deserve John and conflict raged within her. He had never asked her, but she was a Catholic and would die a Catholic. She could never love him more than God. She played a game with herself, and with John, one minute helping him, believing there was hope in the relationship, but the next she lied, and the more she lied, the more she knew she could never change. It left her in despair.

"…Some still tempt me with external and transient power. It would be so easy, but I have no wish to be a King and certainly not a God. I am satisfied if I can take my place as a Priest and Teacher. It is the legacy for which I yearn. I seek only true power, which comes from our spirituality and makes us humble. They even suggest I am of Immaculate Conception. My brothers, James and Judas Thomas, laugh because they know my many imperfections. They know too, that my mother lay with my father Joseph, but the suggestion has sinister overtones. It distresses me, for if they persist with this ridiculous doctrine, then women may become subordinate to men for centuries. The feminine teach us the way of intuition, which is the only authentic voice of the higher non-physical self. It is the vehicle of communication between the soul and its physical incarnation.   Only through listening to your inner voice with your heart, can you escape the limitations of the physical world and move towards the One. I tell my disciples that to them that knoweth, ALL things are possible and they can move mountains if they can only believe. If intuition is closed down, then learning will develop only through the pain and crises of traumatic physical events. The battle between the forces of the Light and Darkness is necessary, if there is to be free will. It is only through a shift in consciousness can we move into the world of paradox, where we discover what the intellect tells us cannot be, actually is. This is the illusion and the matrix, which exists before our eyes. It is a play and we are the actors. Eventually, we understand that what is small in this world, is large in the spiritual world and what may be significant here, may be of little substance there."

CHAPTER 10

Rachel breezed into the hotel room, bright and chirpy, though her eyes were puffy and glazed. Perspiration darkened the edge of her hair and one cheek seemed slightly red and swollen. She strained in her breath and her voice was ragged and uneven, but I dismissed the symptoms. In circumstances where I had a compelling need for love, ignorance was sometimes bliss.

"There's a plain clothes police officer in reception who'll watch the place. He'll follow, if we go out," I said, remaining on the bed, diligently reading through more of the interpretations of the scrolls and making notes. They captured my imagination. The more I read, the more their truths stirred something deep within me, like a child in awe of something secret and magical.

I placed my paperwork to one side, kicking off my shoes, and turning to face her. "You really can't keep walking out on me, on a whim, as you do. It isn't fair to me."

Rachel sat on the bed alongside me. "I'm sorry, I don't seem to be making the right decisions," she said.

"Perhaps it's a matter of trust, but in the circumstances it's difficult," I confided, holding my arms out to her. "Give me a hug." I moved in close, so my chin fitted snugly to the side of her neck. I always enjoyed the warmth of her body, but her heart beat unusually fast. Again I dismissed it.

"I've telephoned Julian, my solicitor in London. He's arriving tomorrow and he said there've been no problems with the originals. They're safe." I took a deep breath. "I wish I'd trusted you." I whispered.

"Stop!" Rachel pushed her hand out and moved away.

"I'm the one, who should apologise." She steeled herself, as she spoke. "Whether you believe me or not, I've begun to fall in love with you."

"Then why the apology?" I said, puzzled.

"John, please hear me out. I'm going to hurt you." For a moment, she placed her two hands over her face. As she removed them, she looked towards me with tears in her eyes.

"Carry on", I said, sensing her discomfort and moving off the bed to give her space. I walked to the window and turned around. I felt as if I was back in the confessional, except this time I could not be objective. In the distance, the sound of the traffic and bustle, associated with all large cities, intruded unpleasantly, but my surroundings were of no consequence.

"I've not told them the whereabouts of the scrolls and I contacted Jean DeValois in a genuine attempt to help you," she said.

"Then what's the problem?" I held my hands out in front of me, palms upward, shaking my head.

"John, I've told you I love you, but you're not making this easy."

"Sorry." I said.

"I don't want you to apologise." She raised her voice and turned away in exasperation, clenching her hands into a fist in the process.

"What do you want me to say?" I asked, despairingly. "Love is not about orgasm. It's about surrender to the other person and it's Holy." I hesitated and took a deep breath. "I'm trying to tell you how much I love you."

"You must let me finish." She turned back, stamping her right foot on the floor. "This just makes it more difficult for me. Now is not the time for these meaning of life conversations."

"Alright, Alright, go ahead. I'll not interrupt again." I sat back on the bed.

She composed herself and took a huge breath, then spurted it out. "Marco Rosseli has been my boyfriend and I worked for him for three years. He asked me to work for your uncle undercover and report back to him. I agreed." She hesitated and my mouth opened, unable to speak for a moment. "There you have it, now say something," she said.

My shoulders hunched, as if afraid to take in the truth and my face dropped. "I don't believe it." My voice wavered and the words barely left my throat.

"It's true, but I grew to like your uncle and I became disillusioned." She stopped, anticipating an immediate response, but I couldn't speak.

"Unfortunately, I didn't know how to extricate myself. The opportunity to work for you appeared to be the perfect solution. I still need your help." She spoke plaintively, almost pleading, but moved no closer. My mouth opened again, but no words came out.

"If you want, I'll spend the rest of my life making it up to you. You'll want time to come to terms with this. Until then, use me in any way you want. If it's my body, that's fine, because I love you."

"Huh," I scoffed, disdainfully. "Love. What do you really know about love?" I found my voice again.

"Then use me to find out what Marco is planning. It's the least I can do. I don't care about the risks."

I buried my head in my hands, more confused than ever. "What sort of a person are you?" I asked, if only as a channel to vent anger.

"I understand you want to hurt me back. It's alright," she replied. "Judge me in any way you want, but I care for you more than I care for myself. You must remember the things I've done recently to help you."

I looked at her, through pitiful eyes. "What am I supposed to say?"

"It's your choice. I'll entrust all decisions to you. If you want me to go, I'll leave immediately and you'll never hear from me again."

She waited, like a waif and stray. A part of me wanted to tell her to go, yet another part still desperately needed her and wanted to believe she could change. The thought of never seeing her again was unbearable. I didn't have the emotional strength to make such a choice. She moved towards me placing her arms around my shoulders and cradling my head in her chest. The anger could barely be contained. I wanted to reject and hurt her, but I resisted the urge.

"Every time you leave, I'll wonder where you are and what you're doing." I said quietly, unable to repress the emotion. "I can't fight it," I sobbed.

Rachel rocked me in her arms. "I know," she replied, with soothing recognition. "But we'll do it together. You're such a gentle man."

I lifted my head, taking a deep breath. "First, I need the truth, all of it, with no embellishment or lies creeping in." I stared at her, with an intensity capable of melting steel. "Either we build on firm foundations or there's no future. It's as simple as that. I must embrace the pain and know it's over. I can't do it any other way. I warn you, if you don't tell me everything now, then in the long term our relationship cannot last. It's your choice."

"Don't push me into a corner," she said, her eyes darting rapidly around the room, then back to me.

"I'm not, but you must understand that if you create a barrier between us, then I'll know intuitively and I can never be as close to you again."

"I understand, but it's not easy for me either. Let's take it one step at a time. You develop a habit of deception and it's difficult to change."

An impression of something, other than the whole truth, still leaked from the subconscious. "Just stay with me. The real test will come later", I said, pushing the remnants of tears away, with my index finger. "Tell me what you know?"

"At the beginning, I was told your uncle had taken important artefacts from the Vatican and my assignment involved their location and return. They said my only involvement would be the passing of information. Marco often did independent contract work and this seemed no different. He had been working for three years or so in this freelance capacity."

"So what did you tell them?" I asked, believing that if she willingly assisted me, it had to be a sign of good faith.

"Very little at the start, but when other agents were placed with his staff, matters became heated. There were constant arguments and I told your uncle I feared for his safety. I also told him why I had been placed there. He was remarkably magnanimous, in the circumstances, and asked me to stay." She hesitated, only momentarily. "When I started quarrelling with people, who were supposed to be colleagues, they wanted me out of there. I'd told them about you and the high regard your uncle had for your abilities. They started making enquiries into your background. I was told you had been a priest and had left the Church under some sort of cloud." She stopped again.

"What happened then?" I asked, impatiently.

"They began to mistrust me. It didn't help. When the opportunity came to work with you, they agreed, as they anticipated your uncle intended to pass the documents to you."

"What did they want you to do with me?" I asked, sullen features reflecting my mood.

"Just pass on information, which I did, until I told them we were in Paris. I had a telephone number to ring Marco. Then I stopped telling them anything. It's as simple as that."

"Were you supposed to make love to me?" I asked, painfully.

"Certainly not, Marco was very possessive. I know he'd harm me, if he knew." She replied, firmly. It rang true. "And he'd definitely harm you, as well, but he doesn't want to believe it. Women understand these things."

"Then I'll trust Jean DeValois. My uncle wanted me to contact his esoteric order and he's not part of the Establishment. What do you think?" I asked.

She moved upright again. "His name hasn't been mentioned to me, so perhaps you're right, but Marco did tell me they had a contact in Paris, who would help them. His name wasn't mentioned."

She looked down, for a moment. "Do you want me to contact Marco and try to find out?"

"No, I don't." I replied, instantly and loudly, my heart still ruling my head. "I don't want you to telephone that number ever again."

"Then perhaps their contact is Monsieur Flaviel?" She raised her eyebrows. "They were certainly unhappy at seeing DeValois. I could see it in their eyes and the way they looked at each other."

"But they also didn't like the idea of trusting a government." I said.

"You're right," she agreed. She moved towards me. The warmth from her body drew me to her, as always. I had a need to channel energy away from the pain and betrayal, to something more positive. I began making love to her, more forcefully than before, as a healing process. I needed to release the hurt. She accepted it willingly. As tempting as it may have been to draw attention to dampness and signs of previous lovemaking, I resisted it. Like Marco, I couldn't face the pain.

"I love you, John," she whispered.

"Please don't say it, don't say anything for now. Just be quiet."

Afterwards I didn't move. "Some things can never be the same can they?" I sighed, breaking the silence.

"No, but they can be different and that means better. I never wanted to be placed on a pedestal. It's hard being up there." She said, poignantly.

"Point taken." I said. "You know it's not the physical thing. It's the deceit, which is always so painful, the breach of trust. Sometimes I wish I could return to the simple and uncomplicated life I had as a priest in South America."

"What can I do to make it up to you? I never intended to fall in love with you." She said, sincerely. Perhaps this time I could trust her, but there could be no more lies.

"Let's sort out the publication of the scrolls. Afterwards, there'll be time enough for personal decisions." I said, snuggling close. I wanted sleep for a short while; it was always the healer and perhaps the anaesthetic too.

***

I finished a summary of the scrolls, as noon approached, heartened by my work and by Julian's arrival. I sat down opposite him in the conference room and spread my papers on the table between us. He was a big man, hardened by years of semi-professional rugby. Blonde and good-looking, he had a ready smile and a presence, which bred confidence. I showed him copies of the documents, which he had previously secured, explaining their nature and significance and the interest shown by various organisations. Rachel sat cross-legged and quiet, apparently content at a table to the side of us.

I looked up from the documents. "Please don't give your surname at the meeting, or if you feel compelled to do it, tell them its Smith. I don't want them to be able to trace you or the documents. In fact, it may be worth moving them to a safe deposit box in one of the major banks in the City. What do you think?" I asked.

Julian thought, for a moment, folding his arms. He had a reputation for the weight of his intellect and though, as with all lawyers, he was intrinsically cautious, his voice resonated with self-belief. Being of similar age, I always felt we had much in common. "I've given you a receipt for the documents, but I'd rather you sort that out personally, when you return. Until then, I'll employ a personal security guard to guarantee their safety. I'll telephone my partner to warn him of the danger and arrange it, before the meeting."

I reached out my hand and placed it on his arm, squeezing it. "I'm pleased you're here," I confided. "There's so much to organise, and I needed someone I could trust."

"If you had to choose a city to visit on business, Paris would be right up there, with the best." He smiled. "What sort of money is in this?" He asked.

191

I withdrew my hand. "Typical lawyer," I replied.

"Well, it'll give me an idea of the stakes involved," he laughed.

"They're very valuable, but I'm not interested in the money, just their publication. It's the one thing I must safeguard and the only basis upon which I'd hand over the originals," I said, straight-faced.

"I understand," he said, more soberly.

"How do you think I can do it?" I asked.

He placed his chin in the cup formed by the palm of his hand. "The only way you'll have guarantees is to allow me to examine and draft contracts with any publishers. They don't even need to see the originals, until the point of publication. It may be the best way forward."

I raised my eyebrows. "If the Vatican agreed to publish them, it would be the perfect solution. That way, I'd have honoured my promise to my uncle and the hassle disappears at the same time."

"Well, there'll still be a need for contracts of some sort with the Vatican authorities, if you insist on publication."

"Whatever you think is best." I agreed.

"Of course, a further option is to give any publishers access to the originals, under guard, but without them actually leaving your possession." He said.

"Either way, provided publication is protected, I'd be content." I felt happier with a friend, who could assist in decision- making. I placed an arm around his shoulder. "I need your help in resolving this. I've been out of my depth."

"It's not a problem." He smiled again, turning to peruse the documents and summaries. "Do you know how much money some of the

Qumran scrolls were fetching on the black market?"
He asked, looking up again.

"I'm not a fool, I'll not turn down money for
the sake of it, but it's only a small part of the
equation. Everything else has to be right first,
primarily publication. So let's go."

"And Rachel. Is she coming to the
meeting?" He gestured towards her, as she sat
passively to the side of us, throughout our
conversation, a strange obsessive silence emanating
from her throughout.

"She doesn't leave my side," I said,
possessively.

She smiled, holding my hand, as we left.

***

Everyone, except Marco, arrived promptly at
the offices of Jean DeValois, so discussions could
begin. The meeting took place in a small library
area, which I hadn't seen previously. It had
mahogany panelling and packed shelves in the
background. The mustiness of old books and
magazines floated obtrusively in the air,
accentuating the taut energy created by the friction
between the parties around the circular table. We sat
with Julian on one side of me, Jean DeValois on the
other, then Rachel and Dominique. David sat
opposite.

"Does your lawyer know you're in
possession of stolen property?" David asked.
"Legal proceedings will commence if the
documents aren't returned."

"Details." I replied, before Julian could
answer, cutting him off completely. "It's time for
decisions. What's your position?" I asked
Dominique.

"I've told you, I'm authorised to offer you two million euros and the protection you seek." He said, still no flicker of emotion breaking the rigid exterior.

"Can you show me this authority? You could be anybody?" Julian asked, looking for reactions.

The shell broke for the first time. It surprised me. He flustered and tutted, for a moment, shifting in his chair, until a reasoned response came. "I'm happy for you to meet me at a government office. I can provide you with written authorities, if you require them. I didn't realise my character was under suspicion today." A pompous indignation showed, as his face reddened. His demeanour concerned me.

"What about my condition of publication?" I asked.

"I've discussed this with my employers and they've instructed me to agree no additional conditions on the acquisition." He shrugged, adding, "It's out of my hands now."

"I see no point in continuing the discussions, unless you reconsider." Gut instinct made me reject his offer. Even if he could have agreed publication terms, there was something about Dominique, which didn't ring true, but I couldn't put my finger on it.

"Then I can no longer protect you and you may regret it. You've my card if you change your mind." He stood up and turned to the door, but with one glance in my direction. "The authorities may themselves take direct action against you. If so, you'll receive no payment. I make no further promises." He added, before leaving.

I looked at Julian, who gently shook his head, to reassure me there could be no legal threat.

"Well David, have you thought about the terms I need for the return of the scrolls to Rome?" I turned to him.

"I don't think you really anticipated a positive response, did you?" he replied, with resignation.

"Perhaps not, but I live in hope." I said.

"You don't understand the bureaucracy behind the Vatican. If you think instant decisions can be made, on questions of immense consequence, in a short period of time, you're absolutely mad." He said, his voice raised, then adding more quietly. "The best I may be able to obtain is a promise to place the matter before an Ecumenical Council."

I closed my eyes for a moment. "That would take years." I replied, expecting nothing better.

"If Pacelli in 1933, before he became Pope, could reach a Concordat with the Third Reich, which were the darkest forces of the era, then you can do better than that. The Vatican have colluded with tyranny and violence, yet all I'm asking for is a collusion with truth."

He tilted his head to one side. "That's different." He hesitated. "Wouldn't it be worth waiting? You've started the process. I've placed your proposition to my superiors, as forcibly as I can, but I'm a pawn and not a man with any influence in the halls of power."

I believed him, perhaps for the first time. "I'll not close the door yet. Why don't you provide me with a letter from the Vatican, with their proposals for publication? I'd want to see the official seal. The First Vatican Council of 1870 declared the Pope infallible in matters of faith and morals, even though it is referred to as a triumph of dogma over history. So, if he was motivated enough, he could push this through very quickly, as you know."

I looked at Jean, who sat silently throughout, arms folded. "How would you feel if the Church made such a promise?" I asked.

"If the truth came out, it would justify our existence. We may also publish historical documents of our own, simultaneously. We'd be content, as we could concentrate on politics. Until then, we, as an organisation, will give you such support as we can."

"Then David, it's up to you." I said. "Please push this through for me. I don't want to fight the Vatican, but I made certain promises to my uncle before he died and I will if I have to."

He stood up from the table. "I'm not sure I can. I may be asked to recover these documents, at any cost. If so, you must understand, you'll be isolated. Despite what Monsieur DeValois has said, his Order is only a fringe occult organisation. It may have greater political designs, but is of little significance in the scheme of things." He pointed to me. " I believe you're a principled man, but I warn you, I cannot afford luxuries."

"What do you mean?" I asked.

"Work it out for yourself," he replied.

I remained unmoved, but Julian, who had been busy taking minutes of the meeting, intervened. "If that's a threat, let me warn you, if the slightest harm comes to my client, I'll take all steps necessary to inform the authorities and the press of these comments."

David shook his head. "You're being unbelievably naïve. I'll tell them you misunderstood and took my statements totally out of context. The Vatican will deny any knowledge of me or else they'll say I was a rogue, with no position within the Vatican, and acting purely of my own volition." He turned to Julian. "Remember you're not immune either, so keep looking over your shoulder."

"Outrageous." Julian responded, indignantly.

"You've been warned." David smiled calmly and quietly left the room. There was something sinister in his lack of emotion, something already dead.

The conversation became more amiable after his departure, with the four of us present, though Rachel dwelt in her own world, a million miles from everybody else. Jean leant back on his chair. "I've spoken to some of my senior colleagues and many are businessmen, who could raise money for the publication of the scrolls, but they feel there'd be an enormous outcry."

I nodded. "That was always going to be the case."

He shrugged. "For this reason, they're a little hesitant and feel experts are necessary to authenticate it first. They believe an international consortium of experts would be essential." He coughed painfully, his body leaning forward in his attempt to clear his lungs. Paradoxically it signalled the taking of another Gitane out of his pocket. "Do you mind?" He recovered some oxygen and gestured with the cigarette.

I shook my head. "So you couldn't organise the actual publication?" I asked.

Jean inhaled deeply on his cigarette. "Not on our own, but we'd want your permission to approach like-minded organisations. There are more of them, than you think. I know an American publisher from such an associated organization. I've asked him if he could attend a meeting at short notice. There was insufficient time for him to come here today. His interests are similar to ours."

"Take my permission as granted." I said.

"I need a summary of the contents of the scrolls, to show the interested parties," he said.

"I've made a summary. It's with Julian, that's not a problem." Julian took a copy out of his attaché case and handed it to Jean.

"If there are some people, who want more detail, how can we arrange it?" He asked, as he took a copy of the summary of the scrolls I had prepared.

"If you wish, I'll do a presentation for you next week, but I'll only provide the copies of the scrolls and their interpretations when everything else is in place and contracts for publication have been signed." I said. "Julian has confirmed a condition can be inserted in the agreement for access to the originals."

Jean inhaled deeply and typically on his Gitane. "That's a good idea. It'll take about a week to arrange. Then I can come to London with the details, if you want." He shrugged gesturing openly with his hands, ash from his cigarette dropping onto the floor. "It's for you to decide the location."

"We'll say noon, a week today, at my home," I said, offering Jean my card, with address and contact details. "If there's a problem, you have my telephone, fax and E-mail address on the card."

"Very good. It's been a profitable meeting for all of us," Jean agreed, as he ushered us out of his offices. He handed me a card, which included his private address and telephone number. In the street, Julian handed back all copies of the scroll summaries. "I think I'd be happier if you kept these for now," he said "Shall we get together for dinner tonight?"

"I'll ring you, at your hotel, to make the arrangements." I said, before he walked away in the direction of his hotel. Rachel and I moved towards a taxi rank.

As I hailed a taxi, I heard someone shout my name. I turned around, only to see the outline of what appeared to be Julian, being bundled into the back of a familiar limousine. Marco's features, staring wildly and pointing his finger, were unmistakable.

"Oh, No." Rachel sighed, spotting him, even before I did.

" … The Romans try to destroy the integrity of our beliefs, but the soul cannot tolerate their pain or brutality. Yet they unconsciously cry out for love and their failure to find it, results in such anger and fear, though they will deny it. Even the propensity for sexual promiscuity is a reaching out for love and harmony in that striving for that Oneness which is the truth of our existence. It is the peace that passeth all understanding, but they are blind to the ways of the soul and severed from spiritual reality. In sexual union, the spiritual energy fields merge with the physical. I anticipate their addiction to an archaic and flawed religious tradition will destroy their civilisation. The Roman psyche does not permit them to acknowledge the parity of women with men, but we cannot change truth merely for convenience. Neither can they accept a religion, which would require neither a Church, nor a priest as an intermediary between the individual and God. The kingdom of heaven is truly within us, if we are made in the image and likeness of God. Paul may want to adapt the truth to make our teaching acceptable to them, but he is quite simply wrong and he can do great harm. It will not cure the emotional disease, with which they are afflicted. We must bend our back to all discipline, for we are never penniless, nor can we ever be poor in spirit."

CHAPTER 11

The offices of the Commissariat were cold and austere, much like the attitude of the Inspector facing us. It exasperated me. I sat in front of a large desk, with Rachel alongside me. The walls of the office were bare of any paintings or personal memorabilia, just files stacked up and cabinets, with more files on them. The accumulated dust suggested they had been there a long time. In the corner on a windowsill, more dust covered a half-empty bottle of Cognac nestling amongst stained, dirty glasses. The Gallic smell of the familiar Gitane floated intrusively in the air. I desperately wanted to navigate my own destiny and bring some control into my life, but I feared instead I could become the architect of my destruction. Bureaucracy in Britain constantly created problems for me, but in a foreign country, the culture barriers often appeared insurmountable, even when the language did not.

"But you admit yourself sir, you only saw an outline of someone entering a car. Perhaps it wasn't him at all or, if it was, he may have been getting into the car of his own free will."

"You don't understand, he was in distress, shouting to me and was bundled into the car. We've contacted his hotel and there's been no sign of him for the last four hours, since we saw him being manhandled." I said, vainly explaining the urgency, something obviously being lost in translation. I looked at Rachel, with eyes to the heavens, which she copied. I persevered. "We've told you, one of the persons in the car was definitely Marco Rosseli and we've given you the registration number of the car. Can you address these matters immediately, whilst there's time?" I asked firmly, but politely.

He shrugged, as only Frenchmen can. "But, of course. However, this is Paris and I'm sure your friend, the lawyer, will want to enjoy himself. There's so much to see and do. I think you'll find he'll be safe and well. We can't do very much, if a person has been missing only four hours."

I shook my head. "You must listen to me. I'd like you to do what you can, because I warn you,

I'm very concerned for his safety. I need to know you've made a record of this complaint." It was time for removing the façade of politeness.

The Inspector changed the expression on his face, raising his voice. "I've tried to explain our procedures to you, as pleasantly as I can, but you're taking more time, than I can give. There are many other urgent matters to consider." He stood up, pointing to the door.

We took the hint. "Very well, if you've any information, will you please contact us at the hotel?" I asked, as we left.

"You'll be contacted," he said, coldly.

Back in the hotel room we both lay flat on the bed in silence. We stayed in this position for at least fifteen minutes. Then, I snuggled up to Rachel, in a foetal position, whilst waiting for inspiration. Soon I drifted off to sleep, only to be woken by the sound of the telephone. I jerked awake, uncoordinated and uncomfortably reaching for it, almost knocking the telephone onto the floor, but catching it at the second attempt.

"May I speak to Rachel?" The sour tones of Marco's unmistakeable voice asked.

"She's not here," I lied.

"Oh yes she is. Now let me speak to her, unless you want your lawyer friend to have an unfortunate accident." His voice conveyed a sinister message.

"If anything happens to Julian, I'll chase you to Hell and back." I said, angrily.

"I've been there. Have you?" He replied, calmly for once. "I'm becoming very impatient, so please let me speak to Rachel."

I nodded and handed her the telephone. "It's Marco, demanding to speak to you," I said.

Her face dropped and paled.

"What do you want?" She asked. Her eyes moved rapidly, taking on the look of a trapped animal. A very emphatic 'No' followed a series of 'Yes' answers. Finally, she shouted 'No way' down the telephone, before hanging up the receiver.

"What was all that about?" I asked.

"He has Julian," she replied.

"So I gather. What does he want us to do?"

"He said no harm would come to him provided you co-operate in the return of the scrolls." She looked ashen and drained.

"What else did he say?"

"He told me that my job was over and I had to leave, except he wanted me to take you out one last time tonight." She hesitated, "to lead you into a trap. That's when I said 'No way'." She whimpered.

"Is that it?" I asked.

"Not exactly, he threatened me, if I didn't do exactly what he asked, I'd regret it. That's when I hung up." She buried her head in my chest and cried. "I'm frightened, really frightened." She spoke in staccato tones, between sobs. "I know him too well."

"He'll only get to you over my dead body," I reassured her.

"That's what worries me," she said.

"I'm not going to hide, but I'm not going to be blackmailed either. Whatever the cost." I said, confidently.

"Then, let's leave Paris tonight?" She asked, holding my arm tightly. Fear gripped her voice, settled in bulging eyes, staring and demanding an answer.

"I'll ring the Police Nationale and tell them what's happened. If they think I can help by staying in Paris, then I will, but provided they don't object, we'll leave tonight, though it makes more sense to wait until the morning. The problem is that if the scrolls are handed over, they are far more likely to harm us and Julian."

"Do you intend to tell the Police about the scrolls, otherwise they'll not understand?" She asked, already opening her case and moving towards the wardrobe.

"That'll create problems, but I'm not prepared to leave Paris and abandon Julian, without someone working towards his release.... He's my friend." I grasped the telephone to make the call. I took the name of the person making the report, as the original Inspector was unavailable. He insisted a personal report would have to be filed and confirmed nine o'clock in the morning would be an appropriate time, but they'd act on the information immediately. Rachel heard the end of the conversation and slumped onto the bed.

I replaced the receiver. "Sorry, but if it helps Julian, it must be done."

She nodded. "I suppose so, but I definitely want to leave in the morning."

"Yes," I agreed. "Now I'm going to ring Jean DeValois. There's an argument for ringing Dominique Flaviel also, if only to gauge his response. It'll flush him out, especially if I ask him to ring the Police Nationale too."

"If he's working with David and Marco, they'll know we've contacted the Police," she said, her voice trembling.

"They'll know anyway, I suspect," I said. "I just don't think they care whether we ring the Police or not. They obviously think they're immune, but I want to rattle a few cages."

"Ask Jean if he thinks you should ring Dominique Flaviel," she suggested.

"I'll do that." After a brief conversation with Jean, he agreed to make a few telephone calls. I felt a sense of having done everything possible, at least for the time being. I rang Dominique and explained the events, but the conversation was strangely stilted.

"I've explained there is nothing I can do, unless you change your mind. If you're prepared to accept our offer I'll promise immediate action." I didn't like the inference.

"It sounds as if you're condoning kidnap and violence," I said.

"Life isn't that simple, is it?" He replied, cold as ever.

I felt like being offensive, but knew there would be little point.

"Very well," I said, ending the conversation and hanging up the telephone.

"I'm not going to treat this room as a bunker," I said to Rachel, gathering enthusiasm for a foray into the night. "Let's go out. I have to think things through, but let's do it in a pleasant environment."

She looked anxious and vulnerable. I placed my arms around her, hugging her.

"Don't let Marco take me, please," she pleaded, childlike. "I couldn't bear it. He's not like any normal ex-boyfriend."

"It'll not happen," I said. "I'll ask them to keep our documents in the hotel safe, as usual. They're only copies, but I've used them to prepare the presentation. I can't see them doing anything in public places."

Rachel frowned, apparently unconvinced.

* * *

The meal had been exceptional, though the mood sombre. The evening had been otherwise uneventful, as we walked, hand in hand, through the narrow streets of the Left Bank, pleasantly lost. I had forgotten precisely where I parked the car, but I didn't care. I may have thought I knew Paris, but it remained a big city. I relaxed, happy to enjoy Rachel's company, squeezing her for reassurance, at every opportunity. I needed her to know I cared. In Paris, all couples showed love demonstratively; content to express it in full public display. This was no different. These may have been difficult times, but for a moment, time had no meaning, escaping its clutches in mutual feeling. We passed a series of small restaurants; music magically spilling out from all of them and exotic smells from most. Happy people smiled, exchanging greetings. Every bar celebrated nothing in particular, yet everything. Invitations to join them were politely declined, as heavy hearts would have affected their mood and spoiled their moment. The atmosphere somehow reinforced the feelings, darkness cocooning us into a private little world. Every touch exaggerating the passion I felt, which stirred as lust. I wanted her. I slipped my hand underneath her clothing, but she stopped my hand wandering further, too vigilant for pleasure.

"You must put the past behind you. Let this be a new beginning," I said, smiling half-heartedly.

For a moment, she didn't respond. When she did, she spoke nervously. "I wish I could, but life isn't that simple. I'd love this to be a new start, but I don't believe it."

I looked around. "I think this road is familiar," I said, noticing a certain landmark, particularly a bar with a night burner suspended underneath the awning. It allowed students to drink on the pavement tables until the early hours, even in winter. We walked on and on the right I saw the L'Arbuci restaurant and took my bearings. "This is the Rue de Buci."

Rachel's eyes darted everywhere. I realised fear stalked close to the surface and she gripped my arm tightly, her body rigid.

"There!" She pointed to Marco, and a colleague, at the end of the street, close to where the car had been parked. I looked at Marco's features. They cracked with a wry smile. I grabbed Rachel, pulling her down a side street. I noticed a motorcycle, parked outside a bistro. Keys had been left carelessly in the ignition. This was an emergency and the temptation was too great.

"Get on, quickly." I shouted. She was too frightened to argue. "Hold on very tight."

"Quickly," she shrieked, as Marco ran towards us. The engine ticked over first time. I engaged first gear, shooting off down the street, almost coming off, as a result of too much throttle and a nervous hand on the clutch. I banked the machine to make the next corner, placing my left foot to the floor in my anxiety. We were in a one-way street, going down the wrong way, too late to do anything about it. I heard Marco shout to his colleague to get the car. He still pursued us on foot, albeit it some distance behind. I saw a pedestrianised area, with bollards preventing cars using it. I took it, luckily avoiding both the bollards and pedestrians, swearing excitedly in French, gesticulating angrily. I slowed to avoid another group, glancing behind and noticing Marco had stopped running, waiting patiently for the car. The pavement twisted around, through more bollards, linking again with a road taking vehicular traffic. I had time to stop at its entrance.

"I'm going to take the direction, farthest away from Marco," I said.

"Yes." Rachel shouted. "Just get away from him." Her body shook as she gripped my waist so tightly that it hurt.

I turned the throttle and eased out the clutch, expertly this time. I accelerated away, furtively looking over my shoulder, when circumstances allowed. I pulled out of traffic and darted back in again, as I sped off, determined to put as much distance between Marco and us, as possible. A build up of traffic halted my progress and it became difficult to move forward in the same direction. People milled around busily. I guessed I had reached the market area of Montparnasse, but my sense of direction had been blown to bits in my urgency to escape. Traders were already setting up their stalls for the morning market and I needed to dispose of the motorcycle. I stopped to look around.

"Where's the metro?" I shouted to Rachel.

"I don't know," she replied, still clutching my waist, desperately. "This isn't exactly how I wanted to see Paris."

"Oh, No." I said, noticing a familiar car some distance behind.

"What's the matter?" She asked, her hands tensing again, in their grip.

"Nothing, but I must find a Metro. I'll try along here." I calmly manoeuvred the motorcycle, driving down an adjoining street. I looked in the side mirror; Marco's car had followed. There could be no doubt. I continued to weave in and out of the traffic, taking too many chances, braking heavily to avoid one irate pedestrian and cutting across another car, in the process. I ignored the tooting horns and sharp expletives, determined to escape into the night. I saw a police vehicle coming in the opposite direction and frantically waved to it, attempting to flag it down. I slowed down, but it sped past, ignoring my flailing arm.

I drove off again, then slowed, before screwing left at the next junction. I noticed Marco's car in the mirror, gaining on me. I saw an illuminated Metro sign and screeched to a halt.

"Get off." I shouted, pushing the bike into a small alley. I snatched Rachel's hand, shooting down the steps of the Metro, out of sight of the street. I had no idea whether Marco had seen us or not.

"We're not going back to the hotel tonight. We'll find a hotel in another part of the City. There's a Novotel in St. Denis and a Metro only half a mile from it."

Rachel still shook uncontrollably, too shocked to cry or to answer. After jumping the last couple of steps onto the platform, there was no sign of any train and insufficient people to hide. I heard the sound of someone racing down the steps. I pulled at Rachel's hand again and moved towards an exit at the far side of the platform.

"We can stay around the corner of the exit. This way we'll not be seen. When the metro arrives, it'll be easy to jump on. In the meantime, we're in a position to escape through the exit."

She nodded, but gripped my hand tighter, breathing heavier than me, seemingly badly out of condition. I looked around the corner after we had settled. Marco arrived on the platform with a colleague. He pointed and shouted for him to look at our end of the platform. His voice echoed. I found myself nervously gripping Rachel's hand tighter. She placed her free arm around me. Her whole body trembled. Her face had turned white with terror. Marco's colleague began to creep nearer. I was about to suggest we move down the exit tunnel when a metro arrived in the nick of time, noisily clanking its way on to the station.

"Look, we'll have to time this precisely," I whispered to Rachel. "I'll watch around the corner for the last person getting on, when I say 'run', you must run with me, as fast as you can. Is that alright?"

"Yes, I understand." She said, in a faltering voice. Everything appeared to happen in slow motion. At the signal, we shot into the nearest compartment. I urged the doors to shut quickly behind us and my prayers were answered. All Marco and his colleague could do was run down the platform and bang on the window. When we were safe inside the train, I couldn't resist a taunting wave and smiled. I cradled Rachel's head, stroking her hair, until the trembling subsided.

"I'll pay for the hotel in cash. Credit cards are too dangerous. I must telephone the Police to tell them to protect the car, but I'll not tell them where we're staying."

It had been a long, exasperating day. When we reached the Novotel in St. Denis, we were both totally drained. As she sank into my arms, it was for comfort and sleep, not stimulation.

A taxi took us to the offices of the Police Nationale marginally before nine o'clock the following morning. It was obvious we were expected and were directed to the same large office. This time, we not only met the original Inspector, to whom we had reported Julian's kidnap, but a more senior ranking officer. He was a tall gangly man, with a dark moustache and large nose, but otherwise nondescript.

"I am Commissaire Moreau," he said, his voice resonating deeply. "All the reports in this matter have been passed to me and I shall be taking personal conduct of the case. I need you to come with me to my offices at 36 Quai des Orfevres, on the Isle de la Cite. It's close to the Notre Dame Cathedral."

I nodded. I had begun to believe the influence of the Vatican and their reported intelligence agencies had spread to the French police force. "I was disappointed with your response when we complained of Julian's kidnapping. I think government intelligence units are involved and I need reassurance."

He cleared his throat. "Not French government agencies, I can assure you. I remind you it was our late President De Gaulle and French Intelligence, who exposed the crime syndicates and private intelligence organisations who, in 1962, made the assassination attempts on his life. They are no friends of France. We stood, almost alone, in this condemnation. We are fully aware that these syndicates and corporations have probably been restructured and relocated from their base then in Montreal. We are not naïve in these matters and have been monitoring the situation and doing more than you think in this case."

To a degree, I felt reassured.

He took us immediately to his headquarters, speaking only briefly on the short journey, when politeness demanded.

"You've heard of the famous Quai des Orfevres?" He asked, during the journey.

"Vaguely," I replied.

At his offices, we settled down again. This was more like the offices of a high-ranking gendarme, with leather chairs and a teak desk with deep drawers. Even the walls had been recently painted a pristine white. Framed photographs on his desk appeared to be family.

"Have you obtained any information about my friend who was kidnapped?" I asked, as he opened his file of papers.

"The hotel have heard nothing and neither have we," he replied, shifting papers from the file on to the desk, in front of him. "I'm also investigating the taking of a motorcycle and the damage to your car. When we discovered it, the car had already been pulled apart, as if they were looking for something. I must tell you, we've also been to your hotel. Your room has been ransacked, although we've recovered your clothes and belongings. We've also taken possession of your passports and some documents you lodged in the hotel safe. They seem to be copies of some historical documents."

I looked at Rachel, still dazed, and I took her hand, before turning to the Commissaire. "I'm sure your biggest concern will be the welfare of my friend Julian, although you'll appreciate, all these matters are linked," I said.

He wrote something down in the file on his desk. He had unusually long, spindly fingers. "First, tell me about the papers, which we found in the hotel safe?" He asked.

"They're simply copies of documents, which were given to me by my late uncle, Cardinal O'Rourke," I replied, truthfully. "May I have them returned to me, please?"

"Are the originals valuable?" He said, quietly, ignoring my request for their return.

"Possibly, but the originals are in London, not here."

A long silence followed, as he shuffled, then read again, the papers in front of him. "The names you've given me have been checked with our Interpol records." He spoke deliberately and mostly in complete sentences. It gave me the impression of an orderly mind. I felt I could trust him.

"And these records, which we've investigated, suggest neither of these two people exist. Certainly, no passports have ever been issued to them."

Rachel, who had sat there previously devoid of emotion, stirred. "I've seen Marco Rosseli's passport many times, but…" She didn't finish the sentence, but choked on her words.

"Is there something else you were going to say?" He asked.

"No, No," she replied, almost stammering.

"I can assure you, my dear, our information is accurate," he said. "Would you like to explain how you've seen this man's passport, so many times? What's your relationship with him?" The Commissaire sat, unblinking, waiting for a response. He was obviously a patient man.

"I lived with him for three years, but despite that, I really don't know him well or what he did," she replied.

"I see." The Commissaire said coldly, in a tone implying disbelief. He turned to me. "Where do these documents originate Monsieur O'Rourke?"

I smiled, looked at Rachel, then back at the Commissaire. "Do you mean before they came into the possession of my uncle?"

"Yes I do," he replied.

"Well, I suspect the originals were taken from beneath the Temple in Jerusalem at the end of the First Crusade by the first Knights Templar Grand Master, Hugues de Payen, when he discovered secret passages deep beneath the crypt. He had found a secret passage that led them there."

"And from there?"

"They were taken from the Knights Templar in the 14th Century, here in Paris, at the time of their purge." I gave a potted history, to cloud any issue relating to possession of stolen property, omitting reference to the nature of my uncle's acquisition of the scrolls.

"Do you know how your uncle came into possession of the scrolls?" The Commissaire asked, immediately realising the omission.

"I assume, as part of his duties as a Cardinal," I replied, vaguely.

"Very well, Monsieur O'Rourke, you can leave now, but I need you to remain in Paris, and at an address where we can contact you, at short notice. I anticipate the copy documents can be returned to you, in due course. We can take copies for our records. I will see you, tomorrow."

"Good. I use them for presentational purposes, so an early return would be appreciated," I said.

"Tomorrow then," he confirmed.

I nodded. "When will we be able to leave? I've business in London, which is important?" I asked, mindful of the need for safeguarding the original scrolls, although conscious of the fact that Julian had arranged additional security, before his disappearance.

"If we're able to resolve certain key issues in the next twenty four hours, it'll be in order for you to leave. We can return your documents and passport at that time," he said. "You can have your car today. It's been towed to the pound," he added.

He looked at Rachel. "Mademoiselle, how do you contact Monsieur Rosseli?"

She looked at me and again at the Commissaire. I nodded to encourage her co-operation. "I've a telephone number for him. You can have it, if you wish," she replied.

He wrote the number down on a piece of paper as she dictated it.

I stood up to leave, with Rachel in tow, grasping her hand tightly.

"Forgive me, Monsieur O'Rourke, I indicated you may leave, but not the young lady." He paused and stood, before walking around to the front of his desk. "She's been travelling on an illegal passport and there are matters, which have to be investigated. We require her to remain in custody to assist us with our enquiries. If it means we must arrest her to detain her, we shall do it."

"... I am often tempted to abandon my teaching mission, as I observe evil profligate. It is flaunted as truth, with a flagrant disregard for the integrity of my message. Though duality may be needed for the dynamic of learning and the experience of darkness essential for the understanding of light, Paradise can still become Hell, if it is static. I must seek evidence of the success of my mission, or else I am doomed to a fate, which others will control. Even my own disciples sometimes fail to grasp the essence of my teaching, despite the use of images, which should reach deeper into the soul. If I cannot make them understand, how can I reach those of lesser intellect and prejudice? They must open the path to their sacred essence by understanding the importance of conscious and responsible choice. Sometimes, I fear I do not have the patience to teach this unifying message. Perhaps others will succeed where I have failed and reveal how the Egyptian and Nazarene philosophy has synthesised the truths in all religions of both East and West. I realise my doubts block the path to intuition and to the soul, but this is my humanity. For this reason, perhaps it is my destiny for my disciples to learn more from my death, than from my life. I must write my truths, rather than teach them, for I fear I am not a natural teacher."

CHAPTER 12

The country may be different, but the words always sounded the same. My mind raced in circles for answers, but none came. I ended up back at the point where I started, still unenlightened and no further forward. Rachel's knees buckled, her face dropping, as I helped her back onto the chair comforting her. Her head turned to me and tears flowed. Desperation painted an unpleasant picture on her face. Her eyes looked down and her chin dropped to her chest.

"Can I arrange for a lawyer to see her?" I asked the Commissaire.

He nodded. "But of course."

I tried in vain to soothe Rachel's distress. "I'll stay with you," I said.

She looked up at me, pitifully, making no attempt to wipe away the tears. "I promise you, I didn't know there was anything wrong with my passport. I signed the application form and gave it to Marco, with two photographs. He's done this."

I glared at the Commissaire. "I honestly don't believe she has intentionally broken the law. Don't you think she's suffered enough? If you need me to put up some sort of bail bond, I'll be more than happy to do so."

The Gallic shrug, which had become all too familiar, conveyed an indifference to her plight. "I can give you ten minutes with her, but then you'll have to leave. She has to be interviewed without you present, but she'll be given access to a lawyer of her choice," he explained. He left the room, closing, and then locking the door behind him.

"I'll ring Jean DeValois and you'll have a lawyer. I'll do all in my power to have you out of here, as quickly as I can." I promised. I offered my little finger and hooked it around hers, as I had done once before.

"I can't handle this any more," she sobbed.

"Be patient and be strong." I said, squeezing her hand, my heart reaching out to her. "The ordeal will soon be over." I mustered confidence in my speech, realizing her life appeared more complex than mine. "At least, you're safe here." I said, reassuringly.

The Commissaire took me to one side, as I left. He was one of few men who actually looked down on me. "It would expedite our enquiries if we could detain Monsieur Rosseli. Do you understand?" He merely stated the obvious. "I have been collaborating with the Direction Centrale Police Judiciaire."

"Who or what are they?" I asked.

He tilted his head. "I suppose they're the equivalent of the American F.B.I."

"I understand," I replied.

"Then would you be prepared to telephone the man and set up a meeting with him. It will be under controlled conditions and we would be close the whole time, but I cannot pretend it would not involve you in danger." He didn't flinch, as he spoke.

As I had felt in constant danger, since the scrolls had been in my possession, it was nothing new. My life could never be the same again. "If can promise to arrange Rachel's release, as soon as possible, I'll do it." This pre-condition gave me back a feeling of control, however illusory.

"If you act in good faith, I'll arrange for her release, some time after her interview, later today," he agreed.

"I want to see Rachel, to tell her what I intend to do. She'll be in custody, so she can't tell anybody." I said.

He hesitated. "I don't think this is a good idea. You could be taking an unnecessary risk."

"If you let me discuss it with her, I'll do it." For some reason, I felt I needed her approval.

"Very well, but I'll give you only five minutes. What if she tries to dissuade you?" He asked.

"If I give my word to do something, I'll honour it," I said, unblinking. He nodded. Within minutes I was back with Rachel, explaining the proposal.

"I don't want you to do it. Not for me, it's too dangerous. You don't know the man." She insisted, grabbing my arm. "Please don't do it, he has reason to hurt you."

"I've made a promise and so I must do it. They've agreed, in return, to release you later today. I'll not change my mind."

She looked down. "Then do any deals with my…" She stopped mid-sentence. "You must only negotiate with David. I knew him well and I don't think he'll hurt you," she said.

I agreed and returned to the Commissaire.

"I assume you'll want David to be present, as well as Marco Rosseli?" I asked.

"Yes, of course. We'd also want the meeting in a public place."

"When do you want me to ring him?" Any dregs of fear had been flushed away by events and concerns for Rachel's predicament.

"I'd like you to do it immediately, using one of our telephones," he replied.

"Well, at least I won't feel so helpless," I said, as he directed me to another office equipped with sophisticated monitoring devices.

Marco sounded restrained during the telephone conversation. It was not like him and I wondered if he knew he was being set up. He gave nothing away, but repeatedly asked to speak to Rachel. The only way I could explain my possession of the telephone number was to tell him the truth. She had given it to me to ring him, as she had been arrested for possession of an illegal passport. Eventually, I persuaded him to meet me at the square in front of Notre Dame Cathedral. He assured me David would also be present. When I asked him about Julian, he paused, before indicating he didn't know what I was talking about. Perhaps he had more intelligence, than I had given him credit.

Within an hour, I was sitting on a bench in front of the Cathedral. Scaffolding covered huge areas of the façade to the side, with material draped over it. Its sadness reflected mine. We were both pitiful sights. The sun warmed the body, if not the heart. I felt wired up like a trussed chicken and conscious of the wires, even though I knew they were minuscule at about two inches square, but there was a wire protruding from that with a foil-like substance at the end of the wire. I had been told that even if they swept for a surveillance device, it would not be detected, as it would not be switched on until after the initial meeting. Prior to that, visual contact would be the sole means of tracking me. These assurances appeared hollow, as I waited, vulnerable and isolated.

I had been offered a simple GP5 tracking dot, a little metallic button the size of a watch battery, which would have transmitted my location to a Global Positioning Satellite System, but no voice would have been heard. I had been persuaded to use a transmitter. At that moment, I felt it was an unwise decision, but I had experienced a lifetime of foolish decisions, so it was nothing new.

Thirty minutes elapsed from the time set for the meeting. It felt longer and I feared they knew the truth. Birds sang in the trees behind me, oblivious to the drama beneath them. Different languages drifted in the air, as tourists scurried excitedly and busied themselves, in close proximity. The scene unfolded, as if I was detached from it, watching on a large screen. I relaxed and closed my eyes for a moment.

"I don't like you." I recognised the familiar voice and aggressive tones immediately and opened my eyes, jolting upright. Marco sat next to me; close enough to smell the staleness on his breath, but no sign of David.

"I can assure you the feeling is completely mutual," I said, gathering my senses.

His face glowered with pent-up anger and stained teeth bared. .

"Where's David?" I asked.

He pointed to a car, parked on the bridge nearby. "We'd like you to join us. We'll feel safer there."

"What's happened to Julian?" I didn't move an inch.

"He's safe. If you want to see him, it can be arranged, but you must come with us." Marco put his hands on my arm and stood up, attempting to pull me up with him. I felt the power in his arms, but resisted stubbornly.

"The last person to get into your car has disappeared and I don't trust you. Ask David to come here. It's a public place, so he's nothing to fear."

"You're testing my patience," Marco said, pointing his finger at me and lowering his face close to mine. "Don't push me too far." He spoke, slowly.

"I'm here to arrange Julian's release. I feel safe in a public place. David is bound to understand." I said, in more conciliatory manner. He backed off, walking slowly to the large black car on the bridge. When he returned, David accompanied him and they sat either side of me.

"Where is Julian?" I asked David.

"Are you ready to release the documents, which belong to us?" He asked, bypassing my question.

"Have you discussed the publication of the material with your paymasters?" I replied.

221

David looked straight ahead. "They'd be prepared to set up a team of Catholic academics to consider the documents, but there would be no time-scale involved and no guarantees about publication." He said, unemotionally.

"I need to speak to Julian about this. It sounds too much like the Qumran scrolls." I said, reverting to my original question.

"Then you'll have to come with us in the car." David said. "I really can do not more".

Animated tourists continued to mill around, chatting endlessly, taking photographs and feeding the strutting birds.

"What will happen if I come with you? Will you release me afterwards and where will you take me?" I asked three questions, hoping at least one of them would be answered.

"You're not in a position to demand answers," Marco intervened, loudly.

David turned to face me. "If you co-operate, you and Julian will both be released very quickly and without harm," he said.

"And if I don't co-operate?"

"You will." Marco interrupted again.

David nodded to Marco and he prodded something hard in my ribs. I turned and he opened his coat, revealing a handgun, with what appeared to be a silencer attached to it.

"Why do you need the gun?" I asked, loud enough to emphasise it to those listening on the device, if it was switched on.

"I promise no-one would hear anything other than a thud. We would prop you up, one each side, and nobody would know," Marco said, with conviction, as if he had done this before. I believed him. He lifted me up with his spare hand and this time I did not resist. David took hold of my other arm.

"Just walk between us," Marco said, "and there'll be no problems."

I looked around, hoping for signs of assistance, but none arrived.

"Where's Rachel?" David asked.

"She's at Quai des Orfevres," I replied. "But what's it got to do with you?"

"You're stupid." David said to Marco, ignoring my question.

"It's his fault." He replied, nodding towards me.

Marco catapulted me into the rear of the black car and into the arms of another heavy. David sat in the front alongside the driver and the car sped off. They underestimated me or else Marco allowed his anger towards me to cloud his judgement. I wasn't frisked or searched, in any way. My heart pumped wildly and I prayed the French police had the professionalism and sophistication to protect me.

I took a deep breath and attempted to remain calm. "Where are you taking me?" I asked again, hoping for some information to relay to the Police.

"You'll soon see," Marco replied.

"I want to know what's going to happen to me?" I persisted. "Why are we going south of the river? Where you are taking me?"

David nodded in my direction and I felt Marco's hand around my throat, unable to breathe. "Shut up and do what you're told or you'll be blindfolded and gagged." He smiled, as if unleashed, revelling in the situation. I coughed and spluttered, as he released his grip.

I wanted to give more verbal clues as to our whereabouts, but decided to wait until we were at our destination and monitored the route. We slowed. I recognised the Montparnasse area again and wondered how I could mention it, without attracting suspicion.

"There are wonderful fish restaurants in Montparnasse," I said, innocuously.

"If you help us, you'll have every opportunity to sample them," David turned and replied. The car stopped.

"The market is just south of us isn't it?" I asked.

David looked at me, but didn't reply. I was manhandled out of the vehicle and through a narrow door at the side of a boulangerie, and up a set of wooden stairs, which echoed to the footsteps.

"The bread smells wonderful," I said, continuing to scatter clues.

I felt a painful fist in the ribs. I grimaced, bending over double and gasping for breath. "When I tell you to shut up, you must listen." Marco taunted me, in his element. "Now tell me how much you don't like me?"

Two of his colleagues took hold of me and dragged me up the rest of the stairs and across a landing, into a large room. It had a large table in the centre and four chairs spread in different positions. Wallpaper peeled off the walls and the floor was bare. In the corner, on a single bed, Julian lay bound, gagged and blindfolded. Dried blood stained his face, as the apparent price for non-co-operation. He seemed unconscious.

"Julian." I said, more for the benefit of the Police, than genuine surprise. Marco dumped me into one of the chairs. The force almost toppled the chair over backwards. He took off his coat and sat facing me.

"You're very cocky, when you have three other people to back you up." I said, intending to relay further information to the police.

He sneered, hitting me hard with one punch to the side of the face and eye. I didn't even see it coming and toppled backwards over the chair and on to the floor. I lifted my hand to my face, as sharp pain shot through my head. Blood streamed down my face and onto my clothes. He picked me up by the lapels, equally roughly, and dumped me in the chair again.

"I'll ask you just once," he said. "Are you going to return the scrolls? We can do this the easy way or the hard way. I'd like it to be the hard way. So do me a favour."

I didn't doubt his intentions and knew I couldn't resist. I took a handkerchief out of my pocket and mopped up the blood. I needed the Police and became concerned at their absence.

"Very well, but I'd still like you to honour the proposal of a committee considering publication." I played for time.

Marco looked towards David, exchanging places with him. "Good," David said, looking at me intently. "Now, where are the scrolls? Your friend tells us he has no idea of their location. He didn't know what we were talking about."

"They're in London." I stated the obvious, still needing time.

"Where?" He raised his voice immediately.

"Ouch!" I shouted, as Marco kicked me in the ankle.

"Answer him," he demanded. He looked at David, his face still taut with anger. "Let me put one bullet in him, maim him first. He'll know he's got to die, but it'll take a long time. He'll beg for it in the end and you'll get all the information you want." My heart raced; missing a beat, sweat pouring out of every pore. It was like the helpless feeling, just before you wake up from a nightmare. But I couldn't wake up or escape.

"Marco, have you learnt nothing in three years." He shook his head. "You have no subtlety."

I thought for a moment, whilst I nursed my ankle, rubbing it to ease the pain. I had no idea how to delay further and realised I was out of my league. I could only rely on the professionals. A groan squeezed out of Julian's limp body and I glanced towards him.

David noticed the concern. "He'll be fine, now I want an answer."

I needed the Police to arrive and felt desperate. I had to say something. "I've placed them in a safe deposit box at Nat West Bank's Head Office at 41 Lothbury, London." I lied again. I had considered placing them there initially, as it was my Bank, so I knew their procedures, but they were no longer regarded as the specialists in safe deposit boxes. I was pleased I had made the enquiry.

"Where's your key?" David asked, firmly, but politely.

"Julian has the one key and the Bank, of course, have the other. In fairness to him, I left a small envelope with him. He wouldn't have known what it contained."

This would give me time. They would have to wait until Julian recovered consciousness. I could only hope the Police would arrive, before he awoke. Suddenly, the door seemed to explode inwards, knocking Marco and one of his colleagues backwards into the room. Something landed in the room. Thick and foul smelling smoke spurted everywhere. I coughed and spluttered almost immediately, but it clung to my lungs and eyes painfully.

"Police!" Someone shouted. I heard footsteps in the room and saw the outline of masked officers with heavy clothing, automatic weapons at the ready. Black masks covering their faces. Then I saw the dim shape of Marco, recovering from the initial shock, pointing his gun at me.

"You bastard!" Even in this hopeless situation, hatred flared. He still found the need to act to type, with an urge to take someone with him.

I dived to the side, as he shouted, but not before a shot had been fired from his gun. Simultaneously, a round of automatic gunfire echoed, and I saw the shape of Marco slump to the floor. At the same time, I felt a thud and a sharp pain in my arm, which rolled me over. It was not the impact I anticipated from gunfire, but the shock held me fixed to the floor, unable to move. Around me, I heard further gunfire. All double-tap, two shots in quick succession, the second intended to ensure the victim falls. At one point, I saw David, with a handkerchief to his mouth, moving quickly to the rear of the room. I must have lost consciousness and an awareness of floating away from the conflict was the last thing I remembered.

"... I remember with affection my learning in the East. Their way is a path of abstaining from life and observing objectively. It is their karma. The way of the West must always be to participate in life. It is our responsibility, though one day the mystical traditions of the East and the West will be as one, but I fear it will not be in my lifetime. There are times I yearn for a return to the East, with its gentle attention to life and its awareness of the constant interaction between the personality and the soul, but it cannot be. I must accept it. In the West suffering appears to be a pre-requisite of any understanding of spirituality or of love or truth. Perhaps others can explain the paradox of spiritual values, where I have failed. My destiny may have been set since the stars appeared in the astrological heavens at the time of my birth, but I will pursue an alternative path, whilst there remains hope. I have explained how the matrix is the karma of a multitude of souls interacting with each other. Karma is affected by all movement of the matrix. Any major decision or change of path (as with ritual) pulls it into a deviation. There is trauma, if the deviation cannot hold its position. This deviation and karma is mainly worked out in the physical world, where the body can cope with the trauma. It explains the inevitable flaws, which will always exist within the personality of man. However, it can be alleviated by work on the astral levels, which reduces the pain, normally associated with the working out of karmic debts. In this way, redemption and perfection must be attainable. It is the glimpse of the joy of this perfection, which lightens the load and leads us to this Light that dwells within our hearts."

CHAPTER 13

Pain jolted me into consciousness again, though my eyes were sore and I could hardly see. I found myself manhandled roughly, from one man to another, so typical of the close quarter training of our own SAS. It triggered spasms of extreme discomfort up my arm and across my shoulder.

I coughed until I wretched painfully. My whole body ached and I found myself groaning by instinct. "I've been shot!" I screamed, hoping for gentler treatment, but none came. Within seconds, I found myself being propped up against a wall at the top of the stairs. Julian was being carried over someone's shoulder and placed alongside me. His bindings and gag had been removed, but he groaned, as he sagged against the wall, lifelessly. Elation, at being alive and free, mingled with the physical discomfort in a strange and confused composition of senses and emotions.

The familiar gangly figure of Commissaire Moreau walked up the stairs. "Do you have confidence now in the French police? These are the Groupe Intervention Gendarmerie Nationale. They are as famous in France as your own S.A.S." He smiled, bending down to look at my arm. He examined the wound carefully and gently moved my arm up and then down. "I think the bullet has only grazed the bone and caused a minor flesh wound. The bullet had gone through. It's superficial," he said, dismissively. I wanted to disagree, but saved my breath. He turned around and spoke to the other officers, before turning once again to me. "How many were in the room?"

"Marco, David and two others. Of course, Julian and myself," I replied.

"One more." He shouted. The heavily armoured and black-masked officers returned inside. There was a clicking of weapons, and an exchange of instructions in urgent tones, before the sound of heavy boots running through the rooms behind us. Within a few minutes, another officer approached Commissaire Moreau.

"It's secure, but there are signs one man may have escaped through the skylight and across the roof. We've radioed to the other units. The area will be cordoned off."

The Inspector grimaced. "Merde!" he muttered. He looked at me. "Are you well enough to identify the people inside?"

"Of course." I replied, lifting myself up with assistance on still-shaking legs, protecting my one arm and shoulder.

He led me inside, offering a handkerchief to protect me from the lingering fumes. The two men, whose names I didn't know, were lying face down on the floor and handcuffed with their arms behind their backs. Each had their hair pulled back roughly to show their faces to me. I identified them as being part of the kidnap, if only in a subordinate role. I turned towards a body on the floor, lying in a pool of blood, which had seeped from its carcass, staining the floor. Marco's features were unmistakable, even in death. I looked around. "This one is Marco. I mentioned him to you, but David isn't here." I said, disappointment etched in my tone.

"There's time. Let's take you and your friend to the hospital," he said.

We returned to the area at the top of the stairs where paramedics were already attending to Julian. He had been drugged, but began to show more signs of life. One of the paramedics approached me and looked at my arm, placing a pad on the wound and pressing it hard with his hand. I recoiled, but he ignored my reaction, strapping it in place and expertly fitting a sling, before taking me down the stairs where police officers had to create a path through an inquisitive crowd, to a waiting ambulance. The Commissaire accompanied me to the hospital, but within a short time, I had been discharged. By evening, I had returned to rejoin Rachel, at Quai des Orfevres, where a lawyer, who had been instructed by Jean, had joined us. Julian would have to remain in hospital until the effect of his sedation wore off and was still not in a fit state to see anyone.

The Commissaire addressed us collectively. "As David has continued to evade us, I'd like you both to stay in Paris, for the time being." He paused, looked at the lawyer, and added. "I've cause to keep her in custody, but intend to release her, as I have promised, on one condition. We may need her assistance when we discover the true identity of the late Marco Rosseli."

"When will she be free to leave Paris?" I asked, determined I would not leave without her.

"I anticipate within the next forty-eight hours, although she may have to return at some point in the future," he replied.

"What about our passports and my documents. You still retain them, in your possession?" I asked.

"The lady's passport is invalid, Monsieur." He replied, firmly.

This time the lawyer, who had been writing notes, interrupted and looked at me. "She'll have to contact the High Commissioner for your country, in Paris. They'll arrange the necessary papers for her return," he said.

The Commissaire stood up, smiled and offered his hand to me. "We appreciate the assistance you've given us, Monsieur," he said. "You've helped us and, in return, we shall do what we can to prevent this young lady from being prosecuted, subject to no other complications arising."

"And my documents?" I persisted, shaking his hand.

"Yes, we've copied them, so there's no reason why they can't be returned to you immediately, and your passport. They'll be waiting for you downstairs. I'll arrange it."

At least this time, we could leave together. Rachel rose timidly from her chair, looking quizzically at all three of us, before walking trance like to the door.

"What about Julian?" I turned and asked the Commissaire.

"He'll not be fit for interview until tomorrow. We intend to prosecute the two men, currently in custody, so we must take a detailed statement from him, in the morning."

"Yes, I understand."

He closed the file on his desk. "You can assist us when he discharges himself. As soon as we have the statement, he can leave the country, as far as we're concerned."

At the front desk, I collected my papers and the three of us left together.

"Jean has been kept informed of developments." The lawyer directed us to a pound, where he had arranged the release of our car, still in need of repair due to the forced entry. "I can arrange for its repair, if you wish?"

"Yes, please. It would be helpful," I said.

"Shall I drop you at your Hotel. I can have the car back to you in twenty-four hours."

"Formidable," I replied, giving him the keys. He sat in the driver's seat with Rachel in the back.

"Right-hand drive," he stated the obvious, as he made himself familiar with the controls. "By the way, Jean has certain people interested in the scrolls. Would you be in a position to do your presentation in the morning, at his offices?" He looked for a response.

"It's not a problem. If it's necessary for me to stay in Paris, there's nothing I have to do, until I see Julian later tomorrow," I said. "Tell him I'd be happy to do it."

"Shall I tell him ten o'clock in the morning, then?" He drove off carefully and slowly, his lack of familiarity with the vehicle self-evident.

"That's fine." I replied.

Rachel sat staring straight ahead, stunned and silent. A vacant expression spread across her face. Even by morning, she remained subdued, speaking only one-syllable answers to the simplest of questions.

She agreed to stay in the hotel and rest, while I attended the meeting, promptly at ten o'clock.

* * * *

Inside the library, coffee, juice and biscuits had been made available. All the guests had already arrived and were involved in animated conversations, with only the slightest pause on my appearance. English Minton china, incongruously, decorated the mantel above a grey marble fireplace. Smoke, friendly and familiar, from the intrusive Gitanes drifted gently, almost innocuously, across the room. Jean, revelling in the occasion, with the broadest of smiles and cigarette in left hand, introduced me to the various people present. Thirteen guests had encouragingly felt the visit important enough, or were sufficiently interested, to attend at short notice. One, an ageing North American publisher, with sparkling eyes and a pointed grey chin beard, had even travelled across the Atlantic to make his appearance. He happily discussed his interest in the western mystical tradition and the authors he had helped on the path to fame and fortune.

After pleasantries were over, we all moved into the Hall with the black and white squared marble floor. Chairs had been placed haphazardly in front of the lectern, where my papers had been carefully placed. A glass of water had thoughtfully been placed on a table to the side. The hum of conversation subsided, as I stood up to address an audience of intellectuals who should have been educated sufficiently to appreciate the significance of the documents in my possession. I settled into a comfortable position with my hands either side of the lectern.

"Gentlemen." I looked to the side at the one lady present, "and Lady. I intend to outline the various texts and scrolls in my possession. Before doing so, I'd like to compare them with the Qumran texts, commonly known as the Dead Sea Scrolls." I began my address by reading a carefully prepared outline.

"But they've already been thoroughly researched. If the scrolls you have in your possession are no different, this is a waste of time." The interruption came from an elderly Frenchman, with snow-white hair and swarthy complexion. He leaned forward in his chair, placing both hands on a carved walking stick, with silver handle, propped up in front of him.

"Monsieur Clerc, the least you can do is allow our speaker to finish," Jean said, firmly. "He's hardly begun and there'll be ample time for questions later.

I waited for a moment. "My late uncle, Cardinal O'Rourke, gave me these scrolls, including a sexual rite, and gave his life to protect them." I pointed to my arm, which remained in its sling and still ached from a restless night. "If the documents were of little value, it's unfortunate that I, and one of my friends, have had to suffer such indignity."

"Please proceed Monsieur," a member of the audience encouraged.

I did as instructed. "It's now becoming apparent the sectarian material, rather than the so-called biblical texts, within the Dead Sea Scrolls are far more significant than we were led to believe. The Essenes were not a fringe cult, as the establishment would have you believe, but the influence and impetus behind true mystical knowledge, which Christ reflected in his teaching. Those of you who are theologians and students of religious history will already be aware of these facts and know that much of the documentation discovered in modern times sheds a different light on religious history. Nevertheless, the sectarian material discovered has huge relevance, as it is the religious essence behind the Essenes and the Nazarene movement, which was the true nature of Christianity until the time of Constantine."

My address, almost surreally, brought back memories of the years, as a priest, when I had stood piously at the pulpit, with such youthful hopes and ambition.

I stopped to ensure I had retained the audience's attention. No-one moved or spoke, so I continued. "When I first began reading copies of the scrolls in my possession, it started with a covenant for Initiates, but what I realised, by the time I'd read the second of the twenty four scrolls, was that the scribe and Initiate in question, was actually Christ."

My audience stirred and I gave them a moment to settle. "Now this time, if the Establishment attempt to undermine this particular sectarian material, as they did by reference to the Essenes, they're effectively marginalising Christ himself. This is the difference." I cleared my throat and bent over to take a sip of the water from the adjoining table, before continuing. "In a moment, I'll outline the nature of the teachings, disciplines and wisdom course within these scrolls, but I promise you their content will disable the power of orthodox Christianity, as we know it. If the Church try to infer the Nazarenes, and remember Christ was a prominent member, were merely a cult, all it will do is paint Christ as an occultist, in the true meaning of the word."

"Didn't they emphasize the importance of the feminine?" A question materialised from the back.

I hesitated and smiled. "Isn't it strange how, despite our intellectual understanding of sexist behaviour, the worshipping of a male God is called a religion, but that of any feminine aspect is immediately classified as a cult."

A ripple of laughter moved across the room, though Monsieur Clerc felt an urge to interrupt again. "How do you know the Initiate you refer to was Christ?"

"Because the second scroll authenticates it." I replied simply. "He's the compiler and commentator on the wisdom course, within part of the scrolls. He relates seven degrees of initiation, strangely similar to the seven chakra points of eastern mysticism. Interestingly, it also confirms he travelled east to synthesise their wisdom with the wisdom of the West to establish the common root of all religion. I suspect it's where he was taught the significance of the eastern mystical tradition's tantra and the reason he believed the highest spiritual sacrament was sexual in nature, using the enduring and universal energy of love, which permeates the whole fabric of our Universe."

I paused for its impact to hit home.

"Are these the infamous Q documents, which portray Mary Magdalene as the great visionary?" someone asked inevitably.

"Perhaps. They do contain the sayings of Jesus, as the Q documents allegedly do, but I have no way of knowing for certain. There are aspects of cabbalistic teaching and even some Grail lore, just as with the Q documents. My Uncle died before I had the time to question him about these matters in any detail. If I were to guess, I'd say they were."

A droning of exchanged whispers followed and several seconds elapsed before I could continue. "Intellectually, I cannot understand how people can possibly believe that one religion is better or superior to another and, deviate into extremism or fundamentalism. If religion is the cause, then let's go straight to the heart of what is truly spiritual. These scrolls reveal a path for the recovery of the spiritual faculty. We should build rainbow bridges between all the religions, by the use of reason and the intellect."

One man stood up, but before he could speak, I gestured for him to sit down. "I promise, there'll be ample time to take all your questions at the end, if you don't mind. It'll be easier for me."

He grunted and sat down. "After Christ's death, Mary Magdalene, the Apostle of Apostles, took over the task of writing the scrolls. She emphasised the myth of Christ, as with the myth of all other resurrected Gods, Osiris, Dionysus, etc, symbolised the spiritual rebirth, which is possible within our own psyche, in this world, not the next. This is part of the inner mysteries, which the Initiates Christ and Mary taught. It's the message it still teaches today, the essence of which is that the individual has to die to his lower self, to resurrect as the Christ within. When the former Bishop of Durham, in England, dared to explain this symbolism in simple terms, the English tabloid media had a field day."

Again they stirred, a few whispers escalating to general chatter. When it subsided, I persevered. "Some of the literature is of a graded nature, as within the ancient mystery schools, and others relate to the structured nature of reincarnation and the mystery of how time itself is transformed into space. Indeed, there's much ritual material of what today we'd call esoteric or magical work. There are details of an oracle, performed as a ritual for channelling prophecies and some of the predictions are contained in the scrolls. One accurately describes the destruction of Solomon's Temple and the murder and enslavement of the Jews by the Roman legions of Titus in AD 70 and the subsequent secretion of these scrolls."

"What other prophecies are there?" The North American publisher asked.

I indulged him. "I'll give you one example, but I should emphasise that some of the entries come across almost as diaries and they bring through his humanity, his doubts and anxieties. One prophecy suggests it'll take two thousand years of bloodshed in the name of religion before efforts will be made to synthesise the religions of the East and the West again. It will be a new renaissance and it predicts the crumbling of the Western Church establishment, at about the same time. It also warns of the emergence of a destructive force, perhaps what we would call an Anti-Christ, which will vent violence and hatred on the world, before the people unite against the evil perpetuated. He will commit murder and violence on a global scale. He and his followers will have no feeling for humanity, for they will become soulless entities, as they separate themselves from those to whom they inflict meaningless suffering and pain. They will scoff and laugh, even rejoice, at others suffering." I waited for a response, which I felt such provocative statements would be bound to invoke.

"It sounds familiar and undoubtedly we could all guess at the identity of such a figure and such an organisation, but are you really saying this is contained in documents two thousand years old." A member of the audience asked.

"That is precisely what I am saying, " I replied, simply.

"Why haven't these rituals persisted in some form of oral tradition?" The person who had stood up earlier asked.

"I'm sure they have." I smiled. I had anticipated resistance. "Perhaps there isn't the discipline today, with all the distractions of modern-day life. Isn't the freemasonry image of the Apprentice, wounded in the right temple, reflecting the right lobe of the brain, intended to reflect the loss of the spiritual and intuitive faculty to materialism? This was the ritual used by the Oracles of Delphi to make their prophecies. There's an outline of the purifying process, which can be used by anyone who wishes to replicate the procedure. It was done in similar ritual form by the famous Abramelin the Mage, all of which is documented in the public domain." I said.

"But a publisher will be subject to ridicule, if these scrolls are demeaned in this way. It's placing

Christ on the same level as Nostradamus?" The North American suggested.

I nodded. "Possibly, but if this was the same ritual used by seers such as Malachy and Nostradamus and it is beneficial to publish it, then isn't it for others to judge?" There was only muted response, so I continued. "Contrary to how most people envisage time, it's explained in a non-linear module." I laughed. "Who knows, this may be the secret of time travel and perhaps these seers actually did travel into the future?"

I stopped to allow my audience the opportunity to consider the lateral ideas I was presenting and took another sip of water from the table to the side of me.

"What you described earlier as written by Mary is classic Gnostic teachings and well-known. If the scrolls contain material similar to the Gnostic gospels of Mary, Philip and Thomas, there is nothing new in them." The one female in the room spoke, a bespectacled English lady, slim build with blonde hair cropped short. She appeared classy and sophisticated in both the clothes she wore and the way in which she projected her voice. I guessed a regular visitor to the fashion houses of Paris, but hoped there was also substance behind the veneer.

I shook my head. "The scrolls contain wisdom and knowledge, much of which is both Gnostic and pagan in its content. In the past, the Roman Church has ruthlessly and relentlessly destroyed thousands of years of such priceless knowledge. Entire libraries have been burned and ancient Temples desecrated. I have in my possession some of that ageless wisdom. It's sad you dismiss it, so lightly. Do you want the superstition, vilification and strife, which brought the last Dark Ages?"

"I'm not dismissing it, but merely questioning it," she said, indignantly, removing her spectacles and pointing them at me.

"Good," I replied, impatiently. "The content of the scrolls show the old pagan mysteries were nearer the truth, whether they were the mysteries of Mithras or Dionysus. I believe the popularity of the Mysteries in the ancient world will be imitated in the new Millennium as we move to another cycle, albeit at a higher vibration."

"Some of what you say appears to me to be contradictory," she persisted.

"If it is, then it's my presentation of it which is flawed, not the scrolls. Early Christianity was full of inconsistencies, exaggerations and lies. I think all the books of the New Testament were at some stage branded as either forged or heretical, so I'm in good company."

"What's the most fundamental significance of the scrolls?" Jean asked, unable to resist the interruption, in the short pause, which followed.

The question required serious thought, as it needed a brief analysis of theological history. "The most fundamental, will be the fact of Christ as an occultist and prophet, rather than as the Son of God. Perhaps the most significant from the point of view of the Catholic Church, and undoubtedly the media, will be the return of the sacred marriage by the placing of the sexual rite as the highest sacrament, symbolising the mystical union of opposites. Related to this, within these scrolls is the explanation of Original Sin, which has nothing whatsoever to do with the sexual behaviour of Adam and Eve. The Church and the Establishment media will misrepresent and undermine it. They'll not understand its spiritual significance or, if they do, they'll have a vested interest in maintaining the

241

status quo, with truth the victim. If you add to that, the fact of Christ's Egyptian origins, you have a provocative mixture, especially as the scrolls emphasise the importance of the female bloodline. In this, it follows the old Egyptian traditions."

"You'll have to prove all this," someone else said coldly.

"Of course," I replied firmly and with a tone of disdain, before returning to my text. "The black virgins are referred to as representing the cult of Isis. Perhaps Christ's mission for the salvation of the personality, rather than the soul, will be equally significant. The harmonious position of the microcosm of the individual within the macrocosm of the Universe, so that the outer world manifests the inner world precisely, may be an intellectual step theological scholars will accept, as scientists and astrophysicists can mainly prove it. Yet, significantly, this is expounded in scrolls, written two thousand years ago."

"Nonsense," a voice shouted, though I could not identify the source.

"Is it?" I replied, reasonably, leaning heavily on the lectern. "Physicists, since the time of Planck over one hundred years ago, have been overturning the old Newtonian physics. They're already proving exactly this fact and that the belief of the person involved will influence the outcome of the experiment, mainly using experiments with sub-atomic particles as the evidence of an outer world corresponding precisely with the inner world, even changing, as the thoughts of the observer changes. In fact, as Niels Bohr would say, particles only become real when they are observed. This is scientific evidence that all of us are strictly the consequences of our thoughts. This was one of the conclusions of the physicist Hugh Everett in his experiments as long ago as the seventies. Of course, if something is real only because we observe it or we believe it, then it also means the laws of physics are only real, if people believe they are!"

A calmer, more sincere voice intruded. "If our expectation of what happens becomes our reality, then this would happen, even on death?"

I looked up from my papers, content to joke with a kindred spirit. "Be careful with your view of the Pearly Gates. It may be an epic and could become your reality, but change your dream and you change your reality."

This may have been deep philosophy, but it was difficult to respond simply and I had to believe that my audience were professional enough to appreciate the enormous significance of these scrolls. In the main, they remained attentive, so I cleared my throat and continued. "The traditional Hebrew God-name Yod-Hay-Vav-Hay initially represented Father, Mother, Son and Daughter, but the feminine has been lost and needs to be restored, in all her glory. The first time there is any mention of the Holy Ghost, as part of a Holy Trinity, rather than as a feminine figure, is in AD 325, at the Council of Nicaea. It's often forgotten that Constantine, who summoned this Council, was the Chief Priest of the pagan Sun God, the Sol Invictus cult, yet he arranged for his employee Eusebius to write an edited and corrupted version of Christianity. In the same way, the feminine full moon feast of Shabattu has been converted by the Jews to a weekly Sabbath, losing much of its sacred nature and significance, in the process."

A telephone sounded in the office adjoining, piercing the silence within the room and interrupting my concentration. Jean left the room to answer it.

"Please continue," he said, closing the doors behind him.

I returned to my notes. "The scrolls outline the history of their wisdom heritage, establishing Egypt as the centre of their tradition. Some of the rituals may be regarded as pagan in their origins."

"What effect is this going to have on traditional Christianity?" Monsieur Clerk asked.

"I suspect they'll fight to preserve the status quo. We all know they'll continue to discredit Mary Magdalene, in the same way as they've attempted to suppress the marital status of Christ over the centuries. There are signs of hope, if you consider the recent pronouncements, particularly in relation to women, but the wheels of the Vatican move slowly. I take a different view of the third secret of Fatima, than the late Pope John Paul II. If it symbolises the end of the Roman Church, rather than the mere death of a Pontiff, then only radical steps will preserve its structure. If they struggle to merely retain the status quo, then I believe revolution within the Church will follow."

The doors opened again and Jean came back into the room. He pointed to a piece of paper in his hand, placing it in his pocket and sitting down on the chair he had previously occupied.

I persevered. "In the past, the Catholic Church has slaughtered anyone, or everyone, who has dared to have an independent thought of their own." I hesitated. "Perhaps that's excessive and unfair, but I was referring to the past, rather than the present….I hope. If something violent happens to me or anyone connected to me, then at least everyone in this room will know that times haven't changed. I don't want this to be another one of those self-fulfilling prophecies." I smiled, before returning to the substance of my address. "As these scrolls emphasise, the Church isn't needed as an intermediary between the individual and God, as the

Kingdom of Heaven truly is within the individual."

"Classic Gnostic teaching," I heard someone say, but again without noticing which person.

"It may be, but you can be prepared for opposition and indignation from the Church, nevertheless. Have no doubt, they'll challenge the authenticity of these scrolls, but the time has come to root out the fanaticism and intolerance of so-called orthodoxy whether it's in the guise of Christianity or Islam."

I stopped for a moment and Jean approached the lectern, taking the note from his pocket and placing it in front of me. I read the note, offering apologies for the pause in the presentation. It contained a note to ring Rachel, with a telephone number endorsed on it.

I turned to Jean. "Is this urgent?"

He shook his head. "She told me to allow you to finish your presentation."

"Very well." I hesitated. "But I hate intrigue," I added.

I turned back to the audience, reluctantly proceeding with the task in hand. I shuffled my papers, looking for the point where I had stopped. "Now where was I?" I asked.

"You were talking about the likely opposition from the Church," a friendly voice replied.

"Yes, I remember," I said, locating the point in my notes. "In the same way, as with the third secret of Fatima, a different interpretation will be placed on the prophecies contained within the scrolls, relating to this Millennium, though their reference to the end of the established Church are, to my mind, unequivocal. There is emphasis on the importance of a unity with the cosmic, rather than a subservience to it."

"Where did these scrolls originate?" Someone shouted at the back.

"I believe the first Knights Templar Grand Master recovered them from beneath the Temple in Jerusalem at the end of the First Crusade, though his brief was to search for the Ark of the Covenant. The Catholic Church probably took them from the Knights Templar at the time of their purge. Cardinal O'Rourke laboriously copied, by handwriting, the entirety of the Journal kept by the Knights Templar Grand Masters. He assured me the original remains in the Vatican vaults."

"What's in the Journal?" The female asked.

"It begins with entries by the first Grand Master of the Knights Templar, Hugues de Payen. It was written prior to the formation of the Templars from within the vault, beneath the Temple in Jerusalem. He explains the scrolls he discovered there and also their significance. It refers to other matters too."

"Do you have copies?" She asked.

"Yes. It's in my uncle's handwriting. I'll read the first two pages, if you wish?"

"Please do," she insisted, "I think we'd all like to hear it," she smiled and gestured towards her colleagues with one hand.

I brought out some loose pages from the briefcase at my side and placed them carefully on the lectern in front of me.

"You must carefully, for a moment, imagine the hardship Hugues de Payne suffered to retrieve these scrolls for us and the enormous personal danger for him from a jealous and ruthless Church."

I paused to allow them time to consider the scene beneath the Temple in Jerusalem at the beginning of the twelfth century. I read slowly from the pages.

"I am writing this Journal in a dank room, deep beneath the Temple. If we had not discovered the secret passage, it would have been impossible to locate this treasure. I have marks on my hand where my one and only candle drips wax over my hand, as I write. I have laboured hard in the tunnels beneath the crypt. My health is deteriorating in the life underground and my sight too will suffer, if we cannot finish our work soon. We must close down the hidden chambers, discovered in the depths. We have located the Ark of the Covenant and I have seen the greater treasure, which was so cleverly concealed when Titus overrun the Temple in AD 70. I must keep records of our discoveries. The only other light is from the reedlamps on the wall, so I write with my face against the candle. I must conceal the truth of our purpose, for the safety of all, at least, until we are strong. We must maintain an oasis of illumination, within the darkness, if we are to prevent the physical destruction of our world, which would follow if the gulf between our spiritual and material existence grows."

"It sounds dramatic," the North American said, interrupting my concentration.

I looked up from the pages, grunted and carried on. "The world is full of suffering and perversions. Life is bereft of meaning. For some, there is an awareness of disaster. There is such a need for spiritual enlightenment to illuminate the lives of weary souls, struggling for survival in this drab and violent Society."

I glanced towards my audience. "When I first read this document, I thought they were describing life today."

One or two in the gathering nodded in agreement.

"Yet the date on the document is 1100." I pointed to the top of the page.

"Why was it written? The female asked.

I turned towards her. "The elation of the success of the First Crusade had been tempered by the hard work of excavation to recover their treasure. They wanted to keep a record, but they knew they had to be cautious, as they always feared capture and exposure. Hugues de Payen wrote the first entries. He described himself as Knight, Nobleman and Mystic. Many believe the treasure, or at least some of it, remained in France and point to the sudden wealth of the French Priest Sauniere at Rennes-Le-Chateau in the Languedoc. The place has many clues to the mystery and, though a priest, Sauniere dabbled in the fashionable occult circles of Paris, at the time."

She nodded and smiled. I read on. "Our excavations at the Temple in Jerusalem have taken months, but no-one yet suspects our purpose. We have found the scrolls written by Christ and his Nazarene sect. They undermine the Church's interpretation of the mission of Christ and show it is part of a heresy, the Roman Church knowingly perpetuates. We have taken possession of a relic, which will prove it, but I dare not reveal it, even in this document."

I stopped at an incomprehensible word and struggled with my handwritten translation. "You must forgive my translation from the original French, which may leave room for minor error. It's some years since I took my degree in modern languages."

I smiled, but persevered. "The values of the Church are disintegrating with decadence and immorality? They know the truth, but use atrocity to bury it. We need a structure to protect the true teachings and essence of the old religion, as Christ would have wanted. We must hide our purpose, with the cloak of secrecy, or all will be lost. Our vow must be to shed light on the darkness, which pervades the modern world. It is a time of destiny, but also a time for subterfuge, as this message of divine wisdom will resound through the centuries. There is another path, other than the outer way of churches and dogma. Eventually, the inner way will teach us, we are all brothers and sisters. Only then can the dark forces of evil in the world be eliminated."

I stopped and lifted my head, as someone asked another question. My concentration wavered, as I puzzled at what could be so important for Rachel to ring me here. "I'm sorry, could you repeat the question?" I asked.

"If this was written at the end of the First Crusade, was this the reason for it, or was it a coincidence?"

I shook my head. "I can't be certain. Perhaps this is an area for further research.," I replied. "But there is an inner wisdom and mystery within the Christian myth, which was buried by the Roman Church to protect their external power in the scheme of things. When it is re-discovered it will reveal the one fundamental truth, which links all religions and all myths. It is a knowledge we all share because at one level we are one, so we know everything. Those searching for the scrolls at the beginning of the twelfth century knew this. Almost one thousand years later and we're still struggling with the concept of a universal brotherhood of humanity."

"I was always told there's no such thing as coincidence," the person smiled.

"I agree. Jung and the physicist Dr. Wolfgang Pauli developed the principle of synchronicity to reveal how the whole of life has a pattern and intent to it. It's a comforting thought that nothing is haphazard." I hesitated. "Now, may I finish the extract from the Journal?"

There was no response, so I continued. "I shall summon Rashi, the foremost authority on esoteric wisdom, and Bernard de Cluny to a conclave here." My eyes narrowed and I sighed rudely at another interruption.

"Who were Bernard de Cluny and Rashi?"

I took a deep breath. "Well, I think de Cluny was the same as de Clairvaux, the Cistercian, who prepared the Templars constitution. Significantly, it was Clairvaux in one of his sermons referred to Mary Magdalene as the Bride of Christ. As for Rashi, coincidentally, he lived close to the estate of Hugues de Payen in France, but happened to be the most knowledgeable expert on the Cabbala at that time." I smiled mischievously. "There's another coincidence or synchronicity for those of you who are interested in these things."

Some members of the audience smiled with me. When it quietened, I read on. "If Nivard de Sion and some of my fellow knights join us, we shall have the mystical thirteen. If Christ wanted to resurrect the Mother Goddess and believed it would transform him, then we have a duty to follow his path." I stopped at the end of the document, but this time no-one spoke.

"This is the first entry in the Journal and the last one is written by Jacques de Molay immediately prior to his torture and crucifixion on the door of the Paris Temple."

"Crucifixion?" Someone queried.

"Yes, but that's common knowledge and historical fact. There are far more interesting things in the Journal," I said dismissively.

As I remained intrigued by the message from Rachel, I felt this was an ideal opportunity to break. I leaned over towards Jean. "What did Rachel want?" I asked in a whisper.

"She didn't say, but said it was important she speak to you."

"I'm going to stop, but tell your guests I'll take questions later."

Jean nodded.

I apologised to those assembled for the need to take an important call, but felt sure I had given sufficient information to whet their appetite. They would, undoubtedly, want to discuss it between themselves. I almost tripped over my briefcase, as I scrambled away from the lectern, towards the double doors.

I telephoned the number on the note. It was a number I didn't recognize. "What's the problem?" I asked Rachel.

There was a brief pause. "I've had a telephone call from Commissaire Moreau. As a result of what's happened, I think it's better for me to step out of your life. I didn't want you to think I'd been kidnapped too, or anything like that." She spoke in strained tones.

"I don't understand what you're talking about." I said, anxiously. "Is there anyone there with you?" I asked.

"No," she replied immediately.

"Then please wait for me. I'll come back to the hotel and speak to you about this, as soon as this meeting is over."

There was another silence, before she replied. "I'm sorry. I'll not be in the hotel, when you return. Believe me, everything is not what it seems."

I sensed the presence of someone else with her. "I'm sure someone is there with you. Don't do this?" I begged, my voice surging gradually higher.

There was a familiar pause, followed by the dial tone of the telephone. I was left stunned, unable to think or even replace the receiver.

"... My journey to the East and my learning in the Mystery schools of Egypt, and by the Essenes, reveal the source of all religions is obviously the same. In our search for the truth, which sets you free, we are taught to know thyself. The inner journey is patently so much more important than the external one, as the outer world will always reflect the individual's inner world. It is the source of true healing. As the microcosm reflects the macrocosm, the truth appears clear, but already the orthodox authorities deny the obvious, in favour of the divisive. I foresee fragmentation of this unequivocal teaching, if the Nazarene and Essenes texts are lost or even if they fall into the wrong hands, where they could be corrupted and misinterpreted. If this happens, nation will fight nation and sect will battle sect, all in the name of religion. If I fail in my mission, I foresee two thousand years of bloodshed in the name of religion, before the religions of the East and West may again be synthesized and people again discover the peace that passeth all understanding. It may even need the destruction of the formal Church for people to search within themselves. I pray the work of the Mystery schools preserves the true sacred essence of life, for the sake of humanity. There must remain rainbow bridges between people of all religious persuasions, just as the half a million items of literary work of many traditions are stored together, under the one roof, in the great library of Alexandria. The alternative is unthinkable. By the Age of Aquarius, we shall not require a mirror to reflect the image of God. The middle pillar of the meditation glyph of the Tree of Life will be the spiritual arrow needed to reach such a high ideal."

CHAPTER 14

My heart cried out, but my voice squandered the opportunity for expression. No longer standing by the lectern, but sitting on a chair in front of my audience, at Jean's suggestion, I felt numb and confused.

I looked around the room, with its mahogany shelving, regalia and antiques. There were paintings on the walls, significantly by the mystical artists, Poussin, Cocteau and Teniers, with all their inherent symbolism encrypted within them. There was evidence of Da Vinci, with prints of the Madonna on the Rocks and the Last Supper, with what many believe to be the flowing tresses of Mary Magdalene sitting on the immediate right hand of Christ. It had been Poussin, of course, who had painted the famous picture of the shepherd near Rennes-Le-Chateau, Et Arcadia Ego, with its esoteric message linking Arcadia with the region. I wondered how many illustrious people had sat in my position before. Drained and vulnerable, I reminded myself only those on the true path are tested in this way, so it was a positive experience, not a negative one. Unfortunately, I always found myself the most difficult convert to mystical truths. I had little inclination to answer questions, but found myself nodding and agreeing to do so, though my mind hovered elsewhere.

I yearned for a simpler life, with someone of reliability in it, but I felt like a grown-up orphan. My need to escape the pain and complication, which constantly sabotaged this quest, remained unrequited. I had believed entering the Church, would provide the haven, I sought. Then it was the turn of marriage to be the shelter, but neither proved the solution. As someone trained for the priesthood,

author, Christ himself, his Nazarenes and later Mary."

A murmuring developed into a drone and, for a moment, it became impossible to speak.

As the noise subsided, Monsieur Clerc rose to his feet. "Can you authenticate your last comment? Are you able to prove the scrolls were written by Christ and the Nazarene sect?"

"I wouldn't expect them to be published, without first proving their source and authenticity." I replied, instantly. Monsieur Clerc sat down again. "It's fair to say the writings are Gnostic in their content, but this time they'll have great difficulty in treating them as heresy." I added.

"I'll publish the documents." The familiar American voice spoke from the back, "subject to my Board agreeing and to authentication."

"Do you want to bring down the Catholic Church?" Another man interrupted. It was the first time he had spoken.

"I don't want to bring anything or anyone down, but to record truth. Isn't the test for all religious organisations that they should be flexible and able to keep their "heretics" within their fold and adapt? The Koran already refers to Christ as a great prophet. Does he have to be the Son of God for his teachings to be followed?"

"What is your religion?" The same person asked.

"I was brought up a Christian and regard myself as a follower of Christ's true teachings, but obviously the Church would not regard me as orthodox. To them, I would be an unashamed heretic."

"Are you a Rosicrucian?" The female asked innocuously, though I had already appreciated that no question from her was as simple as it may have appeared.

"Why do you ask?" I replied.

"Because they were set up in 1866 as a branch of the Scottish Rite Masons and I suspect you are being controlled by the Establishment."

I gave no time for thought and reacted instinctively. "I'm not a Rosicrucian, nor have I ever been involved in the Scottish Rite, though I have researched it. As for being controlled, I can only say that if so, I'm totally unaware of it." I showed my contempt by refusing to answer any further questions from her on the basis she had a closed mind.

It seemed as good a place as any to stop. They had sufficient information to make decisions and I had become fazed by events, suffering a dull headache, which would have made me too impatient to handle fools.

I had asked Jean to liaise with the lawyer and to speak to the Commissaire. My brain barely functioned and the animated, smiling faces, milling around afterwards, became a blur. Questions still shot at me relentlessly, like bullets, one after the other, some friendly, some not.

Jean returned to the room and rescued me, taking me into his private office. "Our lawyer has telephoned again." He pointed to the chair, his face unsmiling. "Please sit down."

"What's the matter?" I asked, impatiently, as I almost collapsed into the chair.

"The Commissaire has discovered the true identity of Marco Rosseli. His name is false, as is the surname of your friend Rachel."

"I don't understand." I gestured, with my hands in the air.

Jean inhaled deeply from his Gitanes. "They believe Rachel was actually married to Marco, so it was her husband who died yesterday. His Christian name is Mark and their true surname is Rosser."

I realised my head was shaking constantly, but I couldn't stop. Jean sat down opposite. "They want to detain her again, for further questioning, but she's disappeared. They have reason to believe the person observed picking her up at the hotel was David."

I brought my hands up to my face and closed my eyes. I wanted to scream, but convention held me back.

"The Commissaire will be here shortly, to speak to you," he added.

I looked up from a face red and twisted with suffering. I felt destined to endure more disappointment. Perhaps some karmic debt had ensnared me. No doubt a psychoanalyst would tell me I had created a pattern of behaviour, which became self-perpetuating or else he would regress me to childhood and blame parenting for the problem. If only life were that simple.

"So they've not arrested David?" My voice trembled, barely audible, over the chatter and clatter from the group in the adjoining room.

"No, I don't think so," he replied, quietly.

"I've been naïve." I said, quietly, looking directly at Jean for support. My head dropped.

"There are worse things," he shrugged, reaching over with his hand and squeezing my arm.

"I think you should be aware that my Order has its own intelligence apparatus. We know many organisations, including the Vatican, which are infiltrated with agents of governments. The private secret societies and corporations are even more in control. This nether world of the intelligence community has threads of influence through world trade marts, charitable and commerce centres. Their computerised databank functions through one of the largest privately owned satellite systems in existence. Its trading system is more sophisticated and technologically advanced, than the capabilities at the disposal of any government. Relief, cultural and trade links are merely fronts for espionage, sabotage and assassinations. So we have to tread very carefully. I think you should now face the enormity of your task."

"I know," I replied. A feeling of hopelessness overwhelmed me.

"Our people also suspect, as in the past, there are many organisations, which have been used to front agents, including many church research groups, Christian fundamentalists, the World Council of Churches and the National Council. Universal freemasonry, at the higher levels is tainted. As is the Biblical Archaeology bodies, some Templar organisations and other Christian groups. There are many innocuous sounding think tanks and institutions, which are used by the intelligence community to influence and control political events." He paused only briefly, but I had nothing to contribute, mental exhaustion taking its inevitable toll.

"The Russian Orthodox Church and the old orthodox Catholic Church of North America have been used by Agents, whilst New Orleans District Attorney, James Garrison, incriminated their affiliated organisation, the American Council of Christian Churches. He said they were involved in the Kennedy Assassination conspiracy. After all, it was set up by a friend and contract agent of the then Head of the F.B.I., J. Edgar Hoover. Agents could operate safely under the cover of Christian missionaries or even priests. David Ferrie was a counter-intelligence Division Five operative, ordained as a priest in this way, until he was mysteriously murdered within days of being subpoenaed by Garrison. These are but a few examples. It doesn't mean there are no people of integrity within the organisations, but they'll have no knowledge of their infiltration. Similarly, a number of Universities are breeding grounds for the future brains of this controlling intelligence elite. In your country, you would be aware of Cambridge and Oxford, but Aberystwyth in Wales is another." His candour may have stemmed from honourable intentions, but I still felt completely deflated.

Within a few minutes, Jean's secretary announced the arrival of the Commissaire and Jean moved over to allow him to take his seat. The Commissaire's familiar gangly features had become reassuring and he took off his cap, placing it on the desk.. He showed me copy printouts. "The fingerprints and other tests conducted by forensic experts reveal, without a shadow of a doubt, the man killed yesterday was Mark Rosser and not Marco Rosseli. Rosser is wanted by the British Police, in connection with enquiries into a gangland killing, three years ago in London. He had a long list of convictions, mainly for violence and for possession and supply of unlawful drugs." He tapped the printout. "You can see for yourself. Strangely, there have been no convictions in the last three years. We believe he married your friend Rachel less than three years ago, so she may not have known about it8."

I perused the documents he placed in front of me. "I could believe it of him, but what about Rachel?"

He shook his head. "There's no record of any convictions against her and she seems to be clean. She may have been able to assist us in respect of Mark Rosser, but as you may know she's vanished. We think she's still in Paris, with the person you refer to as David. Observations are being made on premises about a kilometre from the Bois de Boulogne. We would like you to come with us, to identify him, as we have no photographic records for him. The house is registered to an Italian company, but little is known about the occupants, though we currently have the premises under observation."

"Commissaire, have you been able to identify the person called Dominique Flaviel from the Bibliotheque Nationale?" Jean asked, stubbing out another cigarette in an ashtray, already full, on his desk.

"There is someone of that name, but his work is with a National Intelligence Agency and so I cannot give you any further information," he shrugged, without any change of expression. "I can tell you we have nothing to connect him with the men you refer to as Marco and David."

"I should have guessed he was intelligence." I sighed, with a sense of resignation.

Jean pointed to the adjoining room, where chatter and laughter still echoed and looked at me. "I have matters to organise with my guests, or else I would happily accompany you," he said.

"It's alright, I want to get to the bottom of this," I said. The physical and emotional traumas of the previous twenty-four hours had emptied me of all, but a doggedness of character, the trademark of a journalistic career. "How's my lawyer friend?" I asked the Commissaire.

"He's been most helpful this morning, but we may need to interview him beyond this afternoon. Can you delay your return until tomorrow? It will be easier for him. I've explained your role in his release and he wants to thank you personally."

"How does Julian feel about the delay?" I asked.

"He wants to ensure we have enough information to complete our enquiries, but he's anxious to return to London."

"So am I." I said, walking to the door.

"If we can detain the man David, it will facilitate your return," he insisted.

"If you don't detain him, remember I can identify him," Jean reminded the Commissaire, as he ushered us out of his office. "So it need not hold John in Paris."

I appreciated his assistance, acknowledging it with a smile and a nod. There were few people I trusted, but he was one of them. "I'll stay in Paris until tomorrow," I reluctantly agreed.

Being chauffeur-driven in French police vehicles had become a habit I wanted to break. The street-life of Paris, with its unique architecture and ambience passed me by unnoticed, as the emotional baggage I carried, obscured its magic. I could have been anywhere in the world. When we arrived at our destination I was led into an old, scruffy tenement block, out of character with many of the more substantial surrounding buildings, which were set back from the road, with mature gardens providing more privacy. Inside one of the attic rooms, an array of equipment reflected the seriousness, with which the Police were treating the matter. Headphones were placed around my head and I listened to voices talking, as if they were in the same room. The smell of strong French coffee pervaded my senses, but I focused on my task.

"Do you recognise the voices?" The Commissaire asked, impatiently.

I tried to analyse and assess the accents. "Well, the one could be David, but there are no female voices," I said, turning to face him.

Almost in unison two police officers, looking out of the window with large and powerful binoculars shouted to him. "Quickly, look at this." The one officer stood up, allowing the Commissaire to take a seat and look through the binoculars, which had been fixed on a tripod.

"Merde!" He cursed.

"What's the matter?" I asked, bemused by the developments.

Before anyone could reply, I heard a doorbell ring on my headphones. The Commissaire picked up a telephone and shouted.

"Stop, Stop, we cannot proceed. A cardinal and his retinue are just entering the building." He replaced the telephone and spoke to his men. "I can call at the premises and ask to speak to the person we believe is David, but if he declines, all we can do is carry out the observations, until another opportunity arises."

"I don't understand," I said. "How does this change anything?"

He looked down at me. "It just delays matters, that's all, but there's no way would we storm a building with armed men, if there's a Cardinal inside." He paused. "Just for a moment, think about the public relations consequences for us. Bear in mind, this Cardinal is widely thought to be influential within the Vatican hierarchy. Do you understand?" He tilted his head, at the same time as preening his moustache with the index finger and thumb of his right hand.

I remained fazed, unable to respond. He paced the room and everyone waited for his command. He turned to me. "I would like you to come with me, if you don't mind. First, we can ask to speak to the Cardinal inside. This may give you the opportunity to identify the occupants."

"Anything which will help, I'll do. Let's go." I replied, impatiently, already walking towards the door. Two of the officers laughed at my impertinence, though the Commissaire merely smiled.

"Very well, tell the others to remain in position, until we return." He gave his last instructions and turned to follow me. We passed a parked black limousine and entered through the clanking gate of a large sandstone residence, with gardens already in bloom. The old house had shutters down, on all the windows, and facing us were two wooden doors with a garish intercom device to the side. He pressed it and when a reply came he spoke. "My name is Commissaire Moreau, I am making enquiries into a serious incident, which happened yesterday and I believe you may be able to help with our enquiries. Would you be kind enough to give us access?" For a moment, there was utter quiet, I could only imagine the scene of panic, which must have been unfolding inside. When a response came, it was restrained and measured.

"Yes, someone will come down shortly. If you bear with us, as Cardinal Montagne is here and he'll want to speak to you. You can be taken straight in to see him."

"But this is not the Cardinal's normal residence in Paris," the Commissaire replied.

"No, but he'll be down directly."

We waited for perhaps five minutes. The Commissaire began muttering under his breath, walking back a metre or so and looking around, towards the road. Suddenly, the door opened and a man, in an elegantly cut dark suit, invited us inside. The door opened onto a large hall, with an open staircase, which faced the door and a stained-glass window at the top of the stairs. A gallery stretched out in both directions from the stairs.

"The Cardinal will see you in his study. Will you follow me?" We were taken to the side of the house, to the left of the stairs. No other persons were visible. As a door opened to the study, the Cardinal met us. He stood in front of his desk, offering us his hand. The Commissaire accepted it and introduced me.

The Cardinal raised his eyebrows in obvious recognition. "Are you the nephew of the late Cardinal O'Rourke?" he asked. He was a slim man, with white hair and narrow eyes, which didn't hold my stare. He must have been about sixty-five years of age. He was tanned, but lines around his eyes and neck and brown sunspots betrayed his age.

"Yes, how well did you know him?" I asked, feeling confident with the Commissaire at my side and a large contingent of trained police outside.

"Not all that well, but when I met him, I liked what I saw," he said, sympathetically. "I've also heard something of you. Aren't you a journalist?"

"Do you know how my uncle died?" I asked bluntly, without taking my eyes from his. I knew the question may have been provocative and noticed agitation, as he turned away to speak to the Commissaire.

"Is this the reason you're here? Is it to do with the death of Cardinal O'Rourke?" He asked.

"No, I'm here as a result of a criminal investigation into an incident in Paris yesterday, when one person died. We've traced another person, who calls himself David, to this house. I'd like to know if you've ever heard of anyone called Marco Rosseli, otherwise known as Mark Rosser?"

The Cardinal didn't blink, but pointed to two regency-style chairs in front of his desk. "Would you like to sit down?" He turned and sat at a leather-inlaid desk, whilst we both sat in the chairs proffered. The study was decorated in an old-fashioned way, with walls of faded magnolia. It smelt of mothballs and stale pipe-smoke. The furniture was old and worn, although expensive paintings littered the walls. A gold old-fashioned inkwell and fountain pen was positioned in the middle of the desk. Two trays, at the side, contained a number of letters and envelopes.

He fiddled with a paperweight on his desk, before replying. "Though this is not my usual residence in Paris, perhaps I should tell you that everyone in this house has a diplomatic passport. As an act of good faith, I'm more than happy to provide you with a list of the occupants, which will include my staff."

"May I also see their passports please?" The Commissaire asked politely. The Cardinal did not immediately reply. "Your co-operation would be greatly appreciated," he added, belatedly, but firmly.

He shook his head. "Very well, but I'm disappointed you don't take my word for this," he replied indignantly. I lifted my eyebrows in surprise, at the emotion and ego he betrayed.

"You understand I'm only doing my job."

"Of course." The Cardinal said. "I'll make sure the Ministre de L'Interieur appreciates how well you do it. I know him personally. He may also want to speak to the Commissaire Divisionnaire about your efficiency, bearing in mind my own diplomatic position."

The Commissaire sat rigid. "Are you trying to intimidate me?" He asked, in steely tones. "Have I done anything other than request your co-operation.?"

"Certainly not." The Cardinal picked up the telephone on his desk and spoke to a member of his staff, giving instructions for a list of occupants and passports to be brought to his study. He emphasised in relation to one response. "All of them," before replacing the receiver.

"When you've satisfied your enquiries, would you have any objection if I spoke to Monsieur O'Rourke privately?" he asked, looking first at the Commissaire, then at me. "I feel I should speak to him, especially as his uncle was a fellow Cardinal, whom I knew."

"I've no objection." I shrugged in true French fashion.

"Very well," he replied.

At that moment, a member of the Cardinal's staff entered the room handing him a piece of paper and a bundle of passports. He looked at them briefly, before passing them to the Commissaire, who examined them more carefully. "There's no record of anyone called David here," he observed. He showed me the passports, one at a time, after he had inspected them first. "Are you sure there's no-one here by the name of David?" I looked directly at the Cardinal and waited for his response.

"To the best of my knowledge, there's no-one here by that name." He replied, quietly, but firmly. Each of the passports was covered by diplomatic immunity, and stamped as such, but I checked each of the photographs carefully. One resembled David unmistakably, but the name on the passport referred to a Robert David Emmanuel. It was definitely the David I knew. I pointed to the photograph and showed it to the Commissaire, who, in turn, showed it to the Cardinal.

"That man is called David," I said.

The Cardinal looked at the photograph before speaking, quietly as before. "This man is referred to as Robert. I didn't know his middle name was David. He works for the Vatican Institute for Religious Works."

"The Vatican Bank." I groaned.

His eyes widened. "In any event, I assure you he's not here, at the moment, otherwise I'd encourage him to speak to you."

"Then you would have no objection if I keep these passports, until the morning. Perhaps you can arrange for Robert to attend at my office at Quai des Orfevres at say ten o'clock. We can speak to him and I'll happily return all of the passports."

"Will he need a lawyer?" The Cardinal looked at the Commissaire unblinking, before adding. "You must understand this man has diplomatic immunity."

"Why would he need a lawyer?" He replied, raising his eyebrows innocently.

"Then I'll arrange it, provided I can contact him and he's still in Paris," the Cardinal said.

"I'll leave John with you and wait outside." He stood up and walked towards the door. "I can see myself out," he said, closing the study door behind him.

For a few moments, neither of us spoke, before the Cardinal, still holding the paperweight, leant back in his chair and broke the ice. "Let's discuss the problem you've created," he said. "As intellectuals," he added, almost by way of justification.

"I haven't created any problem, as you so subtly put it," I replied calmly, pausing. "And I'm more than happy to discuss any matters, whether as intellectuals or not."

He replaced the paperweight and leaned forward again, clasping his hands together, then resting his head on them. His tone appeared reasonable and his manner affable, although his lower lip quivered and he dribbled slightly, as older men were prone to do.

I felt minded to argue my position. "Why don't you embrace the true teachings of Christ and allow me to publish the scrolls?" I said, leaning back into my chair. "Or better still, agree to publish yourself. Don't you think you've imposed enough guilt on Christians, over the centuries. It hasn't worked. All it's succeeded in doing is making women subordinate to men, masking the spiritual mimicry of sexual orgasm."

He lifted his head, studying me through world-weary eyes. "You're being extremely naïve. There are political, as well as religious reasons, which prevent their publication. What makes you think you have an exclusive line to Christ? I don't think you've thought through the consequences of your actions. Even if I was in a position of power, and at this moment in time I assure you I'm not, this would have to be implemented through procedural channels, involving consultation with representatives of the Church, all over the world. It's an unwieldy organisation and we both know there are vested interests, which will oppose change. All I can say is if I find myself in a position of power, I'd be sympathetic to change provided the transition could be made in a peaceful and positive way. Does that reassure you?"

He had a comforting manner and spoke slowly, like an honest man. The substance, however, was empty promises, which meant nothing. I sensed he wanted to bury the scrolls again.

"Let the people read the scrolls. They'll decide. We live in a democracy and documents such as these shouldn't be suppressed."

He smiled. "You can't believe that. The teachings would be corrupted and the idea of the

Church being unnecessary, as an aid to salvation, would only result in the Church committing symbolic suicide. If it did, what would fill the vacuum? The Anti-Christ? Islam would have a free run at Society and we both know where their fundamentalist fanatics would take us."

"Their religion is as flawed in the way it's interpreted as any other," I replied.

He nodded. "Then we'd have oblivion and the destruction of a decent and honourable way of living."

He had a point, but there had to be a compromise. "Ideally, I'd like the Church to transform itself and merely reform, just as the individual must do from time to time," I said.

"But the people would see it as a licence to behave exactly as they wanted, with no control or standards. Making sex the highest sacrament would have the same result. It would be abused and it would cease to be a sacrament. There'd be a repeat of Sodom and Gomorrah. You also have no concept of the extent to which the Church has battled against the cartels of crime and drug-trafficking at the highest levels." His comments made it obvious he knew precisely the nature and content of the scrolls and their significance.

" No, No." I said immediately. "The pagan principles, which Christ embraced, would prevent it. It would be unchristian to harm anyone. It's a basic tenet of paganism. You must remember, Christ taught an expansive philosophy, away from group consciousness, which was weak and impotent, with limited personal evolution. Where's his spiritual revolution within the Church? If there's a quantum leap in the individual consciousness of man, it'll contribute to a similar shift in group consciousness. It has to be that way around. This is the salvation of the personality, which Christ sought."

"The Church exists to bind people together in a society, based on spiritual union. The problem with Gnostic-type philosophies is they ignore the need for a structure in this way." He moved his hands as he spoke and held my gaze.

I leant forward. "Religion serves to bind people together to the natural world. The danger with the Church is it talks too much about heaven and forgets its sacred duties to the Earth. The God of Jesus doesn't need a Pope to create the rules of access to him. All the Church has achieved is a materialistic society, where the joys of life are suppressed in favour of a future paradise. The people can have the joy here and now, a linking with spiritual forces will create it, without the guilt." I said, more in hope than expectation. I guessed he knew the fundamental flaw in his faith, but chose to ignore it. He was a kindly man and obviously not evil, unless evil was simply error, or the failure to acknowledge it.

He shook his head. "The womb would cease to be the sacred chakra, to use eastern parlance, and there'd be no discipline, which the Church currently exercises," he said. "Society would crumble in the absence of the stable influence of the Church. Religion is like society. It needs structure or it would further deviate from truth."

"Christ and the Nazarenes had discipline. He knew his mission involved the salvation of the personality and the restoration of the feminine. He wanted the spiritual nature of literature, art, poetry and music to become self-evident, as gifts of a culturally-sound society. It's dogma, which has created the wasteland of Grail lore. It's this wound, crying out for healing, which is the wound of the Fisher King of legend. There'll never be a better opportunity for man and woman's proper place, in harmony with the cosmic, rather than subservient to it, to be rehabilitated. The Church can still provide a lead, to control excesses. What is it you fear?" I asked, placing my hands on his desk. "Shouldn't the Church be a follower of Light, rather than a supporter of darkness and evil? If you look around, you'll notice that excesses already exist. Jesus Christ, no stranger to politics, spoke of the arrogant power of the rulers of darkness, who thrive on spiritual wickedness."

"I'm not wicked or arrogant, though we're all imperfect and it's not a question of fear, but of responsibility. Your uncle would have known that." He said, angrily, perhaps attempting, from habit, to impose his will. He gritted his teeth

I felt my colour redden and my pulse increase, as I realised any reasoned discussion was doomed to failure. "That's self-evident nonsense," I said. "If he had, why was he prepared to give his life for truth, as a true Christian martyr? Can you tell me who's responsible for his death? You must know?"

He tilted his head forward, looking down at his desk. "I've genuinely no idea how your uncle died or who is responsible, if anyone." He spoke softly again, looking back at me. Sincerity reflected in his eyes. "You must realise neither the Pope, nor any Cardinal, would ever sanction publication, but there are political influences, with vested interests, which control much of the diplomatic decisions made by the Vatican," he said. "As far as the scrolls are concerned, the Church will never accept Christ as anything other than the Son of God."

"What can you do about my uncle's death? If my uncle was murdered, will you sit back and accept it, with no conscience?" I asked.

"I don't think you should be lecturing me on conscience, with your past, do you? He asked.

"That's a cheap shot," I replied, incensed.

"Then tell me, do you have any loyalty for the Church, which you once served and which fostered you, as its offspring?"

I looked away. The guilt hurt, he knew it, and I hesitated before turning back to face him. "I'm human, with human flaws and frailties, but we're talking about something far greater than individuals. We're discussing truth."

"Very well, what do you intend to do with the scrolls?" He still did not answer my original question about my uncle's death.

"I've not decided what to do yet." I replied, even though I had a good idea. I hoped the Police were still monitoring the conversations in the house. I wondered if I should try to invoke some admission from the Cardinal. "Just between the two of us, what do you know about the activities of David, or Robert, if you wish to call him that?"

He shifted uncomfortably in his chair, before replying. "I knew a certain group, with ties to the Vatican Bank, were attempting to recover the scrolls and other documents. They believed your uncle had taken them from the Vatican vaults, but I knew nothing about his death. I'm prepared to come back to you personally, once I've made certain enquiries, as I could never accept assassinations as a legitimate option, for whatever reason. I'm certain no Cardinal would ever sanction violence."

"What do you intend to do about David or Robert?"

He stood up and walked around to my side of the desk and sat on the edge of the desk facing me. "I've told you, I had no part in any harm caused to your uncle." Again he sounded sincere, but I had become a poor judge.

"Well, you would say that, wouldn't you?"

He grimaced. "I suggest you wake up from this fantasy world of yours to reality. There's only one force that can stand up to this ultimate secret society of intelligence elite, which controls all the political decisions in the world. They're above governments and control all the other secret societies. Their influence permeates everywhere. I'm not sure you're ready for this, but the force, which can combat it, is a united Christian Church. If it's weakened, penetrated or subverted, it'll not have the strength or willpower for such an enormous task. The late Pope John Paul II tried and failed. What you are doing is likely to destabilise the only organisation it fears. Who do you think has led the ideological battle against communism? The late Pope's major legacy. Only the Vatican can lead this intellectual struggle. "

My mouth dropped open, at the thought I could be a pawn in a game, whose rules I did not understand. There was nothing I could say.

The Cardinal nodded, as he realised his bullet had hit its target. "I've no family, other than the Church, and so have no fear. If you have family, I sincerely suggest you take steps to protect them. You may not like the form of the New World Order, which would take our place, if the battle were lost. Are you absolutely sure you're right?" He spoke softly, with no hint of the strident zealot. In fact, the question and its tone had an independent impulse, with compelling conviction. My thoughts turned inward and I didn't reply.

"You've seen what can happen from the eleventh September atrocity. What if your New World Order or the Anti-Christ was fundamental

Islamic? You would discover a new meaning for bigotry and intransigence and would the world necessarily be a better place?" He hesitated and took a deep breath, before filling the vacuum caused by silence. "Perhaps adverse events provide the thrust for a change to a better world, but maybe not. The two-horned beast of the Revelation can be unusually seductive, as well as terrifying. Do you think the Manhattan project and the work at Los Alamos was for the betterment of mankind or could it have been the deceptive work of the agents of the Devil. Honourable people could have been convinced of the unmanifest danger from Hitler's scientific research. What if this was not crucial and there was another way? What if the dropping of the Atomic Bombs on Hiroshima and Nagasaki was unnecessary to end the war? Have you thought whether it did more harm to the prospect and cause of world peace? Could it have created the gripping fear, which so limited the embrace of the Cold War?"

"Too many questions," I replied, when there was no sign of the bombardment abating. "Let's keep it simple."

The Cardinal smiled humbly, with a kindness in his eyes. "But it is simple. You've just not really thought this through?" He looked at me with a will untouched by reason.

In all honesty, I recognized in my arrogance I may not have considered the full implications of my actions, but it was too late to stop my mission. Nevertheless, I felt subdued and unable to respond.

The Cardinal, however, was in full flow. "A Russian mystic once said the Earth, as a living organism, was the body of Christ and the cosmic Christ became the spirit of the Planet at the moment the blood flowed from the thrust of the Spear of

Longinus on to the Earth. It's this spiritual reality, which underpins the physical reality our quantum physicists study. It's also the Catholic message. You believe the same thing, I'm sure you do."

"Well perhaps the message is being lost in its interpretation." I said smugly, unable to add anything meaningful to the debate.

The Cardinal shook his head. "As for the death of your uncle, I'll have the strongest possible words with Robert, as to his involvement in this affair and with his daughter. Beyond this my hands are tied," he said.

"His daughter?" I queried, as a moronic expression revealed my surprise and destroyed any remnant of will to protract the conversation.

*" The discipline of the Mystery schools is my
teaching. It is the inner way, as vicarious salvation
is a myth with no foundation. My way is of Gnosis
(the path of attaining wisdom or higher knowledge).
It is a path of inward cleansing, purification and
direct contact with God. It is a difficult path to
follow and not all will make the sacrifices necessary
to attain it, but there is no race involved and some
will insist on learning through physical hardship in
their time. So many of the ancient scriptures
confirm we are all gods and sons of the Most High,
but the words are corrupted in their interpretation.
One day, science will again establish it, as they did
in the earlier civilisations before the Flood. I hope
the Gnostic way can survive, in the face of the
personal ambition of men, who claim to be only
seekers of knowledge, when they actually seek
external power. They deviate from truth and, in so
doing, fracture and separate from their spirituality.
Suffering was bound to be a consequence of the
imperfection of their work. The world would be a
more dangerous place if the esoteric way of the
Mysteries is buried and sought its security
underground. The coming of the Messiah was
always intended to reflect the arrival of a state of
freedom from pain, suffering and death, not the
coming of some transforming powerful individual."*

CHAPTER 15

A chill evening breeze brought a shiver, as I walked
moodily and alone down fashionable Boulevard St.
Germaine. Shadows lengthened, then disappeared,
as a heavy shower cloud obscured the setting sun
and began to deposit unwelcome rain, adding to my
depression. Discordant music, which had lost its

magic, and occasional laughter filtered from restaurants and zinc-topped bars. It all seemed surreal and distant, but it intruded unpleasantly on jangled thought processes. I stifled an urge to scream and resisted the temptation to seek shelter and company inside the awning of the famous Brasserie Lipp. Its mirrored interior walls suddenly appeared uninviting. Water spilled over the guttering, as the spewing skies closed in around me. I walked on, oblivious to it, intending to lose myself in the straggling network of little streets, beyond the Rue de Buci. No matter which road I took, I always emerged by the river and taxis jostled eagerly for custom on the Quai St. Michel. Not even the exquisite courtyard of the Musée de Cluny could lift my spirits.

A classy-looking hooker flirted in front of me, offering services, but not the friendship and devotion I craved. A grubby-looking Frenchman, huddled and unshaven, bumped into me, knocking me painfully sideways. He stank of garlic and chartreuse verte. No apology came as he shuffled away, muttering obscenities under his breath and I had no energy to complain. The pain reminded me of my ordeal. This glimpse of the real character and sadness behind the veneer of Paris reflected a different city, than the bonhomie I had previously experienced. Although it may have been the city for lovers, it could be as unforgiving and lonely as any city. Its boulevards were suddenly stark and never-ending. Their coldness matched my mood, as it was inevitably bound to do, in this upside-down world, full of paradoxes. For the first time, I had to accept the possibility I could be wrong, but it meant abandoning trust in my uncle's judgment and breaking my promise. I still felt these scrolls should be published, but a lingering doubt made me hesitate in my resolve. The thought of being the innocent instrument of subversion, for the forces of evil, sent a shiver down my spine and destiny's mantle hung heavily on my shoulders.

Julian had returned from hospital, but remained ensconced in the Hotel George V, insulated from this Babylone Du Monde. I would have been poor company for anyone. Betrayal had become too familiar. Echoes from the past reverberated, despite conscious attempts to avoid patterns of behaviour, which might allow this dark avenging angel a chink of weakness, with which to exploit and wreak its havoc once again. In some ways, I wanted to embrace the hardships, for it was a price I had to pay. It alleviated me of the guilt, which otherwise haunted me at the deepest level of my psyche. Rosary beads and a few Hail Mary's were never enough. My Catholic upbringing and training insisted I hold on to this guilt for the unforgivable sin of deviation from the literal view of the scriptures. Acknowledgment of guilt was such an intrinsic thread of Catholic dogma and, therefore, a prison, from which escape became difficult, if not impossible.

My head bent against the rain, oblivious to a vehicle following slowly, far too engrossed in my own thoughts to care, until instinct made me lift and turn my head. Rachel drove slowly and alone in a car, with the passenger window open. She stopped the car at my side and leaned across from the driver's side, shouting through the open window.

"Are you prepared to listen to me, without becoming angry? We need to talk."

"When a woman says 'we need to talk', it usually means she wants to talk, and she wants something or she wants to complain," I replied sarcastically. She wore designer clothes, elegant as ever, but feelings stirred, uncomfortable feelings. I doubted whether I had the discipline to resist emotions held deep within, though on the surface I created a barrier against her charms.

"That's not fair," she said coldly.

"You've got a nerve." I said, sullenly and angrily, eyes blazing. I restrained an urge to be more hurtful. "Don't talk to me about fairness. Why should I listen to you, you're just a pathological liar."

She shook her head and looked up to the heavens. "You can say what you like, but get in the car."

"Why should I?"

"You're soaking wet and I've things I want to say."

"I'm not sure I want to listen."

She sighed. "What did you expect of me. Betray my husband and my father. It wasn't easy. You may not believe it, but there were times I did."

I felt a compulsion, which I couldn't resist. Before I had time to think, I found myself sitting in the front passenger seat. "The Police want to speak to you," I said, calmly, even if inside a fury held rein.

She closed her eyes for a moment and when she opened them, a lone tear slid gently down her cheek. "If, after listening to me, you want to call them, I'll not make a fuss. I've no desire to hurt or deceive you." She turned off the ignition of the car and turned her head towards me.

"It had better be good." I said, feeling a muscle spasm in my face and struggling to contain anger. Water dripped from my hair into my eyes and down the nape of my neck, trickling sensually, but uncomfortably, inside my shirt.

"My father asked me to take the post with your uncle for one purpose only, to discover if he still had the documents, which had been stolen from the Vatican vaults. If I located them, it would have been a bonus."

"Well, you did your job remarkably well." I said, disdainfully. "But I already knew that."

She lifted her hands upward in exasperation. "My father emphasised that it had been your uncle who'd been in the wrong, as he'd been in a position of trust. I honestly didn't believe any harm would come to anyone, least of all, your uncle, as I'd grown genuinely fond of him. I wouldn't have done this, if I'd foreseen the consequences, I promise you.."

"Ha, bloody ha." I mocked.

"You self-righteous bastard. What makes you think you're always right?" Her eyes bulged. "Don't you think it's difficult enough for me to cope with the guilt and betrayal?"

"When someone has been kidnapped, drugged, and another person died, the demarcation line between right and wrong is clear enough." I replied, allowing anger and stubbornness more than a modicum of freedom. I convinced myself this selfish release of energy was therapeutic.

"I had nothing to do with that."

"The Police may take a different view."

Her face reddened and lines showed on her face. "Look at the facts. First, I worked for you immediately before your uncle's death. My job was done, yet I went with you, against the wishes of my father and husband, because I'd developed strong feelings for you. Secondly, I didn't tell either of them where you'd deposited the scrolls or the name of your Solicitor. I lied and said I didn't know. If I'd told the truth, they may already have been recovered."

"But after my uncle's death, you still came to Paris with me." I said, unable to look her in the eye.

"I always wanted to go to heaven, but it didn't mean I wanted to die." She replied, paradoxically.

"And what does that mean?" I asked, eyes narrowing and unappreciative of her wit.

"I wasn't supposed to go to Paris. It's the reason my husband sent one of his men to grab me at your house, and again he tried to make me go in the car with him, by the steps of the Sacre Coeur. I genuinely wanted to be with you. I'd been unhappy in my marriage for some time and my father knew this. I made him promise no harm would come to you."

"For some reason, I find no consolation in that."

"Fair enough, but remember, the contact with Jean and his organisation came from me. I knew my husband and father would be angry if they found out, but I felt compelled to help you. That's why I told you to negotiate only with my father."

It sounded convincing, but I was too vulnerable and drained to reply.

"Finally, tell me why I should meet you here, if it wasn't for my feelings for you. I didn't pretend to make love. For me, it was the real thing. So much so, I felt dirty making love to my husband afterwards and decided I'd leave him."

"So you made love to your husband afterwards, did you?"

She lifted her hands in the air. "Men," she shouted.

I wanted the coward's way out and to change the past, rather than to embrace the present. I shook my head continually, in a state of confusion and bewilderment.

"John, I remind you, I was the one who told your uncle about the plotting against him. He encouraged you to take me on as your assistant, immediately afterwards. Do you trust your uncle's judgment?" She asked.

"Cardinal Montagne spoke to my father, after your visit. He told him to return to Italy. He wanted me to go with him, but I insisted I'd rather face the consequences with you. He respected my decision, but warned me of grave risks which could follow."

Eventually, she took a deep breath and the silence instilled a vacuum for thought. I had no focus, only a numb paralysis, which dulled the emotions, but I still wanted her, despite the pain. If the heart is the centre for intuition, it kept telling me to trust her. Outside our little cocoon, heavy rain surreally created opaque patterns on the windows.

"I've little confidence, at the moment, in my judgment of character," I sighed, pushing my head back into the seat.

"I understand, but if you trust me this once, I'll never let you down again, no matter how difficult life becomes. I'll always be there for you, to support you, in whatever you do. I want to share your goals, without any equivocation. You've the whole truth now. On everything I hold sacred, I promise you."

She moved her hand and stretched across to touch my arm. First instinct may have been to pull away, but I breathed in her subtle perfume and like a puppy on a lead, with one tug I jolted back into her arms. When I gave my heart, it always ruled my head and all reason and logic disintegrated, tumbling out of the window. My head still wanted to resist, but my heart couldn't."

"That's not fair." I said, anger melting in the furnace. "If you don't mean what you say, or can't sustain it, under all conditions, then drive away and never contact me again."

She smiled, laying her head on my chest. "I'm yours, do with me as you want. If you want to call the Police, I'll not complain. If not, I'll go there voluntarily, in the morning. I intend to help them with all of their enquiries."

"What about your father?" I asked, all fight drained from my body.

"He must face the consequences of his actions. In the future, I'll take your side against him, if necessary. What more can I say?"

"You know I wanted you, even more than I ever wanted my wife," I confided.

"Does that mean you loved me more than your wife?"

"I don't know. Is it the same thing?"

"No," she replied, immediately.

I placed my hand on her shoulders and felt the surge of warmth she always created. If time could stop, there would be no problem, but life is never that simple. "Wait until the morning, then contact the Police. You must be prepared for difficult questions, especially as your father is likely to be incriminated in serious offences." I said.

"I've already decided not to run away again. I'll encourage my father into co-operating with you." She lifted her head. "I've already spoken to him. He's told me he'll do what he can to help you, though he's not hopeful."

"Where's your father now?" I asked, testing her promises.

"He's already left for Italy, but he'll return, provided it's sanctioned by his superiors. He's been badly influenced, but he stressed he was a mere foot soldier. My father knows my feelings for you and accepts the position I've taken. He respects you for the stand you've taken, even if it's caused him personal problems."

"He's brought these problems on himself," I said.

"He knows that. I think Marco's death made him realise his folly. He told me he was only a bagman for the syndicates who infiltrate the banks, both at the Vatican and the smaller European states, who specialise in banking. He's far removed from power and will be expendable."

"Do you mean his life is in danger?"

"My father is convinced that if the hierarchy want him eliminated, no-one can escape their clutches."

A shiver ran down my spine. It placed my position in greater perspective.

Pain etched in Rachel's face. Her head dropped, and beleaguered eyes looked down. "He's told me my life could also be in danger, by associating with you, but if there's a possibility my presence could protect you, then I'm happy enough."

"You're still prepared to take that risk for me?" I asked, pulling her head up gently.

"Yes, I am," she replied, unblinking. "Because I love you."

"What do you think I should do?" I asked, tentatively. Life was full of risks and it was time to take another.

She shook her head. "I'd have thought you'd be safer in London, provided you take appropriate precautions. Your solicitor can advise you and write to the proper authorities, but it's your decision, not mine. I'll respect it, whatever you decide." She looked at me, studiously. I sat quietly, knowing she had the potential to cause me grief, but I decided I would take the chance.

"I've asked my father to try and persuade those in authority to negotiate with you, but he believes they'll refuse, preferring to undermine the authenticity and interpretation placed on the documents. In the meantime, he thinks your life remains at risk."

"I appreciate your honesty. I must speak to Julian in the morning. I'll not make any promises, until I know I can trust you. Trust, like love, needs nourishment and time. I've had cause to mistrust too many people in my life."

"That's fair enough," she acknowledged.

"Did Cardinal Montagne know of your father's connections? I asked.

"He didn't, but he does now."

"You know I must leave for London in the morning and will be leaving you on your own."

She nodded. "I understand."

I looked at her, quizzically. An emotional turmoil, raged inside. "Are you prepared to attend at Quai des Orfevres by yourself in the morning?" I asked.

"That's not a problem. I can be strong, if I know you love me and will be standing by me. I'll tell the Commissaire the truth. I honestly didn't believe any harm would be caused to anyone. I know very little about my father's affairs, but I'll tell him he intends to return to Paris, after he's spoken to his superiors."

"Then it's settled." I said, taking a deep breath.

"Does this mean I can stay with you tonight?" She asked, plaintively, looking at me with those big doleful eyes. I barely nodded, as rational thought held me back. She embraced me and, for that moment, I was content.

"When you care little, whether you live or die, courage is easy." She said, moving back so that her face was directly in front of mine. "I couldn't say anything before, but I've another document, an old scroll. Your uncle gave it to me for safekeeping. He said it was a key to the other scrolls. I felt it was a test, so I don't know if it has any significance. I've hidden it at my home. I didn't tell either my father or Marco about it. You can have it, when we return to England."

"Better late than never." I replied, stingy with gratitude. She never failed to surprise me, but I still felt mistrust. "Are there any other dark secrets you're hiding, whilst we're on the subject?"

"No, there's nothing else. You know absolutely everything."

I had a need to make love to her violently, almost as part of a healing process, again and again. I needed to reclaim my territory. Perhaps then I could rediscover a peaceful sleep.

***

Next morning, I woke up reluctantly, but stirred quickly into action, dropping Rachel off at Quai des Orfevres, before returning to Hotel George V to collect an understandably subdued Julian. I revealed my plans and agreed on a further meeting in London. He would arrange contact with the police there, as soon as possible. On my return, I telephoned Ronan and immediately travelled to Guildford to meet him. I needed someone to authenticate the origins of the scrolls and hoped he would assist, if only out of loyalty to my uncle. If Rachel's scroll helped my cause, things could begin to knit together.

St. John's seminary, near Guildford, was an old monastery-like building set in beautiful green Surrey countryside. The sound of Gregorian chanting in one of the buildings greeted my arrival and added to its atmosphere. Black-cassocked novice priests scuttled in different directions, their footsteps creating eerie echoes across the cloisters, as if their predecessors remained locked there, in the mists of time. The remnants of incense wafted, stimulating the senses. Pigeons flew from the open cloisters area underneath the arches, then dived back out to escape its gilded cage and into the warm sunshine again. Amongst a group moving towards me, I saw the familiar white hair and distinctive bushy eyebrows, easily identifiable as Ronan.

He shook my hand and guided me to a side room, for visitors. "I've been expecting you," he said. "Although, in truth, I hoped the problem would have resolved itself, without my help."

"Do you know what's happened?" I asked, sitting on a hard bench, alongside him.

"Well, I know you've stirred up a hornet's nest and senior figures are panicking. My place here is in jeopardy. The Police have interviewed me about your uncle's death. There's been a devil of a job to prevent his cremation, to allow a post-mortem examination of his body."

He hitched up his cassock, where it dragged on the floor. "I think your lawyer's letter helped."

"Are the enquiries continuing?" I asked.

He lifted those bushy eyebrows, which appeared to mask a universe. "Haven't you spoken to the Police yet? They're anxious to speak to you. I gained the impression it was high priority."

"I've only arrived back from Paris today. My lawyer will arrange it."

"Well, they've taken a detailed witness statement from me. It took all morning. I've told them about your uncle's fears for his safety, but it's placed me in an invidious position."

The sound of bells interrupted his explanation. It signalled a frenzy of activity outside our room and across the nearby cloisters. Someone opened the door, apologised, and closed it again. "I think they're treating his death suspiciously, as a consequence," he said, after the noise subsided.

"What was the result of the autopsy?" I asked.

"The Police have found the presence of toxins in the body, but there are also remnants of radioactivity."

"What's the significance of that?" I asked.

"I understand this could have triggered a fast-acting cancer. I know they've compared it with the death, by ricin poisoning, many years ago of the Bulgarian dissident working for the BBC, after he was hit in the leg with an umbrella tip. There's some argument as to whether it could have accumulated naturally. I don't believe it's a murder enquiry at this stage." He paused, briefly. "I gain the impression they don't want to create a scandal, without overwhelming evidence."

I nodded. "I think they'll bury the investigation after a period. There are too many vested interests."

"You're probably right."

I stood up, pacing around Ronan in a semi-circle. "There's been desperate activity in Paris, including the kidnapping of my lawyer. He's been freed, but only after one person died in the process."

"Oh my God. Hail Mary." He motioned in the form of a cross, with his right hand.

"The person who died was Rachel's husband."

"Rachel's husband?" he repeated, raising his voice and lifting his eyebrows again. "I didn't even know she was married."

"No-one did."

"What did the incident in Paris have to do with him?" He asked.

"I'm afraid Rachel's position with my uncle had been organised to infiltrate his household, with the intention of recovering the scrolls. He was one of the group, which was pursuing and pressurising me to hand over the documents. Rachel insists she didn't know any harm would be caused to anyone." I said, calmly.

He muttered something under his breath, shaking his head at the same time.

" It gets worse. I actually believe her." I said, smiling at my folly.

He looked at me, strangely, but said nothing.

"I know it's bizarre, but I've fallen in love with the girl, so perhaps my judgment is flawed." I laughed at myself, as I spoke.

"Hail Mary" He raised his voice again, looking up to the ceiling. "Thank God I remained celibate."

"I know, at this moment, she's assisting the Police in Paris with their enquiries." I said, ignoring his rhetoric.

He shook his head again. "It's better I'm just a poor priest, life is less complicated."

"This is where the problem arises. I'm going to further complicate your life. I want you to help me authenticate the scrolls. If you agree, your life may be in danger. I must establish the truth, whatever the cost."

"Oh, mother of Jesus." He blasphemed again, sighed and placed his head in his hands. I waited patiently for a response.

"What do you say?" I asked.

He took his hands away from his face. "I've seen the scrolls. Your uncle trusted me and showed them to me. So I can confirm they're the originals, taken from the Vatican vaults, but where will this leave me?"

"You'll be able to live with your conscience," I replied.

"I'll be an outcast amongst my peers, with nowhere to live and no security. All I've ever known is the Church." He said, staring blankly ahead.

"I understand your problem and I can give you no guarantees."

"That's the problem," he lifted his eyebrows.

"All I can say is I'll provide financial assistance and ask any publisher to offer you both security and protection. At the moment, it looks as if an American publisher may be the favourite to take the plunge, provided his Board agree. I'm a little concerned, as some Christian organisations and publishers are controlled by people who have a different agenda."

He again repeated something barely audible, under his breath. Even when he raised his voice he spoke quickly, with a strong Irish lilt, and I struggled to pick up every word.

"If you say you're not prepared to help me, I'll not press you. All I want to do is honour my uncle's memory, by keeping a promise, which I made to him, on his deathbed. You must have known his wishes."

He nodded. "He believed this knowledge could enable human beings to take an evolutionary leap forward. He used to say the truth always sets you free."

"I believe it does, Ronan. Don't you?"

He smiled knowingly, but wouldn't play my little game.

"He told me he trusted you and you'd help me." I said. "Are you prepared to help?"

I had no qualms about playing the loyalty card, if the long-term benefits outweighed the prejudice. He leant forward, placing his head in his hands again. For several seconds, silence filled the room. I gave him all the time he needed for a decision, which was bound to change his life forever.

He looked up, still shaking his head. "Do you realise what you're asking me to do?"

I didn't flinch. "Yes, I do, but life can't stay the same. It stagnates, we mustn't be afraid of change. There is spirituality and growth only by embracing and overcoming the obstacles placed in our path. Otherwise, there's no purpose to life. Isn't this the spiritual dynamic?" I pursued him relentlessly. The importance of Ronan's testimony in the publication and acceptance of the documents could not be underestimated.

"If I take any money, there'll be accusations of taking the thirty pieces of silver and history will place me in the same category as Judas Iscariot. If I don't help you, I'll be betraying my conscience. I can't win." His voice faltered and cracked.

"My recollection of history is that those tarnished by corruption are mainly forgotten, but the memory of its heroes linger on, deep within the psyche. Those people who've the courage to change the world and the foresight to take difficult decisions are remembered, when others, who've sat back and done nothing, are long forgotten." I said.

"Why don't you leave well-enough alone." He said, even if the tone of his voice echoed a different message, one from deep within his soul.

"I know you don't mean it. Perhaps it might be convenient if I walked away, but it wouldn't be right and you know it." I still turned the screw. "My uncle would have expected you to support me."

A faint smile simmered and he wagged his finger disapprovingly. "You know all the sensitive spots, but you're manipulating me."

It was a gentle reprimand, almost one of respect. He was no fool. Just as well, I thought. "When all the fuss subsides, as one day it will, I'd like to return to Ireland," he said, almost to himself.

I nodded, allowing him to reflect, without further interruption. "I'll do it, but I'll have to leave immediately. Wait for me. My personal possessions are limited and I'll leave my books behind."

I felt instantly less isolated. His request was simple. He stood up and I happily followed him to the door. I realised how difficult this must have been and held out my hand to shake his. He readily took it, but his face reflected an inner sadness, which nothing could erase.

"You must understand, I could have helped you earlier. I knew Rachel's father had been employed by the Vatican Bank and had helped secure her posting. " He shook his head again.

"Did my uncle know the connection?" I asked.

"Yes, he did, but he liked Rachel. Though he suspected her of taking the post initially because of her father's influence and to do his bidding."

"She never told me, but that's in the past," I replied, waving my hand in the air.

"They'll not let go easily and not everything is in the past," he said. He opened the door slightly, before turning to me, speaking quietly. "Your uncle entrusted Rachel with one of the scrolls. He showed it to me only briefly. He insisted it had great significance, but I didn't understand why. Did you know?"

I nodded. "She's offered it to me, when she returns from Paris, but I haven't seen it yet."

"Good. If you leave me in some accommodation first, I'd like you to go to your ex-wife Katie and your daughters. I'm concerned for them. She wrote to me about threats being made, but she asked me not to mention anything to anyone, not even you."

"Oh, no, not them too." I said, remembering the comments of the Cardinal and Rachel's warning. I felt sick to the pit of my stomach.

"Please, we must hurry. You can stay in my house, until I find somewhere more secure." I walked quickly with him to his quarters.

Concern for Katie and the girls made me appreciate I hadn't resolved lingering feelings for my ex-wife and still carried the burden of too much pain, despite bold assurances to the contrary. I found emotional situations complicated, often seeking to avoid them. Sometimes it became impossible, as life and circumstances eventually force you to face your feelings. It was a risk to leave Ronan in my house, but it was one I had to take. A telephone call to Julian updated me on developments and I delayed my appointment with him. There were a number of messages on the answer service, including one to ring Commissaire Moreau in Paris. They would all have to wait. I telephoned my ex-wife, but there was no reply. Within an hour I arrived at her house, but I could find no trace of her or my children. Strangely, her car remained on the drive. I called at a neighbour's house, but they had not seen them for twenty-four hours, when they'd been observed accessing a large black limousine. As there appeared to be no violence, they hadn't thought to report it.

Any remnants of discipline frenzied, finally out of control, as I paid the price for arrogance. A myriad of thoughts spiralled. Some formulated into this matrix for use, but words and feelings didn't crystallise. This was a sensitive area and an Achilles heel. I could face danger myself and accept the adversity, but the sombre thought of harm to my ex-wife and two girls could not be borne easily. They were innocents and deserved better.

The time had arrived, to check those messages and bring in the Police, without further delay. Perhaps Cardinal Montagne could be contacted. He had some influence in the corridors of power. I resolved to do whatever it took to free them quickly.

"… When I teach the meek will inherit the Earth, I do not mean the weak, for I find it difficult to tolerate fools or those who lack discipline. I mean only there must be no anger, no fear and no hatred held in the consciousness of man. It is a pro-active movement within the personality of man. For the law of attraction is clear, within the world of illusion, in which we live. Like so obviously attracts like, in all the spheres of existence. I warn you, those who live in fear or in anger or hold hate in their heart will attract the energy of a similar vibration. It will inevitably bring emotional turmoil and damage the vessel, within which the spirit resides. As with envy, which is the opposite of joy. In the beginning was the word and its vibration was God. So beware feeling unjustly treated. Do not misunderstand this subtlety. You can be strong, yet meek. If you eradicate all doubt and negativity, replacing it with certainty, you shed Light in the world. Live with a compassionate heart and you draw to yourself goodness and Light. By allowing the Divine Light to pass through us, then we become a vehicle for it. This gives us the spiritual maturity necessary to take the great leap forward our civilisation demands. Connect to the Light by proactively restricting self-serving desires. In the process, you make a contribution to the building of the Temple and a paradise on Earth. This is the forward movement of evolution that spiritual transformation brings to the individual and, therefore, to the world."

CHAPTER 16

Life often caused more pain, than the cold embrace of death itself. My family, though living apart, had been a rare source of stability, in an ever-changing world. The universe too often portrayed an unpleasant face. It meant a constant battle raged within my soul, allowing negative thoughts a licence to intrude and manifest their limitations in my life, like a stagnant dark cloud hovering and waiting for its opportunity to spoil and torture. I feared my sins had, in some way, returned to stain their innocence. Too many instances existed of innocent children becoming victims for me to believe I could be immune.

I barged through the front door and into the hall, almost knocking Ronan over, in my urgency to reach the telephone. The torrent of injustice washed over me, like a deluge. Bad energy began to stir into life, with thoughts of revenge, and I could not control it.

"They're not there." I blurted out, as I passed Ronan in the hall. I gritted my teeth.

"Someone's been telephoning, whilst you were out, but I didn't answer it," he replied, anxiously. The concern etched in his face, where frightened eyes peeped out from behind those bushy eyebrows.

Agitated, I pressed the answering service number on the telephone to access the messages and my tired body slumped into the study chair."

First message, I'd heard and forgotten to erase. It was of no consequence.

Second message. The Commissaire wanted to speak to me, he still held Rachel. He'd contacted New Scotland Yard, so they knew the position. I wrote down the number.

Third message, Rachel's father warning me to be careful, as political factions within the Vatican intelligence hierarchy still wanted to recover the documents, at any cost. The scrolls were now an open secret and others would muscle in. Moreover, the intelligence services had employed mercenaries to recover the scrolls. He asked me to tell Rachel he loved her and apologised for his failure to be of assistance. He spoke stoically, as if this would be his last message and nothing further could be done. Poignantly, he asked me to take care of Rachel. He confessed to being a poor father and insisted she had not been the cause of the present situation and deserved better.

Fourth message, Jean asking to return his call. The American was having problems with his Board. He could not publish the scrolls.

Fifth message, Julian had made another appointment for interview by the Police, at nine o'clock tomorrow, without fail. He could attend with me. No problem.

Sixth message, this was the one.

"We've taken your family, for their own protection. Bring all the documents in your possession, at noon tomorrow, to the public telephone immediately opposite the newsagents, at Paddington Railway Station. You'll receive further instructions, provided you're alone and have made no attempt to involve the police. You'll have only one opportunity for compliance. Your home is being monitored and we'll know if you've had this message. If you care about your wife and daughters' welfare, follow the instructions very precisely."

It appeared to be the standard sort of stark message, but this had become personal, and my dilemma specific.

Ronan stood by my side, listening to the messages. "What are you going to do?"

I shrugged. "I'll contact Julian for his advice, but not on this telephone. My inclination is to seek advice with an acquaintance of mine, who's a high-ranking Police officer." I shook my head. "But only if he'll promise confidentiality and allow me to conduct matters without full Police involvement, if necessary.."

Too many uncertainties plagued my mind. I knew from my work that police forces had been infiltrated by the espionage agencies, often through the elite masonry lodges, at the highest level. I had to trust personal judgment.

"How do you know for certain these people have your ex-wife and daughters?" He asked.

"I don't, but I can't take the chance."

"Be careful."

"I will. I'll ring every conceivable friend or relative to ensure it isn't a bluff. Julian will help. He knows from first-hand experience the depths to which these people will stoop. If any harm comes to my family, I'll hunt these people down and harass the Vatican, in ways they can't imagine. If my life has to be sacrificed in the process, then so be it."

"Oh mother of Jesus, you must keep your head. Don't be hasty. Vitriol can lead to impulsive decisions." He placed his hand on my shoulder, but it wasn't his family being threatened.

"I understand, but I've been a journalist for a long time and I'm not without some influence in London."

"They'll know that."

"They couldn't have known when I'd be returning and so the message has given me enough time to do something about it. I'm leaving immediately, if they're watching the house, they may try to ring again and alter the time." I said, gathering my briefcase and a small overnight bag. I placed my hand on the side of Ronan's arm, as I walked out. "I'm sorry to leave you again. If the phone rings, answer it and pretend to be a friend or something. I'll not return tonight, unless I have to, but here's my mobile phone number." I handed him a card with the number written on it.

"Ring me, if there are any messages or in an emergency, but if they ask you to contact me, tell them I'm away until tomorrow night." I turned to walk out, but remembered I needed to contact the Cardinal. "There's one more thing you can do for me. Try and contact Cardinal Montagne. I met him and he promised to come back to me. Tell him what has happened and ask him for help."

His mouth dropped open, a forlorn expression pitifully reflected in his eyes. I had changed his life in an instant and he looked every bit the victim of a revolution, but his assistance was critical.

"Are you going to be alright?" I asked, belatedly, turning back to face him in the hall.

"I'll be fine." His words were positive and spoken with a thread of sympathy, but he spoke quietly, with little conviction.

I nodded and left the house, as quickly as I arrived.

* * *

Julian's office typified the modern lawyer's office, uncluttered modern furniture, computer screens and hi-tech everywhere with books hidden away in a library, rather than for show. Access to most law being through the Internet or by CD-Rom, with training involving staff huddled around a television watching video programmes, all cheating it appeared to me. You didn't have to know the law anymore, just which buttons to press and where to find it. Everything had become audits and supervised quality control, with clients often an obvious inconvenience. Charles Dickens wouldn't have recognised the place or approved, but now service to clients had become the watchword, with administration and overheads consequently spiralling and sadly little room for initiative or the small Practitioner.

What had, hitherto, been frowned upon as touting, with disciplinary proceedings brought by the Law Society the likely outcome, had suddenly reinvented itself, dressed up in a new strategy, deviously referred to as marketing. Soon the law would remain an avenue only for the rich, or the very poor and those in between would miss out completely. It was a revolution by political stealth and the spin-doctors would ensure it could not be recognised until too late to rectify. Unfortunately, lawyers were now businessmen, rather than professionals, even if some argued with the assessment. Elitism and pomposity still abounded, restricting any feel for common sense. This was the price of progress.

Even more important than advising the client, was writing down what advice you gave, so your file could be audited and approved afterwards. I remembered, with affection, my blooding as a fledgling, Court-reporting journalist, where I had first met Julian, recalling fondly his glee in humorous situations and his lack of decorum in the Court environment. He shared my hate of stuffy judges and plum in the mouth lawyers. He always found it impossible to keep a straight face. This streak of humanity endeared him to his loyal clients and attracted me to him. He had been my Solicitor for fifteen years. I hoped he thought of me as a good friend, not just a client, after all this time, but he had already paid his price for that friendship.

His delightful receptionist gestured for me to go into his office, with a peculiar punctuality for a lawyer. Punctuality, I had always been assured, was the sign of an organised and disciplined mind. If so, it said much for the state of mine. It was no wonder I remained a freelance.

"They've got Katie and the girls." I said, explaining the message on the answering service and the attempts made to contact friends and relatives, without success.

"Do you think they know you've had the message?" He asked.

"I can't take any risks, one way or the other." I replied.

He leaned back in his leather chair; placing his index finger over his mouth, looking up to the ceiling for a moment, then back at me. His chair was large enough to suit his stature. Bookshelves stacked behind him, but mostly files, rather than books utilised the space. Though some books, probably unused for years, remained for show. No doubt the larger ones, as they always looked impressive. His computer and dictating machine had been set up on a separate desk, to the side of his main desk. His phone and one file and a pen and notepad only remained on the main desk, which looked suitably uncluttered. He had obviously been attending all his management courses and gaining his compulsory points for doing so.

"If you don't want to take any chances, I'll look at all the original documents and certify the copies as examined against the originals and sign them as such. They'll not be as good as originals and it'll make it easier for the authenticity of the documents to be challenged. Nevertheless, it's the best we can do in the circumstances."

"I may also have a problem with the publisher, but I'm more determined than ever to publish the documents, one way or another. My resolve has been hardened, rather than weakened." I fixed a determined expression, gritting my teeth. "But I'll not take any chances with Katie and the girls."

"I understand your motives completely. Do you intend to bring in the Police?" He asked, straight-faced, without proffering any advice on the options.

I shrugged. "I've certain views, but I thought I'd ask your advice. I'm very friendly with Superintendent Thomas. I thought I'd ring him and ask whether he'd be able to guarantee confidentiality."

"There's always a risk, of course."

"I'd discuss it with him in more detail, if I could be absolutely certain the whisper wouldn't spread through his department, as it so often does. I couldn't take that chance."

Julian nodded. "I know the reputation of the Met has had some bad press lately, but, as with the West Midlands force, it was always the minority which tarred the image of the majority. I know Superintendent Thomas, he's a good man." He said, positively.

"In this instance, it's not the corruption which concerns me, but rather the fact the intelligence services have agents, who infiltrate into positions of influence, including the top echelons of the Police. One former head of Scotland Yard is now on the board of a security company with dubious connections." I folded my arms, before asking the important question. "If I hand over all the documents, will Katie and the girls be returned safely?"

He tapped a pen against his desk, before pointing it at me. "You must bring in the Police. It would be my advice. There'd be too much of a risk, without the sophisticated surveillance and manpower they'd generate. I don't think you've any choice." He spoke unequivocally, his eyes widening.

I nodded. "I feel the same way, but I'm too close. I needed someone I respected to confirm my gut instinct."

"Why don't you ring the Superintendent from here?" He pointed to the telephone, turning it around so it faced me.

I paused, looking up again. "You may as well know, on the way here, I've rung an Editor friend of mine for his help. You know how they love an exclusive."

"Only too well."

"Well, I've explained my predicament to him and promised him the first interview about the scrolls. I explained the extent to which the Vatican have attempted to suppress them."

"What if it harmed your family?" He asked.

"I attached one condition, of course. He must do nothing, until my family is safe. He'll want to speak to Ronan and possibly to you, to verify the story. I told him you'd both agree."

"Are you sure you can trust him?" He asked. "You know what some newspapers are like. He may be subjected to immense pressure to toe a different line."

"I understand your reservations, but there are no certainties in life. This man is a friend and I trust him."

"As long as you're sure."

"My only concern is the proprietor of the newspaper, as I'm aware of the media control exercised by the intelligence services, so I've asked him to promise discretion, at all costs. He'll not tell a soul."

"Good."

"I'm determined to make the Church acknowledge their guilt, even if I spend the rest of my life doing it." I said, angrily.

"Then I wish you a long life," he replied.

"The Editor is all geared up to ring Paris and will contact the head of the Catholic Church, here in London, but he'll do nothing, until I give him the all-clear. He's not a fool. This would be a huge scoop for him and for his newspaper. He needs my co-operation."

"You mustn't do or say anything precipitate, which could harm your family."

"I know that. It goes without saying. Do you really think I'd do anything to harm them?" I said, tetchily.

"Don't shoot the messenger. I'm on your side," he reassured me.

"I understand, but bear with me. I'm not a patient man at the best of times and this is testing me."

"That's O.K," he smiled.

"I did think of asking the Editor to ring the Catholic Church about the story immediately, so they'd know there'd be a price to pay, if anything happened to my family. I assume you'd advise against it?"

"I'm a lawyer and we always take a cautious view."

"I wondered whether this is an appropriate time to start turning the screw. I've also asked Ronan to ring Cardinal Montagne, as I thought it may help."

He thought, but shook his head. "They must know there'll be fall-out if something happened to Katie and the girls, so hold back for the time being. That's my advice, for what it's worth. After my own experience, I'll help in any way, but this is really outside my expertise. I'd like to do something, other than examine and certify documents, because this has become personal for me too."

I nodded. "Good. I don't want to be accessible tonight. Although I can stay at a hotel, I'd like to stay at your place, if it's convenient."

He smiled again. "I should have suggested it myself."

"Perhaps I could help you with the documents, whilst I'm there?" I asked.

"Sure," he replied immediately.

I gestured to the telephone. "I'm anxious to meet Superintendent Thomas this evening. The sooner my course is focused in my mind, the easier it is for me."

"Make your call," he opened his palm towards the telephone.

As always, I passed through two civilian staff, before speaking to him. "Gwyn, it's John O'Rourke. I need a big favour and more than anything else, I need discretion."

"If it's to do with the problems in Paris, one of my colleagues has received a call and some reports from Commissaire Moreau. He spoke to me afterwards, as he knew were a friend, so I'm aware of the background. The Department is anxious to speak to you." He spoke with a Welsh lilt, even after thirty years in London.

"First, I must know our discussion will remain confidential. It's a vital precondition to further conversation."

A pause on the line, allowed time for thought, before he responded. "Provided you're not confessing a crime, I can probably comply."

"I hate the word 'probably'," I replied. "And I've not committed any crime. At least, I don't think so."

"Then I can definitely keep it confidential. Is that better?" He raised his voice, but I had no qualms offending him, discretion being paramount.

"Yes, that's better. I'm in Julian's office. You'll be aware of his kidnapping in Paris. Well, I think they've taken my ex-wife and two daughters." I hesitated, awaiting a response.

"Are you sure?" He asked firmly.

"I'm sure. They're demanding I return the documents my uncle gave me, if I care about my family's welfare. A meeting is arranged for noon tomorrow and I've been warned against contacting the Police, so you'll appreciate my sensitivity."

"I understand."

"I don't want you to discuss this with anyone, at this stage," I insisted.

"There'll be no problem with confidentiality, but it's important I meet you discreetly, without delay. There are set procedures for dealing with these type of cases and, though I might normally be expected to involve Special Branch, I'll help personally, in the circumstances. I'll take the flak afterwards." He spoke confidently. "I promise I'll do nothing without discussing it with you first. Your family's welfare will be my main priority."

"That's good. Where shall we meet?" I asked, my heart feeling lighter.

"I know Julian's office. If he doesn't mind, I'll leave immediately. There's no time to lose. I'll drive an unmarked vehicle and use the rear entrance. It'll take me about twenty minutes."

Julian listened on his conference facility and nodded approval.

"Good. I'll see you shortly," I said.

In the twenty minutes, which elapsed before the Superintendent's arrival, we had time to organize the collection of the original documents and for Julian to telephone his wife to expect a guest for the night. He stopped all calls, making arrangements for a partner to take over his urgent work.

Finally, I needed to return the call of the Commissaire. He confirmed Rachel had assisted them with their enquiries, before being released. He anticipated she would return to London. Without informing him of recent events, I asked if he could assist the Superintendent with information, as the need arose. He readily agreed. I tried to telephone Rachel on the only number she had given me, but there was no reply.

***

The Superintendent carried a large briefcase, from which he removed a tape recorder, placing it gently on the desk, before settling back into one of the modern, functional chairs in Julian's office. His features were largely anonymous. He wore a grey suit and his attire was nondescript. It made him appear ordinary, even inconspicuous, which must have been an obvious advantage in his chosen career. An athletic physique suggested regular gym sessions and a pride in his appearance. He seemed flushed, but a naturally fresh face, framed by auburn hair, would have made him prone to revealing the signs of exertion. He must have been close to retirement or, at least, being farmed out for administration work in one of the Chief Constable's offices, in his beloved Wales. On social occasions he constantly reminded me of this long-held ambition.

He turned immediately to the business at hand, in his normal efficient manner. "The tape recorder will save the time of writing everything down, but it'll remain in my possession and will not be transcribed, without your agreement."

I nodded. Julian took notes, in the manner of his meticulous lawyer's training.

"First, tell me briefly what's so important about these scrolls the Cardinal gave you?" The Superintendent leant forward, switching the machine on and sitting back in his chair.

"Where do you want me to start?" I hesitated, whilst gathering my thoughts. "The impact on society and particularly the Catholic Church, when they're published, is bound to be dramatic." I said.

"Well, I can't pretend to be a theological scholar, but summarize it for me. My knowledge of the bible is limited and stems from Sunday school in the village chapel forty years ago."

I shook my head, taking a deep breath. "Briefly, and I mean briefly, the true teachings of Christ went underground after a struggle, for three centuries after his death, between, what we now refer to as Christianity and Gnosticism, which is a more esoteric aspect of it. It's based on the receiving of wisdom or gnosis and is closer to the ancient pagan principles. The importance of the feminine is emphasised, which is why there's such significance to the figure of Mary Magdalene."

"What do you mean by went underground?" He asked quizzically.

I smiled. "The Knights Templar found these Gnostic writings of Christ literally under the Temple in Jerusalem after the First Crusade, but the Catholic Church, who regarded them as heretical, not least, because they took away their power, recovered them from the Templars. They've tried to suppress the teachings ever since."

"Sorry to interrupt, but why did they need to do that?"

I thought for a moment. "A sexual rite, as a sacrament, and the fact the teachings didn't require the Church as an intermediary between the individual and God made them anathema to them. They wanted to preserve their material and spiritual position in the scheme of things and still do. I don't think they're too keen on the idea of Christ having a Royal bloodline from Egypt either, or the fact he may not be the Son of God."

I stopped and smiled again, noticing the pained expression on the Superintendent's face. "Does that help?"

"I'm not sure, I think I'll pass on that one."

I took a deep breath. "There's precedent from the Dead Sea scrolls, where documents passed by Will, from the team investigating them. So I'd like to retain these scrolls." I said.

"I'll do what I can." He nodded.

"What do you intend to do tomorrow morning, have you made any decisions?" He asked.

I looked at Julian and he replied for me.

"We've discussed it. I've told him I'll certify all the copy documents as being examined against the originals, so he doesn't have to risk holding them back. I know from first-hand experience these people can be ruthless, so the first hurdle can be overcome, but afterwards he's helpless. I can't control the situation to ensure his family are returned safely."

"That's where I can step in," the Superintendent said quietly.

Julian lowered his voice and spoke slowly. "The real problem arises only after he hands the documents over. He can't rely on their integrity. He agrees with me, there's only one option." He paused

311

and gestured with an open palm, to the Superintendent. "He desperately needs your help and expertise, but in a way which doesn't jeopardise the safety of his ex-wife and two children."

The Superintendent nodded. "I've a specialist team who can help, but I'd restrict the information to a group of about six of us and I'd hand-pick them myself. They'll keep it tight and no-one else in the Department will know." He stopped and looked at me, expectantly.

I turned to Julian, who nodded in encouragement. "Very well, I agree. What do we do next?" I asked.

"I've a great deal of work to do, as we must install our equipment at the meeting place and I must brief my men. Where do you have to meet them?" He asked.

"At the telephone kiosk, opposite the newsagents at Paddington Railway Station, at noon tomorrow." I replied.

"They may have a person close, to check you're alone, but it'll not be the final meeting place. You'll have instructions to go somewhere else. I'm sure of it. If it's possible, I want you to insist on speaking to your ex-wife. Tell them anything."

"Like what?" I asked, uncomfortable in instinctive situations.

"You can always say that you don't believe they're holding your family, as they often go away on holiday at short notice or something like that. I'm afraid you'll have to improvise."

"How long do I need to talk to them?"

"The longer you keep them talking on the telephone, the easier the trace will become."

"That part sounds fine, but what happens when I move to the next place and you've no surveillance equipment there?" I asked, needing reassurance as to the precise mechanics of the operation.

"But we'll have the equipment there," he smiled.

"How?" I asked.

"Because it'll be on you," he replied.

I screwed up my eyes. "I've done this before. It makes me feel vulnerable. In Paris, I became conscious of it and, consequently, more nervous. If I'm wired, they're bound to frisk me. I get the impression this group are ruthless and professional."

"I don't know what equipment you used, but it's so sophisticated. It shouldn't be a problem. We have one unit, which can be hidden in your belt buckle, if it makes you feel happier. You'll have to keep any coat open, that's all. Even the most intimate of body searches wouldn't discover it. It's not as effective as some of the larger units, but it'll work. I want the final meeting in a public place, if possible, so they'll not be able to do intimate body searches anyway." He smiled again.

"I can't pretend I'm looking forward to this." I said, facial muscles tensing, rather than finding the grace to reciprocate his smile. "But I suppose it's got to be done."

"We're professionals too and you'll have a good team in support. We'll be closer than you think, but no chances will be taken. We could place a device in the lock of the briefcase, but there is a risk they'll have a sweeper, who could detect it."

I made a feeble attempt to smile, but it failed miserably, crossing my face more as a grimace. "When do we set all this up?" I asked.

"I'll meet you with one of my surveillance men, at about eight o'clock in the morning, discreetly, for obvious reasons," he replied, with infectious confidence.

"Why don't we meet in my house in the morning, as John is staying with me tonight." Julian intervened. He wrote his home address and ex-directory home telephone number, on the back of one of his business cards and handed it to the Superintendent.

"That'll be fine. We'll do our own covert surveillance to ensure your home isn't being watched, before we arrive. I'll give you some further instructions then, but I don't want to complicate things today. What would be helpful is all the information you can provide about the person who telephoned, or anyone you anticipate may be involved. I could then do some checks overnight."

I shrugged. "The person who telephoned had a deep English voice, but it wasn't familiar, in any way. All the other people I previously met are either in custody in Paris, except one who is dead." I replied, inadvertently omitting David. "Except for one person I know as David." I added, belatedly.

"Commissaire Moreau in Paris will be able to give you a photograph, as he took his passport, but I don't believe he'll be involved. His daughter Rachel had been held in Paris, although she's now been released, but she wouldn't be involved in this." I stopped after the words spewed out, without thought, recognizing the wisdom of perhaps giving a fuller explanation. "I became involved with her and, in the end, her father argued my case for publication, with his superiors in the Vatican. He telephoned today; leaving a message on the answering service, warning me his representations had failed. Hardly the actions of someone intending to intimidate me, don't you think? In fact, I suspect his life may now be in danger."

The Superintendent tilted his head in one direction, then the other. "We'll do our own checks,

314

in any event. Special Branch have statements and a file on those people on your late uncle's staff. That'll help."

I remembered Ronan at my home "One of the priests on my uncle's staff, Ronan, is actually at my house, at the moment. He was my uncle's closest confidante and the original documents had been shown to him. He's left the St. John's seminary, near Guildford, with the promise of helping me authenticate the scrolls. He's aware of their origins, though I think he is out of his depth. I'd be happier if someone monitored my house to ensure there's no problem. He could be at risk, too."

I looked at the Superintendent. He nodded.

"He's risked his career and changed his life to help." I added. "I'll be ringing him from time to time, but it's not the same. I'd feel guilty if something happened to him, but it needs to be done discreetly, if my family are not to be placed at risk."

"I understand and there'll be no difficulty. In fact, we'd want to carry out observations on him." He wrote some notes in his notebook and switched off the tape recorder. "I'd also like to find out exactly where this girl Rachel is located and the extent of her involvement, so I'll contact the Commissaire."

"I think it'll help," I said.

"The people, who've taken your family, may, of course, want these scrolls for themselves, especially if they're valuable. They could be totally independent of the Vatican or freelancing. If so, they may be more ruthless and consequently, unconcerned about any public backlash or press coverage." He looked stern.

I shook my head. "My fear would be the involvement of the intelligence services. They have more resources than any independents and are more ruthless than anyone freelancing."

He nodded. "I know it's not the reassurance you want, but I must be frank with you. I need information. Is there any way you can communicate with this man David or the girl Rachel? My instinct tells me they may be involved."

A coldness, bleak and empty, crept into my body and I shivered. I began to grasp a semblance of the implications for my family. "I've one telephone number for Rachel, I tried it a few minutes ago, without success. She's told me, there's another scroll, which she intends to give me, when she returns to London. My uncle entrusted her with it."

"… Your legacy for humankind will be the way in which you have delved into the depths of your soul and left a signpost or contribution to the archetype of collective ideas, for others to follow. Everyone who digs deeper, within the well of their subconscious, does so, not just for himself or herself, but also for all of humankind. Reincarnation is such an intrinsic thread of the ancient wisdom, it is entwined with our spiritual destiny, as part of our karmic history. It is the tapestry of our soul, a map of many places in many colours. Destiny is defined in the Mystery schools as the task given to us by our spirit before we were born. It is the choice we have made freely and karma is the action necessary to realign past mistakes, so we undertake our work of destiny. Eventually, all will escape this wheel of rebirth and find the only meaningful source of joy, but they have free will, though few know how to exercise it. Many will choose the path of ignorance first, until they question the complexity of the process of life. Even they will choose in their time. Until then, they must act out their illusions in all their mediocrity, foolishness and limitation. We can only light the path of truth and wisdom, in the hope we inspire others to rise up and open their eyes and hearts. In the meantime, we can find happiness by making a truce with the world, with no promises made for the future, only the present. For there is no past and no future, there is only the One."

CHAPTER 17

A dull wind blew under the roof of the station, as I stood, briefcase in hand, helpless and afraid. My sinews stiffened at the thought, lurking in the back of my mind, of a botched exchange. I still felt insecure with the surveillance device in the buckle of my belt, but realised its necessity. A thick coat, open at the waist, kept me warm, as my eyes writhed in different directions, seeking a flicker of recognition. The stench of stale beer hovered from the bar opposite, where businessmen and tourists mingled in their separate worlds. On the other side, the Newsagents teemed with life, customers jostling each other in the queue for magazines and newspapers. Agitated, I stood rigidly by the telephone kiosk, treating the space around it as my territory, fixing a glare at anyone drifting too close.

Ten minutes, then twenty minutes passed and the telephone remained annoyingly silent. I hated being out of control and picked up the receiver to check it had a dial tone, then replaced it immediately afterwards. I craved normality, away from this ghastly set of circumstances, but knew my destiny appeared fixed, with options limited. I watched pale and hollow faces pour through the concourse, flaunting dour and plain fashions, symptomatic of a miserable environment. I resented this ordeal and the delay, but it made me more determined to fight these nameless people, who dictated to me and threatened violence, as the price for failure to conform.

I shivered. Momentarily forgetting about the device, I closed and buttoned my coat. I had no idea if it still worked with the coat insulating the device.

Another loudspeaker announcement reminded passengers of the arrival on platform six of the train from Swansea stopping at Cardiff, Bristol and Reading. It drowned the sound of the telephone and I hesitated until the second ring made me snatch it.

"Hello." I shouted.

After a short pause, a gruff voice replied. "Go to the reception at the Hilton Hotel in Park Lane. It's only five minutes in a taxi or ten to fifteen minutes in a number 36 bus. There'll be an envelope in reception for you. Follow the directions precisely. We're watching you very closely and your family will be in danger, if you deviate from these instructions or if there's any sign of Police intervention."

"How do I know my family are safe?" I said, but too late, as the caller hung up mid sentence and I found myself talking to myself.

I replaced the receiver and looked around me, but everything seemed normal. I thought quickly, casually opening my coat, in the event it smothered the effectiveness of the device. "I've been asked to go to the Park Lane Hilton and collect an envelope in Reception. I intend to comply." I spoke loud enough for the listening device, yet still gave a ventriloquist impression, in the event binoculars panned my movements. I mimicked a cough, to excuse the hand over my mouth. Unfortunately, these devices had become too familiar, as had my clandestine behaviour.

A taxi took me to the Park Lane Hilton and I walked through the swing doors and across the marbled opulence to the reception area on the right. A charming girl, smiling innocuously, handed me the envelope, as if routine. I moved across, sitting on one of the claret leather chairs opposite, still looking around furtively, but detecting nothing suspicious, only the whiff of routine conversations between sober-suited businessmen. I opened the envelope, which contained typed directions to take a taxi from outside the Hotel to Hyde Park and Speaker's Corner. At that point, someone would take the documents from me. Once they had been authenticated my family would be released. I read the note loud enough for it to be picked up by the Superintendent. There would be no simultaneous exchange, so no guarantees. I guessed as much. I had no choice, but to rely on the expertise of the Police. My belief system may have suggested the mind had some control over the material conditions of my world, but I felt trapped. All mental discipline disintegrated, leaving me within a madman's dream, unable to wake up. Fear is certainly the mind-killer, as one of Frank Herbert's characters would have said.

"You must follow the man taking the briefcase. Please be careful." I said, for the benefit of the Superintendent, my voice cracking.

A taxi pulled up. The Commissionaire pulled open the rear door, for me to gain entry. Inside, I hung on tightly to the briefcase, holding the original scrolls. I had held one back, as insurance. Unless someone particularly knowledgeable examined them immediately, they would never notice the missing scroll. With Rachel's scroll, it meant two scrolls were absent. I guessed the chances of someone understanding the nature of the scrolls and having the linguistic skills to interpret them on the spot had to be remote. It would give me time and, hopefully, it would be all I needed. The responsibility weighed heavily on my shoulders.

The missing scroll happened to be in the middle of the sequence of scrolls. It contained a rebirth ritual, its origins from Egypt, and related a procession to a tomb, where a neophyte would be incarcerated in the ultimate rite of passage. If he lowered his metabolism and survived both the fear and the astral journey, the personality integrated with the spirit. The neophyte could then join the priesthood, as an Initiate, but when the tomb reopened, most failed and perished. Perhaps of greater impact, and the reason I had been reluctant to release it, was its emphasis of Christ as a Priest-King and High Initiate of the Egyptian Mystery Schools, not as a Son of God. The first time he had ever been referred to as a Son of God followed the Council of Nicaea, some three hundred years after his death, when Constantine had to whittle down eighty or so gospels to the few, which would be politically acceptable for the New Testament at that time. Cleverly, he had managed to transfer the remnants of paganism to Christian symbolism. I recalled from theology studies that the process of excluding some gospels continued throughout that fourth century with the Councils of Hippo and Carthage.

The retained scroll contained his teaching of the ancient Egyptian Mysteries to the uninitiated, much to the chagrin of the authorities, particularly the Sanhedrin. It also referred explicitly to his wife (his companion), and to his treatment by the Establishment, as a heretic, undermining him at every opportunity. I knew how disturbing and uncomfortable it would be for orthodox Christians to accept the concept of Christ as heretic, for it still troubled me and was bound to trigger outrage and hostility.

This ceremony of rebirth had passed into the hands of Christ's Nazarenes. At the end of the First Crusade, Hugues de Payne re-discovered it, beneath the Temple in Jerusalem. According to this scroll, this was the reason part of Christ's mission became the salvation of the personality and not the soul, a subtlety lost on the Orthodox Church. After a few minutes, I jolted back from my thoughts and daydreaming, when the taxi driver addressed me by name.

321

"Are you Mr O'Rourke?" He asked, looking at me in the rear-view mirror. He was a young swarthy man in his thirties, with jet-black hair, unshaven for perhaps three days and wearing a white open-necked shirt and yellow V-neck sweater. His look was intense, though his eyes shifted between the road ahead and the mirror. He chewed gum, as if he was attacking it.

"How do you know my name?"

"I've been instructed to collect a briefcase from you and have been paid in cash to deliver it to an address, in the centre of London. I'll receive a further payment on delivery." He studiously looked in the mirror again. "They told me not to engage in any conversation with you or else the rest of the money will be withheld."

I played for time. "I've strict instructions too, which I must follow, precisely. So I can't pass anything over to you. I hand over my briefcase only at Speaker's Corner in Hyde Park and nowhere else."

"That's stupid, no-one will be there." He said, angrily.

"I intend to do exactly what I've been told to do. Tell me where do you have to deliver the briefcase?" I asked, even if I didn't expect an answer. We had reached Hyde Park Corner and traffic snarled slowly at the intersection, more so than usual.

"I can't tell you that." He replied, moving ahead slowly in the traffic congestion.

"Do you know what's in this briefcase?" I asked.

"No, and I'm not really interested." He became agitated, tooting the horn aggressively at a motorcyclist, weaving in front of him. It was symptomatic of his demeanour.

I leant forward towards the driver's seat. The time had come to take a chance.

"If you don't tell me where you're instructed to deliver this briefcase and its contents, you may find yourself in serious trouble with the Police. My ex-wife and two children have been kidnapped and I'm being blackmailed. If you don't co-operate you may be facing the prospect of a long term of imprisonment, as an accessory to these serious crimes."

He pulled sharply in front of another car and crossed lanes, muttering under his breath, two minutes elapsed before he replied. "I think you're talking bullshit. All I'm doing is collecting a passenger and a parcel and delivering it. If you tell me you're not handing over the briefcase, it's no skin off my nose. I'll just report the facts to them." He raised his voice and took his right hand from the steering wheel, gesturing wildly.

"How will you report to them?" I asked.

He grunted, but didn't reply.

"I warn you, the moment you know what's involved, you cease to be simply collecting a passenger and delivering a parcel. You've become part of the enterprise and culpable."

"If you tell me you're not handing over the briefcase, there isn't a problem." He shrugged.

"I've not said I'll not hand it over, but it will not be here, only at Speaker's Corner. I intend to take all steps necessary, to ensure my family are protected and safe."

"That's nothing to do with me." He said, pulling over to a parking area near Hyde Park.

"I need reassurances about my family. I want to know when and how they'll be released. Why should I hand over these documents, if you're unable to give me this information? You're just a runner for the main man and I'll only hand it over to him."

The tightrope, I walked, had its dangers, but I rationalised my decisions as reasonable in the circumstances and, therefore, likely to have been anticipated. They must have had a contingency plan.

After the taxi had stopped, the driver turned around to face me. "For the last time, are you going to hand over the briefcase?" His eyes darted around outside the taxi and again towards me. He nervously stroked his head.

"I'm going to Speaker's Corner, in accordance with the instructions I've been given. I'm asking you, for the last time. Will you tell me where these documents have to be delivered and how you contact them?"

He looked outside the taxi again, shaking his head. I waited for a reply. When none came, I opened the rear door and began to get out. If I could, at least, drag him away from his taxi, it might give the Police time to place a tracking device on the vehicle.

The driver's window wound down, as I alighted from the rear. He shouted to me. "If I come with you to Speaker's Corner, will you hand over the briefcase then?"

'Good', I thought, as I pondered a response. "If no-one else arrives, within a few minutes, perhaps I'll hand it over, but I'm not happy about it. I want some information from you, first. It's only reasonable to have some reassurance about the well-being of my family. Anyway, what do you have to lose by coming with me?"

For a moment, he looked ahead and didn't move, so I answered my own question. "Are you afraid of a parking ticket or do you think, in just a few minutes, some sort of tracking device could be placed on your taxi. Isn't it obvious, I'm totally on my own." I needed to give a hint, about a tracking device, to the Superintendent. I coaxed and cajoled the taxi-driver, until he opened the driver's door and followed me, still glancing back at his taxi, as we walked away. He was a short man, though stocky. It gave me confidence to look down on him. If the Police were to do their job properly, I had to distract him completely.

"Please give me some information about the people who've paid you. Place yourself in my position. I've an ex-wife and two beautiful girls I must protect." I pleaded and would have begged, if necessary. My free hand moved animatedly, emphasising the words.

He shifted his walking pattern, his eyes suspiciously looking around and upwards for inspiration. The sun peeked out from behind a cloud, as if in response, but he still appeared reluctant to speak.

"What's the problem?" I asked, fixing my eyes on him. The sound of oddballs and preachers, pronouncing the imminent end of the world from their soapboxes intruded harshly into the calm space I was trying to create inside my head.. I had little time. A dog, loose from its leash, snapped at my heels and barked.

"I need your help." I said, worried the noise would prevent any response being picked up on the surveillance device, in my belt. I removed my coat, perspiration made me feel uncomfortable. I stopped a little distance from the orators and turned towards him. He stopped, as if by reflex action. "Please help me?" I pleaded, more passionately than before.

"I can't." He replied immediately, lifting up his gaudy yellow sweater and pointing to a bump in his white shirt.

The idea of the taxi driver having his own surveillance device had not occurred to me. I groaned with a silent prayer into the heavens, as everyone does in times of crisis, fearing I had prejudiced my position and placed Katie and the girls in jeopardy.

"It wouldn't be worth the risk to help you. Believe me, I know these people," he said.

A shiver shot down my spine. I had started the bluff and had to play the game through to the end. I urged my brain into action. "Let me make something clear. I've no objection to handing over the briefcase, but I want to know my family are well. I must know what arrangements are in place to exchange them for the documents. I'm prepared to wait here, until they respond. I'll be reasonable, but I need some good faith from your associates."

He sighed. "They are not my associates." He paused and turned away. "Did you hear that? What do you want me to do?" He asked his phantom colleague on the other end of the device.

He turned back and I pointed to a bench seat on a pathway nearby. "Let's sit down, whilst we await further information." He nodded.

I wished I could have opted for an earpiece as well, to have some dialogue with the Superintendent, but appreciated the additional risk. I had to keep my brain alert and positive, but I wanted to be more proactive, as time passed slowly.

"Can you tell me anything at all about the arrangements for the exchange?" I whispered, bored with the inactivity.

He merely grunted, refusing the bait and looking away.

A stream of unhappy jangled thoughts and unpleasant outcomes flowed through my brain. I tried to resist them, but felt alone, despite being surrounded by crowds of people. I focused my mind, knowing all insoluble problems eventually yielded to determined effort, provided one remained positive. I needed inspiration to unlock the ugly prison of circumstances, which had so cruelly incarcerated me. Half an hour of strained silence elapsed, before a middle-aged man, walking his dog, approached us. He was scruffy, bearded and wore an old coat, desperately in need of dry cleaning.

"I've been asked to hand this to you." He said, offering a small brown envelope to me. He walked away, muttering to himself, as he did. I clawed at the envelope, almost demolishing it, in my struggle to open it. Inside, a note had been written. I recognised Katie's handwriting. I read the note aloud for the benefit of the taxi-driver and for the more sinister reason of relaying the contents to the Police.

"John. The girls and I are safe. You have some documents, which belong to these people. They want you to hand them over to the taxi-driver. Once they've examined them, they have promised we will be released, unharmed, immediately. I'm looking forward to having dinner with you again at our favourite restaurant by the river. Katie."

The last sentence puzzled me. It appeared irrelevant and incongruous, but I handed over the briefcase nevertheless. If the Police hadn't sufficient time to get their act together after this time, they never would. I had to trust their efficiency and could do nothing more. The taxi driver grabbed the briefcase, quickly scuttling back to his taxi. I walked, more sedately, towards the main thoroughfare, waiting for a policeman to make contact. As the taxi-driver moved out of sight I began to talk more freely to the Superintendent.

"Gwyn, I hope you've placed some sort of tracking device on his taxi and everything is properly in place. I'm relying on you."

I pondered on the strange last sentence of the note from Katie, something didn't seem right, but I couldn't put my finger on what, in particular, had been out of place. I walked towards the road, where a taxi waited. The other one had disappeared.

"Mr O'Rourke, Superintendent Thomas asked me to collect you. We use this vehicle for surveillance duties. If someone is watching you, they'll not be suspicious. My name is Sergeant Connor. Forgive the shabby clothes, but it's necessary." He showed me his warrant card. He wore trousers, more suitable for the golf course, a check sports shirt and a naff woollen cardigan. I jumped into the back of the taxi, closing the door behind me and sinking heavily into the seat.

"Katie was trying to pass on some sort of message in her note, but I'm at a loss to understand it." I said to the Sergeant. "There is some sort of subtle nuance, on the last part of the note."

"Don't worry, sir, they'll not lose the taxi-driver. We've sophisticated systems in operation. I've Superintendent Thomas on the other end of this radio transmitter. Will you speak to him?" He handed me the radio, explaining which buttons to use, depending on whether I wanted to talk or listen.

"We're following the taxi at a safe distance," he said. "I thought you'd want to know Cardinal Montagne has telephoned my office. He said the men, who have taken your family, are definitely unconnected to the Vatican. They are all freelance contractors. I'm inclined to believe him. He sounded sincere."

"We'll see. Gwyn, I'm sure there's a hidden message from Katie in the note I read out, but for the life of me, I can't think what it is."

"Well, if you get inspiration, pick up the radio. No one else will be on this frequency. I must concentrate on controlling the situation this end."

I handed the device back to the Sergeant, as messages relayed from time to time on the transmitter, with precise details of their location.

"If you know what direction they're travelling, can you follow?" I asked.

"Yes, we all have orders to converge on a specific signal, but not before." He looked in the mirror and smiled. "Don't worry. I'll be close enough."

I did worry and racked my brains over the message. Katie enjoyed a number of restaurants, but not one I could recall, in particular. She enjoyed a restaurant called, The Tower, but it wasn't by the river, so it didn't make sense. The only restaurant we used to frequent by a river was a floating barge, by the Jolly Farmer pub in Guildford. She couldn't be there and still have written the note and conveyed it to me. There was insufficient time. I listened to the radio messages, crackling with hurried voices and urgent tones. A flurry of vocal activity followed, as the Superintendent advised everyone that the taxi had stopped and parked.

Sergeant O'Connor looked in the mirror. "I'll move in a little closer, but I have instructions that no-one is to close in on the taxi-driver until the Superintendent gives the word."

"Where's the taxi stopped?" I asked, with a degree of calmness.

"I understand it's somewhere close to the Tower of London," he replied.

I thought, for a moment, and it hit me. "Can I have the radio, quickly?" I shouted to him, gesturing to the device, impatiently. I snatched it rudely from his hand and spoke to the

Superintendent immediately. "Gwyn, I think I understand the message. One of her favourite restaurants is 'The Tower', but it's not by the river and so I didn't understand. Another restaurant she favours is on a barge, on a river in Guildford. So I believe it's possible they're being held on a barge, somewhere close to the Tower of London and Tower Bridge. Can you arrange for a police launch to intercept it?" I paused, choking on the words and swallowing hard. "Please, make sure my family are safe." I added, my agitated voice trembling with emotion.

"... One of my disciples once asked me of a man born blind. Who has sinned? Is it this man or his father? I could not be angry with him, as people still cannot see what is in front of their eyes. For him to have sinned when he was born blind must inevitable mean he sinned in another lifetime. Although many accept the principle of living many lives and some recall events from past lives, I fear a more orthodox establishment will bury the knowledge. Do they not see that it is an explanation of the supreme form of justice and equality. For what a person does not learn in one life, he can learn in another. Does he not intuitively realise his consciousness is not part of the physical vessel he inhabits temporarily? A more orthodox church will use knowledge for themselves. It will be their way of retaining external power, with the personal right of the Priest to grant salvation to the soul. I have heard Paul preach of it and it is a betrayal of the truth. They will be the ones who, as with the Pharisees, are spiritually blind. The omens shed dark clouds, which can only bring misery to people's lives, if they allow themselves to be duped into this falsehood. How can they be so foolish? The scriptures must record the evidence, even my cousin John, known as 'the Baptist', is the reincarnation of the prophet Elijah. I have to believe the intrinsic goodness in people will eventually bring them to the Light and allow them to lift up their hearts to the understanding of the glorious and simple truth of spiritual destiny through many lives until they eventually see the illusion of the matrix and return to the only truth and harmony that exists in the One. Without this knowledge, death, in all its finality stalks every tragedy. I teach my disciples that death is the result of so much negative energy accumulating that spiritual transformation is no

longer possible in this lifetime. It triggers the wheels of rebirth, as a natural process. In this context, it is a purifying experience and the journey towards transformation continues in the next incarnation. I hope they understand that evolved people, truly spiritual beings, already have their essence in the Kingdom and departure from the physical body is as simple as going to sleep or thinking your way to a new destination."

CHAPTER 18

I sat back in the taxi, stomach churning, as confusing messages crammed the airwaves, in a commotion of different voices. My head spun. There had to be more I could do, but instinctive impatience could sabotage rational thought. My natural disposition may have leant towards optimism, but the vacuum created by this passive role allowed glimpses of a more malignant outcome to flood into my brain again. I realised both the optimist and the pessimist were right, each from their own point of view, and I determined not to adopt the victim's role. A new cycle of pain and suffering, cascading into the future, could be the consequence of fear accessing the dark recesses of my mind. I barricaded the door.

"Hurry!" I leaned forward in the seat and snapped at the Sergeant, unreasonably.

He didn't reply. I could see the landmark of the Tower of London in the distance, but traffic trundled slowly. The Sergeant flitted in and out of the bus lanes and jumped the lights, tooting his horn loudly, as he incurred the wrath of other road users. Perspiration dripped down my forehead, as nervous energy quickened my pulse and I flustered. I slipped off my coat, placing it on the seat alongside me and readied myself to jump out of the taxi when it stopped. I moved towards the door, placing my hand on the handle. The Sergeant observed in his mirror.

"They'll not do anything, until the Police Launch is in position. So don't ruin their plans, by acting impulsively. You must leave it to the professionals. It's important you are disciplined." He said politely, but firmly. With some difficulty, I sat back in the seat, but rocked back and for nervously. Eventually, we arrived at the Tower. Its aura of history didn't touch me, my mind focusing elsewhere. Out of sight of the river, a cordon of police officers and vehicles blocked our path. Although cloudy again and cold, it remained dry. Only one thing mattered. Inclement weather could not deter me from doing whatever was necessary to protect my family. I exited the taxi with the Sergeant. He displayed his warrant card, to gain us access through to a walled courtyard-like area, where plain-clothed police officers waited quietly in clandestine fashion. Some had bullet-proof vests with heavy guns clearly visible. I ran towards the Superintendent nearby, almost twisting my ankle on the uneven cobbled stones in my haste.

He placed his hand on my arm and gently moved me back against the wall. "We have the grounds covered, but the Police Launch hasn't arrived yet. We must wait a little longer."

I shook my head, feeling my face redden. "No, we can't wait." I said, pushing him to one side. I raced towards the gate, until another police officer rushed across, smothering me, forcing me backwards. We both fell on the floor in a heap, with him on top of me. I winced in pain and groaned, then suppressed it, realising the foolishness of my actions.

The Superintendent moved towards me, helping me to my feet. "The engines of the barge haven't started and so we've time on our side. It can't travel quickly anyway. I must speak to the taxi driver. He's inside and nothing will happen, until he leaves. He can tell us how many people are on board and where your ex-wife and girls are being kept. We'd like that information, for their sake."

"Yes, but…"

"John, listen to me. If you were not a friend, you wouldn't even be here. Trust me."

It sounded sensible, but being so close to the girls, yet so far away, gave me a sense of helplessness. I hated losing control. Sheepishly, I walked, shoulders hunched, behind the wall.

"Our own surveillance devices have picked up a child crying and, at least, three men, " he said.

"Perhaps the taxi driver will still be wired up when he leaves. It was under his ribcage, beneath his shirt," I said, my mind bracing itself for all possibilities.

He looked sympathetic. "We'll check it, but his job is done. There'd be no reason to keep it active." Another officer, near the gate, signalled. He nodded and pointed to two other officers standing on the other side of the gate.

Heavy footsteps echoed on the gangplank, then the sound of someone walking towards the gate. He began whistling. Anger flooded my thoughts, but I resisted the temptation to dash out again. The footsteps quickened. A muffled cry was followed by silence. A group of four men, including the taxi driver, appeared from around the corner. The taxi driver's feet trailed heavily across the ground and a detective's hand covered his mouth, as he was dragged across to face the Superintendent, who identified himself.

"Do you understand the importance of being quiet and co-operating with us?" He whispered.

The taxi-driver nodded and the detective removed his hand from his mouth, but the others still held him firmly.

"Now quickly, tell me how many people are on the barge?" The Superintendent looked stern, unblinking and pointed his finger into the man's face.

"I don't, I don't know," he stammered.

"I'll give you one more chance. If you don't co-operate this moment, you'll find yourself in very serious trouble. I want answers and I want them now. You'll find yourself in prison for several years for jointly conspiring to kidnap, and perhaps worse, if anything happens to those people on the barge. You have one chance to help yourself and you must assist us with our enquiries immediately."

He didn't reply and my patience snapped again. I moved forward quickly and punched the taxi driver in the solar plexus. He doubled over, groaning, a groan stifled only by the actions of the officer in replacing his hand over his mouth again. No one stopped me or criticised my actions. The taxi driver hoisted himself back up, with the help of the officers. He took a series of short breaths and quietly bent over again to regain his breath. The Superintendent lifted his head back up, so his face, still grimacing from the blow, looked straight into his own. I'm not going to stop him, if you don't help us."

"Alright." He agreed, taking a deeper breath.

"I'll help, but I didn't see everyone on the barge."

"Talk and talk quickly," the Superintendent demanded.

"Three men are in the room on the right, as you cross the gangplank. I saw another man in the next room. There seemed to be others in there. I think two children and a woman. It looked as if he may have been guarding them or something." He pulled one arm free and mopped his brow. "I didn't see anybody else and that's the truth."

"Is anyone armed?" The questions continued, more politely.

"I didn't see anyone armed in the first room, but the one who appeared to be guarding the others in the second room had a sawn-off shotgun, or something like it, in his hand."

"What does he look like?" The interrogation seemed tedious, especially as I had been desperate for action.

"Balding, forty-ish, stocky and about six feet tall." He replied, face bowed and still contorted.

"Is there anything else you can tell us?"

"Not really." He screwed up his face. "I know the name of the bald man. He is a well-known villain. You're bound to know him. His name is Palmer."

"Is that Johnny Palmer?" the Superintendent asked.

"Yes, that's him," he replied.

"Take him away, but keep him in the car, just in case we need further information." The Superintendent nodded, gesturing to his officers, indicating for others to relay the information to the team. He handed his radio to the Sergeant. At last, a message came from the Police Launch, confirming its imminent arrival. At the same time, I heard the engine on the barge crank into action.

"Quickly, let's go." The Superintendent shouted and a team of men, mostly armed, came from different directions, all converging, by the riverside. Without asking for permission, I ran with them, relieved by the removal of constrictions. The barge looked as if it had seen better days and I quickly scrutinised the layout. The mooring had green slime on its wooden structure and I realised there could be a danger of slipping, but I couldn't slow down. A pungent and distinctive smell, symptomatic of all large rivers, wafted across. I reached the barge at the same time as an occupant began pulling the gangplank, away from its mooring. He noticed the furore, shouting inside. I ran, selecting the least slippery part as a launchpad, and hurdled the side of the barge, just as it began to pull away. I landed noisily, but upright. I saw at least three officers do the same, but others took no risks, pulling up.

"Stop the barge. We're police officers." One Police Officer shouted, unheeded.

Two men came out of the first room, and then turned, as if to return inside. I rugby-tackled the second one and he hit his head against the side of the door with a sickening thud, a gun falling out of his pocket, as he fell. I grabbed it, following the three police officers inside. I had no time to think of any danger. My heart pumped heavily, as never before, and a rush of adrenaline helped me focus. The risks didn't matter. This time, I was not the prey. I saw the two men in the first room pull out handguns, but before they could raise them another officer shouted. "We're an armed Police unit, drop the guns or we'll fire."

One of the men hesitated, before dropping the gun on the floor, lifting his hands in the air. The second one ignored the advice and pointed his gun. A shot fired. For a moment, I couldn't see who had been shot, but the man refusing to surrender, suddenly slumped to the floor like a carcass of meat, blood oozing from his mouth and from a wound in his chest onto the floor. His eyes remained open, startled like a rabbit caught in the headlights of a car. He breathed one last breath, then nothing.

A scream echoed from the next room. One of the officers kicked away the dead man's gun to the side and moved to the second room. I followed, jumping over the dead man's body. The second Police Officer pushed the man, who had surrendered, up on deck, ordering him to remain in full view of the police marksman, with his hands on his head. Having watched his companion die a dog's death, he was unsurprisingly compliant.

Inside the second room, Katie had been bound and tied to a chair, her clothes in disarray. Her long hair dishevelled and tears had dislodged mascara onto her cheeks. Terrified eyes stared out in front of her. My elder daughter Sophie acknowledged me with her eyes, as she, too, sat bound to the chair, sad and forlorn. She began crying. "Help us!" She pleaded.

I forgot my training as a priest and for the first time in my life, I felt I could kill, without hesitation. I raised my left hand, to reassure her, but kept the gun and the other hand behind my back. Next to them Rachel's father David, bound and gagged, had bruises and blood on his face, which had dripped onto the collar of his white shirt. His eyes darted towards the door, then down. I didn't understand the message. At the exit door beyond, the balding man held a sawn-off shotgun, pointing it at Sophie. He held my younger daughter Rebecca in front of him, as a shield. His arm pivoted around her neck, with his elbow at the front, so she was unable to move.

"Daddy, Daddy!" She screamed, until a yank, from the arm of the balding man, shut her up painfully and tearfully. I moved forward in response, but the gun moved, pointing directly at me.

"I wouldn't, if I were you," he shouted and I stopped instinctively.

Rebecca struggled briefly, but to no avail. He edged backwards, slowly. She started to cry again, as he dragged her back with him. I needed to do something, but couldn't risk the girls being harmed. I breathed in sharply and clenched my teeth. Perhaps ten seconds elapsed. It seemed longer, before the elder of the two police officers spoke first. "There are other police officers on this barge. It's surrounded and we've a Police Launch on the river. You can't escape, so don't do anything foolish, to make things worse for yourself." He spoke softly, using both of his hands, palms downward, in a swaying motion, to calm the situation down. The second police officer followed us into the room, aiming his gun at our antagonist.

"Just think about what you're doing and the consequences. Don't be stupid." He kept talking, quietly edging forward, as the man moved backwards.

"Let the girl go. Do you call yourself a man."? I shouted.

His eyes flashed around the room, then behind him through the door, as another gunshot reverberated from below. At that moment, the sound of a loudhailer, from the adjoining Police Launch, urged him to surrender, but still he refused. Another man's voice, from below the stairs beyond the door, shouted up to him. "There's only one other police officer on the barge and he's a dead one. I'm facing life for this. You too, with your record. There's nothing to gain by surrendering. I'll watch the Police Launch, if you cover those inside. Stay by the door."

The sound of footsteps on the stairs, and the shadow of the henchman passing behind, signalled a response from the balding man. "I'll shoot both of the girls before you could get me, now drop the guns on the floor or they'll get it."

The one Police Officer looked at the other. They both nodded, but the younger Officer spoke first, without moving the gun, still aimed at his head. "This is a barge, it's not a speedboat. You're going nowhere. You've not killed anyone yet. You couldn't have known about your friend's actions downstairs. Now be sensible."

"Bullshit! I'll shoot one of the girls, if you don't drop the gun immediately," he said, venomously. His teeth gritted inside a twisted mouth. He had stopped moving backwards and was gaining in confidence. I believed him. He aimed his shotgun more directly at Sophie.

"O.K. no problem." The elder Police Officer agreed, slowly moving his hand downwards and placing his gun carefully on the floor.

The younger Police Officer began to move his gun downwards, but Rebecca pulled up her arm and jolted her elbow into the balding man's groin. He bent down, loosening his grip on Rebecca and she fell to the floor. The shotgun pointed downwards for a moment and before he could raise it, the same Officer lifted his gun and shot him in the chest. He groaned, but didn't move. Then he lifted the shotgun, aiming at the Officer and pulling the trigger.

The Officer fell backwards against the rear wall and slid down, his gun dropping to the floor, with blood spewing out of his face and in a smear down the wall behind him. The balding man pointed the shotgun next, at Sophie. Katie screamed and, before I could raise my gun, the shotgun fired in her direction. Almost simultaneously, David had rocked his chair and lurched in her direction, taking the full force of the blast in his chest. Sophie screamed hysterically, emotionally tortured, but physically unharmed. I reacted quickly, lifting the gun, pointing it into the face of the balding man and pulling the trigger in one movement. It jolted back with the shot, but this time he slumped to the floor in a heap, life seemingly extinguished. The elder Police Officer grabbed his gun from the floor, straddling the body and running to the deck. An exchange of voices, then two shots from a gun followed, with the voice of the Police Officer shouting down. "Everything's resolved up here." I heard him shout to the Launch for an urgent medical team to deal with gunshot wounds and one Police Officer was down.

After untying the children and Katie, I grabbed and hugged Rebecca, then Sophie and their mother. The Police Officer returned, forlornly checking his colleague. David groaned and his eyes flickered open, barely alive. I cradled his head in my arm. I needed to thank him. "You saved my daughter's life, I'll never forget it."

He moved his head slightly forward in acknowledgement and coughed, clearing his throat. Blood spewed everywhere, his features scarcely recognizable, but it was not a time to be squeamish. He spoke weakly. "Maybe I'll get redemption for it. You must understand, Rachel knew nothing about our plans." He hesitated, as his body shuddered. "Help clear her name. It's important to her and for me. I've been a poor father and a bad role-model." He grimaced and his voice cracked. "These men have worked for the Vatican before, but this was personal and for profit. Cardinal Montagne tried to stop them, unsuccessfully. There's another scroll, which your uncle took from the vaults. Rachel's hidden it. I think she intended to return it to you, because she refused to hand it over to us. Promise me you'll help her?" Sad eyes, with no fear of death in them, looked up at me.

I had fallen into the trap of making promises to a dying man before and reluctantly I felt compelled to do it again. "I'll do what I can." I replied, ambiguously.

There was a slight nod of his head. "I was a dead man anyway." He paused, painfully taking a shallow breath. "At least, this way, I'll not be in an unmarked grave." He struggled to breathe, and his body shook. He coughed, taking repeated, strained breaths. "Don't underestimate the Vatican. The new Pope can't control the organisation, no Pope will. The politics are beyond him; they can even support a right-wing dictator like Pinochet, in Chile. It says it all."

I nodded. "Don't talk now. There's a medical team on the way, any moment."

"It's too late for me." He lifted a finger to point, but it dropped down again from the effort. "The scrolls are over there." His eyes panned towards my briefcase. His body heaved, as he tried to speak. "I've sent a letter, with a Declaration, to Rachel and another document. They'll help you. The Declaration will authenticate the scrolls." He fought for each breath. "You're right and I've been wrong. The spirituality of the Templars and the Nazarenes were both inspired by the mysteries of Egypt. In a way, the Templars were descendants of the Valentinian Gnostics of Alexandria." He stopped abruptly, all colour draining from his face.

"What's the other document?" I asked, knowing he had little time.

"A missing scroll," he spluttered. "It contains variations of the Hebrew Atbash cipher, which the Nazarenes and the Essenes used. The

Knights Templar used the same code. It converted the word Baphomet to Sophia or wisdom, but even with this scroll, the Vatican never discovered the Templars' treasure. It remains a mystery. You must know.." He coughed blood onto my clothes and couldn't finish the sentence, but his sunken glaring eyes looked up, one last time. He wheezed. "Tell Rachel I love…" he whispered an unfinished sentence, in his last breath. His body went limp and still. I laid his head back on the floor, before picking up the briefcase. Katie, one arm around each of my girls, consoled them, allowing them to cry until they felt secure again. Even the Police Officer was too stunned to speak.

"Let's get the girls out of here quickly." I said, hastily, viewing the carnage.

The Police Officer nodded. "No problem. Some officers on the Launch are pulling us to the side." He began to react more positively, ushering us onto the deck and speaking to Katie. "Mrs. O'Rourke, we need some information about your kidnapping to be able to question the prisoners, but a detailed statement can wait until tomorrow, perhaps at your home. We've staff specially trained for counselling. You and the girls will need it."

I carried Sophie, who buried her head in my chest. Katie took Rebecca, and we decked and disembarked. A large crowd gathered, drawn from curiosity, by the gunfire. Someone shouted commands and a hefty push backwards, from three or four burly Police Officers, stopped them encroaching upon my traumatised family.

I had anticipated danger to myself, when I made the promise to my uncle, but not the death of innocent people or the risk to my own children. I had been naïve and couldn't prevaricate any more. Once the scrolls had been published, the risks would diminish. I convinced myself.

The Police Officer helped us ashore, before turning to me. "You've killed someone," he said, bleakly and in a matter of fact way. "A detailed statement will be necessary. It saved lives, so this should be a mere formality, I assure you. Again, tomorrow will do."

I felt disorientated. The fact I had killed someone did not register. As a former priest, and with another commandment broken, perhaps it should have done, but life, at that moment, had other priorities.

Amongst the crowd, I noticed the Superintendent at the front, and walked towards him, introducing my family. The Police Officer from the barge briefly explained the events on board. "I'll need the briefcase, simply for evidential purposes. I'll do my best to return it, as quickly as possible," he asked, respectfully.

I shook my head. "I'm reluctant to hand it over. I mentioned this to you, before your involvement. The Vatican have huge influence and you'll find yourself under pressure to relinquish them."

"But I've promised you, they'll be returned."

"It'll not be as simple as that. You must also understand the scrolls could be damaged by exposure to humidity and air generally. Though they're currently wrapped in silk for protection. They've immense value, way beyond financial considerations. I think you can justify me retaining them, for those reasons."

He thought for a moment before replying. "Yes, very well, but I'll need to examine them and I want an undertaking you'll hold them secure and strictly to my order. They may be needed at Court."

"I'll agree to that. If the Vatican make any claim to them, let them take action in the British

Courts. It'll be the best, and most credible way, of authenticating them." I said.

At New Scotland Yard, the Superintendent took brief details from everyone. He took Katie to one side, informing her a medical examination would be necessary, immediately, by a Police Doctor, who was already present. There would only be a minimal delay. She assured the Superintendent neither she, nor the girls, had been sexually assaulted, in any way. He asked me to remain, to assist further. Katie and the girls were soon free to go.

I spoke to her, before she left. "I want to spend some time with the girls for a while. Can I stay in the guest- room, until the girls have recovered from their ordeal?" I asked

She nodded, as if by instinct and her eyes stared blankly ahead.

"I'll finish the business here, secure the scrolls, and telephone when I'm on my way." I said.

She appeared as if she was in some form of trance and was unable to speak. I hugged the children, before walking into the Superintendent's Office, sitting with my back to the door.

"We managed to pick her up the girl Rachel. I didn't want to say anything, until your ex-wife had left."

"Where is she?" I asked.

"Downstairs," he replied, coldly. "She doesn't know about her father's death. I'd like you to tell her. You can use my room."

"Do you want me to tell her, now?" I screwed up my face at the prospect.

"She's got to be told before she can leave and it's always better coming from someone known to her. One of my officers has been taking a witness statement from her about the death of your uncle.

This time, we've told her she's not to leave the country, without informing us first."

Before I could respond, or even agree, the Superintendent walked out of the room, leaving me stranded and rooted to my chair, unable to think how I could possibly explain her father's death. In no time, I heard the door open behind me and turned around, standing to face a smiling Rachel, elegantly attired, as usual. I didn't know what to say, or what to do. I remained stone-faced, unsmiling. I spoke coldly and quietly. "Sit down. I've something to tell you." I gestured to my chair. "It's bad news."

I pulled up another, so I could sit next to her. I held her hand and looked directly at her, but said nothing. I hoped the body language would convey the message, at a pace, with which she could cope. I thought about the words I could use, but none were appropriate.

"It's my father. Something has happened to him." She blurted out.

I nodded. She buried her head in my chest and sobbed. I stroked her hair. "Just let it all out, it's healthy to cry." She held on tightly.

"If it's any consolation, your father died saving the life of my elder daughter. He threw himself in front of her, when a shotgun was fired. His last words were to tell you he loved you."

The sobbing increased in its intensity and it seemed little comfort. After a few minutes, she lifted her head, drying her eyes with a tissue. "I half expected it," she said, with one last sob, shaking her head. "I tried desperately all my life, to make him love me. He never told me."

"I think your father knew his life was at risk. I don't believe he thought he'd ever see you again." I replied, squeezing her hand.

She nodded. "The last thing my father said to

me, on the telephone, related to Ronan. He'd been
the one who informed the Vatican about the location
of the stolen scrolls in the first place. He said to be
careful of him."

"Is that right?" I shook my head.

"It's what he said." He took a deep breath. "I
also have to collect a parcel, which he's sent to me.
It's at my local Post Office."

"... I have instructed my brother James, who may use the name of Joseph of Arimathea, to act in the event of my premature death. Nicodemus, though a secret disciple, will help him. If the worst happens, he must sever my head, in the way of my forefathers in Egypt and embalm it. Proof will be needed of my mortality and will prevent any attempt by extremists to deify me. If he is not careful, those who now tempt me with Kingship will, on my death, suggest I took a physical assumption to heaven. Though they misunderstand the nature of it, they still long for the promised Messiah and will manipulate the truth in their search and in their impatience. Without this evidence, my beloved Nazarenes, their wisdom teaching and all they have strived for, will be gravely discredited and brought into disrepute. I am not even their leader. It is absurd. I would rather die and be remembered as a revolutionary and a political agitator. At least, in that way, as a religious rebel, a more accurate biography of my life's work would be recorded. Though I fear it will not be so. My mystical training will enable me to create a well of knowledge, which others may eventually discover when they search for truth with a pure heart. They must dig deep, for it will be buried beneath many layers of consciousness. I would welcome my death, if I felt my spiritual work and destiny was complete. Only then would it be time to leave this physical body and enter the higher realms of spiritual existence and merge with the One that exists beyond this illusion in which we live. I meditate on my mission and pray it is not ill-fated and incomplete. It is something, which takes my thoughts in moments of contemplation, when I see my work being contaminated by those who seek personal power and are blind to the true reality".

CHAPTER 19

I retained little confidence in my ability to honour the deathbed promise to my uncle. The price had been too high and lethargy took away my willpower and my courage. I knew evil took its first foothold from apathy, but if given a choice between the retention and publication of the scrolls and the safety of my children, there had to be no contest.

I drifted into Katie's bed, more by familiarity, than intention, but indulged myself with excuses, as all do. Intermittent sleep patterns disrupted poignant dreams and I needed someone beside me. Troubled demons painted conflicting landscapes. Surges of hateful emotion were directed at real and imagined adversaries. It ravaged my mind and body in a tragic testimony to events. Innocence, even of children, created no protection from the torment of nightmares. Fear had left its ugly imprint, visible to everyone and the ritual of routine would take over, anaesthetizing the senses.

In my attempts to publish the scrolls, I had become arrogant. It was a flaw of the ego, which always led to a corrective action. Only the solace of family comforted me, even if my ex-wife's perceived betrayal had first evicted me from the hearth fire.

I had heard nothing from Jean in France or from Rachel. I knew I could not reveal details of the scroll in Rachel's possession. It would place her in danger and I had created enough havoc and turmoil in her life, so I remained silent. The Superintendent had pledged covert surveillance systems. I would have to trust them.

My Editor friend telephoned twice, pressing me for the promised exclusive. I asked him for time, reminded him of the suffering being endured by my family. In fairness to him, he showed patience and sympathized. In the meantime, I sifted through copies of the interpreted scrolls, in an attempt to seek inspiration, but little enthusiasm stirred. A separate journey to the centre of my soul took precedence, though circumstances soon spurred action. A heavy knock on the door, signalled a confrontation with a Chief Inspector of Police. A tall unattractive man with dark hair, yellowish unhealthy skin, I guessed probably from alcohol or liver damage, and deep-sunken eyes. Katie invited him inside and left him alone with me in the dining room, edging into the adjoining kitchen for privacy.

"Superintendent Thomas has asked me to call. Here's my card."

The card had his picture embossed upon it. It looked more like a mug shot. I smiled to myself.

"Chief Inspector McGaughey." I read out the name. "What can I do for you?"

"We need the original scrolls urgently. They're evidence in serious allegations of murder and kidnapping and our forensic laboratory insist they be examined immediately. I've been instructed to collect them, even if they're not in your immediate possession."

Something did not ring true. "I'm sorry, I don't understand. You'll not need the original scrolls to prove these allegations against the man who surrendered on the barge. They're irrelevant. It's not as if you're looking for fingerprints to prove involvement in a crime, is it? You've adequate and ample evidence without them." I said, shaking my head.

"Sir, I'm a police officer, just doing my duty. I must inform you, if you attempt to interfere with my enquiries or withhold evidence, I'm authorised to use such force, as is reasonable, to detain you."

He raised his voice, to match the threat. "Now, do I have to arrest you to get your cooperation?" I ignored the threat and walked to the telephone. "Please, sit down for a minute," I said, dialling the Superintendent's number.

He disregarded the invitation, instead walking towards me, eyes blazing. "What are you doing?" He bellowed.

"I'm ringing Superintendent Thomas. I've an agreement with him and, as a matter of integrity, I don't believe he'd break it."

"Are you calling me a liar?" He asked, snatching the phone out of my hand, before I had been connected.

I didn't budge, but took hold of the receiver again, pushing my face against his. "You'll have to arrest me and I'll resist arrest. Your evidence will have to be compelling; if you intend to satisfy a Court you're acting reasonably. You're in someone's house, acting contrary to an agreement I've reached with a higher ranking officer and you're refusing to allow me to clarify your instructions. You may be used to bullying or controlling people, but you're not going to control me, so stop the drama."

I stared at him, until he relented. He released his grip and stepped back, away from the telephone. I picked up the receiver, to hear an exasperated Superintendent trying to get a response. The Chief Inspector retreated to the side of the room. "I'm sorry, it's John here. I've a Chief Inspector McGaughey here and he's demanding the original scrolls and threatening me. He suggests his instructions originate from you. Is that right?"

The Superintendent replied immediately. "I've been under enormous pressure to recover the scrolls. The Metropolitan Police Commissioner has seconded the Chief Inspector from special duties. I've been ordered to take the scrolls back, but I intended to speak to you personally first. You were obviously right. I didn't anticipate the flak."

"You know I'll not agree to hand them over willingly." I said.

"I didn't authorise the Chief Inspector's visit and wouldn't have done so, without discussing it with you." He paused. I heard something muttered inaudibly, in the background. "John, I want you to put McGaughey on the telephone. Is there a way you can disappear for a few days, while I try to sort something out?"

"What do you mean?" I asked, naively.

"You know what I'm saying. I can keep McGaughey engaged on the telephone, for a few minutes. He's still subordinate to me, so just grab a few basics and leave. I'll try and resolve the difficulties. I'll ask for a personal meeting with the Police Commissioner to tell him I've made a personal promise to you. If he insists I implement a direct order, I'll offer my resignation. Let me speak to McGaughey."

"I appreciate your help." I handed the telephone to the Chief Inspector and drifted into the kitchen to a sad-faced Katie, her eyes on the verge of tears. Stress had caused tension lines to stretch across her forehead.

"Quickly, I don't have much time." I whispered, taking her through to the conservatory, for privacy. "The Superintendent has suggested I leave. He'll try and sort everything out."

Her head dropped and she didn't reply.

"I can ring you tonight, but it's better this way. All I do is cause you aggravation. When the girls get back from school, tell them I'll see them soon. Distract the Chief Inspector for me. Tell him I'm in the bathroom or something."

"I don't want you to go again. It's not fair. You can't keep coming and going like this. If you leave, then don't come back," she said, angrily.

I gestured to the dining room. "Please don't create a scene. It'll cause me a huge problem. I'm just doing what the Superintendent has recommended."

She looked down again, before moving to the bathroom, collecting and handing me a toilet bag and a holdall with some clothes. I gathered my briefcase and car keys. For a moment, she said nothing, but looked soulful.

"Don't make me feel more guilty than I do already." I said, tugging at the front door violently.

"Alright, you take care, but I don't think I want you to stay here again", she whispered.

"You don't mean that," I said.

"Test me," she replied firmly.

"I understand." I sighed, knowing I had little time for argument. She turned and walked back, in the direction of the dining room. I did understand and sympathized. My own emotions had cart-wheeled in many different directions. It did nothing for a stable home. Crises normally brought the best out of my character, but these were not normal circumstances. Traditionally, it seemed to me, it was only in moments of crisis did the personality awaken to the potential of the soul or did anyone devote time to heartfelt prayer. I posed little threat to the Vatican in the subdued frame of mind, in which I had wallowed, since the incident on the barge. Ironically, they were the ones provoking me into positive action. I kick-started my brain, by mapping out a likely safe venue, with a list of people to contact and things to do.

First, a meeting with Rachel had become essential. If she had told the Police about the documents, she may already have surrendered them. I needed to examine the sequestered scroll, together with the documents and scroll posted to her by her father, but she didn't answer her telephone. I returned home to collect more belongings and speak to Ronan. He remained comfortably ensconced, apparently untroubled, and with no signs of Police surveillance.

"Rachel called yesterday. I told her you were spending some time with your children."

"Did she sound distressed at all?" I asked

He shook his head. "She was a little subdued, but she understood." He lifted those bushy eyebrows, his demeanour revealed nothing, no passion, no movement of the eyes, only an unreal blandness.

"Did she leave a message or say what she's doing?" I asked, hopefully.

"She said she'd contact you in a couple of days," he replied.

I moved around the house, gathering items I needed and unlocked the study. Ronan hovered in the background. "Has anyone else called or telephoned?" I asked.

"I've made a list of the telephone calls and messages on the pad there." He pointed to a notepad, next to the telephone, back in the hall. "Only cold-calling salesmen or charity workers have called at the house. No-one has asked for you," he added.

"What about messages on the answer-service?" I queried, bundling some clothes from the airing cupboard into my bag.

"I've usually popped out for a walk and some fresh air in the afternoons, so there may be some messages."

I moved towards the telephone, grabbing the notepad and slipping it into my inside pocket. I dialled the answering service. Three messages, two of no consequence, but the third, from Rachel.

"In the circumstances, I felt it wiser to leave a message on your car phone. I've had no response, so I thought I'd ask you to check it, if you haven't done it already. Bye. Rachel."

I suspected Ronan knew the message, but I had finished my business here and needed to return to my car. "I'll ring you later today or tomorrow at the latest." I said, speeding through the front door. "Is there anything you want?" I asked, opening the car door.

"Not at all. I walk to the shops if I want anything," he replied, closing the front door behind him.

I played back the message from Rachel on the car phone. "The police have telephoned and asked me to attend New Scotland Yard with any scrolls in my possession. I need your advice urgently. I thought it safer to leave the house, so I've posted a registered letter to your office, marked 'strictly private and confidential'. My address will be on it and a telephone number, where I can be contacted. Speak to you soon."

'Smart girl', I thought, and drove directly to my office. I scoured neighbouring properties and motor vehicles for signs of surveillance, without noticing any. Within minutes, I collected all mail, discarding useless blurb and locating two registered letters, but only one marked 'strictly private and confidential'. I ripped open the envelope and read the note inside.

"I'm staying with a first cousin, she's a good friend. Her address is "St. Davids", Glanmor Terrace, New Quay, Ceredigion, West Wales. I've put some distance between the police and myself. Can I speak to you or see you, as quickly as possible? I still have the documents from my father. They've had to do a police post-mortem examination and also a separate one, by an expert on behalf of the defence. Apparently, this is because the man, who surrendered on the barge, has been charged with murder, jointly with the others who died. I don't understand it, but I've been unable to arrange his funeral. It's distressing. Please telephone."

She left her number. I sensed it was unwise to telephone from the office, so walked to the adjoining office, where an acquaintance allowed me the use of his office for the purpose. I soon connected to Rachel. Something stirred; even the sound of her voice had a strange effect on my metabolism. I couldn't control it.

"I must see you. Do you want me to travel down to West Wales?" I asked.

"Unless you'd rather meet me somewhere else," she replied.

"No. I can't stay here anyway. I can get there in about four hours, if I leave immediately. I have a bag with some overnight things in the car. Can your cousin put me up for the night or recommend accommodation?"

Rachel shouted to someone her end and, within seconds, confirmed the arrangements. "Not a problem. You'll love the house. It overlooks the harbour and the village itself is straight out of Dylan Thomas and 'Under Milkwood'. There's even blind Captain Cat's perch, at his window in the Crow's Nest in the Yacht Club. You'll understand, when you see the place."

I laughed at her enthusiasm for the place, but she had that effect on me.

"Don't laugh. It really is exactly as I've described it. He actually lived here for a time. His wife Caitlin said this had been his most creative and prolific period and New Quay, not Laugharn as most people thought, had been his inspiration for 'Under Milkwood.'

I still laughed. "Sounds wonderful. I'll telephone from a call box, when I'm close. It's safer. I'm becoming paranoid about surveillance devices everywhere."

"Good. See you soon," she said, cheerily.

Throughout the journey, I regularly checked any vehicles, which followed for a significant period of time. I slowed down, pulling off the M4 motorway to the services at Newbury, when I noticed a black Mercedes, with tinted windows, behind me. It passed, without exiting, so I rejoined the motorway and drove on. I crossed the new Severn Bridge, but as I reached the services, at junction thirty-three, I screwed up my eyes, peering into the rear-view mirror, certain I recognized the same car. I slowed down again. This time the vehicle drove off at junction thirty-four. I drove on warily and vigilant, cruising at eighty miles per hour until Carmarthen, before deviating northwest on smaller roads. At Llandysul, I stopped at a call box and took last-minute instructions from Rachel.

Within thirty minutes, I found myself trundling down the hill and around the one-way system. Eventually, driving down Glanmor Terrace, until the uniqueness of New Quay opened up, every bit as breathtaking as Rachel's description. The evening sun still allowed views across the bay north towards Aberystwyth and beyond, but a breeze, wafting the smells of the sea on its wings, made warmer clothes a necessity for those sitting out on the cliff-top promenade. The lilt of the Welsh

357

language mingled with the occasional English accent. I noticed the Yacht Club on the left, at the entrance to the harbour and immediately understood the analogy painted on the telephone.

Rachel gave me a warm, if restrained, welcome. She wore an appealing off the shoulder, white, lace-edged dress. "I must look a sight after all the crying I've done."

I felt warm in her presence. "Yes, a sight for sore eyes," I said, holding my arms out for an embrace.

"St. David's" had been built in traditional stone, being larger than the houses alongside it, which appeared stunted in comparison. It had a balcony and main living room located on the first floor for the obvious benefit of elevated and unrestricted views. A woman's influence had been meticulously at work inside, where lush velvet drapes hung in contrasting, but matching hues. Deep sofas, with additional cushions, scattered for comfort, encouraged indolence. Oak beams, painted black, edged across the ceiling and luxury light fittings added substance. Old sea landscapes decorated the wall above a small and old-fashioned sewing machine. At the other end, the door led out to the balcony, which stretched out across the front and the whole of one side of the building. An awning suggested regular use.

Rachel's cousin, Dolores, an older woman, was exuberant, yet sophisticated at the same time. She had short-cropped fair hair, boy-like in its cut. The smell of food, seeping in from the kitchen alongside, distracted me and, rudely, I turned my eyes to its source, inhaling pleasurably. A table had been set for three persons for dinner.

"Forgive the bad manners, but if the food is for me, it smells wonderful. I've eaten nothing since breakfast."

358

Dolores laughed. I liked people who could take you at face value, with no truck for pretensions. Dinner and a mellow Rioja, to aid digestion, facilitated conversation. My paranoia appeared a different life away. I dropped my guard. Rachel trusted her cousin and she knew my predicament. The convivial company and tranquil surroundings satisfied more than just my appetite. I found myself laughing again, happy in the moment, though I needed to broach the subject of the scrolls.

"Do you have the scrolls with you?" I asked, abruptly.

She flicked her hair off her shoulders. "Yes, I do and I also have my father's declaration, confirming their origins. He's written a letter you may find interesting."

"Would you mind if I look at them now?" I asked, impatiently.

"I'll fetch them for you, if you clear away the dishes."

I nodded. "That's a reasonable trade after such hospitality."

The documents were spread on silk across the cleared table and consisted of a lengthy and poignant letter from her father, a declaration of authentication of the scrolls, which he knew I needed, the scroll containing the Hebrew Atbash Cipher and the scroll, which she had previously hidden. A strange logic and bizarre act of faith had caused my uncle to release the document into Rachel's hands for safekeeping.

I examined the letter from David, written as if he would not see his daughter again. At one point, he referred to the intelligence services, confirming they had now perfected mind control and psychotronic research to the degree it had become one hundred per cent effective in carrying out behaviour modifications. Apparently, subliminal command messages could be transmitted through 'white noise' or music and key words would bypass the conscious mind and neurosystem, working by bone conduction. The Moscow Institute of Psychcorrelations had first experimented successfully with the technique. Very low frequency infra sound was used and the results were almost instantaneous. Who knows whether Prince Rainier's wife was killed in this way, perhaps for some lack of co-operation on his or her part? Either way, they would never be able to prove it.

David feared he would be its next victim or else, like one of his predecessors at the Banco Ambrosiano, Robert Calvi, he would be found hanging from Blackfriars Bridge. In Calvi's case, he related, it was after being implicated in an illegal arms for drugs operation. He indicated that Italian Police files also suggest Calvi had used his bank as the conduit for funding a Red Brigades hit team, which had assassinated a string of top Police officials and magistrates in the Milan area.

I placed the letter down for a moment, dwelling on its content and the intrigue surrounding the scrolls, before focusing again and finishing it. The letter absolved Rachel from any knowledge of criminal acts. He supplied and certified proof they were done on the direct instructions of high-ranking officials in the Vatican.

He named names and attached a letter from one Cardinal, responsible with his team, for dogma. The letter had been addressed to David, confirming his orders to take whatever steps became necessary to terminate the interest of Cardinal O'Rourke's nephew and recover the stolen scrolls. The words 'the client is not viable' and 'do you have the capability?' jumped off the page at me. The letters had blue ink signatures on bonded headed-notepaper. It even referred to the address of a dead letter box in London for correspondence, reminding him of the American listening post at Menwith Hill in Yorkshire, which intercepted, through its ultra-secret Echelon satellite surveillance system, more than two million electronic communications an hour. For this reason, he was instructed to be discreet in the use of telephones.

In his letter, David reminded Rachel of the far-reaching influence of the Vatican, including within police forces and the aristocracy, throughout Europe.

He told her he had only acted on written instructions, so his back had always been protected, even though, in normal circumstances, the Vatican would ensure instructions were three or four times removed from them, to avoid incrimination. He insisted he knew nothing about my uncle's death, other than the placement of staff to recover the scrolls, but confirmed Ronan had originally notified them of their whereabouts.

I looked up, for a moment. Dolores was still in the kitchen, but Rachel sat alongside me at the table, tears running freely down her cheeks. She had her thumb one side of her temple and her fingers the other, shielding her eyes. I handed her my handkerchief, but said nothing.

"He was never the perfect father," she sobbed. "But I desperately wanted him to love me."

I leant over, so my head rested against hers. "I'm sure he did. His dying words were to tell you he loved you. You must take some consolation from those words. His love for you shines through this letter."

"But he never told me. That's what I needed." Her voice cracked.

I slid my arm around her instinctively, pulling her body even closer, so her head dropped onto my shoulder. I loved her warmth, the texture of her skin, the subtle perfume. It had all become so familiar. For a few minutes I didn't move. I synchronised my breathing with hers, oblivious to my surroundings, outside time and space for the moment.

"Oops. Am I interrupting anything?" Dolores returned, smiling broadly.

"Nothing at all," I replied, jolting upright. Rachel lifted her head off my shoulder, drying her tears, before returning my handkerchief. I turned back to the documents, then to her. "Your father has explained the nature of the Hebrew Atbash cipher in his letter. There are parts of the Knights Templar Journal, which are written in Hebrew. This cipher will help translate them." I said.

"But he told me the Vatican couldn't recover their treasure, even when they'd taken this cipher." She said, puzzled, placing her chin in the palm of her hand, with her elbow on the table.

I nodded. "I suspect they tracked it down to the Templar's Chapel at Rosslyn in Scotland. Apparently, there's something significant about the freestanding wall there. It was never intended to be part of a room. It's some sort of clue. Even the American University, who agreed to undertake ground scans of the vaults and to examine its walls couldn't discover its secret. There is also a theory that the Apprentice Pillar, representing Boaz, the Pillar of Strength, at this location, has its counterpart Joachim, the Pillar of Wisdom, somewhere in Portugal. They suggest there is an alignment of Cathedrals along sacred sites between the two locations."

She sat up again and moved the letter, pointing to one particular paragraph. "My father said the Vatican are no nearer discovering the treasure now, than when King Philip, used his crude attempts at torturing the Templars, but they're afraid someone else may unlock the code."

I pointed to another part of the letter. "This is what I find particularly interesting."

She read the paragraph, whilst I commented on it. "He explains the reasons why some of the Dead Sea scrolls weren't published, even after fifty years. As I suspected, they reveal the Egyptian mystery tradition behind both the Essenes and the Nazarenes. He also suggests the cipher may assist me in translating some of the strange rites, at the heart of these mystical sects, including the Templars."

She handed me the scroll, attached to the letter, containing the cipher. Even a cursory glance revealed its significance, although considerable graft would still be necessary to apply it to certain of the scrolls and the Journal. She also produced the scroll handed to her by my uncle; silk still protected it.

"This scroll is the one which links the other scrolls to Christ himself and to Mary Magdalene. It complements them, by emphasising the origins of the scrolls." I said. "It also confirms the heritage of John the Baptist, who belonged to the Royal bloodline." I added.

I noticed reference at the end of the scroll to Mary and attempted to read it. I looked at Rachel, wide-eyed and excited.

"What is it?" She asked, picking up on the body language.

"The last part of this scroll, if I understand it properly, authenticates and relates Christ's marriage to Mary Magdalene. It refers to her as the High Priestess and the disciple above all others. It confirms the Gnostic texts. It suggests there are many paths to our heaven, if we follow our bliss." I hesitated, unsure if I had correctly translated the last word. I turned to Rachel again. "I can't be sure of the literal translation, but I think it says we need not limit ourselves, for that is the way of the bigot. It expresses a fear of the destruction of their heritage, to be replaced by authoritarianism. The teachings emphasise tolerance, as a substitute for terror and brutality, with human beings having the right to think their own thoughts."

My mouth opened and shut again. It appeared to anticipate an attempt to suppress the truth, by destruction of the evidence of the mystical Gnostic teachings and their origins in Egypt. I found my voice. "An oath is contained in the document, at pain of death, if the contents of the documents are revealed."

She listened attentively and leant across. Sincerity showed in her face. "These are my gift to you."

"Everything now seems to fit together, my uncle seemed to realise this was a key to the acceptance of the scrolls." I said. A tingle crept up my spine, as I realised the potential significance of the document. For a moment, I sat stunned, unable to speak.

"There's another letter, written about six months ago, which I've kept and you can have it." She left the room, returning quickly with the letter and handing it to me. "There's only one reference to the scrolls in this letter, but he does mention evidence being available about Egypt, being the source of learning. He refers to the knowledge being inherited from a more ancient tradition, relocating there only after the great deluge, which is such an integral part of so many ancient myths, in different cultures around the world."

I read through the long letter and concentrated on the non-personal items, which interested me. "He indicates his belief about the existence of a time capsule, beneath one of the sphinx, which may relate to this ancient culture."

"Yes." Rachel said. "The part you may find interesting was his reference to the Vatican having given up their chase for the Knights Templar treasure. He confirms it reached a complete dead-end in Scotland," she smiled. "Just as you suggested."

"The treasure, which fascinates me more, is the wealth of knowledge and inspirational mystical insights." I stretched out a hand to hold hers. She squeezed it.

"Have you reached the post-script yet?" She asked. "It may be important."

I jumped to the end, reading it out loud. "The hierarchy are negotiating and seeking an alliance with another right-wing organisation, who have their ambitions to control power in Europe. The intention is purely political and not doctrinaire. Nevertheless, doctrine remains an immense obstacle, for the time being, as they are diametrically opposed to the Roman Church. If the Order of the True Rose Croix in France surrender their Gnostic leanings and their public pronouncements about blood-line, they may prove an interesting ally. In return the Order will want support, when the truth emerges. They've been asked to assist in suppressing or, at least, delaying the release of the scrolls, for a minimum of ten years."

"...I find so many limitations before me. The mind is imprisoned in fear and the conscious mind is an illusion of disconnection from the Infinite, which is a balance of all things. Time helps create this illusion and it has forgotten that perfect love casteth out fear. Just as you limit God, by calling him or her God, I can now do little to limit the damage done by those who oppose me. The path is narrowing and I fear that the battle is lost. My enemies already gloat and do not perceive the life of slavery they perpetuate. There are few choices available to me, as my aspirations are being constrained. They spread such madness in their message. Even when I addressed the throng, who followed, after crossing the Lake of Galilee, I simply organised the pooling of the food, so all could share sustenance together. Initially, they had been reluctant and kept their food under their clothing. I persuaded some five thousand to eat and drink with me. Later, the message was lost and I heard talk of miracles. They are determined to follow a path, which will make a martyr of me. I try to teach layer of consciousness, upon another and the anchoring of collective ideas, in the way of my forefathers. Yet they build exaggeration upon exaggeration. We can all create miracles in our lives, which defy logic and rationale, but sorcerer's tricks are illusions and contaminate the truth. We must identify with our spiritual essence and distance ourselves from our experiences, but they do not listen. When I was called to the house of Lazarus, I recognised his deep trance state, as it was similar to a state I had observed many times in the East. Yet when I brought him back to full consciousness, using a technique I have developed, as an Initiate, they falsely claim I had brought him back from the dead. The momentum swings against me and all will be lost, if I am not careful."

CHAPTER 20

My enchantment with Rachel aroused its own responses within my imagination. I surrendered to them blindly, even though, as with everything, there would be a price to pay. I gave no thought to my paranoia or to the evil, which stalked me as its victim.

I had always persuaded myself of a truth, which scientists acknowledged in their experiments with sub-atomic particles. The universe is reflexive, responding to human thoughts, aspirations and desires. It is the reason magic is a natural phenomenon.

Morning brought new light and hope. A number of people, working together towards a fixed goal, invoked hugely increased energy. It surmounted most obstacles. At least, I deluded myself with the sentiment, even if my training had taught me this life brought illusion and pain, as well as joy. It was part of the test for spiritual growth.

I savoured a late breakfast on the balcony with Rachel. A gentle breeze caressed the senses, with a hint of seaweed floating gossamer-like in the air. Small boats bobbed in line in the harbour, the sun glistening off chrome accessories, leaving an image of the hulls on the water. A small group of tourists gathered, perched at the end of the harbour wall, watching two dolphins basking and playing for their amusement. Surely, here I had found a haven, away from the fanatics who pursued me so relentlessly.

I inhaled deeply and soaked up the beauty of being alive. My soul felt whole and recharged again. The arctic blue sky and rugged coastline placed the frailty of human life in perspective. I had no warm clothing, but the minor sacrifice carried its own reward, in this little corner of paradise.

Dolores had eaten, but joined us. "Yesterday, I discussed your situation with Rachel. She has two reasons she'd like to help you publish these documents. You'd have to be blind not to appreciate the first, but she'd also like to vindicate her father's decision, to release the scroll and the information in his letter. I'm willing to help you." She sat opposite and smiled.

"How can you help?" I asked, finishing the last piece of toast and picking up the serviette, anchored to the table by a jug of orange juice.

"Well, by occupation I'm a freelance television producer, usually cultural programmes." She sat back in the chair. I liked Dolores. She had an air of authority about her and generally gave me a good feeling.

"Do you mean you've contacts who can help?" I asked.

She smiled again. "Not only do I have contacts, but I can actually produce a television documentary about the scrolls and arrange its publication."

Tension released from my body and a burden I had shouldered for too long lifted. "It sounds good to me." I said, quickly, before she could change her mind.

"Then it's settled." She agreed. "Why don't you start writing an article about the scrolls, it'll create the interest, which will sell the documentary. Rachel informs me that you've an Editor who can help."

I nodded. "That's right."

"Well, as a writer, you appreciate that you don't wait for inspiration, you create it. So let's get to work and develop a momentum, using television, newspaper and magazines. It'll create a dynamism, which will drive us to our goal. We'll trawl all possible outlets."

"Are you sure we can do this?" I asked, still sceptical.

"Certainly, I'm sure. If you really want to do it."

I smiled. She generated such enthusiasm. I was happy to follow in her footsteps. "You give me such a feeling of confidence."

"Good. I can even create a web-site for marketing purposes."

Perhaps our meeting had been the synchronicity I had been seeking, as a sign of right-action. I sat more upright in the chair. "I'd really like to do this," I said.

"We can all network this material and I can circulate copies of the video across the country in no time." She added, eagerly. "I even have contacts in the U.S."

I turned to Rachel and she nodded positively.

"It's appropriate we're discussing this in Wales," Dolores said.

"What do you mean?" I asked, screwing my eyes together.

"Well, the Celtic Tradition has helped keep the Goddess principle alive, over many centuries, a fortress against the puritanical zeal of the respective Protestant and Catholic Churches."

"Of course." I replied. "It inherited many of the teachings from its pagan predecessors and from the children of Atlantis who fled the great Flood. The Druids did the same."

For the first time, I actually began to believe I could publish the documents. Nostradamus and other seers may have predicted the millennium as a time of revelation and revolution in the consciousness of man. In some insignificant way, this could even be part of the process. I fell silent for a couple of minutes, before Rachel tugged my jumper.

"You're miles away. Do you want a penny for your thoughts?" She asked, wistfully.

"They're worth far more than that." I teased, smiling.

"If you tell me the price, I'll pay it," she said.

I chuckled. "I'll tell you the price later, but I was having serious thoughts. The old Church meant so much to me, but it's disintegrating and scandal follows scandal. The paedophilia scandal in America, and the subsequent resignation of a Cardinal, is the perfect example. All the predictions are coming true." I hesitated, taking a deep breath. "In truth, it doesn't please me and I feel some guilt over it," I added.

"Why don't you ask the Church authorities to participate in this documentary?" Dolores asked.

"But they'll never agree," I replied.

Dolores smiled. "The trick is to tell them, if they don't take part, the programme will mention they were given an opportunity to do so and declined. It would be a damning indictment on them and would speak volumes for the authenticity of the scrolls."

"You're right, they'd have to think about it."

"They may want a meeting beforehand to discuss the content of the programme, but that shouldn't present any problem. What do you have to lose?" She spoke confidently, which transmitted itself readily.

"But what if they had enough contacts within the BBC or in the media generally to stop the publication. Wouldn't we be placing them on notice of our intentions?" I asked, morosely, pausing for a moment, as a shaft of wind blew in from the sea and began to dislodge breakfast napkins. "They may even apply for an injunction in the High Court," I added, once everything had been secured.

"Perhaps, but it has to be worth the risk. The truth would have to come out eventually." She said, positively.

"I must ring Jean, in France, before I start work on the article. I want to challenge him about his contacts with the Church authorities. I trusted him and if he has betrayed me, then I'll have no compunction about incriminating his organization."

"I trust your judgment,' she said.

"Good. My Editor friend will be pleased to hear from me."

I stood up from the table and leant against the railings alongside the balcony. Rachel joined me, slipping her arm in mine and bracing herself against the breeze. "Is there room for me in your future?" She asked.

I squeezed her arm. "I hope so, I feel good about life again and you generate feelings, which have been dormant for a long time."

"Are you telling me you love me?" She asked.

I laughed. "In a clumsy way, I am." I said.

She unhooked her arm from mine and pulled me around to face her. "Then say it,"

I lifted my hands, cupping them around her face, moving closer and kissing her sweetly and gently on the lips, then pulling back. "I love you." The emotional barriers around my heart, created from the pain of the past for protection dissolved, almost instantly, and the furrows deepened on my forehead, merely from the intensity of feeling the words generated. I repeated it, "I love you."

"And I love you," she replied, with equal intensity of feeling, moving closer again and kissing me with a passion, which literally took my breath away.

I recovered my breath, but held her embrace, stroking her hair with affection, as she closed her eyes and rested her head on my shoulder.

After a few moments she looked up at me. "Surely, in this place we're insulated from the havoc, which has been plaguing our lives?" She asked.

"Life has few certainties," I replied, with some knowledge of the subject. "But I'm certain that love endures beyond death."

She shook her head. "Why do we always need to escape the human condition?" She asked, rhetorically, as if she had many more questions about life, still unanswered.

"Because subconsciously we know we have our origins in something better," I replied with conviction.

She smiled. "You're right, of course."

"It's a consolation, in times of crisis," I said.

Her eyes sparkled, unrestrained for the first time I could recall. She gave me one final kiss on the cheek and moved away. "I'll help my cousin organise the documentary, but you'll have to help with its structure," she said, picking up and carrying some used breakfast dishes from the balcony and into the adjoining kitchen. "We can prepare a draft, but you'll have the final say on the form it takes," she added, looking over her shoulder at me, as she walked away.

Everything about this place earthed the spirit. Across Cardigan Bay, I could see as far as the mountains of Snowdonia. It was tempting to stay on the balcony, but life always intruded into pleasure and procrastination was the thief of time. The obligations to my late uncle still weighed heavily on my mind. They demanded action or the thrust-block would be lost again. I took one last glance out to sea. A fishing boat chugging back to its mooring, full with its quota of fish for the day, created the only sound disrupting the tranquillity, but chores had to be settled.

The telephone connected to Jean almost immediately. "Do you have anything you want to say to me?" I asked, firmly.

"What do you mean?" He replied in his gallic-shrouded accent, sounding surprised.

"I mean your contact with the Church. You've discussed political alliances with them. Rachel's father has written a letter to her, before he died. It's been revealing." I waited for a reply, but none came. "Then you don't deny it?" I persisted.

"I'm writing an article and want to know if it's true, before I incriminate you."

"Nothing has been decided yet, so there is nothing to deny?"

"If you don't follow what you know to be the truth, you'll undermine and corrupt your organisation," I said.

"Always remember, there are still good men in the Catholic Church," he said. "Although you're right, in a sense, there are dangers and we must show patience. We'll continue to bide our time." He hesitated. "For your sake, be careful. Your position remains precarious," he spoke in slow monotonous tones.

"Are you threatening me?" I asked, angrily.

"No, quite the contrary. I like you and I wouldn't want anything to happen to you. In different circumstances, I would like to be your friend, but you still don't appreciate the forces you face."

"What do you mean by forces and what dangers?" I asked hurriedly, unnerved in the moment.

"Only that there are times when you must compromise your position, for the better good. In the long term, our aims have not changed and we hope to persuade the Vatican of the need for change, but perhaps this is not the time for progress."

"I'm disappointed," I said. "I think you've lost integrity and that's when organisations lose popular support."

There was a silence, before his voice split the airwaves for the last time. "Hello, Hello. I cannot hear you."

"You can hear me alright, even if you might prefer you didn't," I said, aware of the ruse. "Stand up and be counted."

The telephone hung up, before any response. It justified, in my mind, any reference I now chose to make in the article about his organization.

An invitation to lunch from Dolores sounded attractive, especially after a morning of constant telephone interruptions.

"I've booked the table in the window, overlooking the harbour, in the Hungry Trout." She picked up her keys and walked towards the stairs.

Rachel and I followed her, dutifully. "You can tell me what progress you've made," I said. "And you can give me an honest appraisal of the draft article I've written."

Before we could reach the door the telephone rang again. Dolores debated with herself whether to answer it, but succumbed to curiosity. "Who is speaking? She asked. After a short pause she held the telephone in the air, with her hand over the mouthpiece. "Rachel, this man says he's a friend of your father and wants to speak to you. Do you want to take the call or shall I tell him you're not here?"

She walked to the telephone. " No I'll take it." A relaxed expression changed dramatically. She shook her head animatedly. Frightened eyes widened and she gestured for me to listen.

"How do you know about this?" She asked.

I placed my ear close to the telephone.

"They know he's there with you and these people are ruthless. They'll try and silence him permanently. The contract is out. Nothing will stop them now."

"What's your name and how do you know my father?" Her voice heightened and wavered.

"I dare not tell you, but if I were you, I'd keep your distance from him. There'll be grave danger."

"But…" Rachel began, before the line went dead. She began to tremble and I placed my arms around her, hugging her as tightly as I could.

"Ignore it, we've had sinister threats before and came through it together. This is no different."

"Everything was so final, so certain." She spoke slowly, yet in staccato tones, trembling and fixed to the spot. "They know you're here. There's no peace in this world," she sobbed.

I looked at Dolores and pointed to the drinks-cabinet. "Let's all have a brandy or a gin and tonic. We need it."

Rachel sat down and I joined her. "Let's assess the risks philosophically. This is a small town, not a big city, and little danger can lurk here." I assured her.

Dolores came over to assist me, hugging her. "Rachel, life is full of challenges and obstacles. We must overcome them fearlessly. Don't let the barstards drag you down."

"I've had too may challenges lately and I can't take any more," she said, almost childlike.

Dolores squeezed her again. "It's in the nature of our humanity to have doubts from time to time. We can ring the Police after lunch, if we think there is any substance to this telephone call," she said.

Rachel nodded and sighed. Eventually, her breathing became more regular.

Within about ten minutes, I had taken her hand, as we walked out of the house and belatedly down the hill to the restaurant, walking slowly, with Dolores straggling behind. It must have been no more than fifty to one hundred yards from her door, beyond the bend in the road, where the road narrows. The elation, which had previously motivated us, as a group, had subsided and a more malignant force attacked the senses. My life had been full of contradictory impulses and I coped. I hid my concern over the telephone call, though my eyes darted nervously in different directions and I listened for every footstep. Boats and their owners busied themselves in the bay and the familiar smells of the sea, infiltrated the nostrils. Wind occasionally blew my hair off my forehead. The sounds of locals and holidaymakers abandoning the tensions, inflicted by modern society, gave an interesting insight into the slumbering prisons created in our everyday lives. Each salutation resonated with sincerity or humour, beyond its particulars. The place engendered smiling faces. The thought of danger in such perfect surroundings appeared incongruous. I took a deep breath and relaxed.

"Let's do some brainstorming." Dolores said, as we sat down by the window of the Hungry Trout.

I picked up one of the menus. "This is far too tempting. Let's eat before we start serious discussions. Eating should be a ritual. I want to enjoy the company and the view." I settled comfortably into the chair nearest the window and placed my hand on Rachel's thigh. It seemed natural.

The meal matched the setting, but a chill feeling in the pit of my stomach hinted at a foreboding, though unwisely I dismissed it. This intangible sensation tainted the pleasure in the company of friends. I rejected my doubts, as having no substance. If logic could not explain it, how could I inflict irrational and manic fears on Rachel, especially having witnessed the vulnerable side of her nature. I had spent my life rushing around in restless, frenetic circles and it was time to stop. The hospitality, the banter and the wine deserved the most serious of attention.

It must have been mid-afternoon before we left, with Rachel and Dolores moving ahead of me. I followed, walking down the steps directly onto the road. Seagulls screeched and hovered in the air, children fidgeted and laughed. All appeared normal. For a moment, I was lulled into false security, as all this faded into the background. I noticed a man wearing a dark suit. He appeared calm, but conspicuously out of place. Everything then happened in slow motion, as if unreal, almost like a dream. The clamour from the beach subsided, as my consciousness focused on this man walking towards us. I turned to face him. His features gave the clue, his face sallow and dead. No expression or flicker of acknowledgement slipped through his eyes. No soul connection displayed in his demeanour.

Instinctively, I moved between him and the girls. I didn't notice the gun, until the last moment, when his arm lifted and pointed towards me. Though one's first reaction is to freeze, I had become used to this situation of late and jolted my body into action, ducking underneath his arm.

"Look out!" I shouted, reaching out with my hands towards the man's arms. A scream penetrated the air, but my attention remained solely on the gun.

Two shots fired in quick succession. Rachel rushed forward, but fell to the ground. I had become immune to violence and the situation had become too familiar.

I grabbed his gun hand, but recoiled for a moment, at the explosion and the sound of bullets firing. I hesitated for a moment, until I realized no bullet had hit me. I conjured up every ounce of energy and barged my shoulder into his chest, still holding his gun hand. He fell to the ground, with me on top. The gun clattered noisily across the road. All my anger generated an unforgiving force and I punched him in the throat.

He coughed and blood splattered out of his mouth. Nevertheless, he sustained aggression, pulling his gun arm towards me. I twisted it towards his body and the gun fired again. This time his body heaved and a groan signalled the end, as blood seeped from the carcass and over my clothing.

I took a deep breath and pushed myself off the ground. I turned to face Dolores, who sat sobbing, beside Rachel's lifeless body. For a moment, I could not take in the events. A wound in the chest discoloured her clothing, her eyes, still open, but motionless stared upwards. The scream still captured and imprisoned within the expression on her face.

"Telephone for an ambulance quickly." I shouted at a passer-by, who stood gawping, open-mouthed and transfixed, even though somehow I knew it was futile. I turned back to Rachel.

"Please God, No." I pleaded, to no avail.

"She's gone," Dolores said, starkly.

"No, No, No." I demanded, as it became obvious my prayers would be unanswered. Willpower could change nothing.

I crouched, crying and trembling, despising my inadequacy, desperate to turn back time.

Though a part of me recognized the impossibility, I still willed it in my imagination.

"It's too late. Her father, now her." Dolores said, oblivious to the crowds morbidly gathering, like bees to honey.

I shook my head in disbelief. "He might as well have killed me." I said. A hole somewhere inside, created a vacuum within my heart. I was convinced a part of me could never be whole again. This cold, lifeless body had known little joy and I had been given only a few precious moments to rectify it. I remembered, and immediately regretted, all the hurtful things I had said to her, but it was too late.

"What else is left for me?" I asked no-one in particular.

Dolores looked up through hollow tearful eyes, tinged with sadness, but she had no answer. "Only last night she told me it wouldn't last. She was happy for perhaps the first time in her life, but she didn't think she deserved it and always felt something would happen to destroy it," she shook her head. "I insisted she should enjoy the moment, reminding her it was the journey, and not the destination, which was important."

"Life isn't fair," I said, unable to reason or explain events, despite my training.

"You're right. She touched many lives, but she was a victim in life and in death."

What patterns of behaviour may have led her to this destiny I would never understand and could not imagine. It was all beyond my comprehension.

Ambulance and Police sirens drifted in and out of my head. Agitated people crammed the road; some uniformed, some friendly, others openly distressed. Sad faces intruded into a personal grief. I understood, at that moment, why some people eagerly welcomed death. They sought the connection and source of lost love and friendship and yearned to be welcomed home.

For twenty-four hours I wandered around in a surreal cloud of disbelief, my plans in tatters, with no sleep possible for respite. Uncertainty and exhaustion filled the vacuum. I questioned the endless struggle against complication and the reasons and meaning behind atrocity. My faith was tested, as never before. For hours I endured the nightmare, knowing there would be no relief. I yearned for the simpler life I had enjoyed, before the fateful promise to my uncle, but it could never be. I knew that now. The Cabbala had taught me that these incidents reached us at a deeper level, paradoxically pushing us towards a pace of spiritual growth, otherwise impossible in ordinary events. It closed the distance between the spiritual and physical dimensions, but the anguish was no less painful for the knowledge.

I gave statements; spoke to Police officers until I was unable to speak or to think, too numb to know whether I was alive or dead.

After a second night of fitful sleep, decisions needed to be made.

"Have a look at this." Dolores pushed papers across the breakfast table and sat in old pyjamas alongside me. "For Rachel's sake, I must finish what she started." She sat, stone-faced, staring blankly ahead. Dark rings around her eyes were a testimony to the sadness and suffering she too endured. She wore no make-up and her hair was strangely dishevelled, all pride in her appearance had obviously perished with the brutal death of her cousin. She picked up a mug from the table and began to sip strong coffee. I strained to concentrate, through bleary, bloodshot eyes. In front of me, the form of the planned documentary had been structured.

"Are you still prepared to go ahead with this?" I asked, turning to face her.

"I've spent half the night finishing this script, because Rachel would have wanted me to do it."

She looked older, more haggard. Lines etched deep into her face, but a determined expression filtered through the exhaustion.

I browsed through her work. It started with the occupation of Jerusalem, at the end of the First Crusade, then outlining the history of the Knights Templar, including the purge and the violent transfer of the Nazarene texts to the Vatican vaults. The conflict between Orthodox and Gnostic Christians teachings had been accurately related, with the Gnostic teachings going underground. She made reference to the Dead Sea scrolls and the Nag Hammadi texts.

"I'd like to make some modifications," I said, moving to take a pen from the top pocket of my jacket. "I can improve this, if you don't mind."

"Feel free. I'm not egotistical and I want to get it right, if only as an epitaph," she said, leaning back in her chair.

I looked across the table at her. "Do you realize the risks of getting involved in this?" I asked.

"I'm unconcerned for myself. As Victor Hugo once said, 'we're all on Death Row, even if we don't know the method of execution and the length of reprieve.'"

A modicum of enthusiasm stirred beneath the grief. "It's critical we explain the subtleties behind the Gnostic texts and how the pagan mysteries are interwoven with it. It mediates the higher wisdom through imagery and can alter the consciousness of man and perhaps the consciousness of the planet, so the ramifications of these scrolls needs to be emphasized."

She gestured outwards with the palms of her hands. "Please amend it in any way you want. It's only a draft." She spoke quietly, her voice as strained as her appearance.

"I want people to understand the church-promoted fabrication of Original Sin, as relating somehow to sexuality. It's the distorted interpretation, necessary to subjugate them into compliance with the rigid dogma of the Church. It represents power at its most unscrupulous, even if it's being diluted and humanised by the current hierarchy."

Dolores nodded, but pointed to the preamble. "I understand, but it's important you explain it in simple terms or the message will be lost. You must convince the viewers of the particular significance of the texts. If they realise the scrolls show the source of all religions are the same and that it should end all sectarianism, then they'll understand it. Give them hope for the future."

I walked lethargically to the window and looked out at the raw energy of stormy seas, battling to consume the land beneath me. It reflected my mood. I turned and sat back at the table. "You're right. We have to do this in simple language, but it's difficult to relay hope, when you feel grief and perceive such darkness in your world."

"I'll help. Write your contribution and show it to me," she said, finishing her coffee and replacing the mug on the table.

"I'd like to read the penultimate entry in the Knights Templar Journal, as part of the preamble. It'll explain how the scrolls passed to the Vatican," I said.

"This is an entry you've interpreted from the original French, isn't it?" She asked.

"Meticulously," I replied, hoping no criticism had been implied in the question.

"Read it to me," she asked, folding her arms, as if cold and leaning back in her chair again.

I gathered the notes and read the passage out loud.

'Messages have been sent to the Templars throughout Europe. Philip le Bel is in grave financial difficulties. He covets our wealth. This invite to his sister's wedding in Paris is probably a device to ensure my presence. I cannot refuse, but we must take all precautions to protect our knowledge. Our intelligence at Court is strong, but what can I do? We have decided to send some of the scrolls and this Journal to our Chapter in the Languedoc. Our leader there is the nephew of the Pope, Clement V. I fear he may find family ties too strong and negotiate his safety, by surrendering the scrolls. At least, the Pope will not terrorise his own nephew. It has to be the safest place in France and a democratic decision has been made. A compromise has been readied. Copies of the scrolls have been subscribed by our scholars and sent with St. Clair to Scotland. He has given a sacred vow to guarantee their safekeeping. Much of our wealth has gone with him, in ships, although some will travel south to Portugal. I have the peace of mind, knowing all has been done, which is possible to do. Everything else is now a matter of destiny. I must be strong. The dignity and reputation of the Knights Templar is paramount. The architecture of a new chapel, at St. Claire's estate in Scotland, will replicate the chapel found in the vault beneath the Temple in Jerusalem, by one of my predecessors. There is a key, which will be self-evident, if people recall the model of its construction. I consecrate my body to the service of God, as I have always done, for the benefit of mankind. I would like to admit we have held in our possession, since the excavations in Jerusalem, the embalmed head of Christ. The relic would immediately disprove one of the Church's tenets of faith, but they'll burn me as a heretic, if I tell the truth."

"Perfect." She said, sitting upright and pouring another cup of coffee. "Include it, but don't lose the thread, which explains the spiritual significance of the scrolls, rather than their origins. You must keep it simple, otherwise you'll not sustain attention."

"I need a couple of hours to get an adequate script together," I said.

"A cameraman and crew will be here by late morning, and it'll take all day, so that will give you the time. Let's create a setting and you must learn to act. Be animated. I suggest we use my study, with the bookcase in the background and the one scroll on the desk, I also want you to learn your script."

We moved into the small study. It had primrose walls on three sides and a bookcase lining the remaining wall. We moved the office furniture around, until the desk and chair was positioned in front of the bookcase. Dolores sat at the desk. Another table, some small upright chairs and a filing cabinet was pushed back against the other wall and out of sight of any camera shot.

"Your uncle was the instigator of all this, so personalize the script and mention his background and views?"

I nodded. "I remember him commenting once about the diverse religions simply being different ways to access the same spirituality." My voice dropped and cracked. The pain of Rachel's death affected every bodily function and there was no respite. Tears slipped wilfully down my cheeks, betraying the suffering.

"The Church has a lot to answer for." I said, wiping tears away with a handkerchief. "It tests my faith."

Dolores stood up, placing her hand on my arm. "Her death must motivate you to fight for what is right and for the truth. You were a priest, so you know her spirit survives and resides in a place where there is no suffering. This is no time for self-pity."

"I understand, but it makes it no easier. It's my humanity." My heart was heavy and it made talking difficult. "I feel sorry for myself as much as anything. Only two days ago, I had told her I loved her and she made me happy."

"You were a priest. You know the essence of the woman you loved is indestructible. It has simply surrendered itself to its Creator, as part of a natural process for all of us."

"But the pain of the separation is real," I replied, almost childlike.

Dolores sighed. "The natural rhythms of the Universe will eventually bring acceptance. You must restore your faith and believe in the content of the scrolls. They're not just an intellectual treatise, but a living, breathing testimony of the correspondence between the spiritual and physical worlds. The scrolls can build a rainbow bridge between all the religions and encourage a movement away from institutionalised religion and towards spirituality. They must inspire us to illuminate the path, which will end all human conflict. It'll be her monument and epitaph. You owe it to her, to publish this material. Don't give up now." She spoke firmly, rubbing her hand against my arm, as if waking me from some cataleptic slumber.

"O.K. I'll do this, but I need a little time."

"You'll have some time, but we must act quickly," she said

I nodded. "Yes, I know, but you want me to do an article for the newspaper and this script. Do I have time?"

"I want you to do it for yourself and for Rachel, not for me. Do the work on the script first, it's more important. You can write the article tomorrow."

"You're right. I must stop feeling sorry for myself and get this done."

"Good. You were trained as a priest, so you know when we institutionalise spirituality, history informs us that war and conflict follow."

"Perhaps this is the work of the Satan, the Church invented and transposed retrospectively, as a serpent, into a Genesis account, previously free of any satanic involvement," I said, picking up on Dolores's enthusiasm.

"That's it," she rubbed my arm again. "We must concentrate on the positive. You do not love by despising hate, but by loving and you cannot describe light by reference to darkness. If you do, the demonic world and the Anti-Christ will take sway in these apocalyptic times."

I took a deep breath and steeled myself. "You're absolutely right. The Gnostic texts teach us to merge the physical and spiritual worlds. I can incorporate this into the script. Yesterday's events simply reinforce the illusory nature of this life." I hugged her, needing her strength and wisdom.

"Now, please sit down at the desk, there's no time like the present to begin. I'll get you anything you want and come in and check on you from time to time." I sat down heavily and the chair creaked loudly.

"If we want to change the world, I suppose we

must first change ourselves." I said, moving my attention to the script. Dolores left me to do my work. I began writing my opening sentences.

"There are core elements of ageless wisdom in all religions. Even orthodox Christianity accepted the Kingdom of Heaven was within us, but they also had to accept the individual did not need the church as an intermediary. It was a natural consequence of both the Gnostic and Christian principles."

Barely had I put pen to paper, when the telephone rang. Dolores answered it in another room, but soon I heard her footsteps approaching the study. "It's Ronan for you. You can take it in here, just pick up the telephone."

I shrugged, picking up the telephone on the desk. Uncertainty and mixed emotions stirred. "Hello."

"John, I needed to speak to you. I've heard what's happened to Rachel. I'm so sorry. I can't let them do it again," he said, in his unmistakable Irish lilt.

"What can you do about it?" I asked, interested.

"I've written a letter to the Times, which they've agreed to print. That's a minor miracle in itself. Superintendent Thomas has taken a statement from me, which will not only outline my part in assisting the Vatican, but will incriminate a number of their agents in graver crimes. I made certain promises to your uncle at the end. I will honour them. It's the beginning of the end for the Church I loved. You may not know, but I worked with your uncle in the Vatican for many years. I have information, which could harm them."

"Like what?" I asked.

"Did you know, Mehmet Ali Agca was a drug courier and assassin for the Turkish Mafia and a member of the right-wing extremist paramilitary group Grey Wolves?"

"This is the man that shot the late Pope." I said.

"Yes. It was no coincidence he escaped prison, whilst awaiting execution for the assassination of the editor of the leftist Turkish newspaper Milliyet. Let no one be under any illusions that he may have been acting on his own. These people can reach anyone, including you, and they control many similar characters around the globe."

"Who are the people you refer to?" I asked.

"The private companies and intelligence agencies who control the institutions," he replied.

"This is very helpful," I said, thinking about the documentary and the article.

"There is hardly any mention of it, but exactly one year to the day, after Mehmet Ali Agca's attempted assassination of Pope John Paul II, a Spanish priest also attempted to stab him, as he conducted a Mass over the Statue of Fatima, in Portugal."

"I remember something vaguely." I said.

"What most people don't know is this priest had been linked to a fanatical right-wing movement and had been groomed for nearly a year to do it."

I grunted, wondering how I could use this material. "Ronan, hold on a minute, please." I placed my hand over the speaker and beckoned to Dolores. "Do you want Ronan to be involved in this documentary? He's written to the Times and given a statement to the Superintendent incriminating certain people working for the Vatican?"

"It'll definitely help," she said. "Can you

get him here by this afternoon? The crew will be around until late evening. It isn't quite so crucial, as we have the declaration from David, but it'll corroborate it."

"What he's just told me is fascinating," I said to Dolores.

I removed my hand from the speaker. "Ronan, will you take part in a documentary, which is being prepared for television?" I asked. "I need the scrolls authenticated and you'll add credibility, with your background."

"I'll do anything." He replied, sincerely. "You shouldn't have any guilt over Rachel's death. The killer was probably not trying to kill you, at all, but Rachel, because of her father's betrayal. It's the way they work."

I made arrangements to involve him and agreed to collect him from the train in Carmarthen. I sighed, hoping the tide was finally shifting in my favour.

I turned to Dolores, who had remained in the room. "I have to believe in the existence of a spiritual power, which will, in the ultimate scheme of things, ensure good eventually triumphed over evil and light would always illuminate darkness."

"I'm no saint, but I believe it," she said.

"If everyone took the light into their lives, it had to justify the sacrifices. My uncle had faith in Ronan and Rachel. He has already been proved right with your cousin. I hope his faith in me is equally well-founded."

She smiled. "I'm sure it is. Rachel had so much confidence in you and I trust her judgment. The exercise of free will by one person and its effect on the group mind has shown in the course of human history that the individual, rather than the Church, is sacrosanct." She spoke profoundly and it inspired me.

I sensed a feeling of destiny. "If this is the legacy of the Knights Templar, it must be a living, breathing one. I suspect, though, that there's nothing I could do or write, which would affect the intelligence elite and the Establishment figures, who will continue to orchestrate assassinations and political events, unscathed by the pain so wilfully inflicted on their victims."

She nodded, "You're probably right," she sighed.

"Even now I can't be sure they're not manipulating my actions, because I'm still alive and I don't understand how that can be."

"Perhaps the untouchables have always been untouchable," she replied philosophically.

Dolores sat down opposite me, as I wrote the next part of the script. I found her presence helpful, as I didn't want to be alone again and she had a strength, which bolstered mine. I read the script to her for approval.

"If Christianity returns to its mystical roots, it will unite all the traditions, moving forward as part of a cosmic spiritual evolution, which will gather pace in this new Millennium. A hidden tide from the deep unconscious will erupt and overturn the mundane structures of life, revealing its ancient wisdom. It will embrace other religious traditions, which it has previously branded as the work of the Devil. Dogma was the true work of Satan and it must break free from its flawed past. This is a time for healing, to realise science and spirituality are two aspects of the same mystery. Soon we shall have the cycle of the spiritual scientist again. We must re-awaken and open our hearts to the real wonders of spirituality, so we can return our hands to the plough and take up our work of destiny. This is the task our spirit undertook on entry into manifestation. Such a renaissance must happen, but the test will be the time it takes. Within the inner mysteries of the Christian message we can find the meaning of life. It will alleviate the suffering, which is the price humanity has paid for the excesses and deviation from truth for two thousand years." I paused and looked across to Dolores. "What do you think?"

She nodded. "I like it, though in documentary format, we'll have to concentrate on the facts, without waxing too lyrical. I can see why Rachel had so much respect for you." She smiled.

I turned back to the script. "I'd like to end, by reading the final entry in the Templars Journal, by Jacques De Molay. It reads as follows." I took a copy of the entry and read it slowly and precisely.

'There is a greater risk to our Order tonight, than at any time since its inception. If we have failed, then others must heal the wounds, created by sectarian dogma. Christ's mission for the salvation of the personality, not as subservient, sterile and uncertain, but as harmonious, unified and fertile is an ambition worthy of a great spiritual master. He may not have been the Son of God, any more than I am, but society must still try and match his aspirations to renew the rich bond and rhythm, which exists between man and nature. This is the test for history to judge. I have to believe truth will prevail and those who manipulate power for evil ends will eventually receive justice, if only in their purgatory or their karma for future lives. If we fail, I hope one day that someone remembers the Knights Templar Red Cross, as representing the principle of courage and integrity. I shall turn in my grave, if it is appropriated by a less honourable Order and becomes a symbol for subterfuge.'

EPILOGUE.

"... I write this final message by candlelight on papyrus, smuggled into my cell. I will ask that this codicil be bound in leather and placed securely with my other teachings and diaries. The Nazarenes are already preparing for their sacred scrolls to be safeguarded. They will go underground for who knows how long. Tomorrow I am to be crucified and Paul will have his figurehead. I must face my ordeal with courage and remind myself I am only returning home. I am human and it is not easy to believe that life is an illusion, when your suffering is so real. I pray my brothers continue the struggle in my absence. I can hardly believe this is happening to me and I ask, as all do, 'why me', but the portents were always there. It is the task I set myself before I was born. I have to remember truth and light will eventually emerge from the darkness. Otherwise the true teachings are lost and Paul will create a schism. He may rightly argue that an established Church may have some benefit, but like all organisations, it will lead to a hierarchy in the world, as it corrupts itself. Personal ambition and greed will ultimately overcome the spiritual message, which will be buried into obscurity. The consequence will be centuries of conflict and suppression, until good and evil again defines itself. Only love, in its pro-active state, will bring the peace necessary for conflict to end. In this way, the integrity of the human spirit is not affected by my death. All that is left for me to do is to call on the angelic realm to help me create the singleness of heart, openness of mind and freedom from corruption to ease my path to the Kingdom. My function, having been created by the angelic forces, is to re-integrate with them. One day, people will

understand the divine paradox that we are each of us the centre of the Universe, and are our consciousness, yet we are not separate. We belong to the One. I shall open the quarters, as I was taught in the Mystery schools of Egypt. I call on the Lords of Flame, the Archangel Michael behind me, the Archangel Uriel in front of me, the Archangel Raphael on my right hand and the Archangel Gabriel on my left hand. About me flame the pentagrams, behind me shines the Six-rayed Star and above my head is the glory of God, in whose hands is the Kingdom. I ask humbly you take and honour the spirit from my body. I will answer the Guardian of the Gate that I seek the light of the Mysteries and I am willing to be tested."